THE BIG BOOK OF Summer Love

THE BIG
BOOK OF
Summer
Love

RED FOX

A Red Fox Book

Published by Random House Children's Books
20 Vauxhall Bridge Road, London SW1V 2SA

A division of The Random House Group Ltd
London Melbourne Sydney Auckland
Johannesburg and agencies throughout the world

Collection copyright © Random House Children's Books 2001
Text copyright © Random House Children's Books 1997,1998

3 5 7 9 10 8 6 4

Love Games and *The Red-Hot Love Hunt* first published in Great Britain
by Red Fox in 1997, *Love in Store* first published in Great Britain by
Red Fox in 1998

This edition 2001

Printed and bound in Great Britain by
Bookmarque Ltd, Croydon, Surrey

Papers used by The Random House Group Limited are natural,
recyclable products made from wood grown in sustainable forest.
The manufacturing processes conform to the environmental
regulations of the country of origin.

THE RANDOM HOUSE GROUP Limited Reg. No. 954009

www.randomhouse.co.uk

ISBN 0 09 941758 8

Contents

Love in Store

Linda Sheel

Check Out The Specials

It was going to be a great summer! Tessa took the letter out of her bag and checked for the umpteenth time that it still said the same thing. Yep. A week today she started a holiday job at Sullivans' department store. How she'd managed to swing that she had no idea. Perhaps her best mate, Mayu, had put a word in for her.

'Hiya, Tessa, how're you doing?'

Tessa looked up and gave Nerd of the Year a dazzling smile. She'd been multiplying her hourly rate by thirty-seven and had just come to the conclusion that she was going to be rich.

'D'you fancy coming to the pictures with me tonight?' he asked, obviously not able to believe his luck.

I'd rather have my toenails pulled out with a pair

of pliers, thought Tessa, but for once in her life she didn't say it. 'I'm sorry, I'm meeting somebody,' she said, and smiled again. What the heck, a girl could spread a bit of sunshine about every now and again.

'Tomorrow then?' he asked eagerly. His face looked like her aunty's mongrel's did when it was just about to be fed.

'No thanks,' she mumbled, then darted across the road before he could ask her what she was doing three months from now, and pushed open the door of the Pizza Palace.

Mayu, Chloe, and Heather were already sitting at a table in the middle of the restaurant. Tessa glanced quickly in a mirror, smoothed her fingers through her short blonde hair, and walked across to them. Chloe started waving a menu about as soon as she saw her. 'Right! It's pig-out night, tonight. Agreed?'

'Agreed.' Tessa grinned back and sat down next to her at the table. 'Happy birthday, Chloe,' she said, handing her a present. It was wrapped in Thomas the Tank Engine wrapping paper, which was all she could find at home, but Chloe pretended not to notice as she ripped it off.

'Oh wow! Vanilla musk! My favourite! Matching body spray and body lotion. That's great, Tessa. Thanks.'

Tessa held her breath. It was the present that Mayu had given her for her birthday. She hated doing it but she was skint. Once she was working it would be different. She knew Mayu wouldn't say anything but Heather was a different matter. She never really meant to, but Heather had dropped her in it more times than she could remember.

The moment passed and Tessa relaxed. She started planning all the different ways she could pay back her mates for the times they'd forked out for her in the past. Apart from Mayu, they'd known each other since playschool. Heather used to be her best friend because they lived in the same street, but when Tessa's dad moved out and her mum took up with Mark, they moved into his house a couple of miles away. Somehow it had settled into Chloe and Heather being best mates and her and Mayu as best mates, but they still all got on really well. Chloe had gone straight from school into her dad's travel agency, but the rest of them were at college together.

'Take a look at that. I'll fight you for the dark one.' Heather poked Chloe and pointed outside to where two luscious lads were scanning the menu and deliberating whether to come in or not.

'Come on, come on,' she urged. 'Pepperoni pizza with extra mushrooms and a side order of Heather and Chloe. Can't you just feel your mouth watering?'

'The blond one has a seriously cute bum,' said Tessa, leaning back in her seat for a better view.

'You shouldn't be looking.' Chloe put a hand over Tessa's eyes and took a quick peep herself. 'What about Alec?'

'Alec who?'

'Oh, Tessa, you haven't.'

'Oh, Chloe, I have.'

'When?'

'Ten days ago.'

'Nobody tells me anything!' said Chloe as the waitress came to take their orders.

'You've been swanning it in the Algarve for the past fortnight,' Tessa reminded her as soon as the girl had gone. 'What did you expect me to do? Pinch one of my next-door neighbour's pigeons, tie a note round its ankle and see if it could flap its way to the Hotel Splendide?'

'It was the Hotel Villanova actually,' said Chloe, grinning.

'I know. I phoned up to tell you the news but the receptionist told me that Miss Davenport was lying on her belly on a sun lounger beside the pool and couldn't possibly be disturbed at this crucial stage of tanning.'

Chloe let out a squeal of laughter and everybody in the Pizza Palace stopped what they were doing and looked across. Tessa knew that her laugh wasn't her most attractive feature, but at least she didn't sound like a pig being chased by the farmer.

'Why did you dump him?' asked Chloe, when she'd calmed down again.

'I was sick of counting the flakes of dandruff on the top of his head,' said Tessa, pouncing on her pizza as soon as it arrived.

'He was nice. You could have given him a bottle of Head and Shoulders instead.'

Tessa shrugged. 'It wasn't the dandruff, it was looking at the top of his head that put me off.

Welcome to Grantchester – land of the pigmy. I reckon it must be something in the water around here.'

'Well your mother obviously didn't drink much of the stuff when she was having you,' said Heather.

Tessa stuck her tongue out at her before continuing, 'The midwife told her to have a bottle of Guinness a day to build her up. It must have bypassed her and gone straight to me.'

'It's amazing you came out as fair as you did then,' said Chloe.

Tessa stared at her for a moment. It was often difficult to tell when Chloe was joking; she wasn't exactly Brain of Britain.

'Mmm,' she murmured noncommittally through a mouthful of cheese and tomato.

'I wish they would come in.' Heather gazed longingly at the two lads who were still deliberating over the menu outside.

'Must be Librans – they can never make up their minds.' Tessa stood up. She'd had ample opportunity to study the blond lad. He was about five foot eleven, a good inch taller than her. Chances like this didn't happen every day of your life.

'What are you doing?' asked Chloe, as Tessa snatched a couple of menus off the table.

'I'm going to ask them if they've seen the specials. It might tempt them in.'

'You can't do that!' Chloe squealed.

'Watch me.'

'I'll come with you.' Heather got to her feet.

'Chloe should get the other one. It's her birthday.'

Heather pulled a face but stopped to look across at her friend.

'I'm not going out there,' said Chloe.

Heather shrugged her shoulders. 'Well then,' she said, and followed Tessa.

Tessa's hand was actually on the door handle when she saw the two lads wave to a couple of girls who were running across the car park. 'Would you believe it?' she said to Heather. They did a quick about-turn and walked back to the table.

'God, I feel such a prat! Everyone's looking at us,' said Heather, collapsing on her seat in a fit of giggles.

Tessa glanced around and then raised her voice

for the benefit of a couple of old biddies who were staring at her. 'That's better. Got to stretch the old legs every now and then. Stops the arthritis setting in.'

'Tessa!' Mayu shook her arm to shut her up.

'Well, it's your mother that says I should do more exercise to get rid of some of my energy,' she continued, unrepentant.

The blond lad flashed Tessa a grin as he walked over. He was just as gorgeous close to as he was at a distance.

'Shall we sit here?' His girlfriend pointed to the table next to theirs.

Yeah go on, rub it in, thought Tessa.

He sat down facing her. One blond lock dropped over his eye as he bent to pick up the menu, reminding her of an Old English Sheepdog. Tessa smiled as she speared the chips on her plate. Yeah, he could sleep in a basket at the bottom of her bed any day of the week.

'Tell us about your job then. I thought you said you stood no chance,' said Heather.

Tessa's face lit up. 'I was positive. The old cow that interviewed me must have believed it when I told her it was my life's ambition to work there.'

Mayu started to laugh. 'Mrs Turner,' she said.

Tessa nodded. 'I could hardly keep my face straight the way she went on.' She put down her fork, stuck out her chest and looked down her nose at her mates. 'You must understand, Miss Lewis, that at A J Sullivans we demand total commitment from our personnel. Our customers know that once they enter our portals they can expect a friendly smile and a helpful attitude from each and every member of staff. We pride ourselves . . .' She stopped. Mayu was laughing so much that she seemed about to topple off her chair and Tessa didn't want to miss it.

'You look exactly like her,' choked Mayu.

'Thanks a bunch. She must be nearly sixty.'

'You know what I mean. You've got a real talent, Tess. You should be on the stage.'

Tessa shook her head. 'Nah, too risky. A nice steady job bringing in plenty of dosh, that's what I'm after.'

'Do you think they might have any more vacancies at Sullivans?' asked Heather.

Tessa sprinkled sugar on her cappuccino and watched it dive-bomb through the froth. 'Might have. I'll have a word if you like.'

'Great. Ta.' Heather grinned at her and Tessa smiled back. She stopped abruptly as the lad on the next table smiled at her. She was definitely lad-starved; he was obviously smiling at his girlfriend and it was wishful thinking on her part.

'Do you know what department you're going to be in?' Chloe asked.

'Yeah. I go in on Monday for an induction course and then they're letting me loose on sportswear. Great, isn't it? I had visions of being stuck in the annexe with the lawnmowers and garden furniture.'

'D'you get a discount?' asked Heather.

'Haven't a clue.'

'Ten per cent,' said Mayu, 'but it's for personal purchases only.'

'Stuff that,' said Tessa. 'What do you want?'

'I dunno, but I'm sure I'll think of something.'

Tessa grinned. 'I'll have a look around and tell you what there is.'

'But you're not a size ten, Tess,' said Mayu.

Tessa shrugged. 'I'll tell them I'm on the waiting list for breast reduction.'

Blond boy almost choked on his drink. Serves him right for listening, thought Tessa. She finished her coffee and put her cup down. 'That was great, Chloe, thanks.'

'We're all going to have a sweet, though?' Chloe said.

'Oh well, if everybody else is.' Tessa picked up the menu and happily waded through the desserts. Chocolate fudge cake sounded yummy. She handed back the menu and stood up. 'I'm going to the loo. Anybody coming?'

Mayu followed her.

'I'm sorry about your present,' said Tessa, as soon as the door closed behind them. 'If I'd had anything else I would have given Chloe that, and I couldn't scrounge any more money off my mum. As soon as I get my wages I'm going to buy myself another gift set exactly the same as yours. I promise.'

Mayu smiled. 'It's OK. I knew you were broke.' She took a brush out of her bag and smoothed it through the thick glossy strands of her hair, then checked her face for non-existent spots. Her mum was English and her dad was Japanese, and she seemed to have inherited the best bits from both of them.

Tessa stood well back from the mirror before glancing at her reflection. If she did it quick enough she didn't look too bad. At least those zits had finally been blitzed. 'Who's ravishing then?' she said, blowing her reflection a kiss.

'You could be a model, Tess,' said Mayu.

Tessa was ready with a sarcastic reply but Mayu, bless her, was being serious. Tessa started to cackle. 'Oh yeah. You can just imagine me prancing down the catwalk in a ballgown by Yves St Laurent, catching my foot in the hem, and flattening half the audience.'

They walked back into the restaurant where a large plate of chocolate fudge cake was waiting on the table for her. 'This looks scrummy,' she said, picking up her fork and trying it before she sat down. 'Whose birthday is it next? Can we come back here again?'

'Would you like another coffee?' Chloe beamed around at everybody as though she'd prepared everything personally. Tessa could imagine her in a few years time as the perfect hostess and wondered vaguely if she'd still be included in the invitations.

Two coffees later, after they'd persuaded Chloe to show them her holiday photographs with the promise that they wouldn't laugh and then had practically wet themselves trying not to, they got up to leave. The people on the next table left at the same time and they jostled each other at the door. Tessa stepped back. It didn't bother her to wait for an extra thirty seconds. You'd think they were giving out Mars Bars to the first ones outside.

Suddenly she felt a hand in the back pocket of her jeans and she whirled around, ready to thump whoever it was trying to nick her money. All she had in there was her bus ticket, but even so.

It was the blond lad. He winked at her and then pressed a finger to his lips. Temporarily lost for words, Tessa watched him saunter out of the restaurant, put his arm around his girlfriend's waist, and walk off.

'Prats!' said Heather as Tessa joined her outside. 'Trying to push us out of the way.'

Tessa dug into her pocket and drew out a piece of paper that the blond boy had pushed inside. 'You can say that again,' she said.

'Prats!' said Heather loudly, and grinned. 'What have you got there?'

'Number one prat's name and phone number.' She threw the paper away in disgust.

Heather let out a gasp. 'The blond lad? I thought you said he was gorgeous?'

'Fancy doing something like that when your girlfriend's sitting next to you.' Tessa shook her head in amazement. 'What a slimeball. If they hadn't already gone I'd have run after them and told her.'

'And they have the cheek to call girls fickle!'

Tessa nodded in agreement. In the distance she saw her bus turn the corner, so she said a quick goodbye to the others and pelted across the road. If she caught this one she'd miss the drunks. What it was about her that attracted drunken old men she couldn't fathom, but even when there were empty seats available they'd come and plonk themselves down next to her and start telling her their life history.

As the bus pulled away Tessa spotted blond boy treating his girlfriend to a tongue sandwich at a bus stop further up the road. Ugh! How could she have kidded herself that he was luscious? That shirt he was wearing was pretty gross as well, she decided, turning away in disgust.

Tessa let out a deep sigh. Where had all the decent lads gone? Surely there must be some of them out there somewhere. She wasn't that fussy, was she?

Where There's A Will . . .

Mayu raced into the restaurant the next day and looked around guiltily. She'd spent twenty minutes this morning helping her mum find her contact lens, and now she was late. Luckily nobody seemed to have noticed. She called hello to Kat, who was sorting out her tables at the far side of the restaurant, and started gathering together the salt and pepper pots from her own tables. It was always her first job of the day to fill these, and she piled them hastily on a tray ready to take into the kitchen.

Would that idiotic new chef be in today, she wondered, as she walked towards the swing door that divided the kitchen from the restaurant. He'd spent the whole day yesterday messing about and flirting with all the waitresses. It was a wonder

Mrs Emmanuel put up with him. He was probably from an agency and only here temporarily or she wouldn't.

She rested her tray on one hand and pushed at the swing door with the other. That was strange. It seemed to be stuck. She pushed harder and it gave way. Mayu had a brief impression of size nine boots before they and their owner crumpled to the floor. Will, the idiot chef, was in today all right. He was lying in a heap at her feet.

'That's not fair! It doesn't count if some moron pushes me over!' he shouted to the head chef, who was standing on his hands against the storeroom door. The man weighed about twenty stone, sweat was trickling down his beetroot-red face, and he looked as though he was about to have a coronary.

'You were lucky. I'll give you a return match any time you like.' The chef swung his legs down to the floor, took out a hanky to wipe his face, and walked away.

Mayu put down her tray and stared at the lad she'd just flattened. He hadn't moved and his arm seemed bent at a strange angle. 'Are you all right?'

she asked.

He looked at her for the first time and pulled a face. 'I think I might have done something to my right arm. I can't seem to move it.'

'Oh God.' Mayu dropped to her knees beside him. 'I'm really sorry. Shall I ring for a doctor?'

'No.' He reached out his good hand and grabbed her arm. She didn't like to push him away seeing as she'd been responsible for his accident.

'You won't be able to work if you've hurt your arm,' she said. This was awful. If he was employed by an agency he wouldn't get paid at all.

'It might be all right.' He looked up at her through long brown lashes. His eyes were a deep blue.

'Are you going to try to move it? Is there anything I can do?'

'Maybe.'

'What?' She leaned closer. His hair was the colour of a desk in her dad's study; a rich, polished mahogany. She wondered vaguely if it was dyed. No, probably not.

'You can kiss me better,' he said, puckering his lips and closing his eyes. There was a burst of laughter from above, and for the first time Mayu became aware of the rest of the kitchen staff towering over them and not missing a thing.

'You stupid pig!' she said, and struggled to her feet. Her face was glowing; it was probably the same colour the head chef's had been five minutes ago.

Will leapt to his feet, clutching his arm. 'It's a miracle! I'm cured!' he shouted, and everybody laughed louder.

'What in God's name is going on in here? I'm delayed five minutes and the whole place reverts to a kindergarten.' Mrs Emmanuel, the restaurant manager, stalked into the kitchen and thudded a pile of account books on to the nearest surface. The temperature in the kitchen dropped ten degrees as she glared around at everyone like Vlad the Impaler. Finally her eyes rested on Mayu.

'Just what do you think you're doing in here, Mayu? You have customers, you know.'

'I didn't realise.' Mayu took the opportunity to escape and bolted through the swing door. Luckily her 'customers' was an old lady who came in every morning for a cup of tea. Mayu thought it was probably because she was lonely so she tried to spend as much time talking to her as she could. Today, though, as Mrs Williams talked about her cat, how hot it was at night, and how she was looking forward to visiting her sister in Bournemouth, Mayu found it impossible to concentrate. She was seething with anger. What a stupid trick to play on anybody. He must have spaghetti for brains.

A middle-aged couple walked into the restaurant and Mayu stirred herself. Grief! She hadn't switched on the coffee machine yet. They didn't look the type of people who would happily wait for five minutes while their coffee percolated. She raced over to the machine, switched it on, handed Mrs Williams her bill, then dashed over to the couple. Thankfully, they only wanted a pot of tea and two doughnuts.

She walked over to the urn and picked up a stainless steel teapot. Out of the corner of her eye she saw Will leaning out of the serving hatch, trying to catch her attention. She looked pointedly away. Whatever he was up to she didn't want to know. He was stupid and childish and she hated him. She scrunched two tea bags between her fingers and threw them into the pot.

Just because he was good-looking, did he expect every girl to come running when he snapped his fingers? It had made her sick yesterday watching Rebecca giggling and fluttering her eyelashes every time he poked his head out of the hatch. She wasn't in today; he must be feeling at a loose end without all that adoration.

Mayu picked up the tray of tea and doughnuts and marched determinedly across to the couple. What was wrong with him now? He was pointing down at himself and then pointing across at her. Mayu's cheeks glowed with embarrassment. Was he sick in the head? Normal people didn't go around doing things like that.

'A word, Miss Akira.'

Mayu jumped as Mrs Emmanuel's hot breath hissed down her neck. She was about to hand the man his doughnut but her sudden jump made it launch off the plate and land on his lap instead.

'Good shot!' he said, ignoring his wife's tuts of annoyance.

Mrs Emmanuel was waiting for her on the

other side of the swing door. 'Just how many times must I tell you young girls how important outward appearances are when you're in constant contact with the public?'

About three times every day, thought Mayu, but she kept quiet.

'So why are you improperly dressed?'

Mayu froze. Oh no. Please no. She'd done it once at school and the memory still made her feel weak. Once in anyone's lifetime was enough to walk around with your skirt tucked into your knickers. She looked hesitantly around the kitchen. People were pretending to get on with their work. Not Will though. Oh no, not him. He was staring across at them, lapping up every minute. She stared back defiantly, hating him. No, she didn't hate him. Hate wasn't a strong enough word for the feeling boiling inside her. She detested him. No wonder he'd been making obscene gestures at her. He probably thought she'd done it on purpose to turn him on or something. Grinding her teeth, she lifted her right hand and felt her bottom. Her skirt wasn't caught up on that side so she did the same with her left hand. It wasn't caught there either.

Totally confused, she glanced across at Will and then at Mrs Emmanuel.

'Your apron, Mayu. We issue you with two. One to wear and one to wash so you have no excuse not to be wearing it.'

Enlightenment hit Mayu like a frying pan across the back of the head. She stared shamefacedly at the empty space on her front where the frilly white apron that Sullivans thought their waitresses should wear ought to have been. That was what Will had been doing. He'd been trying to warn her before Mrs Emmanuel swooped. She glanced across at him. He gave a rueful smile and popped more bread into the toaster.

'I must have left it in the cloakroom,' Mayu said miserably.

'And what about these?' Mrs Emmanuel indicated the tray of salt and pepper pots.

'I was going to fill them up.'

'Going to? Going to isn't good enough, young lady. No apron, no condiments, what in heaven's name is the matter with you today? I thought you were one of our more reliable girls. Is there a personal problem I should know about?'

Mayu's head jerked up in alarm. 'No,' she said, shaking it vigorously.

Mrs Emmanuel studied her for a moment, then tilted her head to one side. 'Women's problems, is it, dear?' she asked quietly, but not quietly enough that big ears stacking toast only a few metres away didn't hear. He gave a snort, turned away, and she saw his shoulders shake.

I want to die. Please God, take me quick.

God didn't take any notice. Maybe he'd decided that seventeen was too young, that she had plenty more years of humiliation and embarrassment to endure yet. Behind her, Mayu could hear people coming into the restaurant. When was this woman going to let her leave so she could go and serve them? 'Shall I go and get my apron now?' she asked.

'Not now. They're coming in for breakfast already. Go on your first break. Take these condiments back and fill them up when it's quieter.'

Mayu didn't need telling twice. As she walked back into the restaurant half a dozen heads bobbed up expectantly. Some bright spark in Sullivans had decided that they should do breakfast specials for a bargain price. Mayu wasn't a violent person but if she ever met him she'd definitely be tempted to dismember him. When she'd started her Saturday job nine months ago, there'd been ample time in the morning to prepare for the lunchtime rush, but now there was a constant stream of people queuing for tables until the offer ended at half-past eleven.

Mayu raced over to the first table, took their order, thumped it down on the serving hatch, and hurried over to the next. Where was Vicky? She should have been in by now. She glanced across to the far side of the room where Kat was dashing about like a demented bluebottle. The tables between them were filling up but there was nobody to serve them.

With a martyred sigh, Mrs Emmanuel emerged from the kitchen and began serving. Kat and Mayu exchanged grins. There *was* some justice in the world. All Mrs Emmanuel did normally was buzz about the place like a queen bee, bossing everybody else around.

Being busy took Mayu's mind off what had

happened that morning. She couldn't forget Will entirely. Whenever he handed her a plate through the hatch he would pull a daft face at her or say something stupid. Was he never serious? She was sure he was older than she was, but he acted so infantile.

Half-past eleven came at last. Mayu poured herself a giant Coke, picked up a sandwich, and wrote down in the book what she'd taken. As a perk of the job they were allowed to eat what they wanted at a fraction of the cost to the public.

She pushed open the kitchen door and walked straight through to the fire escape where there were some plastic chairs on a small platform. Fetching her apron would have to wait. At the moment she was gasping for a drink.

'Fresh air!' The metal platform shook as Will jumped outside, tore off his chef's hat, threw back his head, and theatrically gulped in lungfuls of oxygen.

Mayu groaned. If she'd known his break was going to be the same as hers she would have asked for a later one. She clamped her hands around her Coke and sucked on the straw. Unfortunately it caught on the ice at the bottom and gave out a large slurp.

Will grinned but didn't comment. He probably drank like that all the time and didn't think there was anything unusual about it.

'I dunno which prat thought up the idea of these breakfasts but I'd like to get my hands around his neck. If I'd wanted to do conveyor-belt cookery I'd have got a job in McDonald's.' Will picked up his own Coke and clambered on to the safety rail along the side of the fire escape.

Mayu held her breath. Why did boys do such stupid things? They were four floors up. If he slipped he'd kill himself. He settled easily on top of the rail and began drinking. Like a baby, he closed his eyes with satisfaction, as the liquid travelled up the straw and into his mouth.

'Doing the breakfasts brings people into the store. They might buy other things on their way up to the restaurant,' Mayu said, simply so she could disagree with him.

Will's eyes flickered open and he started to laugh. 'You're something else,' he said.

Mayu turned away from the intense blue of his

gaze. She realised that what he really meant was, 'You're a moron,' and she couldn't really disagree with him. Why on earth had she come out with such a ridiculous statement?

'You new?'

Mayu shook her head. 'I started full time last week.'

'That's new.' Before she could explain, Will closed his eyes and bent his head back. A seraphic smile lit up his face. 'I was on holiday last week. Ibiza. Island paradise. With the sun on my face I feel like I'm back there. Sun, sea, and s . . .' He opened his eyes and gave her a wicked grin. 'Sangria,' he continued. 'You been?'

'No.'

'What's your name then?'

Mayu chewed at her bottom lip. She'd read his name on his name badge. He obviously couldn't be bothered to do the same with hers.

'All that partying affect your eyesight?' she said cuttingly.

Will covered one eye and then the other and scanned the distance. 'Nope,' he said, turning back to her.

Mayu glared at him. If they were only one floor up she'd definitely topple him off his perch. 'You just have difficulty with small print, like on name badges?' she prompted.

Will stared at her for a second and then he chuckled softly. God, but he was so irritating.

'Yeah OK, I haven't heard of that one, but I'm game. When do we start?'

'Start what?' He was a total pain in the neck. When he wasn't being irritating he was talking in riddles.

'Hunt the name badge,' he grinned. 'It could be fun.'

'Oh for God's sake!' Mayu looked down at her blouse to point out the badge that always left whopping great pinholes behind in the fabric. All she saw was an unbroken expanse of white.

'Have we started? Can I join in?' Will jangled his boots noisily against the metal.

'It's in the pocket of my apron in the cloakroom,' she said dully. She was a total idiot. The fairies had been in the middle of the night. Because there was no tooth under her pillow they'd taken her brain instead.

'You're no fun.' Will threw his hands in the air in disgust. 'You're not supposed to give the game away like that.'

'You could have told me instead of letting me make a fool of myself.'

He shrugged and leaned back precariously. 'Makes a change. It's usually only me that acts the fool around here.'

'I wish you wouldn't do that.'

'Do what?' He stared at her innocently but leaned back even further.

'It's a long way down.'

'Is it? I hadn't realised.' He twisted to take a look, somehow lost his balance, and toppled backwards.

Mayu screamed, jumped to her feet, and raced over to him. Her help wasn't needed. The top part of him might be upside-down but the bottom part remained exactly where it was.

'That was lucky.' He pulled himself upright again and grinned at her. 'If I hadn't twisted my feet through the bars I'd have gone over for sure.'

'You . . . you . . .' She couldn't think what to call

him, she was shaking so much with fright. 'If you ever do that again I'll push you over myself!'

'It was just a joke.'

'Well, save them for somebody who'll appreciate them. Rebecca's back tomorrow.' She picked up her empty Coke and stomped towards the door.

'Mayu?'

Her name stopped her in her tracks. So he did know what she was called after all. 'What?' she asked more softly.

'Don't forget to put your pinny on.'

She stuck her tongue out at him and turned away. Slowly a sly smile crept across her face.

'Oh, William?' she said, turning back to him.

'Yeah?'

She scooped a piece of ice from her Coke and threw it at him. It ricocheted off his shoulder with a satisfying ping.

'Don't forget to duck!' she giggled, and threw another one at him.

Dish Of The Day

'Hi, Mrs Akira!' shouted Tessa, as she walked into Mayu's house on Wednesday morning. She tossed her trainers to one side and then almost skidded over on the wooden floor of the Akiras' hall. Mrs Akira smiled, and it crossed Tessa's mind to wonder whether she polished the hall more thoroughly than she did the rest of the house just for a laugh. If she did, Tessa couldn't blame her. Living with Mayu's dad, who seemed to have left his sense of humour behind in Japan, couldn't be a bundle of fun.

'She's upstairs, Tessa,' said Mrs Akira, and returned to the kitchen.

'D'you fancy coming for a walk?' Tessa pushed open Mayu's bedroom door and plonked herself on the bed. 'I told Chloe and Heather we might see them in the park. Chloe fancies the lad who does the boats on the lake so that's where they're going. Chloe can't row a boat to save her life. It'll be better than the telly watching them.'

'Oh, I don't know. I don't really feel like going out.' Mayu put down her book and sank back lethargically on the bed.

'Time of the month, is it?' Tessa flicked open one of Mayu's magazines and started reading her stars.

'God, don't *you* start! That's what Mrs Emmanuel was asking yesterday.'

'Were you grumpy yesterday as well?'

'No!'

Tessa stared at her mate's downturned lips. Something was up, but Mayu didn't seem too keen to tell her what it was.

'Mrs Emmanuel. Is she the one that chucked me out that time for standing on the table?'

'Yes.'

'Silly cow. I was only trying to get Sam's balloon back. He would have shut up screaming if I had.'

'Do you mind going to the park by yourself?'

'Yes I do. I wouldn't have come all the way over here if I'd wanted to go by myself. You can't lie on your bed all your day off, Mayu. You'll turn into an old woman. Come on, the fresh air'll do you good.'

'Maybe.' Mayu combed her fingers languidly through her hair.

'Oh for God's sake, Mayu, spit it out! What's the matter with you?'

Mayu let out a deep sigh. 'I got an official warning at work yesterday.'

'No! I don't believe it.' Tessa's jaw dropped open. She was always telling Mayu to lighten up and not be so serious. What on earth had she done?

'Well it's true.'

Tessa was amazed. Mayu was as straight as they came, that's why Tessa was so shocked by what she'd said. 'So what happened? Was it a mistake?'

Mayu shook her head. 'It wasn't a mistake. I forgot to put my apron on in the morning—' She got no further before Tessa's deep laugh boomed around the house.

'Oh well, that explains it. I'm surprised they didn't put you on remand.'

'No, listen, Tessa. It wasn't just that.' Mayu

seemed agitated so Tessa shut up. 'I'd forgotten to fill the salt cellars as well.'

Tessa stared at her, gobsmacked. What was this place she'd just signed up for? 'A hanging matter,' she muttered.

Mayu sighed again. 'But the worst thing was the water all over the fire escape. Someone could have slipped and had an accident. They wouldn't have. It would have evaporated. But that's what Mrs Emmanuel said. She was in a bad mood, you see, because Vicky didn't show up and she had to serve her tables because we were busy.'

'You're not making any sense, Mayu.'

Mayu frowned. 'I'm telling you what happened.'

'Why was the water on the fire escape?' Tessa asked. She settled herself more comfortably on the bed. They could be here all day.

Mayu stared at the ground. 'It was one of the chefs. We were throwing ice cubes at each other.'

'Is he nice?' You had to be careful asking Mayu that question. She always saw the best in anyone and would go out with the type of lad you'd normally cross the road to avoid.

'He's an idiot.'

'Oh.' That sounded promising. Tessa searched her memory banks. She often popped in to see Mayu when she was working, but there was nobody in that restaurant who was the remotest bit fanciable. Still, Mayu's taste was vastly different to hers. It seemed to be one of the reasons they got on so well.

'How many warnings do they give before they boot you out?'

'Three.'

'That's all right then. You're not likely to get any more, are you?'

'But it'll go down on my record, Tess.'

'Oh for Christ's sake, Mayu. Do you think an employer is going to refuse you a job when you finish university because you haven't got a reference from Sullivans?'

A slow smile spread across Mayu's face. 'I'm being too serious again, aren't I?'

Tessa leaned across the bed and gave her a hug. 'Yes, sunshine, you are. Although the bit about the ice cubes shows promise. How old is he?'

'About eighteen or nineteen.'

'Is he good-looking?'

'Yes.'

Tessa considered. With Mayu that could mean anything, but it was still worth checking out. First chance she got. She glanced at her watch. 'So, are we going to see if Chloe and Heather have managed to drown each other or what?'

Mayu got up from the bed and smiled. 'Shall we get a boat as well? It's ages since we've done that.'

'Yeah, OK. We could try ramming them.'

The first thing Mayu heard when she walked into the restaurant the next day was Will's laugh. Was he incapable of being serious? Even when Mrs Emmanuel had been bawling them out he hadn't been able to keep a straight face.

'There you are, Mayu.' Mrs Emmanuel walked over to her, and Mayu checked for the third time that morning that she was wearing everything she should have been.

'This is Diane. She's joining us for the summer. We'll take over your tables this morning while I show her what to do, so you can help out in the

45

kitchen. I'll call you when Rebecca goes for her break.'

Mayu smiled at the girl and said hello. The waitressing Mrs Emmanuel did on Tuesday had certainly upset her; she wasn't going to risk it happening again.

Mayu walked into the kitchen and slipped a plastic apron over her clothes. 'I've come to help. What can I do?' she asked.

The head chef said his usual, that what he'd like her to do wasn't possible in a kitchen, and she waited with her arms crossed and a tight smile on her face until the laughter died down.

'You can give me a hand if you like.' Mayu didn't need to turn around to know who that voice belonged to.

'We're trying out a new dish for lunch and I need a packet of chicken lips from the chest freezer in the storeroom.'

'Chicken lips?' Mayu stared at him, but he didn't look up. He was engrossed in cracking eggs into a bowl.

'Right-hand side, near the bottom,' he said.

Mayu walked into the storeroom, put on a pair

46

of padded gloves, and opened the freezer. She felt at a disadvantage because her mother wouldn't touch convenience food. They must be a new product, like fish fingers or turkey drummers. Methodically, she lifted out packets of sausages and frozen vegetables and stacked them on the shelf beside her. She came to the bottom but didn't come across any packets of chicken lips. Maybe she'd missed them. She sorted through the pile to check.

'They're not there,' she said, looking up to see Will watching her from the door.

'Must be in the left-hand side,' he said, and turned away quickly.

'Moron,' she muttered, replacing one set of food and starting on the other side. The freezer was huge and she had visions of toppling inside as she reached into the very bottom. There were chicken breasts, chicken legs, chicken drumsticks, chicken wings, and even chicken nuggets, but there was nothing remotely resembling chicken lips. The suspicion that he was winding her up filtered into her brain.

'Haven't you got them yet?' A huge grin was splattered all over Will's face as he walked into the storeroom. The rest of the kitchen staff were gathered in the doorway and were also beaming like idiots.

'They're not in there,' she said, and they all burst out laughing.

'I can't believe you fell for that,' he spluttered, holding his sides, as she piled everything back into the freezer. 'I thought you were brainy and went to college.'

'Who told you that?'

'Nobody. I'm clairvoyant.'

'Clairvoyant?' She slammed the lid of the freezer down. 'That means you can see the future before it happens?'

'Yeah.'

As she passed him on her way to the door, Mayu gave him a swift kick on the shins. 'Well you didn't see that about to happen, did you?' she said.

Mayu was back in the restaurant when Tessa came in. The lunchtime rush was over and there were only a few customers.

'Any chance of a coffee?' Tessa plonked herself on a seat in the centre of the room.

'That's not one of my tables.'

'I know, but I can't see into the kitchen from your bit.'

Mayu groaned. She might have known what Tessa had come in for.

'Call him out then.' Tessa hoovered up the froth from the top of her cappuccino.

'I can't call him out. What do you think he is, my pet Labrador?'

Tessa started to giggle. 'Go on.'

'No.'

'Hey Rover! Walkies!' she boomed out.

Mayu turned away. Thank God Mrs Emmanuel was on a late lunch. Tessa's laughter ceased and Mayu saw that she was staring at the service hatch. She didn't need three guesses to know who had popped his head out.

'My, my, my, that's what I call dish of the day,' she heard Tessa mutter as she picked up her coffee and wandered over.

Ten minutes later she wandered back, and perched on the edge of one of Mayu's tables. 'He's nice,' she said, scraping her finger around the cup to capture the last traces of froth.

'You try working with him,' said Mayu.

'It'd be fun. You should go out with him, Mayu. It would make a change from the boring creeps you usually go for.'

'Thank you, Tessa.' Mayu flicked her with her cloth. Tessa might be her best mate, but she could go too far sometimes.

'Thanks accepted,' grinned Tessa.

'You seemed to be getting on with him OK. I'm surprised *you* don't want to go out with him.'

Tessa shrugged. 'I could tell straight away that he didn't fancy me, and life's too short to waste on lost causes. He was friendly enough, but he was looking over my shoulder all the time we were talking. I reckon he was watching you.'

Mayu snorted. 'If he was then it was only because he was trying to think up new ways of tormenting me.' She told Tessa about what had happened that morning and went off to take table three's money while Tessa was laughing.

'Oh God, Mayu, you really are an idiot. Fancy falling for something like that.'

'Well I didn't know, did I? Your brothers are always eating the strangest things when I come round. Dinosaur- or alphabet-shaped stuff.'

'Yeah, I know, but chicken *lips*. Honestly, girl.'

Mayu bit her lip. She knew exactly what kind of fool she'd made of herself that morning thanks to Will stupid idiot chef. She didn't need Tessa to rub it in.

'I still reckon he fancies you though. He asked me if you'd said anything about him.'

'Oh, yeah, yeah. Give me a break, Tessa. I don't need you winding me up as well.'

'Would I do such a thing?' Tessa demanded with fake innocence, and Mayu laughed.

'Yes.'

'Not this time. I swear to you that's what he said. They're so vain, lads, have you noticed? They think we spend all our spare time talking about them.' She started to giggle. 'I don't know where they get that idea from.'

'What did you tell him then?' asked Mayu, playing along with her.

'I said you had the hots for him.'

'Oh my God, Tessa, you bitch!'

Tessa started to cackle. 'Well, maybe that wasn't exactly what I said. I think it was more along the lines that you kept things to yourself, that you were an enigma – that's a good word, don't you think? That should get him going. Lads love a challenge. They want to be the first to unravel a girl's mystery. And it's true – you are a secretive cow, Mayu. Why didn't you tell me about him before?'

'Why should I tell you about somebody that's about as interesting and as irritating as a midge bite? And he's never been here before on a Saturday anyway.'

'Oh yeah, that's right. He said. He always has Saturdays off because him and his mates go clubbing on a Friday night. That's convenient: he won't interfere with our girls' night out on a Friday.'

Mayu let out a loud groan and threw her tea towel at Tessa. 'This isn't funny any more, Tessa. Do me a favour and shut up about him. And if you ever talk to him again I'd be grateful if you didn't mention me.'

'Yeah OK.' Tessa stood up and slung her bag over her shoulder. 'I take it you didn't read your stars in that magazine you gave me?'

'No. Why?'

'Love is in store for you this month when a dark-haired stranger picks you to be his. Remember that the course of true love never runs smooth.'

Mayu frowned. 'Is that what it said?'

Tessa grinned then shook her head. 'Nah, I just made it up.'

'Tessa!' Mayu grabbed her spray gun, but Tessa was already out of range by the time the shower of detergent spattered through the air. Mayu heard her cackling all the way down the stairs.

Tessa Meets Her Match

Tessa couldn't wait to start work properly on Tuesday. The induction course had bored her out of her head, but as they were paying her to attend she wasn't going to complain. She felt a bit self-conscious in her shop clothes. Navy skirt and white blouse, the letter had said, so she'd thought: great, her old school clothes would do. She'd forgotten how much she'd grown. Her step-dad had told her that she looked like a tart as she'd left the house – they were big on parental support in her family. He did have a point though. Part of her first wages would definitely have to go on a new skirt.

'Tessa Lewis, I presume?' The voice came from behind the till in the sportswear department.

'You presume right,' she said, as she sized up

its owner. About twenty, five foot eleven (what a waste), oil-slick gelled hair, and an overpowering smell of deodorant or aftershave which usually meant with lads that they couldn't be bothered to wash and thought that would do instead.

'I'm Brett Oliver.'

Tessa smiled. Brett Oliver. BO. Nice one.

He held out a clammy paw and as Tessa shook it her smile vanished. He was definitely the type of lad who'd sit next to you on the bus and get his kicks by squashing you into the window every time the bus turned a corner.

'I'm the sportswear department manager.' His chest puffed up with pride.

'Oh? It says assistant manager on your badge. Have you just been promoted?' she asked innocently.

Two red streaks flashed across his cheek. 'Mr Edmonds is on holiday. I'm acting manager.'

'Right.'

'Shall we get you settled in, then? I'll show you around the storeroom while there's nobody about.'

Tessa didn't like the sound of that. Would she

get the sack for headbutting the assistant manager if he tried it on? She considered for a moment and decided she probably would.

'. . . and these are the T-shirts. The main thing you must remember is that everything is stored in alphabetical order . . .' BO's voice was like a bumble bee; it droned on and on. Tessa leaned against the shelves and fought the urge to close her eyes. And she thought the induction course had been boring.

'. . . So Adidas is always stored before Nike, for instance. Do you think you'll be able to remember that?'

'I'll try my best.' Patronising prat! Did he think she had the brain power of an amoeba or what?

'. . . and now the trainers. Same thing here but complicated by the fact we're dealing with numbers as well. Are you listening? This is important.'

Tessa jumped. She'd been thinking about the film they'd all gone to see on Friday night. 'Yes, it's just my way of concentrating.'

BO looked unconvinced. 'I think I'll give you a little test to make sure.'

'Like at school, you mean?'

The sarcasm was lost on him. 'That's right. Men's size ten Reebok "Slice Canvas" trainers. Fetch them please.'

Tessa positioned the stepladders under the right shelf and clambered up. Moron! Him and his fetch. What did he want her to do, shove the trainers in her mouth and come down on all fours?

The trainers were on the very top shelf. She reached them easily, but poor old Mayu would have stood no chance. It had gone quiet below so she glanced down to see what was up. BO was squatted down, tying his laces. From that angle he had a perfect worm's-eye view up her skirt, and she could tell that was exactly what he was doing by the stupid grin splattered all over his face.

Without a second thought, Tessa let the trainers drop. Pity they hadn't been in the electrical department and the trainers weren't a microwave, but they weren't exactly lightweight. They bounced off BO's head with a satisfying thud.

'Ooo sorry,' she trilled. 'I get a bit wobbly on ladders.'

His face was a funny shade of purple as he glared up at her. For a second she was sure he was going to topple the ladders over with her on them. Yeah go for it, she thought. Sullivans might give her a bundle of dosh in compensation.

But he turned and walked away.

'Do you want me to find anything else?' she called after him.

'No,' came the strangled reply from the door.

Tessa clamped both hands over her mouth and the ladders shook with her laughter. What a meanie! He hadn't even told her whether she'd passed her test or not.

It seemed that that was to be the highlight of her day. BO exacted revenge in typical slimeball fashion. Whenever he got the chance he would swoop over when she was with a customer and explain things so painstakingly slowly to her that they must have thought she was on a special needs programme. Most of the decent lads that came into the department seemed to be joined at the hip to their girlfriends, but those that weren't were definitely put off.

Lunchtime came. Tessa gobbled down her sandwiches and went upstairs in search of Mayu. Her mate wouldn't be too chuffed to see her during one of her busiest times, but she had to moan to somebody.

She squeezed herself around a table beside a mum and dad and their kid who looked as though he was in training to be a Sumo wrestler. Mayu gave her a fleeting smile, zoomed past, and returned carrying three plates of chicken dinners that she put down in front of the family. Fat boy pounced on his as though he hadn't eaten for a week, and ripped the flesh from the chicken like a tiger at the zoo. Tessa had to look away. She'd been thinking of becoming a vegetarian for some time and he'd definitely brought the decision closer.

'I can't really talk,' whispered Mayu, coming back with a cup of coffee for her.

'I know. I've just come up to see a friendly face,' she whined pathetically.

'Oh, Tessa, it's not that bad surely? It's only your first day. Once you settle in things will seem different.' She squeezed her arm and Tessa cheered up.

'Maybe. I shouldn't have dropped those trainers on his head. It's really pissed him off.'

Mayu's eyes widened in surprise, but a couple

three tables away were calling her and she had to go. Once she was there they couldn't make up their minds what to have. It didn't seem to bother Mayu like it would have Tessa. Mayu kept a smile plastered on her face while she wiped the table and waited patiently for them to order.

Tessa spotted a free table. She picked up her coffee and nabbed it before anyone else could.

'What are you doing moving around? I thought you'd gone,' said Mayu.

'I had to get away from piranha jaws. You should give him his own trough in the corner.'

Mayu started to giggle and turned her face to the wall so no one could see. 'Shh! Your voice comes out louder than you think, Tess.'

Tessa grinned. 'OK, I'll behave.'

Mayu turned back and cleared the dirty dishes from the table.

'Has he asked you out yet?' Tessa asked, as she spotted Will at the serving hatch.

'Yes. We're getting married next week,' said Mayu sarcastically as she picked up her tray.

'Can I be your chief bridesmaid?' Tessa called after her, but Mayu didn't deign to reply. Tessa leaned back in her seat and watched as her mate manoeuvred her way around the tables. There was something relaxing about watching somebody else work, and Mayu in particular. She made waitressing seem easy and effortless, but Tessa could see what hard work it was. Life in the sportswear department was a doddle in comparison.

As she got up to go, Will's face appeared at the serving hatch and he grinned over at her. She waved back. It was a pity Mayu didn't fancy him at all. She could do a lot worse.

'See you later.' Tessa waved to Mayu as she walked out. She had ten minutes to go to the loo, check her make-up, and go down to the perfume counter where she intended spraying herself all over with the pongiest perfume she could find.

She'd figured out why BO overdosed on the aftershave. It wasn't to hide his body odour but other people's. She knew it was warm outside and people tended to sweat a bit in the summer, but you'd think if they knew they were going to try on trainers they'd change the socks they'd had on for the past month first. The old bloke this morning had been the worst. His big toe had stuck right out of his sock and she could see the dirt encrusted under the nail. The smell was disgusting and she'd been in danger of splattering him with her morning crispies. Funny how BO had kept out of the way when she was serving him.

'There you are.' BO looked pointedly at his watch as she came in, but he couldn't say anything, she had at least three-quarters of a second of her lunch break left.

As she got closer his head seemed to jerk back. This *Midnight in Paradise* she'd tipped over herself was a bit strong. She hoped it would wear off soon; it was making her feel sick.

'Here I am,' she said brightly, standing right next to him. She'd suffered his awful aftershave all morning. They could suffer *Midnight in Paradise* together.

'I'll go for my lunch now.' Coward. He'd said earlier that he was going at two o'clock. 'Daphne is just around the corner. If you get stuck or need anything ring your bell.'

Tessa waited for him to show her for the fifth time that day how to use the bell, but he didn't. He bolted away like a horse at the Derby.

'God, I stink,' she muttered, as the combined fragrance of jasmine, freesia, rose, lavender, and every flower on God's earth drifted upwards. It hadn't smelt so bad in the bottle. It was obviously one that Sullivans kept especially for people like her, who came in to use the perfumes with no intention of buying any. She'd tried washing it off in the ladies afterwards but it hadn't made any difference.

Luckily this department wasn't very busy. She was daydreaming quietly behind the till when her first customer came in. Tessa became rigid. It wasn't fair! He had the body of an Olympic athlete and the face of a male model. He could have done with an extra couple of inches in height, but somehow it didn't seem to matter, he was still drop-dead gorgeous.

'Go away. Please go away,' she whispered, but he took no notice. He walked over to the display of trainers and started looking at them closely as though he meant business. He looked enquiringly over in her direction, but she looked down and pretended to change the till roll.

It wasn't fair! Normally she'd have been over there before he'd made it to the display, pushed him into a chair, and insisted that he try on every trainer in his size. But she couldn't move. If she took three steps in his direction he'd keel over with the smell.

He glanced over again and she ripped the till roll out of the machine. God, she hoped she could remember how to put it back. He'd be as thick as a brick, of course. Lads like him usually were. They spent all their time at the gym and found the instructions on the Coke machine mentally challenging. But if boys could appreciate bimbos why couldn't girls drool over fit lads?

He was looking around to see if anybody else could serve him. Maybe he'd get sick of waiting and come back when she didn't stink. She didn't know why she was getting herself in such a state. He was probably engaged or he'd be so big-headed because of his looks that she'd hate him.

'I'm sorry to bother you, I can see that you're busy.' The voice was deep but surprisingly gentle for someone of his build. Tessa felt really guilty. If somebody had ignored her like that she wouldn't have been so polite.

'These till rolls can be a pig,' she said, closing the lid.

'Aren't they?' His lips curved into a warm smile. 'I worked in a supermarket once. I could never figure the damn things out.'

Tessa smiled back. Close to, he was even more gorgeous than she'd imagined. His hair was a thick glossy chestnut, his skin looked as smooth and soft as her kid brother Sam's, and his eyes were the colour of melted chocolate. Her legs felt a bit wobbly. She leaned against the counter to support herself.

'Do you have these in a size nine?' He placed a pair of trainers on the counter.

Tessa picked them up and looked at them. 'Are these for tennis?' she asked. 'Because the soles are smooth and they won't give you a good enough grip for most other sports.'

He nodded then grinned at her, and her legs wobbled even more. What amazingly luscious lips he had. Imagine those coming in for the kill. 'A girl who knows her trainers. Have you worked here long?'

'It's my first day.'

One perfectly formed eyebrow shot into space.

'Trainers come a close second to football as a subject for discussion in our house,' she explained.

'Oh right.' He gave a deep chuckle. It was the sexiest sound she'd ever heard. If she'd been a Victorian lady she'd definitely have gone into a deep swoon.

'I'm sorry about the smell. I spilt a bottle of perfume,' she blurted out.

'I thought it must be standard sportswear department issue.'

'Say again?'

'To guard against smelly feet.'

'Oh no, nothing like that.' Tessa grabbed the trainers and rushed into the storeroom before he noticed that she was blushing. What was wrong with her? She'd stopped going red when she was eleven.

They did stock his size. Tessa didn't know if she was pleased or not. It meant he would stay longer, but she didn't know if she could lace them up for him without making a fool of herself. Her whole body seemed to be quivering with excitement.

He sat down and began unlacing his shoes when he saw her coming back. His sports socks looked new, as though he'd opened a fresh packet and put them on before he'd come out.

She knelt down in front of him and waited for the immortal words that every male under the age of ninety seemed programmed to say: 'That's where I like to see women – on their knees in front of me.'

They didn't come. 'Yeah, these seem fine. What do you think?' he said instead.

'They look great, but so they should for that price.'

He started to laugh. 'Don't let them hear you saying that. I bet they told you to push the more expensive makes.'

Tessa shrugged. They could tell her what they liked, but she wasn't going to rip off somebody as nice as him.

'I need the support in the more expensive ones for work. It's false economy buying the crap ones.'

'What do you do?'

'I've got a summer job coaching part time at the tennis centre.'

'You're not from round here though, are you?'

He grinned. God, she was doing it again. He'd tell her to shut up and stop being such a nosy cow any minute. It wouldn't be the first time it had happened. But if she was interested in someone she had to know everything about them. Have you got a girlfriend? was the question she most wanted to ask, but she didn't dare.

'I come from Sutton, but I'm going to the university here in October. I came down earlier when I heard I'd got this job.'

'What course are you doing?'

'Physics.'

Physics? Christ! Her mouth dropped open.

He pulled a face. 'I know. It's a complete conversation stopper. Like telling people you're a mortician or something. I'm just a boring git, I'm afraid.'

Boring? Him? No way! Tessa knew that she could talk to him for the rest of her life and never be bored. 'I've always liked physics,' she blurted out.

He started to laugh. 'I don't believe you. Name something you like about it.'

Tessa's mind went blank. She'd hated the teacher, she'd failed the subject at GCSE, and deleted any record of it from her memory banks. 'Er, what I meant to say was that I've always liked tennis.'

He laughed even louder. 'Now, that I believe.' He leaned towards her and smiled. His teeth were white and even, and she stared at them, mesmerised.

Slowly his face moved closer. Sullivans' department store and the rest of Grantchester disappeared. They were the only two people left in the universe. Tessa looked deep into his eyes and she knew that she loved him. This was the lad whose name was tattooed on her soul. It was stupid: he hadn't touched her, he hadn't kissed her, but she knew.

'What does a person have to do to get some service around here!'

Tessa jumped as reality kicked her in the face.

'I've been waiting at the till with this track-suit for the past five minutes while you've been canoodling with your boyfriend. I've a good mind to report you to the manager!'

Tessa picked up the trainers and stood up. Her

body felt strange – as if she'd just stepped off the Waltzer at the fairground. She tried to walk over to the till but her legs didn't seem to want to move. Her bones had turned to mush.

'Are you going to serve me or what?' The woman shoved the tracksuit in her face and Tessa came slowly to her senses. She clutched the trainers and gawped at the woman until her brain cells reassembled.

'I'm afraid I have to serve this gentleman first.' Tessa put on her best posh voice. 'I was advising him about trainers. He's a professional tennis player and must have the best. How would you like to pay for them, sir?' She pointed her feet in the direction of the till, and this time they behaved themselves and carried her there.

He followed her over, looking a bit shell-shocked. He paid for the trainers, mumbled something that she didn't catch, gave her a last lingering look, and went.

Gone! Just like that! She wanted to leap over the counter and run after him, but the woman was chuntering on again, and she couldn't.

As soon as it was quiet she opened the till and

looked at his cheque. Ralf! His name was Ralf. Ralf Peters. This was the lad she was destined to share her life with. She closed her eyes and smiled. Tessa Peters. Yeah, she could live with that. Would he come back this afternoon? Maybe he'd just popped upstairs for a coffee until the tracksuit terror had gone.

Tessa's senses remained on red alert for the rest of the day, but Ralf didn't return.

He would come in on Wednesday.

But he didn't.

He had to come in on Thursday. Friday was her day off this week. If he came in then he might think she'd left or got the sack and he might never bother coming back.

He didn't come in.

The universe couldn't be so cruel. It couldn't give you five minutes with the lad of a lifetime and then tear him away for ever.

It couldn't . . . or could it?

If You Can't Beat 'Em . . .

'Looking forward to your girls' night out then?'

Mayu paused on her way to the storeroom and stared at Will. 'How do you know about that?'

'Your mate told me.'

Mayu smiled. Tessa was like a radio transmitter. She gave and received more information in a few minutes than anybody else she knew.

'She hasn't seemed so chirpy the last couple of days.'

Mayu frowned. When Tessa was happy it was like a Mediterranean summer. At the moment they were in the middle of an Arctic winter.

'So what's up?' Will persisted.

'Oh you know.' Mayu walked into the storeroom and took down a box of sugar sachets. Tessa's problems were her own business. She would feel disloyal discussing them with anybody else.

Will was scrubbing down his work surface when she came out. 'I don't actually, but it doesn't seem that you want to tell me,' he said, continuing the conversation.

Mayu hesitated. He'd been less obnoxious than usual over the last few days and it had been nice, but mates were mates and she wasn't going to discuss hers with him just to keep him sweet. She turned away.

'So where are you off to tonight, then?' he continued.

'The bowling alley.'

'You go there every week?'

'No. Sometimes we go to the pictures, sometimes to Barney's. If Tessa has to babysit sometimes we all go round there. It depends.'

'I see.' He juggled his spray bottle in his hand like an outlaw in a film juggling his gun.

'I'll see you on Monday then,' said Mayu. She put her hand on the swing door, ready to push.

'I'll be in tomorrow.'

'Are you working overtime?'

'Nah. She's changed my day off to Wednesday for the time being.'

'That's my day off as well.'

'God! Is it? That means I'll have to suffer you for one more day than I need to.' Will took his cloth and threw it in the sink.

Ditto, thought Mayu. 'As long as you try to suffer in silence,' she said, pushing open the swing door. As she did so she tripped on something. It was her apron caught up around her ankles; Will must have untied it while they were talking, and she hadn't felt a thing.

'You seem to have a problem with that pinny.' Will leaned against the work surface and grinned.

Mayu slowly shook her head. He was a total nutter. She bent to pick up her apron. Oh well, if you couldn't beat them maybe there was no option but to join them.

She plastered a sugary smile on her lips and turned back to Will. 'See you tomorrow then. I'll think of you slaving over a hot stove while I'm enjoying myself at the bowling alley.'

'Come again?'

'Tom Sullivans' retirement do. You'd think with

all the money he has he'd have held it in the Ritz instead of here, wouldn't you?'

Will's face was a blank, and Mayu had to turn her face away to hide her grin. She wasn't very good at this kind of thing.

'Mrs Emmanuel offered me double time to stay behind but I managed to get out of it.' Mayu opened the box of sachets to avoid looking at him. 'They're having outside caterers as well, but she said she wanted you to do the carvery.'

'She never said anything to me.'

'Oh God, Will, where's the meat?' His face was several shades paler. Mayu's jaw muscles ached with the effort of trying not to laugh.

'In the freezer.'

'Do you think it'll defrost in time?' she asked, and then just as Will took off his chef's hat and raked his fingers through his hair she spoiled it all by bursting out laughing.

'Why you little . . .' He leaned back against the sink and watched as the tears rolled down her cheeks. It wasn't really that funny; she didn't know why she was laughing so much. Tessa would have done it so much better. She'd have been in the storeroom throwing joints of meat out of the freezer and clattering roasting dishes about, totally straightfaced. But Will's face had been a picture. He'd completely believed her, and it had felt good turning the tables on him for a change.

Mayu looked sheepishly up at him as she wiped the mascara from underneath her eyes, but he grinned and pointed to a plaque above the door – YOU DON'T HAVE TO BE MAD TO WORK HERE BUT IT HELPS.

Mayu smiled back and rolled her eyes. It was beginning to seem like she was already halfway there.

'Did Ralf come into the restaurant today?' were the first words Tessa said as Mayu met her outside the bowling alley.

'How should I know, Tessa? I don't know what he looks like.'

'You'd recognise him if you saw him. That means he hasn't come in.' A dark cloud seemed to form over Tessa's head.

Mayu waved to Chloe and Heather, who were

already on a lane, and they went to change their shoes.

'Come on, Tessa. Try to forget him just for tonight,' Mayu encouraged her as they walked over to join the others.

'You don't know anything about love,' said Tessa dramatically.

'What's this about love?' Chloe stopped sorting balls and turned to listen.

Tessa told them about Ralf.

'And you didn't hear what he said when he went?' asked Heather.

Tessa shook her head miserably. 'No. I think I was only really functioning on auto-pilot, and this old bag kept rustling her tracksuit and tutting so I couldn't hear properly.'

'Maybe he was asking you to meet him outside at six o'clock, and he hasn't been back 'cause you didn't,' said Heather.

Mayu saw the look of horror that swamped Tessa's face, but before she could kick Heather she must have noticed it too.

'No, no, I'm sure he didn't say that. If he did he would have come back to make sure, wouldn't he? He was probably saying, "I'll see you around," but he hasn't been back because he's been working. Yeah, I bet that's it. He'll be in again next week,' Heather gabbled.

Tessa didn't reply. She stared at the ground, her shoulders hunched, and looked as if she might burst into tears at any moment. Mayu hated seeing her like this. In all the years she'd known Tessa she'd never seen her cry, and it just didn't seem right that she should work herself into such a state for a boy who she'd only met for a few minutes and might never see again.

'Look, Tessa, you keep saying how nice he is. Maybe that's all he was doing: being nice,' she said.

'Yeah. How do you know he hasn't already got a girlfriend?' asked Chloe.

Tessa snatched up a ball. For a moment Mayu thought she was going to aim it at them. 'None of you understand!' she said, and stormed on to the lane. She let go of the ball and it hurtled up the middle. The pins dived for cover and Tessa scored a strike. The lads on the next lane applauded. Tessa told them where to go.

'Thanks, pal,' hissed Heather. 'I had my eye on the dark one.'

Tessa shrugged, dropped into a seat, and folded her arms.

'I was supposed to go first,' said Chloe. 'You were second, then Mayu, then Heather.'

'All right. Don't get your knickers in a twist. We'll say that was your score. I'll have another go and then it'll be right.' Tessa snatched up another ball, threw it at the pins as though they were her worst enemies all lined up in one spot, and scored another strike. The lads on the next lane didn't say a word.

They finished their first game and decided to have a Coke. Tessa's mood was affecting everybody, Mayu noticed. Chloe seemed miserable, but maybe that was because she'd been so thoroughly slammed in the game. They all knew that Tessa was the best player among them, but only Mayu knew that she usually dropped a few shots so that she wouldn't win by too much. Tonight, however, she was playing as if she was on a personal vendetta. Their own scores looked ridiculous in comparison.

'So how's your love life, Mayu?' asked Heather jokingly.

'Mayu's OK. The boy of her dreams would come running if she snapped her fingers.'

'Tessa!' Mayu hadn't said anything to Heather and Chloe about Will because she knew what they were like. They'd blow it out of all proportion, just like Tessa had.

'Go on! Spit it out! We want to know every little thing.' Chloe and Heather gathered around her like vultures. She flashed Tessa a look of annoyance, but Tessa was staring into space and didn't notice.

'And speak of the devil,' said Tessa when Mayu had finished. 'Don't tell me – you told him you were coming here tonight. Right?'

Mayu followed her gaze along the lanes to where Will and a group of his mates were parading about and she felt herself begin to blush. She didn't know why. 'He didn't say he was coming,' she mumbled.

'He probably didn't know whether he could persuade his mates to come,' said Tessa.

'The lads on lane ten? Which one is it? That one

with the dark hair is a bit of all right.' Chloe and Heather jostled each other for a better look.

Mayu groaned. Why didn't they just announce it over the Tannoy?

'That lad with the dark hair has just waved. I think he fancies me. I like his T-shirt.' Heather tossed her hair back and smiled in their direction.

'That's Will,' said Mayu.

'God, it isn't! You lucky cow, Mayu!'

'We just work together. I've told you, he's an idiot.'

'Well if there's nothing going on between you, you won't mind if I wander over.'

'Back off, Heather. This one's got Mayu's name on it,' said Tessa.

'Well she must need glasses then because she doesn't seem to have realised.'

'She's just a slow reader.' Tessa turned to her. 'Go on, Mayu, go for it, before somebody else sinks their claws into him.' She stared at Heather, who turned away and finished her drink.

'I'm not going over.' Mayu could just imagine what would happen if she did: he'd start shouting, 'Oh my God, I can't even get away from her in a place like this,' and hide under the chair or something. It was bad enough at work. She wasn't about to set herself up for public humiliation.

'Why not?' demanded Tessa.

Mayu shrugged. 'He's with all his mates.'

'So? It's just moral support. They take the piss out of us and say we can't even go to the toilet ourselves, but they're worse. D'you want me to come with you?'

'No!' All she wanted was for Tessa to shut up.

'What do you think he's come here for?'

'To have a game of bowls with his mates.'

'Oh yeah. As if.'

'You've got love on the brain, Tessa. It's just a coincidence. And I'm not going over and making a fool of myself.'

'Yeah, OK,' said Tessa, and Mayu breathed a sigh of relief. Normally, when Tessa got her teeth into something she was like Chloe's Yorkshire terrier and wouldn't give it up.

'I'll go over and see why he's come. I don't mind making a fool of myself,' Tessa continued, and Mayu groaned. She might have known.

'Don't you dare,' she said.

'Why? You're looking at your fairy godmother, girl. One wave of my magic wand and you can live happily ever after.'

'I'm happy enough as I am, thanks.' Tessa was bad enough trying to be helpful when she was in a good mood. In the strange mood she was in now anything might happen, but it wouldn't be Tessa that would have to live with the consequences for the rest of the summer. Mayu could just imagine how big-headed and overbearing Will would become if Tessa walked over and announced in front of all his mates that her best friend fancied him. It was a ridiculous idea. How on earth had she got it into her head?

Tessa kicked out at a chair with her foot. 'I'm only trying to help. Just because my life's ruined it doesn't mean I don't want you to be happy.'

'Oh, Tessa.' Mayu sat down beside her and gave her a hug. 'I'm sure everything's going to be all right. I bet you a cinema ticket that he'll come into Sullivans next week to see you again.'

'You don't think he's already got a girlfriend?' Tessa asked.

'No.' Mayu had to cross her fingers behind her

back as she said it. It was only a half-lie. She didn't know for certain whether Ralf did or not, and she was saying it for the best of reasons. Tessa just didn't seem ready to face the possibility that she might never see this lad she believed to be her soulmate again.

'I think something special must have happened for you to react the way you have,' she added. She was speaking the truth there. Something special had happened to Tessa, but whether it had also happened to this Ralf person was another matter.

'I knew you'd understand eventually, Mayu.' Tessa stood up and smiled at her. 'Does anybody fancy another Coke before we have our next game? My mum gave me a sub on my wages.'

'I'll come over and give you a hand,' said Mayu. She didn't trust Tessa not to go over to Will and his mates.

'Shall we ask if the lads want a drink?' whispered Tessa as they came close.

'If you like. As long as you don't mind me never speaking to you again,' answered Mayu.

'Meanie,' hissed Tessa.

Tessa paid for the drinks, but as they turned to

leave Will sauntered over. 'Fancy seeing you here,' he said.

'Fancy.' Tessa rolled her eyes and leaned back against the counter.

'Are you having a good game?' he asked Mayu.

'Yes.' Mayu could hear his mates giggling behind her. What was he up to? Her body tensed as she waited for him to try and get his own back for the trick she'd played on him earlier.

Will stared at her for a moment, then took some money out of his pocket and checked the price board above their heads. 'Oh well, see you tomorrow then,' he said, walking past them to the counter.

'Aw, isn't that nice?' said Tessa as they made their way over to the others.

'What's nice?'

'He's shy, bless him.'

Mayu's jaw dropped open. Shy! Will? She'd never met anybody less shy in her life. 'You're mad,' she said to Tessa.

'No I'm not. It's you that's mad. What were you looking at him like he was Jack the Ripper for? No wonder the poor lad couldn't get his words out.'

Mayu shrugged. She was sure she hadn't been looking at him like that. Tessa always exaggerated.

'He's not as good-looking as Ralf of course, but he's still bloody gorgeous. Don't you think so?'

'I've never said he wasn't good-looking,' said Mayu. In fact she hadn't realised quite how good-looking he was until tonight. She was so used to seeing him in his white chef's overall and stupid hat that it was a shock to see him in jeans and T-shirt.

'Mad, mad, mad,' muttered Tessa, as they walked back down the steps to the bowling lanes.

Ralf Goes Window Shopping

On the way to work next morning, Tessa stopped at The Card Shop and bought Mayu one of the small pottery animals that she collected. She thought she'd been a bit moody last night and this was by way of saying sorry. She'd give it to Mayu at lunchtime and she'd also ring Heather and Chloe to apologise. They were good mates. Not many would have put up with the way she'd acted earlier last night.

She took the stairs two at a time on the way up to the sportswear department. It was the start of a new day. Perhaps Ralf would come in. But if he didn't she hadn't got to let herself get in such a state about it. Lads weren't worth it. No, that wasn't true; this one was. But she mustn't take it out on other people.

'Any messages?' She bounded into the stock-room and gave BO a huge grin. It confused him when she was nice to him. You could see his little brain ticking over.

'What do you think this is, some kind of hotel?'

'You know what I mean. Did anybody come in looking for me yesterday?'

'Like the police, you mean?'

'Ha ha very funny. Have you ever thought of being a stand-up comedian?' That was her quota of being nice to him for the day. 'So did anybody ask for me then?'

'The only person who's been asking for you is the assistant store manager. She wants you to help the window dresser today. I'm to tell you that you'll find her in the window beside the side entrance. So I'll bid you farewell.'

'I want to stay here.' If she moved, Ralf would definitely think she'd left, and they'd never see each other again.

BO started to laugh. 'I'm touched, but as they say: tough. Mr Edmonds is back on Monday and we've the Saturday lad in today. We don't need you.'

Tessa tramped down to the side window with a heavy heart. It put on a few extra tons when she saw what she was supposed to help with. Bridal Wear! Whose idea of a sick joke was that?

'Hi! You must be Tessa.' A bright bubbly blonde, who looked as though she should be hosting a game show, smiled at her. Tessa smiled back. It wasn't her fault she was five foot three, slim, and had hair straight from a Pantene commercial.

'I'm Catriona. I'm so pleased you're tall.'

'Are you? I'm not.'

Tessa heard the tinkling of tiny bells. It was Catriona laughing.

'You can pin these garlands of silk flowers along the line on the wall behind you. It's just out of my reach.'

Tessa picked up the flowers and glanced out of the window. Now she knew what Herbie, her brother's goldfish, felt like. 'Doesn't it get on your nerves people gawping in at you all the time?'

Catriona shook her head. 'You forget they're there most of the time. You're a student, right? Is this a Saturday job or are you here all summer?'

As they worked Catriona chattered constantly.

89

It was quite a shock for Tessa to find someone as nosy as she was, and she took to her instantly. Catriona was right: the people outside soon faded away. Catriona's tales of how she and her boyfriend had hitched around Europe when they left college were much more interesting.

'Have you seen the Sellotape anywhere? I can't get this veil to stick on Cynthia's head.'

Tessa grinned. 'Do you give them all names?'

'Of course. I even talk to them when nobody's here. Present company excepted, you get a lot more sense out of them than most people at Sullivans.'

'I think I saw it in the corner. Hang on a minute, it's rolled behind Davinia here. If I just bend—'

'No, Tessa!'

'It's all right. I've nearly got it. I just need to stretch a little bit more.'

'Tessa, get up! You're showing your knickers!'

'God, I forgot where I was.' Tessa straightened up and turned gingerly to look out of the window. A double-decker bus had pulled up outside. Please God, don't let there be anyone on it from college.

Please let it be a busload of grannies on their way to bingo.

God had packed his case and gone on his holidays. The first person she saw, his eyes as wide as saucers, was Ralf.

Tessa staggered out of view and banged her head methodically on a hardboard dividing wall.

'Hey, come on, it's not that bad.' Catriona raced across and stopped her. 'They were nice knickers – very tasteful.'

'What's he going to think now?' Tessa moaned.

'Who?'

'Ralf. The lad I was telling you about, the one who bought the tennis trainers. He was on the bus.'

'Oh my,' said Catriona.

'The first time I saw him I stunk to high heaven, and the second time I was flashing my knickers. What's he going to think?' she wailed. 'It's a total disaster.'

'No,' said Catriona. 'Of course it isn't,' but she didn't sound that convinced.

*

'I can see the headlines in the *Echo* tonight,' squealed Chloe. 'Shopgirl strips in Sullivans! Read all about it.'

Tessa's expression didn't alter.

Mayu had hoped that Chloe and Heather coming into the restaurant would cheer Tessa up. She'd lightened up last night, but now she was sitting in the corner eating her lunch, throwing off mess-with-me-and-you're-dead vibes. It seemed that short of presenting Tessa with a giftwrapped present of Ralf Peters, nothing was likely to penetrate her gloom.

'Your mate's going to bop the other one in a minute,' said Will, as he handed her two plates of spaghetti bolognese.

Mayu sighed. Tessa wouldn't, but she was likely to say something she'd regret for a long time. She served the spaghetti then zoomed back to the corner.

'Have you seen this figure that Tessa got me?' she asked, hoping to change the subject. 'A kitten in its basket. Isn't it cute?' She offered up a prayer that Heather wouldn't spot it was the same as one she already had. Luckily she didn't.

She left them cooing over the kitten and hurried over to a table where three lads were trying to attract her attention by snapping their fingers. She took their order, trying not to let it show how much she detested it when anybody did that. It seemed harder work today: a restaurant full of customers *and* Tessa to keep happy.

'Will?' Mayu didn't leave the order on the counter as she normally did, but waited until he strolled over.

'What can I do for you, lotus blossom? Shall we leave all this behind and take the next flight to Ibiza?'

'I wish,' she said with feeling. 'How much have you got in your piggy bank?'

He pulled a face. 'Not enough.'

'Table three want to know how hot your curry is.'

He smiled, and she noticed a dimple on his cheek for the first time. It made him look incredibly cute. 'How hot do they want it?' he asked.

'I quote: "We don't want the mild muck we had last time." '

93

Will poked his head out of the hatch, glanced over in the lads' direction and grinned. 'I can make it hot.'

Mayu was getting to know that grin. 'They're customers, Will. Don't do anything stupid.'

His grin widened. 'As if.'

'Caterpillars,' she reminded him. A girl who'd dumped his brother had practically screamed the place down when she'd found a giant specimen snoozing happily under a lettuce leaf on her plate.

'Curried caterpillars,' he mused. 'Difficult ingredient to get hold of, but a master chef always has a jar handy next to his station. Now if they'd wanted woodlice . . .' He went away laughing.

Mayu turned away. She'd have to hope that he was only joking. He could lose his job otherwise. She went back over to her friends.

'He's lovely, Mayu,' said Chloe. 'Has he asked you out yet?'

Mayu groaned. 'I've told you there's nothing going on between us,' she said. She wished they wouldn't keep going on about it. She wished that he *would* ask her out, so then she could say no, and then they'd be satisfied and shut up about it. But he *wasn't* going to ask her out, was he? If he'd wanted to he'd had plenty of opportunities.

'I think I'll just wander over and say hello.' Heather glanced at Tessa to see if she'd stop her, but Tessa was currently inhabiting a different planet to the rest of them and didn't say a word.

As she hurried about, Mayu caught snatches of their conversation. 'So you go to college one day a week on day release? That's great. I'm surprised we haven't seen you in the refectory. Yeah, the stuff they serve up is a bit crap. I wouldn't eat there either if I had the choice. When does your course start again?'

Mayu polished the table next to them and realised that she was rubbing so hard she was almost taking the surface off. So Will went to their college, did he? Nice of him to tell her.

She walked over to Chloe and Tessa's table. 'Has Tessa gone?' she asked.

Chloe nodded. 'I don't know why she's making such a big deal about it. It's the type of thing you expect Tessa to do – show her bum to everybody in the window. Normally she'd be the one who laughed most about it.'

'One of Will's mates fancies me like mad. I said he could ring me.' Heather returned to the table, her cheeks glowing.

'Which one?'

'I'm not sure.' Heather wrinkled her brow in concentration. 'I'm trying to remember what they looked like. None of them were really gross, were they?'

'Depends what you mean by gross,' said Chloe.

Mayu left them to it. Trouble was brewing on table three.

'Will!' she shouted through the hatch.

'Oo, I'm so much in demand today,' he said, putting on an effeminate voice.

'Table three are complaining about their curry.'

He grinned. 'I thought they might.'

'You didn't put caterpillars in it, did you?' she whispered.

He started to laugh. 'What do you think I am? I did go a bit overboard on the chillies and cayenne pepper though. Give them their money back. That should shut them up.'

'They're demanding to see somebody.'

He sighed. 'OK, I'll send Alistair out. He owes me one.'

'It should be you. You did it. You should take the blame.'

He gave her a strange look and then grimaced. 'Well normally I would, but as I went to school with two of them I think they might twig the moment they clocked me that it wasn't an accident. Give us a break, Mayu. They're total losers. I've been waiting to get my own back on them for a long time.'

'All right. I'll tell them somebody will be over to see them in a minute.' She went over to their table to clear their dishes. As she picked up a plate her hand froze. Was that half a caterpillar or a chewed-up chilli on the side? She put it hastily on her tray. She couldn't be sure and she didn't really want to know.

'What type of lads does your mate Heather go for?' Will joined her on the fire escape as she took her last break of the day. The coffee tasted stewed but she drank it anyway. She needed the caffeine.

'Ones with two legs,' she said, and then grimaced. What was wrong with her? She wasn't normally so bitchy. 'I'm sorry, I meant she has no particular preference.'

He laughed, and clambered up on his perch. 'It's been like a zoo out there today. At one point I felt like standing at the hatch and throwing the plates out like frisbees. I might do that on my last day.'

Mayu felt her heart thud down to the ground. 'Are you leaving?' she gasped. Suddenly she realised how much she would miss him if he went and how dull her job at the restaurant would be.

'Would you miss me if I did?' he teased.

'Like a hole in the head,' she said, and he laughed.

'I keep applying for better jobs, but until I get my qualifications I don't think anybody's going to be interested. One of these days I'll have my own restaurant. I might give you a job if you ask nicely.'

'You didn't tell me you were on day release.'

He looked at her closely and then shrugged. 'You never asked.'

'Which of your friends liked Heather?' She decided to change the subject. She suspected her voice had started to whine and she didn't like it.

His brow furrowed in concentration. 'I think it'll have to be Andy.'

'You mean you made it up?'

He looked for a moment like a little boy who'd been caught stealing Smarties.

'Why?'

He shrugged. 'To get her off my back.'

Mayu stared at him in amazement. 'Why?' she asked.

Will jumped down from the rail and the platform reverberated under his feet. 'Because some of us have work to do and can't stand around all day chatting and entertaining.' He continued on into the kitchen.

Mayu frowned at his back. Was she going mad? Wasn't that exactly what he seemed to enjoy doing whenever he got the chance?

She took her cup through and stacked it in the

dishwasher. Will was leaning out of the serving hatch and she could hear Vicky's giggles from the other side.

Mayu was totally confused. It was true that lads were a mystery. And this particular one was more of a mystery than any other.

Fragile – Handle With Care

Tessa waited in Mrs Turner's office to hear which department was going to be the lucky one to have her that week. She hadn't realised that they intended moving her from one to the other. She might be doing a stint with the garden gnomes yet.

'Chinaware, dear. Second floor. Tell Mrs Butler I sent you.' Mrs Turner put down her phone and smiled brightly across her desk at Tessa.

Tessa nodded and walked out, wondering whether she'd still be smiling later that day. 'Tessa's the name, demolition's the game,' she muttered, running up the stairs to the second floor. When she was little and they'd come into Sullivans to buy an ornament for her gran her mum had pinned her arms to her side and marched her straight through to the counter, hissing, 'Don't you dare touch anything!' Even now when she went round with her mates she always got the feeling that she shouldn't really be there.

'Are you Mrs Butler?' she asked the woman behind the counter in the china department.

'No, thank God.'

Tessa smiled. This woman seemed OK. She'd be able to get on with her all right.

'We call her Mrs Bustler around here. Don't take it personal, but she probably won't let you serve anybody. She seems to think that everybody's entitled to the whole history of Wedgwood even when they've just popped in for a Peter Rabbit egg cup.'

'I'll tell her I'm studying modern china at college. I am actually, in business studies, only it's the country and not the teacup variety.'

The woman laughed, but shut up quick enough when a well-padded grey-haired dragon emerged from a door behind her.

'Miss Lewis?' Mrs Butler came over and frowned at Tessa. She looked pissed off with her before she'd even started.

'Tessa.' Tessa tried to smile at the woman but her lips couldn't quite manage it. She had the feeling that she probably looked as though she was about to break wind.

'Miss Lewis.' The woman wrinkled her nose as though Tessa had actually done so.

Tessa was dying to say 'Tessa' again and see how long it would go on for, but she'd had her first pay packet and quite fancied seeing the next one.

'I'll go and get started in the stockroom then, shall I?' The other woman winked at Tessa behind Mrs Butler's back and walked away.

'What would you like me to do?' Tessa attempted another smile and managed to look a little less constipated.

'Dust.'

Dust! Tessa studied the woman to see whether she was joking. Nope. No joke had ever passed those lips.

'Mrs Curtis will show you where the cleaning utensils are kept.' She pointed over to the stockroom.

Oh fun! Oh joy! Tessa went in search of dusters. She thought she'd got out of stuff like this by working. Not that they were that hot on dusting in her house anyway.

'Mrs Curtis, show this young lady where the cleaning utensils are kept, if you please,' Tessa said to the woman in the stockroom, and was pleased to see her jump. Yeah, she had the old bag's voice just right. Maybe a fraction too high.

'Jesus! I thought you were her. I was just about to have a sly fag.'

'Oh sorry. What's with this Miss and Mrs stuff anyway? I thought somebody like her would want to call us by our first names; it usually makes them feel superior.'

'She's probably frightened somebody would start calling her by hers.'

'What is it?'

'You promise you won't let on?'

'Promise.'

'Fanny.'

Tessa took a moment to digest this information before she started to laugh and the crockery on the shelves began to rattle. Mrs Curtis shoved a feather duster into her hands and pushed her back through the door.

The minutes ticked by like hours. Monday mornings were usually quiet, according to Mayu, but this was like working in a mausoleum. Whenever anyone hovered at the edge of the department and looked as though they were thinking of coming in, Fanny bustled over to them. This usually gave them such a fright that they charged off in the opposite direction. Tessa felt like leaping out at them shouting, 'I'll head them off this way,' but she'd lasted two and a half hours without breaking anything and had decided to go for three.

Tessa had lunch, did her best not to moan too much to Mayu, and came back to the china department. What exciting job would Fanny have lined up for her this afternoon?

It was dusting duties again. Tessa had a sinking feeling that when she'd finished everything Fanny would send her back to the first lot and tell her to start all over again.

'This stick should have a government health warning printed on the bottom of it.' She waved the feather duster at Mrs Curtis as she passed carrying a basketful of Crown Derby.

'Yeah. Dusting can seriously affect your brain

cells,' she said before Tessa could. 'At least you're only here for the week, love. I'm here for life.'

The woman's words cheered her up. She'd already made a conscious decision to try and put Ralf out of her mind, but what Mrs Curtis said seemed to put things in greater perspective: her life could be a lot worse.

'Hello again. You get about a bit.'

Even if she'd been blindfolded Tessa would have recognised that voice. A rush of blood swept through her body, her hand shook, and a Royal Doulton figurine almost dropped out of it. She'd developed psychic powers: she'd thought of Ralf and he'd appeared!

'Oh hi,' she mumbled. That dusting had done its damage. Where was all the sparkling repartee she was famous for? Wherever it had gone it didn't have a chance to come back before the Mighty Bustler pounced and dragged him off to her lair beside the till.

'And what is it you're looking for, young man? A christening present? Well you've come to the right place. Have you anything particular in mind?'

Tessa listened as Fanny went through her spiel.

It wasn't her imagination, she was sure it wasn't, that Ralf kept looking over in her direction and smiling. He bought a silver money box in the shape of a teddy bear and paid extra to have it giftwrapped. Tessa thought it was the best christening present in the world.

Finally he was free and Tessa's heart started booming. She knew he was going to come over and she just wished that she didn't look such a prat flitting about with her feather duster.

'I hope he likes it. It's for my sister's kid.' Ralf held up the Sullivans' black and gold bag and smiled. Her insides turned to marshmallow, and it was all she could do to stand. Nobody had ever affected her like this, not even after a marathon snog at the pictures.

'I saw what you bought. I think it's lovely,' she managed.

'Really?'

'Yeah, really.'

'Miss Lewis! Go and help Mrs Curtis in the stockroom please.'

'Right.' Tessa turned back to Ralf.

'Now!'

'I better go.' Ralf stuck his present under his arm, gave her a last heart-stopping smile, and walked away.

Evil bitch! Miserable cow! Tessa marched over to Mrs Butler, silently mouthing a litany of abuse. She gripped the handle of the feather duster and knew exactly where she wanted to shove it. Mrs Butler gave her a tight smile as she stomped past. She looked the happiest she'd done all day; destroying other people's lives definitely agreed with her.

It didn't take Tessa long to calm down. Ralf had come in. That meant he could come in again. And he would. You couldn't send out a smile that singed another person's nerve endings and not like them a tiny bit. He'd be back, and this time she'd have her wits about her. She'd tell him straight off what time her break was and the evil old witch wouldn't be able to do a thing about it.

Tessa was flitting about with her feather duster like the sugar plum fairy when Fanny came over to her just before closing. 'Are you enjoying your work in the china department, Miss Lewis?' she asked with a frown.

Tessa gave her a gushing smile. 'I love it, Mrs Butler.' That should upset the old bag.

'Then I'm afraid I have some bad news for you. The toy department is under-staffed and Mrs Turner wants you to report there tomorrow.'

Luckily she turned away before she saw Tessa's reaction. The feather duster hit the ceiling, did a few frantic pirouettes, and narrowly missed a display of glass birds before Tessa caught it.

'Yes!' she said, throwing it up again. Life was good and getting better by the minute. As far as she could see the one and only advantage of having a little brother was that you got to play with his toys. She would have a whale of a time in the basement, and there'd be no Sam hanging on to her and whining that she wouldn't give him a go.

And Ralf would find her. He'd already said how she got around, so he'd be expecting her to be somewhere else next time he came in. And lads were big kids. Once he saw her in the middle of train sets and construction kits he wouldn't be able to resist joining her.

Yeah, she'd play stickle bricks with him any time he asked her.

'I hope you'll be happy with us, Tessa. I like to think we're one big happy family down here.' The toy department manager shook her hand and beamed at her.

Tessa grinned back. The man must be nearing retirement but he was a real sweetie. Fat and jolly, he was probably dressed up at Christmas as Santa. He looked as though he'd be in his element sitting in a grotto with loads of kids climbing all over him.

'So if you wouldn't mind helping Marlon this morning, that would be wonderful. He's over there pricing up jigsaws.' He pointed vaguely to the far corner.

Tessa walked over, smiling to herself. Would she mind? He was so funny. What would he have done if she'd said she did?

She passed a Sylvanian farmhouse and crouched down to look at the figures inside. She'd bought Sam the squirrel family for his last birthday because she'd fancied playing with them, but he'd chucked them away and said they were a pooey present. It looked as if she'd be able to play with them to her heart's content here.

Where was this person she was supposed to help? What had the manager said his name was? Marlon? God, she hoped it wasn't Marlon Baxter, the biggest prat in their college. He'd be in his element here: he had a mental age of about nine.

There were the jigsaws and a pricing gun lying beside them. Perhaps Marlon was round the corner. Tessa took a look just as the most hideous green scaly monster leapt out at her. As its red-veined eye peered menacingly at her, she let out a blood-curdling scream that Mayu would have heard on the top floor.

'Dear, dear, what's going on?' The manager padded over and started to chuckle when he saw them. 'Naughty, naughty, Marlon,' he said, patting the monster on the shoulder and padding off again.

Tessa waited until he'd gone and her blood pressure had dropped from cardiac arrest before calling Marlon something a little more colourful than 'naughty, naughty'. Bloody Marlon Baxter.

She might have known her luck was too good to last.

He ripped off the mask and grinned. 'I got you though, didn't I?'

Tessa gave a bored sigh. 'Try to act your age, Marlon, not your shoe size,' she said, but he was oblivious to sarcasm.

'You were really scared,' he laughed. 'Wait until I tell the lads about it.'

'I wouldn't if I were you.'

'Why not?'

'Because then I'd have to tell them what Angela White told me when she was going out with you, and I don't really want to because it was said in confidence.'

Marlon stared at the ground and kicked out at a pile of Trivial Pursuit with his foot. 'Yeah OK,' he said, and she had to turn away to hide her grin. What a lucky shot! First day of term she'd get Angela in the cloakroom and find out what had happened.

The day passed like a dream. Tessa kept pinching herself to make sure she wasn't going to wake up and find she should have been in chinaware with

Fanny Bustler, she was enjoying herself so much. Most of the time she even forgot to feel irritated with Marlon. Parents seemed so pleased that she was prepared to open toy boxes and show them what the things inside did. She even challenged one dad to a race on a space hopper and they made it as far as the Wendy house before he fell off.

'I've found my vocation. I'm going to pack in college and open a toy shop,' she joked to Mayu at lunchtime.

Marlon was putting some battery-operated animals on a table beside the till when she got back. 'Take a look at these!' he shouted.

'Oh yeah!' She watched the display of penguins, ducks, dogs, and bears all bumping into each other, and started to laugh. One bear had fallen over and couldn't quite right itself. It was stopping a duck from getting past, and every couple of seconds the duck would let out a loud quack as though it was telling the bear not to be so stupid and to get up. Over in the corner, a penguin had got stuck, was nutting the table, and looking totally pissed off about it. The star of the show, though, was definitely the dog. It walked a couple of steps forward, gave a little bark, stood on its hind legs and then did a complete back flip.

'Oh, I want to take you home with me.' She picked the dog up. It had the cutest face and lovely soft fur.

'Will you take me home instead? I'm fully house-trained.' Marlon dropped to his knees and raised one hand like a paw.

'Nah, you can't do tricks.'

'Wanna bet?' He checked behind him, gave a little woof, and flipped back.

Tessa started to laugh. 'Idiot,' she said. 'Where did you learn how to do that?'

'Junior gymnast, I was,' he grinned. 'Even made it to Wembley one year.'

'Clever doggy.' She bent down and patted his head.

He stuck out his tongue and started to pant.

'Nutter.'

'I need a good home. Don't let them take me back to the pound,' he said, leaping up. He took her off balance and she toppled backwards.

'Get off, stupid!' She tried to push him off as

he leaned over her, panting in her face, but he was heavy and she couldn't shift him.

'Oh sorry,' she heard a voice above her. 'I was looking for one of those activity things for babies.'

The voice was familiar. Marlon leapt to his feet, giving her a clear view of its owner. Never had she seen anyone looking as gobsmacked as Ralf did as he stared at her sprawled on the floor. But then she hadn't taken a look in a mirror at herself.

Anyone For Tennis?

'I've managed to change my day off. I told them my gran had been taken into hospital.' Tessa came rushing into the restaurant at five o'clock that night.

'Tessa!' Mayu was shocked. 'Your gran's been dead three years.'

'Yeah, well, she won't mind me lying about her, will she? So, d'you fancy a trip up to the tennis centre tomorrow morning?'

Mayu took off her apron and folded it. She thought Tessa was mad. From what Tessa'd told her about what had happened in the toy department this Ralf lad would probably run a mile if he saw her. 'Don't you think it might be better to wait for a bit?' she asked.

'Like he's going to forget he saw me flat on

my back with that half-wit Baxter slobbering all over me?'

'No, but—'

'I've got to get this sorted, Mayu. I can't think of anything else.'

'You don't know he'll be there tomorrow. You said he only worked part time.'

'I've got to try, Mayu. I've got to let him know that's there's nothing between me and Marlon. If you don't want to come then I'll go by myself.'

Mayu looked at Tessa's determined expression and sighed. How could you tell your best friend that you thought she was about to make the biggest fool of herself ever?

'I know what you're thinking, Mayu.' Tessa sat down on a table and kicked out at a chair. 'I don't care. It's too important. I know he's the boy I want, and if I let him slip away without doing anything I'm going to regret it for the rest of my life.'

Mayu gave her a quick hug. 'Of course I'll come with you,' she said. Apart from anything else, Tessa would need her to pick up the pieces afterwards if anything went wrong.

Tessa jumped down from the table and grinned. 'Thanks, Mayu. I'd do the same for you. Are you all ready? Shall we go?'

Mayu put her apron in her bag. 'I'm ready.'

'Don't look so worried. Everything's going to be great. I know it is.' Tessa walked towards the stairs, rested her bum sideways on the handrail and hurtled down. She waited until Mayu caught up with her. 'Then all we have to do is get you sorted and we can live happily ever after. You're going to have to say something to him, you know. You have to let a lad know how you feel about them. It's the only way.'

'Maybe,' said Mayu, although she had absolutely no intention of doing so. Agreeing with Tessa was often the only way of shutting her up.

Mayu was still eating her breakfast the next morning when the bell rang. Usually nine o'clock meant ten o'clock with Tessa, and Mayu hadn't hurried herself.

'God, I'm so nervous.' Tessa took off her shoes and threw them down. 'My heart's on hyperdrive.'

She followed Mayu into the kitchen. 'Have you left that?' She picked up Mayu's toast and started eating it. 'I couldn't eat a thing before I left the house and I feel a bit sick now; I thought I was going to puke on the bus. I better use your loo before we go as well. Shall we have a coffee before we go or shall we get one there?'

'Calm down, Tessa!' It was making Mayu feel dizzy watching Tessa pacing backwards and forwards in the kitchen. 'You're getting yourself in a state and you don't even know whether he's going to be there or not.'

'Yeah, you're right. D'you think I should ring up and check? No, they might put me straight through to him and I wouldn't know what to say. I need to see him face to face. Although—'

'Deep breaths. Now!' Mayu grabbed Tessa's shoulders, and for the next few minutes made her breath rhythmically in and out to the sound of her counting.

'OK.' She let her go.

'That stuff really works, doesn't it?' said Tessa, taking a few extra breaths for luck.

'Yes it does, but we'd better go now while you're

feeling the effects. We'll go to the ladies when we get there and we'll do the same again.' With any luck it might stop Tessa looking and behaving so manic that it scared the poor lad off for good.

They got to the tennis centre twenty minutes later, and with Tessa as calm as she was ever going to be they headed for the reception. The bloke behind the glass partition barely lifted his head as Tessa gasped out her request.

'Peters? No, it's his day off,' he said, and returned to filling in his form.

'Are you sure?' Mayu felt Tessa sag, and she kept a tight hold of her arm.

'Sure? Of course I'm sure.'

'Ralf Peters?' demanded Tessa, and Mayu tried to pull her away. She could see the bloke beginning to get annoyed.

'Watch my lips. Ralf Peters. It's his day off today. Is that clear enough for you or do you want me to repeat it again?' he said.

'Moron,' said Tessa, and turned away.

'Sorry, she's a bit upset,' said Mayu apologetically.

'She'll be more than upset if she doesn't stop

kicking that pot plant,' said the man, rising to his feet.

'Tessa!' Mayu dragged her away. 'Let's go upstairs and have a coffee. We can think about what you're going to do next.'

'Like jumping off the roof you mean?' said Tessa as she tramped upstairs. 'Oh God, Mayu, I got myself all worked up for nothing. I'm so stupid.'

'No you're not.' Mayu pushed her into a chair by the window and went over to order their coffees.

'If he had been here it would have been all sorted by now. It's not your fault he wasn't,' Mayu said when she came back.

'I should have rung up to check,' said Tessa, 'but I was so sure he would be here. I'm not so sure of anything any more. Everything's gone wrong. Maybe somebody's trying to tell me something.'

'Like the course of true love never runs smooth, you mean?'

Tessa groaned, but Mayu was pleased to see a faint smile on her face.

'So that's plan A down the drain. What's plan B?'

'I never got that far,' said Tessa. She took a few

sips of her coffee and then her face lit up. 'I'm going to write him a letter! That's probably better than seeing him face to face anyway. It means I can explain everything properly without getting embarrassed about it.'

'Right,' said Mayu guardedly.

'Have you any writing paper in your bag?'

'Mmm. I've got a full set of envelopes too.'

'Great! Let's have them.'

'I was joking, Tess.'

'Oh.' Tessa took a deep swig of her coffee and stood up. 'I better go and see if I can find some then.'

Mayu settled back in her chair. There was a good view from here over the outside tennis courts and she became interested in one of the matches being played. One of the lads had the same hairstyle as Will and she found herself hoping that he would win.

'Brain food,' said Tessa, returning ten minutes later with two huge plates of double chocolate gateau. 'I couldn't resist them when I walked past.'

'That's not brain food.' Mayu picked up a spoon and smiled.

'Course it is. It'll be converted into energy, won't it? And that's what my brain needs at the moment – plenty of energy.'

'Did you get some paper?'

'Sort of. That miserable old git was still on the reception so I knew I'd be wasting my time trying to scrounge any off him. I asked him for an application form instead. I'll have to write on the back of it.'

It took Tessa an hour to compose her letter. Mayu continued watching the Will lookalike match and made Tessa spill her coffee by clapping when he eventually won it.

'I feel shattered,' said Tessa. She put her letter into the envelope, scribbled out the name of the tennis centre and wrote Ralf's name on the front. 'I hope Misery Guts is off the desk by now,' she said, standing up.

But he wasn't.

'He's probably been sitting there since the centre opened and people have forgotten all about him,' said Tessa.

'Shh!' said Mayu. The man was already eyeing them suspiciously, and didn't seem at all pleased with the liberties Tessa had taken with his application form.

'If I ever turn out like that when I'm older, do me a favour and shoot me, Mayu, will you?' said Tessa, as they walked out of the centre and crossed the road.

Mayu sighed. It had been a long morning.

'I wonder if he'll ring me or come into the shop?' said Tessa.

'I don't know, Tess. Whatever he does you're going to have to try to be patient.'

Mayu Crashes Out

Patience, unfortunately, was not Tessa's middle name. From nine o'clock the next morning she was bubbling with expectation that Ralf would come into Sullivans to see her. She raced home and set up vigil beside the telephone to wait for his call. But as the days passed and it looked likely that Ralf had been abducted by aliens, because there was neither sight nor sound of him, Tessa seemed to fold in on herself.

On Thursday morning of the next week, Heather came into the restaurant and slumped over a table. 'A bottle of whisky and a tall glass,' she said, when Mayu came over.

Mayu wiped the table while she waited.

'Yeah OK, a cappuccino, but sprinkle plenty of chocolate over the top.'

'You've been down to see Tessa.' It was a statement rather than a question.

Heather nodded. 'She's doing a roaring trade in euthanasia kits.'

'Don't, Heather. She can't help being upset.'

'She could try a bit harder. Honestly, Mayu, you walk down the steps to the basement and the vibes hit you in the face. It's a wonder the kids don't run away screaming.'

Mayu grimaced. She didn't need anybody to tell her the effect Tessa was having on everybody.

'I could never stand that stupid Marlon lad but I feel quite sorry for him. He followed me out and asked if it was anything to do with him, the way Tessa was.'

'Poor Marlon.' Mayu went off to make Heather's coffee. She felt mean for thinking it, but she was truly grateful that Tessa was still in the toy department and hadn't been moved to the restaurant this week. Things were brilliant for her at Sullivans. Since she'd taken Tessa's advice and lightened up a bit with Will they were getting on great. Waitressing used to be something she only did for extra money, but now she found herself

126

looking forward to coming to work and she didn't think she'd ever laughed so much. If only poor Tessa could be so happy.

'We'll have to think of somewhere better to go this Friday. Somewhere that might cheer her up,' said Heather.

Mayu thought for a moment. 'What about Barney's? It doesn't matter if we don't talk that much because the music's loud, and we might even get Tessa up for a dance.'

'Yeah OK. Anything has to be better than last week.' They fell silent. Like her, Heather was probably remembering last Friday's fiasco. Tessa had insisted on keeping her promise of taking them all out for a meal and they'd gone to a Chinese restaurant. Chloe had summed up the general feeling afterwards by saying that she'd had more fun at her gran's funeral, and she'd really loved her gran.

Mayu served two customers and came back to Heather. 'How did you get on with Andy?' she said, remembering.

'All right.' Heather's face brightened. 'He wants to take me to the pictures on Sunday. I'll probably go. It was funny though,' her forehead creased into a frown, 'he seemed to have the impression that I was mad keen on him and not the other way round. It pissed me off a bit to begin with.'

'Oh well, you know what lads are like,' muttered Mayu vaguely, and zoomed off quickly to serve someone else.

As she passed the serving hatch she did a double-take: an orange furry animal was waving at her. 'Hello, Sooty,' she said, waving back. A little boy had left the glove puppet in the restaurant yesterday. If Ladbrokes were taking bets on who had their fingers inside it she could have made a fortune.

Mayu stacked her salt and pepper pots on a tray. She hadn't had time to fill them this morning, and, as her tables were empty at the moment, she decided to do it now. The fact that Will was in the kitchen and she hadn't seen him for a while didn't enter into her decision. Of course it didn't.

'Are you looking forward to your holiday? What time's your flight?' she said to Kat as she walked past. Kat was off to Majorca and had talked about nothing else for weeks. Mayu loved travelling. So why didn't she feel envious? It was strange, but at this moment, she'd rather be in grotty old Grantchester than anywhere else in the world.

'Remember to send us a postcard,' she said, as she pushed open the kitchen door.

A sense of unease hit her immediately. Everybody was standing around. Nobody was doing any work. Her eyes darted across to who they were looking at.

'Mayu!' Will's voice was a muffled croak. He was slumped over the sink. 'Go away! Don't look!' he said, turning his head to her.

'What?'

'I've had an accident.'

'An accident?' she repeated. Her knuckles were white as she gripped her tray.

'I was carving some meat and I was carrying on a bit.'

All the blood drained from her body. She was icy cold. She couldn't move.

'I think it's deep.' He turned slowly towards her and lifted his arm to show her the wound.

His overall was one huge pool of red as his life blood seeped relentlessly into it.

The crash of broken crockery echoed around the kitchen. 'No, Will, you can't die,' she said, as she followed it to the ground. A black swirling pit had opened in front of her and swallowed her up.

'That's it, keep your head down between your knees,' was the next thing she heard as she surfaced from the scary blackness of the pit.

'Will!' Every atom of her body seemed to scream out his name. How could she have fooled herself that he meant nothing to her? Why had it taken until now, when it might be too late, for her to realise how important he was?

'He's going to be all right, love.' It was the head chef, leaning over her, firmly pressing her head down.

'No! All that blood!' He was lying to her, trying to keep her calm. She struggled upwards, needing to know exactly what had happened.

'Just tomato sauce, love.'

Mayu stared at him blankly. What was he talking about? Will was badly injured. He might be dying.

And then she saw him. Apart from the others, his hands thrust deep into his trousers and his head hung low on his chest. 'I'm sorry,' he mumbled. 'It was only a joke.'

'Joke!' Mayu scrambled to her feet and grabbed hold of a work surface to support her. She took a deep breath and then, for somebody who never swore, gave a performance that would have impressed even Tessa's step-dad.

There was a deathly silence afterwards. People stared at the floor, at the sink, at the food mixers, anywhere but at her.

'Mayu . . .' Will stepped forward, but she ignored him. She also ignored the fact that there were thirty-five minutes left of her shift as she stormed out.

Double Depression

It would get better. Soon it would get better. All the magazines said it would. But it didn't.

Tessa smeared blueberry eyeshadow around her eyes and wondered if she should do everybody a favour and not go out tonight. If she was brave and noble that's what she'd do, but she wasn't. She needed her mates. She needed to be with them, doing normal things, pretending that things were the same as they'd been before she met Ralf.

She finished her make-up and flexed her jaw muscles in an attempt to smile. It had been a long time and they seemed to have forgotten what to do, but she tried again and this time she managed it. She'd read somewhere that if you were miserable and you smiled at yourself in a mirror your brain thought you were happy and sent out happy chemicals into your bloodstream. This fooled your body into thinking that you were happy and you cheered up automatically. Tessa stared at the idiot grinning at her in the glass. It was a load of bull.

She picked up her bag, hurtled downstairs, and slammed the front door. There was probably an article she hadn't read that would tell her that dancing was the ideal solution for a broken heart. She was probably about to prove that one wrong as well.

Why hadn't Ralf been in touch? She'd explained everything in the letter. Did he have a girlfriend after all and when he'd got her letter he'd thought – my God, who *is* this girl? Couldn't he even pass the time of day and be friendly with someone any more without them jumping to the conclusion that he fancied them? Tessa added humiliation to her list of sufferings.

Chloe and Heather were waiting in the queue outside Barney's. Tessa joined them, ignoring the complaints behind her. 'Hi!' she said, fixing a smile on her face. She really must try tonight.

'Is Mayu coming?' asked Chloe.

Mayu? Why shouldn't she be? Tessa looked blank and then her smile froze. Mayu! She'd gone up to the restaurant to see her today and they'd told her she'd phoned in sick with a stomach upset. God, she was a selfish self-centred horrible cow! She'd completely forgotten to ring up and ask how she was.

'Er, the line was engaged and I couldn't get through,' she mumbled, and she saw Chloe and Heather exchange glances. They knew she was lying, and Tessa felt even more ashamed.

Mayu appeared while they were brushing their hair in the cloakroom. 'How's your tummy?' asked Tessa. She'd have to be extra nice to make up.

'There was nothing wrong with it,' said Mayu.

Tessa's mouth dropped open. What was going on here? Mayu never lied. She'd never skived off school or her job in her life.

'Didn't you tell her?' Heather asked.

Mayu shook her head.

'Tell me what?' demanded Tessa.

They all stared at her. Eventually Chloe sighed. 'I'll tell her,' she said.

'What a stupid prat!' said Tessa when Chloe had

finished. 'You must have been in a hell of a state, Mayu.'

'Not that you'd care.' Mayu unfastened her make-up bag and rummaged inside. Tessa had known her long enough to know that she was deeply hurt.

'Of course I care, Mayu. You know I do,' she protested.

'That's why the phone never stopped ringing all day with you phoning up on your breaks to see how I was.'

'I'm sorry.' She was the lowest of the low. Mayu had every right to be pissed off with her.

'I know it's difficult phoning from work some-times, but I thought when you got home . . .'

'I'm sorry,' repeated Tessa. She didn't even try to make excuses this time.

'And I'm sorry that you're so wrapped up in your own problems that you can't spare a second for your supposedly best mate.'

Tessa stared at the floor. Whenever she'd needed Mayu her mate had always been there for her, but today when Mayu had needed her she'd let her down. True friends weren't only there for the good times. Mayu, Chloe and Heather had proved that. They'd stuck with her while she was a total pain. She didn't deserve it.

'You're right. I shouldn't have come.' Tessa picked up her bag and walked out of the cloakroom. The music vibrated through her bones as she pushed her way through the crowds to the exit. A bouncer grabbed her hand, and she didn't have the energy to stop him as he stamped it with a re-entry pass. She lowered her head and walked miserably past the people in the queue outside.

'Hello,' said a voice from one of them.

'I shouldn't have said that to her.' Mayu sat down on a chair in the corner of the cloakroom and felt miserable.

'Of course you should. She's got to learn that she's not the only person who matters in this world,' said Heather.

Mayu shook her head. 'She doesn't think that.'

'Well, she acts like it sometimes. She's been a pain in the bum for months.'

'Days,' said Mayu.

'It's felt like months,' said Heather.

'It hurt a lot that she couldn't be bothered to phone me.'

'Of course it did.' Chloe patted her shoulder. 'You were right to tell her. Maybe it'll make her snap out of it and come back to planet Earth again.'

'Too right,' said Heather. 'I tell you, I nearly put an advert in the *Echo* this week: Will the individual known as Ralf Peters please contact Tessa Lewis currently working or pretending to work at Sullivans' department store, and put us all out of our misery.'

Mayu gave a weak smile. Tessa had been in the wrong but she knew she was sorry. She didn't like to see her upset like that. 'I think I'll go and find her,' she said.

'She's probably already on the dance floor,' said Chloe.

'I think she's gone home.' Mayu checked her watch. She should be able to catch Tessa before her bus came.

'Good luck,' she heard Heather say as she hurried out of the cloakroom.

137

*

'Hello, Tessa,' said the voice again, and Tessa looked up. For a second everything went out of focus and all she was aware of was Ralf's face smiling at her.

Smiling?

Laughing, more like. Embarrassment and humiliation saturated every cell of her body. The things she'd said in that letter! If only she'd taken Mayu's advice and waited until she was thinking more clearly. Tessa noticed his mates grinning at her. Oh God, had they read it as well? She could imagine them rolling around on the floor, practically wetting themselves, as they quoted bits of it to each other.

'Hello,' she said, and turned away. She was dying inside but she wasn't going to let them see that. If any of them said anything she'd say that one of her mates had sent the letter for a laugh.

Why hadn't he replied? Why had he been so cruel? There was no sign of a girlfriend with him, but she supposed that didn't mean anything. This was Friday night. She was probably out with her mates while Ralf was out with his. Tessa lowered her head and hurried her pace.

'Isn't it any good in there tonight, then?' Ralf left his mates and started walking along with her. Why was he bothering being nice? If he was that nice a person he would have rung her up the first day and told her she'd made a mistake instead of letting her hang on for days, hoping.

'It's all right,' she shrugged.

'But you're not?'

She glared at him. If he'd actually bothered to read her letter properly he'd know that she wasn't all right. Was he getting some kind of kick out of this? 'Don't worry, I'm fine,' she hissed. 'I'm well and truly over it now.'

'You've broken up with your boyfriend then?'

'What boyfriend?'

'That prat, I mean that lad you were on the floor with in the toy department at Sullivans.'

'Marlon? He's not my boyfriend. You know that.'

'Do I? And how am I supposed to know? He looked pretty much like a boyfriend to me. Or do you carry on like that with any lad who takes your fancy?'

'Oh just get lost, will you!'

Ralf came to a standstill and stared at her. Tessa stared back. It would be the last she'd ever see of him so she might as well take a good look. Why was he so gorgeous? Why did she still want him so much it hurt when she obviously didn't mean anything to him?

Slowly, he shrugged his broad shoulders. 'If that's what you want,' he said quietly, and turned away. It felt as if he'd ripped out her heart and was dragging it along the pavement behind him.

'You could at least have had the decency to read my letter!' she shouted.

He stopped, turned, and frowned at her. 'Letter? What letter?'

'The one I sent to you. The one you couldn't be bothered to read.'

'What address did you send it to?'

Tessa stared at him in disbelief. Was he pretending? Was there a chance he hadn't received it? 'I didn't actually send it. I left it at the tennis centre for you,' she said.

'You came all the way up to the tennis centre to leave me a letter? Wow!' Ralf's frown disappeared and a slow smile took its place. Tessa's brain fizzled and popped like a cereal commercial as all the nasty thoughts she'd had about him were wiped out.

'Who did you leave it with? Don't tell me. I bet it was that old bloke on the main desk who wants to bring back hanging for driving offences?'

'Sounds like him.' Tessa smiled back. Ralf had left his mates. He was standing here, talking to her. He had to like her a little bit, hadn't he?

Ralf leaned against a lamp post and shoved his hands into his jeans pockets. 'Tell us what was in the letter then.'

Tessa's cheeks simmered gently. 'Every time I've seen you I've been doing something stupid,' she said.

'Mmm,' he agreed, and her cheeks reached boiling point.

'I was looking for the Sellotape when I was in the window and I forgot that everybody could see what I was doing. And Marlon was pretending to be a battery dog when you came into the toy department. He'd just knocked me over and—'

Ralf started to laugh, and a warm glow spread through her body. It started at her toes. 'You're so funny, Tessa,' he said.

'I can be hilarious if I really put my mind to it,' she mumbled.

'Funny's OK for starters,' he said. Tessa watched his lips. He had the most amazing smile. He could be on a toothpaste advert.

'How did you know my name?' she asked, dragging her eyes away.

'I read your name badge. How did you know mine? I presume you did if you wrote me a letter.'

'I read your cheque.'

He laughed again, and reached out for her hand. It disappeared into his great masculine paw, and Tessa felt safe and small at the same time. It was an amazing sensation. She didn't want him ever to let go.

They walked for a while. Tessa didn't have a clue where they were going and she didn't care. In fact she couldn't feel her feet on the pavement. Ralf was probably the one who was walking and she was just floating after him. Somehow they ended up in a shop doorway – Millets Outdoor Leisure. For the rest of her life it would have a special significance.

'You still haven't told me what was in your letter,' he grinned. 'Was it how great I was and how much you fancied me?'

Tessa cringed. It hadn't been far off. She was pleased now he hadn't got it. 'Big-head,' she said. 'I was asking for advice on my backhand.'

He started to laugh. He was standing so close now that she could feel his breath warm against her cheek.

'I haven't been able to get you out of my head, Tessa,' he said, becoming serious, 'but I thought I was wasting my time. I didn't want to muscle in if you already had a boyfriend.'

'I've thought about you quite a bit as well,' she said, and his hot-chocolate eyes crinkled at the edges.

'You've got lovely hair.' He reached out a hand and pushed a strand gently away from her face.

'It's a mess.' Why hadn't she washed it before she'd come out tonight?

'Then I love messy hair,' he said, and she grinned. She'd never met anybody as nice as him. Ever.

'And you have a lovely smile,' he said, tracing his finger around her lips.

Tessa started to tremble. His closeness was doing funny things to her, invading all her senses. His touch was tickly and sent prickly little shivers running down her spine. His voice was deep and. mellow; she could listen to him reading her mum's Kay's catalogue and it would be like listening to poetry.

'You smell lovely,' she whispered. His aftershave mingled with the smell of soap and shampoo. It was as if he'd just stepped straight out of the shower. The thought of it did weird things to her stomach.

'Thanks,' he said. 'And you smell a bit nicer than you did the first time I met you as well.'

'That's why you couldn't get me out of your head – it was the smell.' Tessa started to giggle. She was feeling so tense; she needed to relieve the tension somehow.

Ralf put his arms around her waist. She shut up as instantly as if he'd flicked a switch. This was it! Any second now he was going to pull her towards him and kiss her. Blood thundered around her system. She was so nervous. It was as if nobody had ever kissed her before.

'I wanted to kiss you the first time I saw you,' he murmured. 'If that woman hadn't started ranting on about her tracksuit I think I might have made a fool of myself.'

'I wouldn't have thought you were a fool.' Tessa twined her arms around his neck. She needed the support. If he didn't kiss her soon she was going to pass out.

At last, his strong arms gripped her to him and held her against the taut muscles of his chest. His lips felt smooth and warm as they pressed against hers, and he kissed her more thoroughly and expertly than she'd ever been kissed before. Every other snog had simply been a trial run for this moment. A beautiful warmth flooded her body; it felt as if her insides were turning into runny honey.

A lifetime later, he lifted his head and smiled.

Tessa was beyond words. If this was a film they'd be standing beside a waterfall and there'd be fireworks and rockets crackling in the sky behind them. She had to make do with Millets' shop doorway, but she didn't mind. She didn't want to be anywhere else in the world but here with Ralf at this moment.

Tessa was in love.

Sorry

'I'm sorry for going on and on. Am I being really selfish? It's just that I'm so happy. I wish you could feel the same way, Mayu.'

Mayu smiled across the bed at Tessa. Happy wasn't the word. Tessa looked as though she'd been plugged into the mains and was sparking with vitality. Her skin glowed and her hair shone. If she was a dog and they entered her for Crufts she'd win Best of Breed award for sure.

'I'm really pleased for you, Tessa. He's lovely.' It had been a shock finding them wrapped around each other in a shop doorway on Friday night, but he hadn't seemed put out by her interrupting them. He'd seemed keen to go back to Barney's and meet Tessa's friends. Chloe and Heather had been green with envy after he'd talked to them.

'What are you going to do, Mayu?'

'About what?' Mayu crossed her legs more tightly underneath her. She knew exactly what Tessa was talking about.

'About you know who.'

'I don't know,' said Mayu miserably. 'I can't bear to think of him laughing about how stupid I was.'

'I'm sure he hasn't been laughing, Mayu. I bet he's more embarrassed about it than you. For one thing, you could have cut yourself to pieces falling on top of all that broken crockery.'

'I suppose.' Mayu twisted the corner of her bedspread between her finger and thumb and sighed deeply. 'I really thought he was dying, Tessa. I made such a fool of myself, but when I saw him like that I couldn't help it. I've never been so frightened in all my life. I hate him.'

'You don't hate him, Mayu. If you did you wouldn't have reacted the way you did.'

'No, you're right.' Mayu picked at a loose thread. 'I didn't realise how much I'd grown to like him and how much he meant to me until I thought I might never see him again. But how could he do that to me, Tess? It was awful.'

'I know, but I'm sure he never meant it to turn out the way it did. I'm sure he really likes you, Mayu.'

'Then why did he do it? It was such a horrible thing to do.'

Tessa shrugged her shoulders. 'I don't suppose he really thought about it beforehand. He just did it. Lads are like that. You've seen the wildlife programmes where the male of some species parades about doing really stupid things just to get the female's attention.'

Mayu frowned. 'So you reckon it was some kind of courting ritual?'

'Oh God, Mayu, I don't know.' Tessa threw up her palms in surrender. 'It was probably meant to be a joke. He's probably like me: it seems a good idea at the time and it's not until you're actually doing it that you realise what a stupid half-brained idea it really is. Remember when I tipped that bottle of Fairy Liquid into the fountain on the roundabout by Tesco's?'

Mayu remembered. 'But that was funny, Tess.'

Tessa grinned back. 'Yeah, I know, but what I'm saying is that it didn't happen the way I thought it was going to. I expected it to lather up and there'd be a few bubbles blowing around. I didn't expect that whacking great tidal wave of foam frothing all over the road, the police having to stop the traffic, and all those letters in the *Echo* about bringing back corporal punishment for juvenile delinquents.'

'No,' said Mayu, laughing. It was good to have the old Tessa back again.

'What are you going to do then?' asked Tessa, and Mayu stopped laughing. Her mate was like a summer cold: difficult to shake off.

'I'm not sure.' She stared out of the window, away from Tessa's steady gaze.

'But you are going in tomorrow?'

'Probably.' Mayu stared at the clouds scudding across the sky. She didn't want to tell Tessa that she was thinking of ringing around other restaurants to see if they needed waitresses. She'd call her a coward, and she'd be right.

'OK. I'll come here first and we'll go in together.'

'Why?'

'Because I owe you, Mayu. You're a good mate and you've put up with a lot from me over the last couple of weeks.'

'It's stupid you coming here first, Tessa. I'm not a little girl.'

'No. A little girl would hold her mummy's hand and do exactly what she was told. You had no intention of going in tomorrow, did you?'

'I hadn't decided.' Mayu shifted uncomfortably on the bed.

'You have to face up to things when they happen, Mayu. It's no good running away.'

'Hang on. Don't I usually say things like that?'

'Yeah, you do. So it must be true. Right?'

Mayu was no more decided when Tessa turned up next morning and practically frog-marched her to work. At least she got Mrs Emmanuel over straight away.

'Are you all better, dear? Nasty things these tummy bugs. I'm sure you didn't contract it here. I always tell all my staff to be extra vigilant in the hot weather.' And that was it. No mention of her going off early on Thursday or of the broken salt and pepper pots. She glanced across at her tables. Somebody had set new ones out. She wondered who it was.

Mayu walked down her row, checking her tables, taking sugar sachets from one to put on another. Any other time she'd have gone into the storeroom for another box, but she wasn't setting foot in that kitchen unless she had no other choice. So much for facing up to life.

'Hi, Mayu, you OK?' Vicky's voice wasn't its usual squawk, but soft and gentle, the way you talk to people with terminal illnesses.

'I'm fine, thanks,' she said, trying to stop her fingers trembling. This was awful. She shouldn't have come in. And she hadn't even seen *him* yet.

It got worse. Everybody was treating her as if she was a glass ornament that was about to drop off its shelf. Vicky told her she'd missed her, and Rebecca must have had a personality transplant because she started helping her with her tables when it got busy.

Mayu did her best to avoid Will. She waited until his head disappeared from the hatch before she grabbed her plates, and if she looked up when he was watching her she looked the other way. He looked hurt, but he'd hurt her a lot more than that on Thursday. She didn't go outside for her break as she normally did but sat in the corner of the

152

restaurant to eat her sandwich and drink her Coke. Was she being childish? She wasn't sure. All she knew was that she couldn't make herself go through that swing door and face him.

One roast beef dinner and one chicken and mushroom pie for table six. They should be ready now. She walked over to the hatch to check. Yes, they were waiting. She slid the beef dinner on to her tray, trying not to spill any of the gravy, and picked up the chicken pie. Something caught her eye. Something was written on top in thin coils of pastry: *Sorry*. And then there was a round circle with two dots for the eyes, a small blob of pastry for the nose, and a thin strip turned downwards for an unhappy mouth.

Mayu glanced into the kitchen. Will was watching her. He mouthed the word 'sorry' and then pointed two fingers at his head and pretended to blow his brains out.

Too confused to know what to think, Mayu automatically picked the pastry off the pie and delivered it to table six. With any luck the bits that remained looked as though they were meant to be there.

Ignoring table five, Mayu walked straight into the kitchen. If Will had anything to say she was ready to hear it now. He was standing beside his station, his shoulders hunched. He hadn't seen her come in, and her breath caught in her throat: he looked so sad that she wanted to rush over and hug him.

'Mayu!' His face brightened, and before she knew what was happening he'd grabbed her and a chair and dragged them both into the storeroom where he closed the door and wedged the chair against the handle.

'What on earth are you doing?'

'I'm kidnapping you.'

Mayu groaned. Nothing had changed. He'd said sorry for one joke so he thought it was OK to play another one.

'Don't be so stupid.' She reached out to pull the chair away but he stood in front of it, blocking her. His face was serious. He didn't look as though he was joking.

'Let me go, Will,' she said slowly.

'Just a couple of minutes, Mayu, please. I tried to get your address from personnel but they wouldn't tell me, and I rang directory enquiries for your number but you're ex-directory. I was going out of my head in case you were so pissed off with me you didn't come back to work.'

Mayu stepped back from the door, her mind reeling as it tried to assimilate what he was saying. She was wrong about him; he must care about her to go to so much trouble.

'Thanks.' He gave her a fleeting smile and all the anger she'd felt seemed to melt away. Her stomach churned as she waited to hear what he was going to say. She hadn't felt this nervous since she'd taken her GCSEs.

Will took off his chef's hat, threw it into the corner, and raked his fingers through his hair. 'God, I don't know where to start. I've rehearsed this over and over in my brain, but my mind's a blank now I've got you here.'

'Why?'

'Why? I don't know why. Will Armstrong – Grade-A loser, that's me.'

Mayu rested against a shelf of pickles. She didn't know what to say. She'd never ever seen Will look this agitated or unsure of himself.

'I'm sorry about the other day, Mayu. I think you gave me as much of a shock as I gave you when I saw you pass out like that. I couldn't believe how stupid I'd been. I'm going to change, I really am.'

Mayu gazed into the deep blue of his eyes. There was no doubt in her mind that he was telling her the truth. 'So it was just a joke? You did it without thinking?' she whispered.

'Yes. No. Sort of.'

Mayu stared at him. He made talking look as though it was painful.

'Maybe I did it to prove to myself once and for all that you didn't give a toss about me,' he said eventually. 'I should have asked you out at the bowling alley. I was up for it, but when it came to the crunch I blew it. My mates were wetting themselves behind me, and you and your mate were looking at me as if I had some kind of contagious disease . . .' He gave a deep sign and shrugged his shoulders.

'I'm sorry.' Mayu felt awful. She just hadn't thought what it must be like for him. 'I thought maybe your mates were daring you to come over for a laugh,' she murmured.

Will shook his head. 'I had to bribe them to go there that night, but as I was walking over to you I was thinking: What are you doing this for? You're mad. She's made it plain from the start that she can't stand you and you get on her nerves. And I bottled out.'

'I'm sorry,' said Mayu. 'If only you'd said something sooner.'

'I didn't know sooner, did I? Being the idiot I am I thought it was funny to play jokes on you. All the other waitresses know what I'm like and they don't react any more. You were different.'

'Stupid,' said Mayu.

'No. I'm the one that's stupid. I should have realised earlier what you meant to me, how I was racing into work to be near you, and how seeing you laugh brightened my whole day.'

'Oh.' Mayu's brain felt scrambled. This was all such a shock.

'But by then it was too late. I'd blown it. We seemed to be getting on OK, but I reckoned you'd just decided to humour me. You never let me get too close. Your mates would come over and talk and ask me all sorts of things, but you just weren't interested.'

'I was. I am.' Mayu looked up at him in confusion. 'I just can't be like them. It takes me longer to get to know somebody, but that doesn't mean I don't care.'

A slow smile formed on Will's face and Mayu felt a strange stirring in her stomach. She realised it was happiness.

'What would have happened if I'd asked you out?'

Mayu's heart juddered against her ribcage. 'Why don't you find out?' she whispered.

'God, girl, you don't make it easy, do you?' he said, but he was still smiling. 'So will you . . .?'

'Will I what?'

'You know . . . will you go out with me . . .?'

'OK.' She smiled back at him.

'OK?' He came over, cupped both his hands around her chin and stared deep into her eyes. It was the most romantic thing anyone had ever done. 'You're not joking?' he asked softly.

'No. Are you?'

'No. And I *am* going to change, Mayu. I'm going to stop messing around so much.'

'I don't want you to change, Will. Just give me a bit of notice next time you're thinking of stabbing yourself, OK?'

'I'm sorry, Mayu. I'll never hurt you like that again.'

'You'd better not.' Happiness was making her giddy. She held on to the front of his uniform while the rest of the storeroom spun away and went out of focus. Only Will was solid and real. His face came closer and closer to hers, blotting out everything else.

'I've wanted to do this for a long time,' he murmured, as his lips hovered over hers.

Mayu looked into his eyes. They were the colour of a summer sky as they sparkled down at her. Nothing could be as special as this moment. She would remember it for ever.

'What's going on? Why can't I open this door? Is Mayu there?' The hammering on the storeroom door, Mrs Emmanuel's yelling, and Will's deep groan gradually penetrated Mayu's consciousness.

'I've kidnapped her,' he shouted, and Mayu's eyes opened wide.

'What?' screeched Mrs Emmanuel.

'I said the door seems to have jammed, Mrs E.'

'What's she doing in there? There's a restaurant full of customers outside.'

Mayu heard Mrs Emmanuel's voice, but somehow the importance of what she was saying didn't seem to register. She began to wonder if she was dreaming, and she held on more tightly to Will. He smiled down at her and she felt the resonant thud of his heart under her hand. This was no dream.

'She was helping me to find a packet of chicken lips in the freezer,' said Will.

Mayu buried her face in his chest in case she giggled. His uniform smelt of herbs and spices and a faint trace of deodorant. It was a unique smell. Exactly like Will.

'A packet of what?'

'You know. That new ingredient we're trying out for the kids' menu.'

'If this is one of your jokes, Will . . .'

'You're getting me mixed up with somebody else, Mrs E. Now if you don't mind, it's been nice talking to you, but I need all my concentration for getting this lock open.'

He turned back to her with a grin. 'I think we've been rumbled,' he said. 'I don't think we've got much time.' And then his arms folded around her, he drew her close, and they both discovered just how special a kiss could be. As his lips pressed firmly against hers, Mayu realised how much she'd misunderstood him. But there was no mistaking his message now. She was the one he wanted, he cared about her, and he made her feel so good.

With her own kiss she tried to show him how she felt, and she thought she succeeded. Afterwards he gave a great sigh of contentment and snuggled into her neck, sending shivers of pleasure running all the way down to her toes.

Mayu felt she was going to burst with happiness. The shelf of pickles was digging into her back and would probably leave a permanent ridge there. She didn't care.

Mrs Emmanuel was going ballistic outside, and they'd both probably lose their jobs. She didn't care.

It was a great summer.

The Red-Hot
Love Hunt

Jenni Linden

Grand Plans

'Think she'll make it?' asked Nik, as they waited for Lou to come through the door with her overnight bag in hand. She tipped back her stool, reached out for her mug and stretched her long legs. 'Since that creep Guy walked out on her, she's hardly left the house.'

'Yeah, course she will,' said Holly, nodding her head vigorously so her red hair bounced. 'Where else would she want to be when she's down 'cept with her mates?'

She didn't tell the others that Lou had said she might give tonight's sleepover a miss. She was planning to celebrate the last night of term holed up in her room, playing the music she and Guy had listened to together over and over again.

'Have a good time without me,' she'd added. 'Oh – and thanks for trying to help.' She'd turned to stare out of the window at the sand, the shingle and the glittering sea.

But Holly was in no mood to let it lie.

'Aww, come on, Lou, if your best friends can't help, who can?' she'd asked. In the end, Lou had muttered that since it was all the same to her where she was, she supposed she might as well be on Gina's mattress as anywhere else on the planet.

'Gina says you can sleep in her bed – she'll have the mattress,' Holly had told her, but Lou had just nodded in a faraway manner then turned to look at the sea again. Lou had grey-blue eyes that deepened to bluebell when she was happy and enjoying life. Now her eyes were a rainy-day colour and her usually silky hair hung stringily around her face. There was no doubt about it, she was in a really bad way.

'Dumping her just like that.' Nik shook her sleek brown head. 'Lads – what a waste of space. We'll have to get Lou on the beach tomorrow. Warm and windy, perfect weather for surfing.' She took a gulp of creamy foam, her eyes dreamy with visions of epic two-metre waves.

'That wasn't exactly what I had in mind . . .' Holly started to say, when the door flung open and Gina's Uncle Toni burst in, bent down and started poking around in the fridge.

'Talking about me, ladies?' he enquired, waggling his black-jeaned bottom.

They grinned at him. Uncle Toni was Bexington's own Action Man. He was macho, muscular and the proud owner of the tackiest karaoke bar in town. Right on the beach, it was filled till the early hours of the morning with a selection of the lairiest lads on the planet. Inside his open black leather jacket, Uncle Toni's chest was home to a massive collection of gold-coloured medallions and a Polynesian necklace of sinister shark gnashers. Uncle Toni had all the qualifications for a top-ranking creep, but with his big grin, bounciness and unshakeable conviction that Antonio's karaoke bar was Kensington Palace on Sea, he was more like a friendly, none-too-bright puppy-dog. Everybody liked Gina's Uncle Toni.

He straightened up, a can of Tennent's clasped in his big, hairy mitt.

'You girls fixed up with holiday jobs yet?' he enquired. 'If you play your cards right, you might be lucky enough to end up at Antonio's Top Karaoke Bar for the summer. I'm looking for a waitress, barmaid . . .' he swept his hand round, the rows of heavy rings on his fingers flashing wickedly, 'general factotum,' he ended grandly.

He waited a moment. Gina was gazing at him wide-eyed, her lips parted. Holly bent her head and made a snorting sound into her coffee. Not wanting to hurt Uncle Toni's feelings, she turned it into a cough. Nik put her mug down slowly on the table. For once she seemed lost for words.

'So tomorrow could be your lucky day, *signorine*,' concluded Uncle Toni triumphantly. 'But put on your skates if you want to be first in the queue, there'll be lots of competition. *Ciao, bambine* – business calls!' He waved his can and crashed out of the kitchen.

'D'you think he's serious?' Holly spluttered, 'Can you imagine . . . ?'

Nik grinned. 'You won't have any competition from me,' she assured Holly. 'They've asked me to help out at the windsurf school again this year. Aww – I can't wait to get out and catch those waves.' Neither of them even looked at Gina, who was slowly turning over the brown sugar crystals with her spoon, then patting them into place again. The whole idea of shy, gentle Gina, with her big brown eyes and dark glossy hair, stepping within fifty metres radius of Uncle Toni's karaoke bar was completely ludicrous. She seemed even quieter than usual tonight.

Holly's eyes narrowed thoughtfully.

'Surfing instructor,' she repeated. 'That could be useful. Hey, will you be working with that gorgeous hunk of tan again – what's his name – Matt? You certainly struck lucky with him last year, Nik.'

Nik shrugged. 'Dunno,' she said. 'He doesn't live in Bexington, he just came for the season. He's a qualified instructor, so he can go wherever the wind blows. But I hope so – he's a really good laugh. He's just a mate,' she added hastily, seeing the gleam in Holly's eye. 'Lads – they're all right in their place, but sea and surfing are where it's at in the summer.'

'That sort of attitude will get us nowhere,' said Holly severely. 'With your built-in access to serious lad potential we'll all be looking to you for help during the coming weeks. And, talking of help, where *is* that girl?'

'Hi,' said a melancholy voice from the doorway. They hadn't heard Lou's quick ring at the door and

Gina's mum had let her in. She put her duffle bag down and managed a faint grin. 'Hi, everybody,' she said again.

Nik and Holly slid off their stools. Holly put her arm round her shoulders and Nik gave her a hug and kicked her bag into a corner. 'I'll make us some more coffee,' said Gina. She went to get another mug.

'Make me a cup as well, Gina,' said Gina's mum, who'd followed Lou into the kitchen. 'And one for Aunty Linda. All right, Louise? You look a bit pale to me. You'll have to get that nice boyfriend of yours to take you down to the beach during the holidays.'

'She'll be OK, mum,' said Gina when Lou didn't reply. 'Erm, why don't you all go up to my room and I'll bring a tray?'

Lou nodded mutely and they went upstairs, Holly's arm still round Lou's shoulders, Nik carrying her duffle bag.

'When your friends have gone, Gina, I want to talk to you about you know what,' Gina's mum was saying as they left the kitchen.

'Oh, *Mum* . . .' they heard Gina moaning.

One of the great things about staying over at

Gina's house was her humungous bedroom. She'd started off sharing it, then inherited her sister's space when she went to work in Italy for a year. Sometimes Gina's sister sent her a card threatening to return and reclaim her half-share. Since she also said what a brilliant time she was having as an au pair, and how cool Italian lads were compared to what British boyhood had to offer, Gina wasn't too worried. Some of her posters still decorated the walls in between Gina's own top selection.

The twin beds had enough space between them for two mattresses, so there was plenty of room for all four of them. And so far, however loudly they giggled or played their music, none of Gina's family had ever complained.

Gina had put her best fluffy bunny on Lou's pillow, together with a man-sized box of Kleenex. A favourite CD chirped gently in the background. Lou lay down on the duvet and reached for a wad of tissues. Holly settled herself at the bottom of the bed and Nik sat cross-legged on a mattress facing them.

Lou smiled mistily at her pals. She was so glad Holly had pushed her into coming. It was true – the best place to be when you were down in dumpsville was with your mates. Since Guy had broken it to her that he needed his own space and thought they should cool it, her heart had been so heavy it felt like she was carrying a tonne weight. Everything took twice as long, and she'd fumbled around for ages looking for her hairbrush and getting herself together to catch the bus to Gina's house. She only hoped Holly wasn't going to go into her agony-aunt routine and start dishing out advice. She'd already made her plans. This summer was to be totally dedicated to moping.

'So, how're you feeling, Lou?' asked Nik sympathetically.

Lou had imagined she was all cried out, but when she tried to reply, the tears prickled her eyes and her throat ached so she couldn't speak. She shook her head.

'Hey – enough of that.' Holly poked Lou with her toe. 'Say after me, I, Louise Ingram, am beautiful, talented and irresistible. Guy Wilson is a lowlife prat, totally unworthy of my attentions. As from now, he is but a blip, an accident of history. The whole of my summer hols will be dedicated to forgetting him.'

'I, Louise Ingram . . .' started Lou obediently.

Her voice died away. She still cared for Guy, so what was the point? Holly meant well, but she'd never been in a relationship long enough to know how you got used to having the same person around all the time.

'It's no use, I'm sorry,' she managed. 'There's nothing anyone can do, it's just good to be here with everybody.' She blew her nose on the scrunched-up Kleenex and tried to smile.

'That's where you're wrong,' Holly was just starting when there was the sound of a trainer kicking against the door.

'Can you let me in?' called Gina. 'I've got the drinks here.' She cleared a space among the fruity gels and lotions on the dressing-table, put down her tray and passed another handful of tissues to Lou.

'Never mind, Lou,' she said gently. 'After a whole year together, anybody would be upset.' Her dark eyes were soft with sympathy. She's probably never managed more than a two-minute *conversation* with a boy in her life, thought Lou, but she really seems to understand.

'We were going to that new club. You know, the one just off the sea front – I was wearing that pink dress I bought,' she confided. 'Pink doesn't really suit me, but I'd got it because Guy always said he liked girls to look girly. I was really looking forward to it. Then when he came, he said . . .'

Nik had been lying on her back, pedalling her legs in the air, but now she flipped on to her stomach.

'You shouldn't let blokes control you like that,' she said. 'Holly's right, Lou – you've just got to forget him. Come out with us, have a laugh, don't let him make you miserable.'

'I don't want . . .' Lou started again, but Holly was waving her arms and shaking her head, her hair glowing like a light-bulb.

'No, no, take it from me – the only way to get over a bloke is to replace him with a better model. All that stuff about needing his own space – space to come on to that blonde girl with the butterfly tattoo at the disco, he means. Sorry, Lou,' she added at Lou's stricken face, 'but face it, Guy Wilson isn't fit to lick your trainers. And your friends are here to see you get the boy you deserve. The Spunk of the Century.'

There was no arguing with Holly when she was in full flow. And when she said she knew what she was talking about, she was right. Holly flitted from lad to lad like a bee through a field of clover.

Guy had often tried to prise Lou away from her mates. He'd said Nik was pushy and argumentative; but she was nothing compared with Holly the man-eater, as he'd called her. 'She's so *loud*,' he'd complain. He'd flinched every time Holly laughed, and his worst insult when Lou appeared in something which didn't meet with his approval was that it was just the sort of thing Holly would wear.

'They're my friends,' was all Lou could say when he'd asked why she hung out with them. The only one he'd had any time for was Gina. He'd said she was rather sweet, though Lou wondered if he'd just been describing the way her long black eyelashes swept over her eyes and curled on her cheeks when she looked down and blushed if he said hello.

'So, girls,' continued Holly, raising her voice to a pitch that would have had Guy clapping his hands over his ears and running for cover. 'D'you realise that by some strange quirk of fate we're all in the same boat at the moment – ladless? Some of us through no fault of our own' – Lou turned her head away – 'others through shyness'

– Gina blushed and bit her lip – 'some 'cause they can't be bothered' – Nik grinned and looked up from her mattress – 'and some, like me, 'cause the wells of local talent have long since dried up. So, as well as getting Lou here a one-way ticket out of dumpsville, what say we *all* go out and grab ourselves a "spunky specimen" before the summer ends?'

'Hunt a Hunk,' said Nik, giggling. She rolled off her mattress and squatted beside Lou. 'A Six-Week Search for a Stud! Quite a challenge. What d'you think, Lou?'

A new boyfriend is about the last thing I need at the moment, thought Lou, but I don't want to be any more of a wet blanket. She smiled faintly and nodded.

Holly was well away now, her hair blazing, her arms waving. 'D'you also realise that millions of girls would *kill* to be in our shoes?' she demanded. 'Seaside location, gorgeous blokes from all corners of the country heading in our direction to chill out on the beach? All we have to do is get down there with our fishing nets and scoop them up. Sorted!'

She'd excited herself so much that her hair was almost shooting out sparks.

'OK?' she finished. And, without waiting for an answer, 'We start tomorrow.' Gina, who'd been listening with her mouth open, drew her breath in. 'Lou!' Lou jumped, she'd been mentally planning to have a weep-fest with one of her mum's slushy vids. 'I'll be calling for you in the afternoon. Get into your top lad-pulling gear and we'll hit the beach.'

'Shall I meet you there?' asked Gina. 'I don't . . . I've never . . . I don't know if I can . . .'

'Stick with us, babe, and you'll be fighting them off,' Holly reassured her. 'Right, Nik?'

'OK, after I've checked out my job with the windsurf school. I don't want anybody else nabbing it,' said Nik.

'My mum wants me to get a job,' said Gina. 'She's been going on about it all day. I hope I have time for . . .' She looked down and studied the pattern on the carpet intently.

'Yeah, my folks have been dropping subtle hints about me pulling my weight,' said Holly. 'But let's think positive here. Jobs can be great pulling opportunities. The right kind, of course – like Nik's. Just imagine the gits on offer at Uncle Toni's.' She peered at Lou. 'You paying attention, Ms Ingram?'

Lou's eyes were heavy. The last few nights had been spent tossing and turning, thinking up schemes to get Guy back, wondering if he'd phone the next day to confess he couldn't live without her. She'd close her eyes for a moment before she got into her T-shirt and they started the cleanse, tone and moisturise routine they'd sworn to carry out every night of the hols. She snuggled under the duvet, not noticing the mug that Gina was holding towards her. It would be nice to wake up and see Gina's dark curls, Nik's sleek head and Holly's blazing mop of hair instead of the photo of Guy she hadn't been able to take down yet. What good mates they all were.

Life's Not Fair

Lou had never been able to make up her mind whether it was a good or a bad thing to be an only child. Sometimes she thought one thing, sometimes another. Holly, who had two kid brothers, was in no doubt.

'You don't know how lucky you are,' she said bitterly. 'No horrible kids mucking about with your make-up, no having to take them swimming or play their stupid computer games. Then they're hanging round all the time when you've got someone lush coming, listening to your phone calls . . . No *privacy* . . .' She rolled her eyes.

Lou nodded. She could see what Holly meant, but on the other hand, especially when she'd come back from her or Gina's noisy house, it could seem awfully quiet at home. Perhaps it had something to do with both her parents working full-time.

Sometimes she thought it would be nice to pig out with a bag of popcorn in front of the telly with a sister or brother – somebody you were comfortable. with so you didn't have to make an effort.

At the moment, though, returning from Gina's house, she was glad there was no one at home to ask why she was wandering from room to room, picking things up and putting them down again. What was the *matter* with her, Holly's mum would have demanded? And she knew that Gina would barely have been in the house two minutes before her mum was telling her to go down to the shops or make a salad or chop some herbs. She, on the other hand, could turn on the TV and stare at the illuminated screen vacantly, without really seeing it. She could switch it off, wander into the kitchen, pour a glass of orange juice, take a sip, decide she didn't want it and leave it on the draining-board. Holly's mum would have gone ballistic if Holly had done that.

Benji the cat was rubbing against her legs, miaowing loudly. Lou knew he'd had his breakfast and wasn't entitled to any more till supper-time. She bent down and stroked him. Benji arched his back and purred, then looked meaningfully at the fridge. Why not, thought Lou, why shouldn't someone have a little happiness? She got out some cheese, chopped it into little bits just as Benji liked it and put it in his bowl. He raised his head and looked after her with devotion as she went up to her room and put on her Walkman. But every kind of music brought tears to her eyes now. Lou took off her Walkman, went over to the dressing-table and stared mournfully at herself in the mirror.

Then Lou did something she'd promised herself she'd never do again. She opened the left-hand drawer of her dressing-table, dived to the bottom and brought out all the snaps of her and Guy she'd sworn would remain buried there till she felt strong enough to rip them into tiny pieces. She arranged them in a row on her pillow then lay down beside them. She closed her eyes, imagining it had all been a terrible dream and that Guy still loved her. A tear squeezed its way through her eyelids and down her face.

After a few minutes Lou rolled off the bed. She would have liked to remain in her room until the millennium, playing the most mournful music she could find over and over again. But Holly was coming to pick her up and she'd promised to be ready. She went into the bathroom and washed her face then opened her wardrobe and peered at the contents. She'd also promised Holly she'd make an effort with her appearance, though the whole thing was totally pointless. Right at the back, glowing vibrantly, she saw the bright summer trousers she'd bought and the equally bright top to go with them. When she'd shown them to Guy he'd staggered back with his hand over his eyes as if blinded. Lou had felt ashamed of having purchased such tacky gear and had never worn them since. Now she pulled them out and held them against her. In spite of Guy's reaction she still thought they suited her – they looked rather fun. Not that she was in the mood for fun, but since the others were going to so much trouble she wanted to make an effort for their sake.

First, though, Lou decided to wash her hair and try that new citrus-smelling conditioner she'd bought and never used. Her mum had left a note saying there was some salad stuff in the fridge. Lou had ignored it, feeling she couldn't swallow a mouthful, but now she thought she might have a forkful or two after she'd finished her hair. Outside the sky was blue and the sun was shining. It was the first time she'd noticed the weather since Guy had ditched her. It would be lovely on the beach. With her friends.

'*Hey*! You look terrific!' said Holly when Lou opened the door to her later that afternoon. She too had changed from the jeans and T-shirt she'd been wearing at Gina's into an outfit that even managed to out-loud Lou's. Guy would have had some crushing comments to make along the lines of there being a serious colour clash with Holly's flaming hair, but to Lou she looked fabulous. She grinned at her.

'You look pretty good yourself,' she said.

'Yeah,' said Holly modestly. 'Well, we've got to show these fellas we mean business. You haven't forgotten what we decided last night, have you?' Without waiting for an answer, she added, 'Like my new shoes?' They were outrageous as usual.

Lou nodded. She really did, but there was something she needed to say. 'You know, I'm not so interested in getting another boyfriend,' she said with difficulty. 'After Guy ... I don't think I want anyone else.'

Holly shook her head. 'No, no, no, *no*,' she said. 'I'm not listening. It's down to the beach and a new, improved boy for you, Lou. What did I tell you? Aunty Holly knows best. Before you know it, you'll be saying, "Guy who?" Anyway, we've arranged to meet Gina there.'

Her enthusiasm was infectious. Lou gave up. It was easier to go with the flow. 'OK,' she said. 'But honestly, Holly, d'you think all this is a good idea for Gina? She's so shy.'

'We'll look after her,' Holly reassured her. 'Protect her from the creeps. I said we'd meet her at the ice-cream van – nice and central, so we can do some totty trawling while we're waiting. And we'll see Nik after she's signed on at the surf school.'

She was glad her mum and dad weren't putting on the pressure to find a job thought Lou as they walked along the promenade. That was another perk of being an only child with both parents working. Nik, who lived in a tiny flat with her mum, had always had a holiday job, and last night even Gina had said something about her mum hassling her. And in Holly's family everybody had to pull their weight – even her kid brothers had paper rounds.

'Have you started looking for a job, Hol?' Lou asked.

Holly shrugged. 'Plenty of time yet,' she said. 'I'm not settling for anything unless it's really trendy – something that'll put me in touch with the top talent. Only the best for Holly. When I find the right job I'll see if they've got anything for you.'

'Yeah, thanks,' said Lou. She couldn't be bothered to argue; they'd nearly arrived at the ice-cream van.

'Well, hello – *girls*,' said the scuzzy-looking bod with the greasy pony-tail in charge of dishing out the cornets. His eyes dwelt on Holly's colourful top. 'Fancy a Big Rainbow?'

Holly ignored him. 'We'll wait round the back,' she told Lou.

OK, I might as well be skulking at the rear end of an ice-cream van with the lolly sticks and dead crabs as anywhere else, Lou supposed. She was starting to feel depressed again.

'Look,' said Holly suddenly. Gina was walking

185

in their direction, picking her way through the sandcastles and sunbathing bodies. Mid-afternoon was a top time for totty to gather on the sands and quite a few likely looking lads turned round to stare at her, then whisper to each other. Gina kept her eyes on the sand and seaweed, scuffing her trainers on the shingle. She was frowning.

'She's so attractive,' said Holly. 'If only she had a bit more confidence, she could pull any lad she wanted.'

Gina advanced towards them. The others wouldn't believe it when she told them, she thought. She could hardly believe it herself. She kept hoping she'd wake up and find it was all a bad dream.

She hadn't believed her mum really *meant* it either, when she said she was going to ask Uncle Toni as a special favour if he'd give her a job at the karaoke bar. Taking Gina's speechless horror to mean she was overcome with gratitude, her mum had said that naturally the proprietor of a prestigious establishment like his could take his pick, but she knew Uncle Toni had a soft spot for Gina. She wouldn't promise, but she was almost sure she could persuade him. But why had Gina looked at her like that?

I must be the only one of the family who doesn't share Mum's high opinion of Uncle Toni's bar, thought Gina, stepping absent-mindedly round two blond, Swedish-looking types holding out a dripping ice cream temptingly towards her. Uncle Toni was the family success story, the one who'd made good. Hadn't he got a long stretch limo with blacked-out windows, rather like the ones in the *Godfather* films? It played havoc with the narrow sandy road leading down to the bar, but it looked magnificent parked outside it – a statement to all the world that Uncle Toni had made it big-time.

Gina's family loved to ride in it, with people turning round to gawp and speculate which celebs it contained. Gina was only glad, as she shrank back against the plush grey upholstery, that nobody could actually see inside.

She had no doubt that her mum would be able to persuade Uncle Toni to take on his favourite niece at Antonio's Top Karaoke Bar. It was impossible to get through to her the total tackiness of the place – to Gina's mum, everything belonging to Uncle Toni was perfect.

But surely even she could see how hopelessly unsuitable she'd be – Holly and Lou would hate it, but at least they'd be able to cope. Gina imagined the lairy lads urging each other on to performances of 'My Way', demanding drinks she'd never heard of, and shuddered. She cast around wildly for an excuse.

'I'll get all the cash muddled up,' she said. 'And I don't know the different drinks. I don't want to let Uncle Toni down,' she added cunningly.

'Don't be silly, Gina,' said her mum. 'Uncle Toni will train you. He's a real professional. How do you think he rose to the top of the entertainment business? You couldn't have a better teacher.'

It was useless arguing. Gina could only hope that, like a nightmare, the whole thing would fade away or that her mum would forget it.

So when Uncle Toni had come bouncing into the kitchen while they were waiting for Lou, Gina had kept her head down and her mouth shut, willing one of the others to volunteer. They hadn't, of course – nobody would be that stupid. Her mum obviously hadn't spoken to him yet, and until this morning Uncle Toni had still lacked an assistant. Then Gina's mum had put on her jacket, walked over to the bar and carried out her threat.

She came back beaming all over her face. 'He said yes immediately,' she reported. 'He told me he'd had lots of offers – naturally – but if he couldn't help his own family, what was the world coming to? That's your Uncle Toni all over,' she said fondly, 'Always puts his family first. You're a very lucky girl, Gina.'

Gina had looked at her in despair. How would her mates react when she told them what she'd been pushed into? Nik would probably say she should have stood up for herself, Holly would suggest she should act so useless that even Uncle Toni would lose patience and sling her out. They'd no idea how impossible it was. None of them had got a family like hers.

'If only we could get her to come out of her shell,' said Holly, as Gina walked slowly towards them. 'Hey,' she called out, 'lighten up, Gina, today's the first day of the holidays – and the first day of your new life. Holly will see to that. Trust me.'

'What's the matter, Gina? What's happened?'

asked Lou gently as they walked over to the big black rock and sat down. Gina gulped. Then she told them everything.

There was nothing to say. Gina – shy, gentle Gina – entombed in that tacky bar amid the moans and bellows and sick-cat screeches thudding out of the speakers and the local thugs jostling each other to do their dodgy impersonations of even dodgier crooners. Lou and Holly looked at each other. How would she cope with trouble? To do Uncle Toni justice, there was never any real trouble in Antonio's Top Karaoke Bar. If any of his customers showed signs of getting out of hand because they hadn't been called on to perform yet, Uncle Toni simply propelled them out of the door and on to the beach. He came back rubbing his hands and chuckling. Sooner or later they all crept back, and Uncle Toni was content to let it lie until they misbehaved again. But how would Gina handle the rowdy element if Uncle Toni wasn't around? How would she handle even the quiet ones?

Lou was the first to break the silence. 'Perhaps it won't be all that bad when you're actually working there,' she said unconvincingly. 'None of us has ever been inside. It probably looks – and sounds – a lot worse than it is. And Uncle Toni's really nice. You'll learn a lot, Gina.'

Gina looked at her. 'It'll be terrible,' she said. 'And I've got to go along there now. Uncle Toni's going to show me the ropes.' She picked up a piece of seaweed and started to shred it into tatters. At least her mates hadn't told her how pathetic she was to go along with her family's plans. She was grateful to them for that.

Holly took a deep breath. 'We'll come with you,' she said. 'All of us. Give you moral support. As soon as Nik gets here . . . There she is. Hey, Nik!' She jumped to her feet and started waving. Nik sprinted over the wet sand towards them.

'Hi,' she said breathlessly when she arrived. 'They've taken me on at the surfing centre, isn't it great? I'll be doing some instructing and helping with the board hire and that sort of thing. We – I – can start tomorrow.'

She hoped the others hadn't noticed her slip of the tongue. She didn't want Holly going on about fwoarsome, sporty boys when she heard that Matt would be starting there the same time as Nik. There was nothing like that between them. It never seemed to enter Holly's head that you could be matey with a boy without him being a boyfriend. To Holly, all fanciable lads were potential pulling material.

All the same, Nik couldn't help this big grin spreading over her face whenever she thought of Matt. Sure, it had to be admitted, he *was* rather gorgeous, all tanned and toned, and the beginners fought to have him help them get their boards up and running off the shingly shores of Bexington. But, as well as that, he was a really nice guy, never losing his cool when he had to rescue learners who'd slipped beneath their rigs or become enfolded in their sails. And once or twice, when they'd had time off together, they'd gone to some windy surf spots further up the coast and had unforgettably fantastic afternoons on the water. Windsurfing is the best sport in the world, thought Nik dreamily. It really gets into your soul.

She hadn't dared to hope that Matt would be back again this year. With his experience, he could have gone anywhere – he'd been talking about Fiji and Barbados. But waiting at the surf school, her heart had skipped a beat when she saw a familiar figure in front. Even in wetsuit gear, with his back to her, she'd recognised those broad shoulders and dark slicked-back hair.

'Matt?' she'd said, putting her hand on his shoulder, and he'd spun round.

'Nik!' he'd exclaimed, with a delighted grin that told her he was as pleased as she was. 'I hoped you'd be here again this year – wow, this is great!' She hadn't been able to stay chatting with him long because of meeting the others. But now she knew he was staying the whole of the summer it didn't matter, she'd see him every day. Life is good, thought Nik, sitting down and clasping her hands round her knees. But there's just this stupid Hunk Hunt of Holly's – aww well, if it gets Lou on the road to recovery from that creep Guy it will be worth it. Nik shrugged her shoulders philosophically.

The others were strangely quiet, she noticed. They'd nodded and murmured 'great' at her news, but she was a tad hurt they hadn't been more enthusiastic. And what was the matter with Gina? She seemed even more down than Lou, who was looking fantastic in a top and pants Nik had never seen before.

'There's a new instructor at the surf centre,' she

said. 'A New Zealand guy. Quiet and rather shy, but a really nice bloke. Just your type I'd say, Gina. If you come over tomorrow I'll introduce you. Holly can bring you,' she added. She wanted the others to know she hadn't been so caught up in her brilliant new job that she'd forgotten them.

'She won't be available tomorrow,' Holly said in a hushed, sepulchral voice. When Nik looked at her mystified, she added, 'We'll tell you on the way.'

Antonio's Bar looked at its very worst in the bright afternoon sunshine. The tables outside were overflowing with people's feet and bottles, bikes were strewn around and stereos were on at top volume. *Smart dress please* read a printed notice on the wall, to which Uncle Toni had added in his loopy handwriting, *Thank you, Antonio*. As they were reading this, he emerged.

'Ah, Gina,' he beamed, 'Such a lucky girl, eh?' Turning to the others he spread his hands out. 'I'm sorry, *signorine*, I would take you all if I could, but I promised Gina's mamma. Uncle Toni will keep you in mind, though,' he assured them as he ushered Gina into the bar. 'I have big plans for expansion.'

The last thing they saw was Gina's face turned towards them in a frantic look of appeal as she disappeared into the gloom.

The Power Of Positive Thinking

'Think positive,' Holly muttered as she cycled along the prom. She'd been telling herself this all day, but it was getting more and more difficult to keep smiling. When she'd set out this morning, she'd never imagined that bagging a summer job would turn out to be such a hassle.

Holly had aimed high at first, choosing the big hotel on the front where Nik's mum worked as a secretary. She wouldn't mind a job in the reception area, where she could keep a lookout for any passing totty – there'd probably be loads of tasty student types working there as well. Yeah, it was the Grand for her, decided Holly. She propped her bike against the railings and went inside to tell them the good news.

She knew she'd made a mistake as soon as she

set foot on the marble-tiled floor. The snooty-looking woman at the reception desk looked as if it had been so long since she'd clocked a human being under the age of twenty she'd forgotten what they looked like.

'Jobs?' she said. Her thin, pencilled eyebrows had risen until they disappeared into a hairdo that looked like Blackpool Tower. She had stared at Holly, slowly looking her up and down. 'I don't think . . . perhaps in the kitchen . . . Sometimes we have vacancies for washers up . . .' Her eyes fell on Holly's brightly coloured nails. She shook her head and the hairdo swayed. 'No,' she said definitely.

'OK,' said Holly. It was the Grand's loss, not hers, and it was beneath her dignity to argue. Anyway, she'd lost interest in this oldsters' paradise. The pulling facilities were obviously zilch. The caff in the park was the place for her – she couldn't imagine why she hadn't just gone there first.

Yeah, waitressing at the caff would be a really cool move, decided Holly, as she retrieved her bike and set off. The place was buzzing with cute lads slurping their cappuccinos and sporty types in droves quenching their thirst. The park itself was packed with guys chilling out on the grass, soaking up the sunshine and checking out the girls. It was the perfect Spunk Spotting ground.

Holly parked her bike against a big oak tree. In its shade, some tanned, bare-chested lads were fiddling with their stereo. The cutest gave an enormous wolf whistle when he spotted Holly. Holly felt a flutter of excitement as she grinned back, but she didn't linger. A quick glance round had shown there were plenty more where he came from and he'd keep till she'd fixed up her waitress job. She walked over to the caff and pushed her way through the crowd to the counter.

'No jobs,' said the guy behind the till as Holly approached. She hadn't even got as far as opening her mouth. 'Try again at Christmas.'

Christmas! Holly was gutted, she'd been counting on the caff. She looked at the waitresses, drifting around in their trendy gear, flirting with all the lads. It would have been the ideal launching pad for the Spunk Campaign.

'Anything else?' said the man at the till as Holly struggled to tear herself away.

'No,' said Holly. 'Ta,' she added politely. There was no harm in leaving a good impression. After all, come Crimbo all the skateboarders and footie freaks would be congregating there for warming drinks. Summoning all her powers of positive thinking, Holly flashed him a brilliant smile and turned away.

She almost decided to take time out to join the totty under the oak tree - but no, she'd given strict instructions to the others to secure themselves cool jobs. Now she had to get one for herself.

'Think positive,' she urged herself again. The park was out for the moment, but what about the beach? Plenty of oppos for lad interaction there. Ice-cream seller? Deckchair attendant? Holly propelled her bike towards the sea.

The deckchair man had a little hut on one of the windiest parts of the beach. Stinging sand blew into Holly's eyes as he told her that he worked on his own and always had. People had been wasting his time all morning asking for jobs. She should have got her finger out and started looking earlier. She'd be very lucky if she found anything now. There were billions around like her, he informed her. He sounded like Holly's dad.

Holly rode thoughtfully along the prom. She

199

was definitely getting rattled. Securing a job wasn't proving to be the pushover she'd imagined. Obviously a touch of lateral thinking was required. Time to move inland. There were clothes shops full of sussed-up lads and hairdressers where she'd have the guys at her mercy. Holly turned her back on the sea and rode into the town centre.

. It was mid-afternoon before she finally admitted defeat. She'd been round all the trendy clothes shops and even, to her shame, a few sad ones she'd never imagined she'd be desperate enough to enter. They'd all started shaking their heads before she'd even got halfway through her request. She'd left it much too late. Even the smallest backstreet hairdresser had a waiting list a mile long and that was to sweep up hair and make tea. Holly decided to pack it in. All these rejection experiences were doing her ego no good. She'd just have to start again tomorrow.

On the way home, her thoughts turned to the others. She wondered how they were getting on. She'd seen the fluttering flags of the surf club when she was talking to the deckchair man on the beach. She'd even caught a glimpse of Nik, kitted up in wetsuit and surrounded by a group of eager-looking beginners clutching their boards. There were heaps of gorgeous guys bounding about the place, but to a man they all appeared to be concentrating their energies on windsurfing activities. And then – Holly had narrowed her eyes – she'd spotted someone who looked suspiciously like the sporty stud Nik had palled up with last year.

As Holly was bending an ear to the deckchair man's ravings, she had watched Nik's so-called mate walk over to Nik and start chatting. Just good friends, huh? Holly had a built-in radar for girl/boy interaction and even from this distance her antennae were quivering. She hadn't been able to see Nik's face properly, but there was something in the way Matt was gazing into her eyes, their total absorption in each other, that had sent out vibes right the way across the beach.

So why had Nik kept it to herself that Matt was working at the surf school again this year? Holly shook her head and grinned. Nik would have some explaining to do when she met up with her.

But if Nik was now immersed in the job of her dreams, Gina's was the employment from hell. Holly, who'd hardly seen her over the past few days, couldn't imagine how she was coping. She'd looked so pathetic as she disappeared into the depths of Uncle Toni's establishment. We'll all have to take turns to check on her, thought Holly. Poor Gina. We'll have to find her a delish boyfriend to make up for her entombment in the karaoke bar.

And what about Lou? Had she been following Holly's instructions to get out there and start living again, or was she taking a fast train back to deep depression? She'd have to take control, work out a foolproof boy-trapping plan for the lot of them. Fortunately, Holly was never short of ideas . . .

Holly had been feeling hot and sticky, but pedalling now along an avenue of trees, the coolness of their dappled shade revived her. She lifted her head and looked around.

Just in front there was a break in the trees, and Holly saw the familiar big gravel driveway and open gates of the local garden centre. On one of the gateposts a large notice was pinned. Holly threw it a quick glance, then braked so hard she nearly went over the top of her handlebars. She couldn't believe what she'd read.

She got off her bike, went up to the notice and

looked at it carefully: *Chestnuts Garden Centre. Temporary staff required*. Holly walked through the entrance, crunched up the gravel drive and propped her bike against a spare garden trolley. She surveyed the scene before her. It was about as familiar as the dark side of the moon.

Just in front was a big glass and wooden building surrounded by neat rows of shrubs and trees. Polythene tunnels stretched into the distance. There was no doubt about it, on the scale of hipness the Chestnuts Garden Centre would register absolute zero. It did however, Holly reminded herself, offer something she now admitted she was desperate for – employment.

Holly walked in through the big glass doors and found herself in the gifts section.

In the middle, surrounded by wicker baskets full of teddies and tinkling bamboo wind-chimes, there was a little glass office place. Holly drifted towards it and peered inside. Hunched in front of a computer screen was a lanky man with bushy eyebrows and a speckly beard. He raised his cold grey eyes and regarded her through black-rimmed specs. He was the spitting image of Mr Franklin, her ex geography teacher.

Holly snapped out of her trance. She'd got on well with Mr Franklin during his brief stay at her school and had been sad when he'd moved on. They'd had an understanding: Holly didn't trouble Mr Franklin too much if Mr Franklin didn't trouble her. It wasn't easy to ignore Holly, but Mr Franklin had managed somehow and she admired him for it. She knocked briskly on the door and walked inside.

'Hi,' she said to the figure at the desk. The lanky man looked up. 'In search of a job, young lady?' he asked. 'Sit down and tell me about yourself.'

Like Mr Franklin, he was a man of few words, and ten minutes later Holly found herself a temporary employee of the Chestnuts Garden Centre. She would be available for general duties, the Franklin clone had told her. They liked their employees to wear neat, practical clothes – green or black trousers, for instance, and a nice green blouse. He spoke slowly and clearly, with spaces between his words, as if addressing an idiot. Holly didn't mind. She smiled and nodded encouragingly at him while secretly wondering just *how* she'd managed to get herself a job in such a pathetic, half-dead dump.

He was a very busy man, concluded Mr Mack – for that was the name on the label on his desk – but his assistant, Derek, would show Holly round. He rang a bell and waved her towards the door.

Derek wore green wellies, green cords and a green sweatshirt with a large picture of a chestnut tree on the front. Holly tramped round the garden centre after him while he showed her more varieties of vegetation than she'd ever wished to see in her life. All of them had both a short name and a longer one. Derek made absolutely sure he told Holly every single one of these.

As Derek's words trickled gently into Holly's brain and out again Holly used the time to run over her lad-pulling strategies. She didn't have to be an Einstein to realise that these would need to be conducted out of working hours.

'Have you got a garden at home?' Derek enquired.

He gave her a funny look, a bit like Mr Mack's, when she thought for a moment before nodding. There *was* a garden at Holly's place. She used it in the summer as a background for a sun lounger or when she wanted to paint her nails in the sunshine. Sometimes when she felt like getting away from her brothers she sat on the old swing and pushed herself backwards and forwards.

Derek paused before a tableful of bright red geraniums in little pots. 'You'll know the names of all this lot before you finish,' he said. 'They'll be like a second family to you.'

'Yeah,' said Holly. Derek was as sad as they came.

They went through into the garden chemicals section, where Derek stopped. 'You'll be working here at first,' he said. Holly looked round at the shelves of fungicides, fertilisers and weedkillers and for one crazy moment she almost envied Gina. At least she was working in an environment where things *moved*. But, when she really thought about it, even the bug-blasters won over Uncle Toni's lowlife clientele.

Derek was yammering on. 'Come and look at these cute little fellows,' he told Holly, and she followed him into a kind of courtyard. For a moment she couldn't believe what she was seeing. All around her were grinning little figures with bright-red cheeks, white beards and pointed hats. None of them came higher than her waist. Some held fishing rods, some were winding buckets down wishing-wells, some sat on red-spotted toadstools. It looked like a cross between Disneyland and the *X-Files*.

'Garden gnomes are right back in fashion again, I'm glad to say,' Derek told Holly. 'I've always had a weakness for the little folk.'

Holly thought they were all totally hideous. Her attention was caught by a particularly weedy-looking specimen at the back. Unlike all the others, who were holding forks or trowels or doing something, it was just standing there. By some trick of the light, it seemed to be staring straight in their direction. Imagine having that infesting your front garden, thought Holly.

She watched in amazement as a smile spread slowly across the gnome's face. It got up from its knees, rose to its full height and advanced towards them. Holly looked to Derek for help.

'Ah, good,' he said. 'Holly, I want you to meet Stewart, he's just started in the garden gnomes section. You'll be able to look after Holly, Stewart – she's new, too. She's starting in garden chemicals tomorrow.'

Stewart looked Holly up and down. His mouth

had fallen open and a strange, glazed look had entered his eyes.

'Yeah,' he told Derek. 'Yeah . . . I'll look after her . . . Yeah,' he repeated.

'I've got to go now, if it's OK,' Holly said to Derek. 'See you tomorrow.'

'Yes, see you tomorrow, Holly,' Derek replied.

'See you tomorrow, Hol,' echoed the Gnome Boy in a disturbingly syrupy voice.

Holly got on her bike and pedalled over the gravel towards the open gate and freedom. She turned round for one last look at the Chestnuts Garden Centre, its greenhouses glinting in the sunshine. There, knee-high in gnomes, stood Stewart the Gnome Boy. He was staring after her, and even at this distance she could see the gleam in his eye.

Holly put her head down and pedalled faster. She'd recognised that gleam immediately. She'd seen it many, many times before.

It was the light of love.

Dream On

For the first time since she'd started work at Uncle Toni's, Gina woke up smiling. She snuggled under her duvet and wiggled her toes with happiness. Who'd have imagined that she'd find the sexiest, most gorgeous guy in the whole world at Antonio's Top Karaoke Bar?

She thought of her dream. It had been lovely, and it was almost as nice remembering it. Gina sighed, feeling all warm and tingly. Then she lifted her head, looked at her bedside clock and shot out of bed. She was on the day shift today and she had a lot more than usual to do before she set out for work. She wanted to wash her hair, then put it up into a high, glossy pony-tail. As well as being cooler, it would emphasise her cheek-bones and sparkling brown eyes. She'd slick on some copper-coloured lip gloss as well.

Gina hadn't been bothering much about her appearance recently. She didn't want to inflame the saddos who stamped and whistled every time she entered the bar, or the lads around the pool table, who pretended to trip her up as she went past. And, as far as Uncle Toni was concerned, everything she wore was perfect. Uncle Toni thought about Gina as he did about his karaoke bar – neither could put a foot wrong.

Today, though, everything was different. Gina decided to put on the new white top that showed off her smooth brown skin and dark, shiny hair. She looked at the clock again. There was a lot to do and she didn't want to be late. It wasn't fair to take advantage of Uncle Toni's good nature, she told herself virtuously.

Gina usually walked along the prom to the tacky end of the beach and Uncle Toni's bar in a haze of misery. She hardly noticed her surroundings. She looked around now, though, and saw the sea was extra-blue, the sand more golden. The white wings of the seagulls riding on the waves shimmered in the sun. She skipped out of the way of the mini-train that trundled up and down the prom and stopped to watch the painted horses of the carousel dip up and down.

Just across the road was a little green kiosk belonging to Madame Esmeralda, the noted palmist, Adviser to Royalty and the Stars. *I have helped many over troubled waters*, said the sign outside. Gina lingered to look at it, but when Madame Esmeralda herself poked her head out of the window and crooked a finger at her she smiled and shook her head, then hurried on.

Lou had said she might walk over to Uncle Toni's bar later today. Gina hoped she'd manage it. Her friends seemed to be the only ones who had any idea of the total hell of working there. It got a zillion times worse when Vince, the local disc jockey, took over the karaoke. Vince was heckled mercilessly as he cracked his feeble little jokes, and if she hadn't been so wrapped up in her own embarrassment Gina would almost have felt sorry for him.

Vince didn't need her pity, though. He called the heckling 'interacting with his audience' and took it as proof of his success. Sometimes he suggested that 'the lovely Gina' should sing the ice-cream song for them, and everybody shouted 'Yes!' and punched the air while Uncle Toni beamed proudly at his pretty niece's popularity. Shaking her head, Gina would try to act cool and unconcerned, wishing that the ground would open and swallow her up.

Lou had told Gina that she hadn't got a job lined up, but she hadn't seemed worried. She'd said that Holly was bursting with plans to get them all sorted 'spunkwise', since they were making such a pathetic job of it themselves. She didn't mind going along with Holly's crazy ideas, it might be a laugh, Lou had added. Gina had been amazed: who'd have thought a week or two ago that Lou would be talking about enjoying herself or having a laugh without Guy?

Lou had never ventured inside Uncle Toni's bar – one quick glance through the window had been enough to show her what lay in wait inside – and Gina didn't blame her. Instead she usually sat at one of the tables outside. As soon as he spotted her, Uncle Toni would bring her one of his special ice-creams and call Gina to come and have a chat with her friend.

Uncle Toni understood why Lou was such a regular visitor to his bar and why she looked so sad and far away sometimes. He knew that what Lou really wanted was to be taken on the staff of Antonio's Top Karaoke Bar, and it grieved his tender heart to have to disappoint her.

'Soon,' he promised, waggling a ring-encrusted finger at Lou. 'Be patient, *cara*, your time will come. Uncle Toni will not forget you.' Giggling with Lou in the sunshine, trying not to let Uncle Toni see, had been up to now the only bright spot in Gina's day.

Gina had almost arrived at the bar now. Her heart was thumping and her stomach felt as if a colony of butterflies had taken up residence. When Lou came later this afternoon, should she tell her about what had happened yesterday? She *had* to – she was dying to confide in someone.

Yes, Gina decided, she'd tell Lou, but not the others yet. It was all too new and overwhelming, and she knew she'd start blushing and stammering as soon as she tried to explain how she felt. Arriving at Uncle Toni's, Gina gulped, stood there for a moment, then plunged inside.

'Yo, sexy!' came the shout, followed by the usual chorus of whistles. Gina ducked her head and dived into the kitchen, hoping, as she did every time, to lurk there and escape notice. Like every other time, she failed, and Uncle Toni shooed her fondly back into the bar.

'No, no, Gina, see how the customers look forward to seeing you,' he said, then raised his hand. 'Quiet now!' he bellowed, and the whistles died away. Uncle Toni beamed around and retreated to the kitchen.

Ohhh, thought Gina, picking up a bottle and trying to unwrap some git's fingers from on top of hers, he was so *cool*. He was ... absolutely perfect. He was also, face it, totally out of her league. If she had any sense, the best thing she could do was forget him. But even while she was saying this to herself, a vision of his dark-grey eyes, high cheek-bones and slight frown came into her mind. She tore the bottle out of the git's hand, gave a quick wipe to the table and returned to the kitchen.

Although he came every day to deliver the ice, Gina had never had the chance to have a really good look at him until yesterday. He usually went round the back, where Uncle Toni attended to him. But yesterday Uncle Toni's presence had been required in the bar, where some creeps were having a punch-up with a fruit machine. He had asked Gina to tell the Ice Boy to tip some of the ice in the sink and store the rest in the freezer.

Any excuse for getting out of the bar was welcome, and Gina had slipped thankfully into the kitchen, to be faced with the most gorgeous guy she had ever laid eyes on. Her stomach wibbled and her throat went dry. Delicious little shivers ran up and down her spine. This was the one, she knew it immediately. The boy of her dreams.

He was tall, with eyes the colour of storm clouds, and he'd stood leaning against Uncle Toni's microwave, waiting for Gina to direct him. As she had gazed at him, unable to speak, paralysed with shyness, he had gestured impatiently towards the deep freeze.

'In there?' he'd asked. Gina had cleared her throat, made a huge effort and managed to nod – her heart doing somersaults in her chest. Even though Uncle Toni had said he wanted some ice in the sink, she would have agreed with anything the Ice Boy suggested. He'd opened the top of the freezer, dropped the whole bag of ice into it and lowered the lid.

'OK?' he'd said. Then he'd done something totally devastating. He'd smiled. It was like a burst of sunshine in a wintry landscape and it finished Gina off completely. She'd read about it, dreamt of it, thought she'd never find it and now finally it had happened. The real thing. Love. She was hopelessly in love with the Ice Boy. Even thinking about him now made her feel wobbly at the knees. He was gorgeous and she was going to see him every day!

He was due at Uncle Toni's any minute. Gina wove her way between the huge feet that occupied most of the floor space while keeping an eye on the door to the kitchen. Straining her ears, she heard a kind of heavy clunking sound followed by voices talking together. Drawn by a force it was impossible to resist, Gina pushed open the kitchen door and walked inside.

Neither Uncle Toni nor the Ice Boy seemed surprised to see her.

'Ah, Gina,' said Uncle Toni genially, waving her further into the kitchen. 'Such a lot of ice we use this hot weather. I tell him,' he gestured vaguely towards the Ice Boy, 'maybe he bring us more. What do you think? I always consult my niece about my business decisions,' he informed the Ice Boy.

'Yes. It's a good idea, Uncle Toni,' said Gina. Her voice was husky, she felt hot and light-headed and her heart was thumping so much she couldn't look him in the eye, but at least she'd been able to produce a few words. She hadn't known when she'd opened her mouth whether her vocal cords would function or not.

'I can bring you some more later today,' said the Ice Boy. He had turned towards Gina when she spoke, but his gaze was fixed on a spot several centimetres above her head.

'Mmm,' said Gina. After the ordeal she'd put it through, her voice had finally packed up. She put her hand up to tuck in any wisps that might have strayed out of her pony-tail and realised she was still holding the dishcloth for mopping the tables. She couldn't move over to the sink with it because she couldn't decide which foot to pick up first. Her legs had turned into cotton wool anyway. She stood there totally paralysed, unable to move or speak. If the Ice Boy didn't go soon she knew she'd start blushing, yet she'd have given anything to keep him there for ever.

'*Bene, bene*,' said Uncle Toni, bustling forward. 'You will come again later then. Gina,' he said, in his best captain of industry voice, 'I make you in charge of the ice supplies from now on. Delegate, delegate – the secret of success,' he explained to the Ice Boy.

The Ice Boy nodded, arms folded across his chunky chest. It was impossible to tell if he approved of Uncle Toni's business methods or not.

'See you later, then,' he said. Gina wondered how she could bear seeing him twice in one day. On the other hand, how could she wait till later? She muttered something in a strangled voice, and with a cool half-smile to them both the Ice Boy departed. Slowly – very, very slowly – Gina's heartbeat returned to normal.

'Nice boy,' said Uncle Toni. 'If you handle the ice supplies well, Gina, I give you even more responsibility. Perhaps in time you become my personal assistant and your nice friend can have your job. She not look so sad then.' He beamed and rubbed his hands. Uncle Toni enjoyed giving pleasure to people. 'She coming today?' he asked.

'I hope so,' said Gina. Now she'd decided to

confide in Lou, she could hardly wait to tell her everything. Of all her friends, Lou would understand best what it was like to be dying of lovesickness and not capable of doing anything about it.

Passing the open door of Uncle Toni's bar, Lou glanced inside. Music was thumping out and the fruit machines were clicking and whirring. One of the lads at the pool table twirled a cue at her, another waved a half-eaten pizza. Lou hurried past, telling herself again how lucky she was. She might have lost the only boy she'd ever loved, but at least she didn't have to work at Uncle Toni's. Poor Gina . . .

Gina had seen her and came outside. Uncle Toni's voice floated after her, telling her to rest a while, sit in the afternoon sun with her friend. She had worked hard and she deserved a break before Vince arrived and the glorious karaoke really got going. She and Lou found an empty table as far as they could from the bar door and sat down with their cans of Coke.

Lou thought Gina looked fabulous: her hairstyle

suited her thick, glossy hair, her cheeks were pink and her eyes shining. She'd been looking rather tired and pale recently, and Lou had been worried about her. Was she settling down at the karaoke bar – maybe even getting to like it? No, decided Lou, watching Uncle Toni absent-mindedly brushing feet off his tables, whatever caused the glow radiating from Gina today it was certainly not the joy of working in Uncle Toni's bar.

'How're you getting on, Lou? What have you been doing?' Gina asked.

Lou put down her can and shrugged. 'This and that,' she said vaguely. 'I took next door's dog for a walk this morning. We went across the fields and along the prom.' She didn't tell Gina that when she'd reached the pier she'd caught sight of Guy and immediately switched direction. Digger the cocker spaniel had had to walk back through the town instead of along the coastal path as she'd intended. She and Guy had agreed they'd still be friends, but Lou wasn't up to saying hello and chatting casually with him yet. At least the sight of him hadn't sent her into a deep depression, as it would have done a week or two ago.

'Still missing Guy?' asked Gina gently. It was as if she'd guessed what Lou was thinking.

'Mmm,' said Lou. For a moment the old ache at the back of her throat came back, then she shook her head. She'd come here to cheer up Gina. But why was she so different today? 'How's it been?' she asked sympathetically.

Gina took a deep breath then told her.

After the first pause, her words came tumbling out, while Lou sat there trying to take it in. The last thing she'd imagined was that Gina would develop a desperate crush on someone she'd met at Uncle Toni's bar. He didn't sound anything like the lairy crowd who usually gathered there. But was he Gina's type? If he was as cool and aloof as she suggested, how would they ever communicate with each other?

'And I don't even know his name!' Gina wailed finally. 'And he's so cool he hardly knows I exist. He doesn't even look properly at me – he probably wouldn't recognise me outside Uncle Toni's.'

Lou was sure that the Ice Boy *did* know Gina existed. She looked so gorgeous today, how could any guy resist her? 'Perhaps he's shy, too,' she suggested. 'That's why he doesn't look at you directly and why he seems so remote. Perhaps he doesn't know what to say.'

This was obviously a new idea to Gina. She considered it, then shook her head. 'No,' she said, 'No – he's just totally cool. And I can hardly say a word to him. He probably thinks I'm a complete idiot.'

'Take it easy,' advised Lou. 'Don't get desperate about it. Then, when you feel a bit more sure of yourself, you – you'll have to take the initiative. Just make it clear you like him, that's all. Take the initiative,' she repeated, knowing they'd probably reach the millennium before Gina would be confident enough to do that. 'I know how you feel,' she added, and Gina nodded gratefully.

It was nice to see Gina in love, even though she was obviously suffering so much. Lou'd never realised herself how painful love could be until she and Guy had split. She was meeting Holly and Nik for a pizza tonight, but she'd leave it to Gina to tell them about the Ice Boy when she was ready. With Gina being so shy and the Ice Boy so unapproachable, it might never come to anything, and she didn't want Holly charging in and scaring him away.

Lou was looking forward to seeing Holly and Nik. It was nice to have a laugh with her mates – well not a laugh exactly; more to listen to Holly complaining about the prize geek pursuing her at the garden centre and Nik describing the incredible exhilaration of surfing. When Nik got going about water sports, it was almost like listening to poetry.

When Lou got up to leave, Gina stood looking after her for a moment before returning reluctantly to the bar. It had been nice of her to listen so sympathetically. Gina knew her advice had been sound, but she also knew she was incapable of revealing even a glimpse of her true feelings to the Ice Boy. When he returned later with more ice, her throat would seize up, that half-sweet, half-painful trembly feeling would come over her and she'd be just as pathetic as she'd been before.

To comfort herself, Gina thought back to her dream. In it, the Ice Boy had turned to her, looked into her eyes and told her how he'd melted at the very first sight of her. Gina had smiled radiantly in reply, and without further words he had taken her into his arms. He had held her very, very tightly. Gina shivered as she remembered how his strong arms had closed round her, how her heart had leapt when he'd bent his head and their lips had met in a long, long kiss. She closed her eyes, trying to hold on to the memory.

It had been wonderful. It had been the most marvellous dream she'd ever had. And that's all it would ever be.

Nightmare!

The wind had been blowing hard all day, sending spray over the sea wall and on to the prom. It was far too gusty to let the new arrivals at the surf school loose on the water.

Nik looked longingly at the lines of waves racing along the shore. She'd spent most of the day sorting out the videos and teaching the newcomers how to balance and control their boards. They hadn't seemed to mind – there was plenty of social interaction breaking out already – but Nik would have given anything to be on the waves.

She checked out all the training rigs and boards, had a hot shower and went into the club-room. One or two of the instructors and some beginners were sitting round a table.

'Coming to join us, Nik?' someone called out. Nik smiled and shook her head.

'Waiting for a friend,' she told them.

She went over to the bar, got herself a hot chocolate and sat down by the window, where she'd be able to see Holly coming over the beach. Holly had said she'd call in at the surfing school on her way home from work – she said she'd burst if she didn't have a moan about what she was going through at the garden centre.

Whatever it was, Nik felt sure Holly would be able to handle it. Holly was always in control. She went straight for what she wanted and never had any doubts. Up until now, Nik would have said she was the same herself.

She stirred the foam on her chocolate round and round into a whirlpool, and stared out of the window. She'd been feeling restless and jumpy all day long, and it wasn't just that she hadn't been able to get on the water. She was totally fed up with people jumping to conclusions about her relationship with Matt. Why couldn't you just be friends with a guy without the whole world assuming you were up to your neck in a hot romance?

'Hey, Nik!' someone called across the room and she jumped. 'Matt coming in later by any chance?' the girl asked casually.

'How should I know?' snapped Nik, and immediately wished she hadn't.

'Sor*ree*,' said the girl, looking surprised. It wasn't like Nik to be so touchy.

'I've no idea where he is,' said Nik. She wondered why she was lying. She did in fact know exactly where Matt was. He'd told her he was off for some jet-ski action a few kilometres away. The blustery wind that made the waves too high and bumpy for the beginner-surfers was epic for jet-skiing, he'd said.

Although she liked him better than any other guy she knew, it was just as well Matt hadn't been around today. It was nothing to do with him – he was still the same friendly, uncomplicated person he'd ever been. It was other people's attitudes and comments that were really getting to her.

Nik stared through the clubhouse window at the white foamy tops on the waves, the clouds scudding across the bright-blue sky. When Matt returned, perhaps she'd suggest taking their boards on the water – early evening was high tide, perfect for wave-sailing. Nik's eyes shone, imagining surfing across the bay with Matt and returning as the sun sank low in the sky, cutting a golden pathway across the sea. He knew exactly how she felt about windsurfing, she couldn't imagine anyone better to share it with.

Then she shook her head impatiently, annoyed with herself. There she went again ... No wonder people were getting the wrong idea: she'd been seeing far too much of Matt recently. Yesterday, the girl who'd asked if Matt was coming in, a leggy blonde with big blue eyes called Cherry, had described Matt to Nik as 'your sexy boyfriend'. When Nik had put her right, Cherry had nodded thoughtfully, then asked if he'd be around tomorrow. An unmistakable look of disappointment had crossed her face when Nik had told her it was his day off, then she shrugged.

'Oh well, I can wait another day,' Cherry had said.

Surely Matt would have the sense not to fall for those baby-blue eyes and all that eyelash batting, thought Nik. Then she was angry with herself again. What business of hers was it who Matt fancied? He was so gorgeous that girls were falling for him all the time. He was always nice to them, but so far he'd given them a kind (but unmistakable) brush-off. One of these days, though, some girl was going to throw herself at him and he wouldn't walk away . . .

Nik shifted restlessly in her seat and picked up her hot chocolate. She'd been so busy thinking about Matt that she'd let it get almost cold. Why didn't she like the idea of Cherry getting her hooks into Matt? Nik told herself firmly that it was simply because she wasn't good enough for him. Nothing else.

Suddenly a blob of red appeared on the beach. Nik peered closer. Coming towards the clubhouse, the wind whipping her thick red hair into points and whirls about her face, was Holly. She was wearing a dangerously short scarlet dress.

Nik jumped to her feet, went to the door and waved. Seeing her, Holly waved back and sprinted the last few metres.

'Hi, windy or what?' she gasped. Her cheeks were bright pink. She wasn't as brown as Nik, but her arms and legs were a warm golden colour. Everybody in the clubhouse turned to look at her and a silence fell as she came inside. She totally dominated the room. 'Can't stay long,' she said, after they'd got themselves another drink. 'I've got to babysit my kid brothers – my mum and dad are going out for a meal. Garden centre all day, Josh and Jordan at night,' she continued bitterly. 'Great summer this is turning out to be.'

'I like your dress,' said Nik. 'D'you wear that at work?'

'I went home and changed,' said Holly. She couldn't wait a second longer than was necessary to get out of her green T-shirt and trousers. She was utterly sick of green. Sometimes it seemed to Holly that the whole world was turning into a giant vegetable.

For the first time since she'd come in, Holly took a good look around the club. Everyone was wearing jeans and T-shirts, but she didn't care. Sometimes a girl had to make her own statement. The place was full of surfers, most of whom still had their eyes glued on her. 'Where's Matt?' she asked. 'I still don't know why you kept him hidden for so long, Nik. Why didn't you tell us he was working here this summer?'

'Day off,' said Nik wearily. If Holly was sick of the garden centre, she was just as fed up of being asked about Matt. If anybody else enquired where he was, she'd scream.

'You could pass him on to your mates if you're

really not interested,' said Holly, but she spoke without much conviction. She still hadn't forgotten the way Matt and Nik had been looking at each other when she'd seen them on the beach.

After another quick scan of the room for any stray talent she might have missed first time around, Holly fell silent. She'd changed her mind about revealing the horrors of the Chestnuts Garden Centre. It was bad enough having to work in the dump, without wasting her free time remembering it.

After she'd looked back to see the Gnome Boy gazing after her with that unearthly light in his eyes, Holly's instinct had been to pedal down the avenue as hard as she could and never return. Only the thought of having to set out on another dreary round of job-hunting had persuaded her to report back to Derek the following day. Now she knew her instincts had been right.

The chemicals section was not the liveliest part of the garden centre. All those death-dealing sprays and pellets had cast a gloom upon the place. Dressed obediently in green, Holly had stood in the middle of these instruments of destruction and waited for customers.

Derek had presented Holly with several books and catalogues that he promised would make her job more interesting. Holly had put them on a table piled high with puffers for the slaughter of greenfly, whitefly and blackfly – and immediately forgotten them. She had far more important things to occupy her mind.

Her first customers had been a pair of wrinklies in search of something to stop the leaves of their roses going curly. They had approached Holly and asked her advice. Holly was startled. She'd been wondering if the shy New Zealander Nik had told them about at the surf centre might be adapted for Lou's use if Gina wasn't interested. She had waved a hand towards some plastic containers with pictures of roses on them and they had pottered off contentedly.

Holly had felt a thrill of satisfaction at a job well done. Garden chemicals were a doddle. Derek, who had been hovering nearby, moved over and started boring the wrinklies' pants off them with a load of stuff about quantities and dilutions. Holly hadn't been offended that he'd taken over her customers. That was the sort of thing Derek did best. To each his own . . .

She'd been staring into space wondering if it would soon be time to knock off for lunch, when suddenly a blast of hot breath scorched her neck. Startled, Holly whirled round and there – much, *much* too close and with a sheepish, adoring smile – stood the geeky Gnome Boy. 'Hi, Hol,' he muttered.

First moving to a safe distance, Holly had opened her mouth to enquire how he'd escaped from the gnome farm, but in a flash Derek was at her side.

'Yes, Stewart?' he asked coldly. Muttering something about coming over to help Hol settle in, the Gnome Boy had slunk back to his lair, but not before hissing 'Catch you later, Hol'.

'All right, Holly?' enquired Derek. 'I will not have my staff's time wasted. Any more nonsense, report to me.'

'Yeah, ta, Derek,' said Holly. She reckoned that now she knew the danger, she was more than capable of dealing with the geek of the century without any further help from Derek.

Little did she know.

From day one it had been evident that Stewart

had the hots for Holly in spades. Cunningly selecting a time when Derek was occupied elsewhere, he would make his way to garden chemicals like a homing pigeon. Once there, he would hang around fiddling with the spray guns and staring at Holly as if he couldn't get enough, his eyes bulging like a lovesick bullfrog's.

'You and me – we really get on well together, don't we, Hol?' he would mumble hopefully. When Holly, taking a deep breath, had pointed out that this was definitely not the case, since she would sooner die than spend any more time with an idiot like him, he had simply shaken his head as if he hadn't even heard.

At first Holly couldn't believe that Derek's words of warning had totally washed over this geek. But then she realised the truth. Stewart was in the grip of forces beyond his control. He was totally smitten.

Nothing put him off. Even though Holly spent her whole time being obnoxious to him, he just grinned adoringly and said that as soon as he'd clocked her red hair he'd known she had a temper. He liked his women sassy, he confided.

Then two days ago Holly had been moved to

outside duties, filling up trays and tables with little pots of plants. At first she'd been pleased. Away from the heady atmosphere of garden chemicals and in the open air, she'd imagined that Stewart would find it more difficult to hunt her down. But like a rogue elephant on the trail of his mate, he pursued Holly to the four corners of the Chestnuts Garden Centre. Nowhere was safe. And it was beneath Holly's dignity to summon Derek to her aid.

This afternoon, before she'd come to see Nik, Holly had been walking back from lunch through the garden statues section when she'd spotted Stewart racing eagerly towards her. She jumped right to avoid him and Stewart, grinning inanely, had jumped left to cut her off. They continued dodging round each other until Holly made a sudden sprint sideways and fled past him.

As she sped between the stone nymphs and cherubs, the sundials and the bird-baths, Holly looked wildly round for Derek. He was usually nearby keeping an eye on her: he would pretend he was checking whether the plants needed watering, but Holly was never fooled. Where was he now, though, when he might have come in handy? Nowhere to be seen. Typical, thought Holly bitterly, putting on a spurt and arriving at the garden sheds section.

Stewart was gaining on her – she could hear him breathlessly bleating her name and the squeak of his wellies. Just in front was a potting shed. Holly flung herself inside it and slammed the door.

The potting shed was nice and cool and dark. Holly stood there motionless. Sanctuary at last! There was a scrabbling sound at the door and Holly leapt forward to lock it. Too late she realised it had no lock or bolt. It opened and Stewart's face, red and pleading, appeared in the entrance.

'Are you avoiding me, Hol?' he demanded plaintively. 'I know, why don't we go out sometime? Get to know each other a bit better? How about a nice game of crazy golf?'

Arrgu! It was coming to something when you couldn't even get any privacy in a shed. She moved back into the furthest corner.

'Get lost, Stewart,' she said wearily.

'I only want to *talk*, Hol,' Stewart protested. He advanced further inside, and with another nifty sideways move Holly sprang past him, banging the door behind her. If there'd been a key in the door she would have turned it.

When she finally got back to her trays of plants, Holly's hair stood up around her face like the petals of the dahlias in Derek's big glass frames. Her cheeks were the colour of the trailing nasturtiums in the hanging baskets she'd been making up that morning. Derek looked at her curiously but made no comment. Holly wondered if *anything* would dampen Stewart's ardour, as she rearranged a pile of plastic pots that he'd knocked over while gawping at her the previous day. As if she didn't have enough to plan . . .

Nik noticed that Holly wasn't her usual bubbly self. She seemed to have changed her mind about revealing the dark secrets of the Chestnuts Garden Centre. She hadn't even noticed the New Zealand guy who'd just walked in. He had turned to gawp at Holly in her bright-red dress with open admiration. Not really Holly's type, too shy and serious, thought Nik. She wouldn't introduce him; she didn't want to lumber Holly with another unwanted admirer, not after the hints she'd dropped about the nerd at the garden centre. Then Holly lifted her head and spoke.

'We've *got* to get moving,' she said. She spoke slowly and emphatically. 'Time's running out and *none* of us has pulled yet. These guys won't come after us, you know – at least those worth having won't,' she added hastily. 'We've got to get out there and grab them.' She'd recovered all her sparkle and, like a small, furry mammal mesmerised by a beautiful golden eagle, the Kiwi cutie couldn't keep his peepers off her.

Nik grinned at her. 'OK,' she said. 'But what's the hurry? Plenty of time left till the end of the holidays.'

It's all right for Nik, thought Holly. Matt was a spunk by any standards, even though Nik seemed to have become very touchy on the subject, and it seemed the light of love had yet to dawn on them both. She wouldn't be surprised if Nik got sorted soon, but the rest of them were as far from pulling as they'd been at the start of the holidays.

An unfamiliar feeling of desperation was creeping over Holly. In fact, the time might come when she was the most desperate of them all . . . Thinking of the long days at the Chestnuts Garden Centre dodging Stewart's unwanted attentions, Holly felt almost sorry for herself.

Then her natural optimism returned. She had pulled far and wide, all over Bexington – why should it be any different now? All that was needed was the opportunity, and she, Holly, was the one to provide it for all four of them. She glanced around the room again and this time caught the New Zealand guy's eye. He blushed, looked away, then back again. He was obviously utterly and completely smitten.

See? Holly told herself. Cute, but not her type, alas – a tad too serious. It proved, though, that she was still in top pulling shape. She smiled brilliantly at him just for practice and he looked as if he'd copped the lottery. That should keep him happy for the rest of the day, thought Holly, getting to her feet in a glow of virtue.

'Got to go,' she told Nik. 'See you soon. I've got to get moving,' she repeated.

On the way out, she passed Matt, back from his jet-ski activities and out of his wetsuit gear. He was so busy scanning the room that, to Holly's total amazement, he didn't even notice her – or the blonde, baby-faced girl who was trying to attract his attention.

Holly watched as he caught sight of Nik, his

face lit up and he hurried to join her. Their dark heads were close together and they were laughing and chatting happily as Holly closed the door and hurried home across the windy beach.

Lou Acts Cool

Lou sat high on the hill, overlooking the bay. Digger, next door's spaniel, panted happily beside her. His life had been transformed since Lou had started taking him for walks. Instead of one walk a day, he was getting two – and each one was different. There was no knowing which way Lou's wanderings would take her.

'Good dog,' said Lou absently, reaching out to pat his glossy black and white coat. He squirmed nearer and put his head on her knee. He gazed up soulfully into her eyes while Lou stroked his ears and stared out to sea.

Every so often a windsurfing sail could be seen crossing the bay. Sometimes it would disappear beneath a wave and a few seconds later a figure would clamber from underneath and haul it upright again. Lou thought of Nik at the far end of the bay, where the beach sloped gently into the sea, and of Gina at the other end, imprisoned in Uncle Toni's karaoke bar. Inland, making a kind of triangle between them, Holly toiled reluctantly at the Chestnuts Garden Centre. All of them had a job except Lou, but, in spite of Holly's efforts, all four were still totally ladless.

Jobless and boyless – it sounds really sad, thought Lou. But she didn't feel sad. She wasn't quite sure how she felt, sitting dreamily in the sunshine, the wind lifting her hair and Digger drooling contentedly on her knee.

It was nice to have Digger on loan for walks. Nobody asked where you were going, or why, if you had a dog attached to you. Sometimes she went one way, sometimes another. Her skin had turned brown and little freckles had popped out on her nose and cheeks.

Usually, when she stopped to sit in the sun or to give Digger a rest, Lou's thoughts turned automatically to Guy. She still missed him, but things didn't seem quite so desperate now. She no longer felt that if another day went by without seeing him she'd just have to pick up the phone and call him. There were still places she couldn't go to, roads she couldn't walk down, because they'd been there together, but if she met him unexpectedly now she wouldn't have to turn away. She thought maybe she could handle it.

'We'll still be friends, Lou,' Guy had promised when he'd told her it was time to cool it. Lou had been so devastated she'd just nodded, but later she'd thought it was one of the stupidest things she'd ever heard. Even if she could bear it, how could they be friends after he'd chucked her like an empty crisp packet? Anyway, apart from that one time when she'd panicked near the pier, she hadn't seen him around at all.

At first Lou would have given anything to know where Guy was – and who was with him. She longed to ask her mates if they'd seen him with another girl, but because they didn't want to hurt her they'd been extra careful not to mention his name. Lou hadn't missed the warning look Nik had flashed at Holly when she'd started sounding off about this brilliant club she'd been to. Lou guessed it was probably because she'd seen Guy there – with someone else. The blonde with the butterfly tattoo? She'd been dying to know, but at the same time she couldn't bear to have her worst fears confirmed.

Holly's hand had flown to her mouth and she had changed the subject very obviously. Lou sighed, then shook her head and grinned. Holly was a good mate, but she wasn't exactly subtle . . .

If she bumped into Guy now, would she be able to talk naturally to him? Lou had the feeling that he'd said all that stuff about staying friends because he felt guilty. If he saw her first, he'd probably leg it, just like she'd done.

Lou was tired of the same thoughts going round and round in her brain. She decided to walk down to the beach and see if anybody she knew was about. At least she'd got past the stage of wanting to stay home and mope.

'Come on,' she said to Digger, removing his head carefully from her lap. Digger whined softly, licked her hand, then sat up quivering, ready to begin the next part of his lovely walk. He thumped his tail gently as Lou fixed the lead to his collar. Together they set off down the path to where the fishing boats were moored, the nets and lobster pots heaped up beside them.

'Hi, Lou,' said a familiar voice behind her. Lou's stomach lurched and her legs went weak. Digger stopped dead in his tracks. It was impossible to pretend she hadn't heard, or to start walking the other way. Lou turned round and looked straight into Guy's grey-green eyes.

It was a shock to realise he was even more good-looking than she'd remembered. He was smiling his usual easy, confident grin. The breeze ruffled his hair and he put up his hand to smooth it. With a jolt, Lou remembered the times she'd sat flipping through a mag or watching telly while Guy stood in front of the mirror brushing mousse and hairspray into his hair. If Lou forgot and reached up to touch it after he'd spent ages styling it, he would jerk his head back impatiently. Every time they walked past a shop window he would glance in to check it. He would even bend down to peer into a car mirror.

At the time she'd just thought how lucky she was to have such a tasty boyfriend. Girls were always eyeing him up, and when they were in a club some would even come over and start dancing with him, ignoring Lou. The last had been the butterfly-tattoo girl. Lou had tried to make it clear he was with her, but it had taken her a long time to get the message.

When Lou had tackled Guy about it, asking why

he'd played along with her, they'd almost had a row. Guy had shrugged and said he couldn't help girls chasing him. What was she worried about, didn't she trust him? Did she really think he was going to go off with someone else? She had a major jealousy problem, he'd told her. Lou remembered that it had ended with her apologising madly – and felt like kicking herself.

Guy finished patting his hair into place and was gazing at her intently. 'How're you doing, Lou?' he asked.

How do you think I'm doing, Lou felt like replying. It was typical of Guy to creep up on her like this. It was the first time they'd met since they'd split, but it had obviously never occurred to him that she might be upset at seeing him again.

He acts as though other people's feelings don't count, thought Lou angrily, remembering the comments he'd made about her friends. Holly had once described him as 'the guy who loves himself'. Lou had defended him, protesting that Guy wasn't really like that, but now she thought Holly might have a point.

She shook back her hair and met his eyes. 'I'm

fine, how are you?' she was pleased to hear herself answer coolly.

'You look great, Lou,' he said unexpectedly. He was staring at her as if he'd never properly noticed her before, as if he'd only just met her.

Lou nodded. She knew she was looking good. She might not yet be obeying Holly's instructions to get out there and bag a bloke, but the days of not caring about her appearance were in the past. She was wearing her new jeans and the top she'd bought the day before. She'd had her hair cut shorter, too, and it shone and swung about her face. 'Yeah,' she told Guy. 'I'm fine,' she repeated. Digger, tired of waiting and bored with snuffling around Guy's feet, scratched the grass impatiently and looked longingly down at the fishing boats.

'Well . . .' said Lou brightly, 'see you around then.' She was amazed at how well she'd done. Her heart was thumping and her throat was getting dry – she had to get away now before she started croaking – but nobody would have guessed it. Certainly not Guy, who mumbled, 'Yeah, see you around, Lou,' then stood there hesitating as if he didn't know what to do next. Lou turned briskly round, gave Digger's lead a tug and walked away.

She could feel his eyes on her back as she went down the path, and it made her step out more confidently, hold her head higher. She might be crying inside, but she'd kept her dignity. She hadn't let Guy know what he'd done to her.

Her heart was beating normally now and she was congratulating herself on how well she'd handled things when suddenly there was a shout behind her.

'Lou!' called Guy. She looked back and watched him running down the hill towards her. What did he want now?

'Erm . . .' he said, when he reached her. His face was flushed, not just with running but with something else – embarrassment? Guy prided himself on being Mr Cool. It wasn't often you saw him flustered.

'Your fringe has gone tangly,' Lou told him, and he brushed it back impatiently, almost as if it didn't matter. What was the matter with him?

'Are . . . are you walking down to the beach?' he asked. He was almost stammering.

'That's where this path goes,' Lou told him politely.

'Well . . . I was wondering . . . if you're free, we

could have a coffee in the park or somewhere. There's no reason why we can't be friends. Is there?' he said. His eyes were almost pleading. He gestured towards Digger, who was totally fed up with all the delays and was whining and pawing at Lou's jeans. 'We can tie him to a tree or something,' he said.

Lou considered Guy's suggestion carefully, taking her time. Then she shook her head. It was a wonderful moment. 'Sorry, Guy, I've arranged to meet someone,' she said. She made it sound as mysterious as possible. 'And Digger doesn't like being tied up,' she added. Digger had caught a whiff of fish from the boats and was straining at his leash.

Guy hovered uncertainly. He seemed unable to tear himself away. 'Oh . . . right,' he said. 'Well, some other time.' He recovered some of his old poise. 'Like I said, no reason why we can't continue to be friends, is there?' he added. If he says that one more time, I'll set Digger on him, thought Lou. All she did, though, was smile enigmatically and move away. She wanted to finish the walk and get home. Holly had wangled a long lunch-break and had said she was going to call round at Lou's place. She had something majorly important to discuss.

In spite of the brush-off she'd just handed him, there'd been a moment when Lou had actually been tempted to go to the park with Guy. Perhaps, a little voice inside her whispered, perhaps when they got there he would blurt out how much he'd missed her, and that he wanted her back. Lou stopped for a moment while Digger tried to pull her on. Had she made a terrible mistake, lost her one chance to get Guy back? No – there was no way she was going to let him think he could drop her and pick her up again just like that. Being on her own, with lots of time to ponder, had made many things clear to Lou. One was that never again was she going to allow Guy Wilson – or any other bloke – to mess her about. She'd rather go it alone.

She delivered Digger back home and waved at Benji, who was glaring jealously through the window at them. When Lou got inside he gave her a reproachful look then turned his back on her. Lou put a few fragments of cheese in his dish, but it was several minutes before he forgave her sufficiently to start purring.

'I've got Friday off next week,' announced Holly as she whirled through the door.

'Yeah?' said Lou. 'Green suits you,' she told her. Holly waved the compliment away impatiently. 'So's Gina – and so's Nik,' she said triumphantly. 'We've *all* got the same day off. So . . .'

'So what?' said Lou.

'So it's action time,' said Holly dramatically. 'Time to reveal Holly's master-plan. Since none of us – even me – has pulled yet, I've decided to take control. Give you the benefit of my vast experience. All you have to do is follow my instructions and by the end of the day I guarantee everyone will have scored. It can't fail.' She looked around the kitchen. 'OK if I make myself a peanut butter sarnie?'

'How do the others feel?' asked Lou. 'Are you sure Gina still wants—?'

Holly put down the jar of peanut butter.

'The others feel like we do,' she assured her. 'And don't worry about Gina. I know exactly what Gina wants.'

'Holly . . .' started Lou, then she grinned.

'OK,' she said. 'Let's hear about this brilliant plan, then. What do we have to do?' She got out a loaf of granary bread and passed it to Holly. 'Make one for me, too, while you're at it,' she said.

'Simple but attractive,' said Holly. 'Like many lads we know!' She passed Lou a doorstep of a sandwich and took a bite out of her own. 'You don't know how lucky you are having the house to yourself like this,' she continued indistinctly. 'Can I have a banana with it?' She reached out for a banana, peeled it, opened her sandwich, squashed in the banana and pressed it shut.

'*Mmm*,' she mumbled. 'I needed that. You wouldn't believe the morning I've had.'

'Was it awful?' asked Lou sympathetically.

'You wouldn't believe,' repeated Holly. 'I've been moved to fish and aquatic plants.' She brooded for a moment, then her face brightened. 'Mind you, some of those tanks and ponds are mega-deep,' she said thoughtfully. 'It wouldn't take much for someone to drown in there. It could easily happen.' A faraway look came over her face. 'It'd be so easy,' she repeated dreamily. 'One push . . .'

Lou looked at her puzzled. It wasn't like Holly to have these macabre fantasies. 'You're – you're not thinking of pretending to drown so some lifeguard types can come and save us, are you?' she asked. ''Cause you won't get Nik . . .'

Holly shook her head, swallowed the last of her sandwich and slotted her plate in the dishwasher.

'Nik will just have to make sacrifices like the rest of us,' she said. 'We top totty-pullers can't afford to be squeamish. Gotta get back,' she continued. 'OK if we all meet here next Friday? I'll give you your instructions then. Oh – and get hold of a beach ball. I'll nick a few Frisbees off Josh and Jordan.'

'A beach ball,' said Lou slowly. 'So we're going on the beach, are we?'

Holly nodded. 'Yup, that's where all the top totty hangs out, right?' she said. 'So where else?' She made for the door, then, about to turn the handle, she paused. She turned round to face Lou again.

'You look fantastic today, Lou,' she said slowly. 'Has anything . . . happened – you know?'

'Like what?' asked Lou, playing for time.

'You haven't met anyone on those long walks with that animal next door, have you?' asked Holly. 'Hey, that's not a bad idea – you can go anywhere with a dog, and no questions asked.' She peered hard at Lou. 'Your eyes are sparkling,' she accused her.

'And there's something . . . Louise Ingram, what's been going on? Have you been stalking some lad or something?'

'I haven't been doing any stalking,' said Lou. 'I just met . . .' She hesitated, then decided to tell Holly everything. Why not? She was proud of the way she'd seen off Guy. She was certain Holly would approve. She was right.

'Yes!' said Holly. 'That'll show God's gift to women he can't mess you around. You're well getting over that creep, Lou. You're in prime shape for a brand-new boy. Great! By the end of next week you'll have a totally new model. Must go – Derek will be throwing a wobbly.' She grinned encouragingly at Lou and whirled out of the house.

Lou went over to the telly and switched it on. She stared at it without really seeing the image. If Holly hadn't been in such a hurry, she would have tried to explain that the last thing she wanted – after finally beginning to clear Guy out of her brain – was another boyfriend.

Still, a day on the beach with her mates would be fun, whatever happened. Fun? thought Lou in surprise. Yes – it had to be admitted. She was almost looking forward to next Friday.

Holly's Guide To Beach Pulling

'Right,' said Holly briskly. She inspected the others, sprawled around Lou's living-room. It was clear she had taken control not a moment too soon.

Gina was fiddling with a bright-red Frisbee, turning it dreamily round and round between her fingers. Nik was frowning slightly. She patted the enormous yellow beach ball so it bounced lightly on the carpet. Lou, wearing a deep-blue top and shorts, sat up and looked at Holly attentively. She seems the most positive of the lot, thought Holly.

'Right,' she repeated, raising her voice slightly. 'Listen up. Holly's guide to pulling on the beach. Based on boys' most primitive urge.' Gina blinked and laid the Frisbee on the sofa. 'Which is' – she paused dramatically – 'to show the entire universe what big, tough guys they are. Basically, they're all longing for us girlies to mess up so they can rush to the rescue. All we have to do is act helpless and they'll descend in droves. And then – *wham!*' She banged her bottle of Factor 8 on the telly and Gina jumped. 'We've got them. They're ours to do what we like with. Putty in our hands.'

She gazed at them triumphantly. 'And there you have it. OK?' She reached out for her beach towel and tucked it under her arm. 'So what are we waiting for? To the beach!'

The others remained where they were, their mouths open.

'Helpless?' said Nik slowly. She spoke as if the word was in a foreign language she didn't understand. 'I don't *believe* you, Holly. You can't seriously mean behave like bimbos?'

Holly nodded vigorously. 'Yup,' she said. 'It never fails. It appeals to their deepest macho instincts. They can't help it; that's the way they're programmed.'

'But how, what . . . ?' started Gina.

Holly sighed. She put down her towel and reached for the Frisbees. 'See these little plastic disks?' she said, brandishing them at Gina. 'Clock this suntan lotion?' She picked up the bottle and Gina flinched. 'And this big, bouncy ball? These are our secret weapons. First we scan the beach for the highest concentration of totty. Then we take up our position close by. Not too obviously, of course.' She ignored Nik's snort. 'And *then* . . . we go into action.'

'Action?' asked Lou. Holly turned towards her.

'Don't you just love throwing a big coloured ball to your mates?' she demanded. 'It's such *fun*! You jump up and down squealing so everyone knows what a good time you're having. Only you're such a pathetic litle butterfingers you sometimes miss and it just happens to tumble in the midst of these delicious boys.'

She stopped for breath, while the others stared at her. Nik was shaking her head.

'And then,' she continued, 'you're so mortified you don't know *what* to do, and you stand there blushing . . . and surprise, surprise, the tastiest of the lot picks it up and brings it back. Oh, you're so grateful. *Or*,' she continued, ignoring Nik's sick-making face, 'you catch it, but it knocks you right off your tiny feet so you stagger straight into the arms of said tasty geezer. You look up at him, thank him in your best girly voice, and—'

'OK, OK,' interrupted Nik. She brooded for a

moment. 'Stagger,' she repeated. '*Stagger*?' Her voice rose.

'Like this,' said Holly, falling neatly into Lou's arms. 'Ooh, Ms Ingram, what *would* I have done if your big, strong arms hadn't been there to catch me? Oh, *thank* you, thank you.' She straightened up. 'And so on,' she said.

They gazed at her in horror.

'I can't stagger,' said Nik abruptly. 'Honestly, Hol, it's a lousy idea.'

'It'll work,' said Holly, 'And that's all that matters.' She held up a Frisbee. 'And Gina, when I throw this to you – Gina!' she repeated sharply. Gina was bending down to tickle Benji's tum. The dreamy, faraway expression had returned to her face. 'When I throw this to you, Gina, I'm so useless that naturally I miss, and – *quelle coïncidence*! – it lands on the towel of the best-looking boy on the beach. I rush up, apologising madly, and nature takes its course.'

'What about the sun lotion?' said Lou, squinting at it.

'Obvious,' said Holly scornfully. 'How can a girl anoint her own back? We can but try, but it's *très, très difficile* – impossible, I reckon –

without a little help. Preferably from a carefully selected spunk who just happens to be sauntering by.' She handed it over to Lou. 'Any red-blooded lad will come to a girl's assistance when he sees her struggling. And then – *voilà*, nabbed again!' She picked up her towel. 'Ready? Nik?'

Nik brooded, twirling the beach ball round and round with her finger. Then suddenly she nodded. 'Aww, why not?' she said unexpectedly. 'Might be interesting to be a pathetic beach babe for the afternoon. Yeah, it'll be a whole new experience. I'll give it a go.' She picked up the ball. Holly handed out a Frisbee to Lou and Gina, slid on her sunglasses and dropped the lotion into her beach bag.

'Right!' she said. This time they all got up and followed her.

It was a perfect day for beach activities – the sun was shining and the sea was the same beautiful deep-blue colour as the sky. There wasn't a cloud to be seen.

Leaning over the sea wall, they examined the scene before them. The beach was seething. Drawn by the sun and the sand, groups of lads had sprung up everywhere. Bare-chested, anointing their pecs with oil, exercising their muscles in time to loud, booming music, stretched out on towels or feeding their faces with ice-cream, they soaked up the sunshine and eyed up the girls. There were almost too many of them, and they came in such a wide selection of colours, shapes and sizes that it was difficult to sort out the studs from the saddos. Then Holly raised her arm and pointed.

'There!' she said.

The others peered across the beach. On a nice flat stretch of sand, not too far from the sea, a cluster of blokes were arranging themselves on their towels. Some lay on their backs, some sprawled on their stomachs. All were wearing shorts and, as far as could be seen, there wasn't a dud or weedy one among them. They were all mouth-wateringly luscious.

Holly leaned over even further, screwing her eyes up. 'Just clock those legs,' she hissed. 'Nice and brown and muscley.' She looked at the others. 'Let's go,' she said.

Carefully weaving their way through the other bodies on the beach, they found a space nearby.

Gina spread out her towel, lay down on her front and closed her eyes. Nik sat hunched up, staring in the opposite direction.

Holly poked them both. 'Hey,' she said. 'There's work to be done. There they are – as promised. A whole load of totty waiting to be pulled. So let's get out there and bag them. Gina, here.' Gina rolled over and sat up and Holly handed her a Frisbee.

'I'll have that one with the micro-shorts,' she said. 'Which do you fancy, Gina?'

'Umm, I don't know. That one?' said Gina wildly, pointing at a guy spread-eagled on his stomach. From the back his hair looked rather nice – crisp and brown and curly.

'Mmm, good torso,' said Holly grudgingly. 'Well, if you're sure . . . you can always change him later. Aim for his towel. And *scream* when it lands. So he knows it's you.' Gina looked terrified.

The others watched as Gina and Holly took up their positions. Holly threw her Frisbee towards the guy she'd selected, but it landed several metres away. She squealed loudly and jumped up and down. The only people who reacted were a group of girls nearby, who glared at her pointedly.

Gina was staring in the direction of Antonio's Top Karaoke Bar, a soppy smile on her face.

'Gina!' snapped Holly.

Gina jumped.

'Throw it,' commanded Holly.

Gina aimed vaguely in the boys' direction. The Frisbee skimmed towards a mum and dad with two kids, slicing the turrets off their magnificent sandcastle.

Gina rushed towards them. 'I'm *sorry*,' she breathed, as the kids burst into loud sobs. She started frantically patting the sandcastle together.

Holly strode forward. 'It doesn't matter,' she said impatiently. 'They can rebuild it.'

'Here's your . . . thing,' said the dad coldly, holding out the Frisbee.

'Ta,' said Holly, taking it from him and returning it to Gina. 'Let's keep it up, Gina. You'll strike gold soon. Wait there while I sort out the others.' She returned to Lou and Nik.

'Let's go,' she said. She tossed the beach ball into the air and it landed near a guy flat on his back waving his foot in time to his Walkman. He gave them a filthy look, put out his foot and knocked it back to them, then closed his eyes.

'Just practising,' said Holly. She threw the ball to Lou, who rushed forward to catch it then remembered to stagger back and drop it. She gave a tiny scream. Holly nodded encouragingly.

Lou sent the beach ball towards Nik, who, making a tremendous effort, managed to miss it. She was amazed how easy it was to be a useless bimbo if you really put your heart into it.

They were causing havoc on the beach. Holly was right – acting pathetic is certainly the way to get noticed, thought Lou. She watched as Holly, pretending to be winded when Nik threw her the ball, staggered neatly into the centre of the selected hunks.

'Sorry, how *stupid* of me,' she trilled, batting her eyelashes madly at the guy in the tiny shorts.

He didn't reply. Nobody did. After waiting a moment, Holly rejoined the others.

'We might have to try some other lads,' she said thoughtfully. 'Plenty more around. Anyway, he had knobbly knees.'

They were all well into the pathetic-beach-babe routine now, jumping and screaming and throwing the beach ball more and more wildly. Even Gina was attracting a lot of attention as she cast the ball far and wide, but it wasn't exactly the kind Holly had promised. In the end, unable to take the glares and mutterings any longer, she made the excuse of exhaustion and crept back to her towel.

She rested her head on her arms and immediately her thoughts turned to the Ice Boy. Tomorrow's the day, she told herself. Yes, tomorrow I'll pluck up the courage to ask his name. She imagined how she'd put it: 'Oh, by the way, I don't think I know your name . . .' She'd say it coolly, as if it didn't really matter, as if it had only just occurred to her. As though she hadn't been thinking about him every single minute she was in Uncle Toni's bar and every moment she was out of it.

And then, maybe he'd ask *her* name. And then . . . Gina sighed and picked up the suntan lotion. She smeared some on her shoulders and tried unsuccessfully to rub some on her back. Supposing he came along the beach now . . .

'Like some help?'

Startled, Gina squinted sideways and found herself staring straight into a pair of twinkling hazel eyes. She was positive they belonged to the curly-haired guy she'd pointed out to Holly. She'd done it! She'd followed Holly's instructions and, behold, she had pulled! *If* she wanted to.

She sneaked a look towards Holly, Lou and Nik. They were so busy they hadn't even noticed what was going on. Gina turned back to smile into the eyes of the boy crouching down beside her. 'No, I'm all right, thanks,' she said.

His face fell several metres. 'Sure?' he asked, getting to his feet again.

'Absolutely,' said Gina firmly. She was so certain she didn't want to bag this good-looking boy that her shyness had miraculously vanished.

'Pity,' he said as he moved away.

Gina felt her face turn red with guilt. She'd been brought here by Holly to pull, she'd been on the brink of success and at the last moment she'd bottled out. She watched the curly-haired one return to his mates, give them the thumbs-down sign and pick up a sports mag. Gina thought he seemed nice, but however nice he'd turned out to be she still wouldn't have wanted him. The only guy she wanted was the Ice Boy.

The others were tossing the ball all over the beach. Nik had just fluffed catching the huge, impossible-to-miss beach ball for the third time.

Giggling and staggering like a complete bimbo, she became aware that somebody was watching her, had been standing watching her for some time. His expression was one of total disbelief.

There was a sick, churning feeling in Nik's stomach. She stopped in mid-stagger, shut her eyes, willing it all to be a dreadful mistake, then opened them again. It wasn't.

'Matt!' she gasped. She'd never been more mortified in her life.

'Nik?' said Matt slowly. He blinked, as though he still couldn't believe what his eyes were telling him. He looked at the beach ball, then at her. 'Nik?' he repeated.

She stared at him in anguish. Like a flash of lightning she realised that she cared very much what Matt thought about her. He was, in fact, the last person in the world she wanted to see her making a complete prat of herself.

Matt was grinning at her now. He seemed not only baffled, but amused. His teeth were very white in his brown face. People were always saying he belonged on the set of *Baywatch*. Nik thought they were right.

'What are you doing?' he asked.

Nik, her face flushed and her heart hammering, rushed to explain. It was all for the sake of securing Lou a boyfriend, she started off. Holly had organised this beach-bimbo business, and it was all totally stupid, of course, but they'd gone along with it ... She watched Matt miserably, waiting for his expression to turn to one of complete contempt.

But Matt didn't look contemptuous. He was looking even more amused, and something else – relieved. 'You were making a brilliant job of it,' he said, his dark eyes glinting with laughter. 'But it's not exactly your kind of thing, is it, Nik?'

'No, it's not my kind of thing at all,' Nik agreed hastily. 'Not at all.' She shook her head vigorously several times. 'No, it isn't,' she repeated, in case he hadn't understood the first and second times. She could have strangled Holly at that moment.

'You're much too honest and straightforward to play those sorts of games,' said Matt thoughtfully. He was gazing at Nik as though now he'd stopped to consider exactly what kind of person she was, he'd realised there was something very special about her. As if he liked her very much, and found her rather endearing. And her smile. And her lips ...

He put out a hand to touch her arm and Nik closed her eyes. Even though the sun was blazing down, she shivered and swayed towards him. Everyone else on the beach faded away and they were alone in the middle of a huge silence. They remained like that for a moment and then Matt said suddenly, 'You look great, Nik.' Nik felt her heart stop in her chest as Matt leaned slowly forward. It seemed like a lifetime before, with a shiver of delight, she felt his lips finally touch hers and melt into a gentle, wonderful kiss. They drew apart and stood smiling at each other. Then Matt said in a voice that was suddenly husky, 'Fancy coming for something to eat when you've finished . . .' He grinned and swept his hand around the beach. 'All this?' he ended.

Nik caught her breath. 'I've finished now,' she told him, breathlessly. 'And I'd love to. Be with you in a minute.' She ran over to where Lou and Holly had tactfully returned to Gina.

'Erm . . .' she started, putting the beach ball down on Holly's towel. Holly waved her hand.

'Say no more,' she said smugly. 'We saw it all. What did I tell you? It never fails. You were just a good mate – a *very* good mate – to that gorgeous lad until suddenly he saw you in a totally new light. You deserve him, Nik,' she said generously. 'You certainly gave it your all.'

'It wasn't really like that,' protested Nik, then she smiled and shrugged. She was so happy, what did it matter? 'See you later,' she called, as she ran back to where Matt was waiting for her. The others, watching them walk away across the sand, saw Matt slip his arm around Nik's shoulders and Nik snuggle close to him as if she'd been waiting for nothing else all summer. Just by the sea wall they stopped and looked at each other as if, once again, they were the only ones on the beach. Matt and Nik drew together into another kiss that seemed to last an eternity until they finally drew apart and continued over the beach entwined together.

Even Holly seemed stunned by the swiftness with which things had developed. 'They could snog for England,' she said eventually as they gathered their things together, ready to call it a day. 'Well, at least Nik's sorted. It was obviously meant to be, but it might never have happened if I hadn't pushed things along. Nik put everything into it and it worked. If others had done the same, they might have pulled as well.' She looked severely at Gina, who blushed guiltily.

'It was fun anyway,' said Lou unexpectedly. She was smiling and bouncing the beach ball as they walked along.

'Fun?' said Holly. '*Fun*? We're not here to have fun – we're here to pull. But don't worry. Holly has many, many more excellent plans up her sleeve.' Gina and Lou looked at her apprehensively. 'Make sure Uncle Toni doesn't want you to work next Friday evening, Gina, and we'll meet up at my place. We're going on the town. In style. Bexington won't know what's hit it,' she promised them.

Disco Divas

When Lou rang Holly's doorbell there were the usual shouts and scuffles as Holly's kid brothers fought to the death to answer it.

'Leave it – it's for me!' she could hear Holly yelling above the uproar, but when the door finally opened all Holly's family were crowded in the hall, waiting to see who it was. Holly's family liked to know what was going on.

'Hello, Louise,' said Holly's mum. 'How are you? You look very nice. Have you been working over the holidays?'

'She's fine,' said Holly. 'And no, she hasn't been forced into a boring, no-hope job by her parents, unlike some people. Come up to my room, Lou. It's the only place we'll get any privacy round here.'

Halfway up the stairs she turned round. 'I'm

expecting two more friends,' she called down. 'So when the doorbell rings again, I'll get it. Then we're going out. OK?'

'Where?' started Holly's dad, but Lou and Holly had reached the top of the stairs by now.

'Out!' shouted Holly.

She swept Lou inside her room and slammed the door. '*Honestly*!' she sighed, rolling her eyes. Then she looked Lou up and down. Lou wriggled uncomfortably under her gaze. She was wearing one of her favourite dresses – black, sleeveless and simple. She'd thought it would be ideal for clubbing. It made her feel confident and sexy and it looked good with her tan.

Holly was shaking her head. Her expression was sad.

'What's the matter?' asked Lou.

'My mum was right,' said Holly. 'You look very nice. Nice,' she repeated. 'Tonight – we – are – going – to – pull. You don't pull by looking safe and nice. You pull by looking glamorous and sassy and . . . sexy! If you want guys to notice you, you've got to stand out from the crowd. Luckily, I've had a trawl through my wardrobe and I've dug out some really impressive items.'

'Holly, just 'cause they look good on you doesn't mean they'll be right for me,' protested Lou.

'This will make anyone stand out,' said Holly. She held up a tomato-coloured, severely-short dress that made Lou gasp. 'And to go with it . . .' She fished out a pair of strappy scarlet shoes. 'Perfect! Now *that* is dressing to impress!'

'I can't—' started Lou, when the doorbell rang.

'I'll get it!' screamed Holly, hotfooting it to the door. But already they could hear Josh and Jordan clattering through the hall; then Nik and Gina's voices.

'That's very pretty, Gina,' Holly's mum was saying. 'I wish Holly would wear something like that. And what a lovely colour, Nik.'

'Are those silver elephants on your bangles, Nik?' Josh was asking. 'Holly's got silver trousers, hasn't she, Mum?'

'Aargh!' screamed Holly. She leaned over the banister. 'Leave them alone! Come on up, Nik and Gina! Just ignore the *children*.'

Gina came up smiling. 'I don't mind them,' she said. She was wearing a pink top and pants. Nik was glowing in an orangey-yellow outfit she'd picked up courtesy of Oxfam. Lou thought they both looked very nice, glancing apprehensively at Holly, who was muttering 'Hopeless' under her breath.

'What's this?' asked Nik, picking up the bright-red excuse for a dress. 'Wow! Are you really going to wear this, Holly? You're the only one of us who could carry it off.'

'No, Lou is,' said Holly, and Nik gasped. 'Get into it, Lou, then we'll get going on your mush. Lots of glitter and scarlet lippy, I reckon,' she said thoughtfully.

She turned to Gina. 'Gina, try these on.' She held up a shiny, almost non-existent skirt and top. 'We might tattoo your tum, since there'll be so much on display,' she said. 'Something tasteful – a flower or a bird – but it'll make you stand out.'

'No!' shrieked Gina. 'I'd rather wear what I've got on, Holly. I can't wear that, and I don't want a tattoo.'

'Not a real tattoo, just a transfer,' said Holly soothingly. 'And we can't have this negative attitude, girls. If my plan is going to work, you've got to put your all into it. Unlike last week on the beach.'

'Come on, Holly, we did try,' protested Lou.

Holly shook her head, sadly. 'Not hard enough,' she said. 'It was a foolproof plan. If you'd followed my instructions we'd have pulled in no time.'

'Nik pulled,' said Lou. 'Hey, Nik, whatever happened to lads being a total waste of space?'

Nik grinned. 'Aww – some guys are different,' she said.

'Yes, yes,' said Holly. 'You're well sorted, Nik, so you're let off the hook. But the rest of us have serious work to do. The idea is to knock these blokes senseless by the sheer power of our sex appeal.' She indicated the alarmingly tiny outfits. 'If you've got it, serve it up on a plate. And we've certainly got it, girls. So off we go!'

'Look, Holly,' said Lou. 'I can't.' She pulled the red dress up at the front then tried to tug it down again. The heels of the shoes she'd put on were so high they should have come with a health warning.

'Great!' said Holly. 'You look almost as good as I do in it. Here's some lip liner. Draw yourself some really curvy smackers, then fill them in. Black eye-liner, eyelash curlers and mascara over there, so get dramatic with them. Same goes for you, Gina.'

She passed over two little pots of shiny eye-shadow. 'Purple for you, Gina, pewter for Lou,' she ordered. 'Now get plastering – and don't forget the blusher.'

By now Gina, swept along by the tornado-like force of Holly's personality, was inside the micro-skirt and top. She too was teetering dangerously in a pair of Holly's typically outrageous shoes. Holly had changed into some disturbingly tight trousers and an equally figure-hugging top.

'I always feel *powerful* in this clobber,' she said happily. 'Nails.' She passed a kaleidoscope of nail-varnishes over to Gina. 'Take your pick,' she commanded. 'Lou – be bold!'

'It'll never move again,' moaned Lou, after a session with the curling tongs followed by a blast of extra-strong hairspray. She shook her hair experimentally. It remained totally rigid.

Holly scanned them both with satisfaction. 'That's better,' she said. 'Now, those are *real* pulling clothes. They say these babes mean business. But it's not enough to *look* good . . .' The others gazed at her, hypnotised. The gold spray on the tips of her red hair glowed. She'd been musing about having dreadlocks, but had had to give up the idea for lack of time. Her outfit is every bit as outrageous as ours, thought Lou, but somehow Holly has the attitude to carry it off.

'We've got to have a plan of action,' continued Holly. 'So – first we suss out the talent. *Then* we loiter by the bar, looking *très* helpless. "Oh dear, what does a girl have to do round here to get a drinkie?"'

'We've tried helpless,' said Lou, giggling. 'On the beach.'

'Yep, and Nik will tell you that it worked,' said Holly. 'Just ask her.' Nik opened her mouth as if to argue, then shut it again and looked out of the window. 'But tonight a leetle more action is called for than just batting a ball or spinning a Frisbee.'

'I've never been to the Kiss Club,' said Gina, struggling vainly to cover a little more thigh area with Holly's tiny skirt. The others looked at her and smiled. Gina had never been much of a one for clubs.

'You'll have a great time,' Holly assured her. 'And you'll wow them in that gear.' She looked at Gina ruminatively. 'Mustn't forget that tattoo. Makes a girl look really wild.'

'Tattoos are tacky,' said Lou suddenly.

'Uh?' said Holly. 'What? Oh yeah – well, perhaps we'll forget the tattoo this time.' Gina gave a sigh of relief and looked gratefully at Lou. 'Kiss is perfect spunk territory, but remember, we've got to get out there and sell ourselves. Loadsa eye contact – and when you're on the dance floor give it *everything*: sexy gyrations, hand moves, the lot.'

She picked up her purse, went over to the door, opened it and peered round. 'Looks safe. Let's go,' she said.

They tiptoed down the stairs, but as soon as they reached the bottom, the kitchen door was flung open and Josh and Jordan burst through. They stopped dead as the girls wobbled towards the door.

'Why's Holly's hair a different colour at the edges? Gina's falling off her shoes! I can see Lou's chest and Gina's *belly button*!' they yelled. Gina and Lou turned crimson with mortification. 'Mum, Mum! Come and look!' they shouted.

They had reached the door by now. Putting on a burst of speed, Holly opened it and they teetered down the path.

'Holly! Where are you going? You'll cripple yourself! Put on a jacket! When will you be back?'

floated after them. Without looking back, Holly waved her hand, opened the gate and they turned the corner.

'It's like getting out of Fort Knox,' said Holly. 'Dream boys, here we come!'

Kiss was a great club. It had a really good atmosphere. Gina's eyes shone as she imagined going there with the Ice Boy. Aww, he was probably too cool to frequent the local clubs, but it was nice to dream. Lou peered at the mass of people on the dance floor. She blinked as a flash of light suddenly revealed Guy's face. And then, of course, she saw it wasn't him at all. Holly would never have chosen this club if there'd been any chance of Guy being here. But the strange thing was that all she'd felt had been a tiny flutter of surprise. Interesting . . .

Holly was hissing in her ear. 'Come on,' she said, 'Let's move towards the bar.'

Slowly, they wandered around the club to the bar, where a selection of tasty lads were loitering. The barman smiled and came forward, but Holly shook her head.

'Helpless,' she mouthed above the music. 'Eye contact,' she reminded them. There was a cute-looking guy in baggy, surfie gear nearby with a couple of his mates. Lou tried looking at him and holding his gaze. He looked nice and cool, the sort of boy she wouldn't mind spending some time chatting to, since she was free. Yeah – free! It was the first time she'd thought of it like that, and it made her feel light-hearted and confident. It didn't matter what stupid things Holly got them to do, she knew she was going to enjoy herself tonight.

She continued to stare directly into the surfie guy's peepers. She hoped Holly was taking note of the masterful way she was maintaining eye contact. He was gazing back, his eyes wide. Lou felt a thrill of triumph. Yeah, she wouldn't mind chatting this one up . . . Then she saw that in fact his eyes weren't fixed on hers but on the scarlet dress. And they were wide because he was truly gobsmacked. Lou followed the direction of his gaze and her face flamed. For a moment she'd forgotten she wasn't wearing her own black dress. She moved back into the shadows and he blinked and turned away.

Gina wasn't doing much better. Holly had

sculpted her glossy brown hair into a frozen tidal wave. She was doing her best to exchange eye contact with a guy whose eyes were superglued to her bare tum. In the end a girl came up to him, passed her hand several times in front of his face, then turned and glared at Gina. Gina dropped her eyes, and when she looked up again they'd both disappeared.

Nik watched her sympathetically. Strangely enough, she was attracting a lot of interest herself, without really going out for it. Her shining hair, happy face and the glow of confidence that surrounded her seemed to be doing the trick without any effort at all on her part.

Holly was doing her stuff on the dance floor. She spun and glittered, her red hair like a flame. She waved at the three of them to join her. Gina and Lou did their best, wiggling and gyrating in their tiny outfits, but Nik thought neither of them was really cut out for that sort of thing.

Nik looked at the guys who were standing watching them. Their expressions ranged from amused to stunned to lecherous. A few Neanderthal types were making 'Phwoor!' noises every time they moved. Holly took it in her stride and it didn't seem to bother Lou one way or the other, but it was obviously getting to Gina, in spite of her efforts to look cool.

There were plenty of sexy-looking lads around, but the only boys they seemed to be attracting were one step up from primeval slime. When they gathered at the bar again, one of the creeps eased up to Holly.

'Hello, gorgeous. D'you know you're the classiest chick here tonight?' he leered. Holly sent him reeling back with a few well-chosen words, but, like all slime, he oozed back again. This time he started making up to Gina.

'You're the best-looking girl . . .' he began, but Gina moved quickly away. He looked at Lou, who said, 'Let's get back on the floor.'

This time, Gina thought, she was really going to make an effort and give it all she'd got. Lou was grinning at her, and seemed to be enjoying herself, so why not? Waving her arms in what she hoped was a sexy, abandoned manner she gave a tremendous wiggle and lost her balance, almost falling over. As the room spun round her, she spotted someone out of the corner of her eye. No, it *couldn't* be . . . She'd just imagined it because she'd been thinking about him all night and wondering why she still hadn't got round to asking his name.

The room slowed down – and yes, it *was* him, and there wasn't even time to get off the floor and hide. It was far, far too late anyway, because the Ice Boy had obviously seen her and was looking right at her. In fact he was staring, and that didn't look like lust on his face. If his mouth had fallen open any further he'd have been in serious danger of dislocating his jaw.

For a moment their eyes met, then Gina wrenched her own away. There was only one thing to do, one place to run to. She put her head down and rushed blindly through the crowd to the toilets.

The others stopped and looked at each other in surprise.

'What's the matter with Gina?' asked Holly.

'Something's upset her. Come on,' said Nik, and they followed her out to the ladies' loos.

Gina was washing her face at a basin. Lou put her arm round her, but it took quite a long time to get the full story, because every time she started she choked and tears came to her eyes.

'Take it slowly, Gina,' said Lou gently. 'And don't worry, we're all here for you.'

'Did one of those creeps say anything to you?' asked Holly. ''Cause if so, I'll go out there and—'

'No, no,' wailed Gina, shaking her head. 'It's just – the Ice Boy,' she spluttered.

'He . . . he isn't *here*, is he, Gina?' asked Lou. Gina nodded miserably.

'What happened?' asked Lou.

'He – he looked at me,' hiccuped Gina. She looked down at her outfit. 'He was obviously totally disgusted.'

'Who? What?' said Holly. 'What's going on here? The Ice Boy – who's that?'

When Lou explained, she frowned. 'Yeah, I see,' she said slowly. 'I wish you'd told me before, Gina, I could have fixed it for you. I'll go and sort him out, shall I?'

'No. *No!*' wailed Gina again. 'It's too late, I've completely blown it, I've lost any chance . . .' She accepted a tissue from Nik and dabbed her eyes.

'Aww, Gina, it's not as bad as that,' said Nik. 'You can tell him you were just having a girls' night out. What's wrong with that?'

'I can't—' started Gina.

284

'She hasn't talked much to him yet,' explained Lou. The others nodded. 'He was just surprised, that's all, Gina. He's only seen you in Uncle Toni's bar before. You can have a laugh about it – it'll break the ice,' she said comfortingly.

'D'you think so?' mumbled Gina hopefully, and Holly nodded.

'Lou's right,' she said briskly. 'It's probably the best thing that could have happened. Come on, Gina, just go up to him and start chatting.' Gina swallowed and looked anxious. 'We'll be with you,' she added encouragingly.

Gina had calmed down now. She peered and dabbed at her face in the mirror. Most of the make-up and mascara had washed off by now. Eventually, after a lot of persuasion, they got her to emerge.

The club was still pulsating. There seemed to be even more people than before. They looked where Gina had sighted the Ice Boy, but he was no longer there. They went up to the bar, they walked around the edges of the dance floor, they penetrated into the furthest and darkest corners of the club, but eventually it had to be admitted – the Ice Boy had departed.

They stood around in depression. Nobody had any idea what to do next. Gina was biting her lip and staring at the floor, trying to keep back another flood of tears.

'Tomorrow, how can I *look* at him . . .' she started, then gulped and shook her head. 'He was *disgusted*,' she sobbed, 'He didn't want to talk to me because he was so *disgusted*.'

'I wouldn't think so, Gina . . .' Lou started.

'But you didn't see his *face*,' wailed Gina.

They did their best, but Gina was inconsolable. Even Holly, for the first time ever, seemed to have run out of ideas. The evening was ruined.

In the end, though, it was Holly who came up with an unexpected suggestion. It was one they'd never heard from her before.

'Let's go home,' she said.

The Ice Melts

'So, Gina. You enjoy yourself last night? You see any *ragazzi* dance as good as your Uncle Toni?' Uncle Toni shimmied in and out of the tables in the bar, round the pool table, over the stage and back again, moving his shoulders and waving his fingers in the air. He seemed in a particularly manic mood.

'Maybe we introduce dancing to Antonio's Bar,' he said breathlessly, whirling to a halt and clutching his gold medallions for support. 'What you think, Gina?'

Gina tried to smile. She was pale and her eyes felt heavy. After she'd got back from the club she'd hardly slept. She'd kept thinking about the moment when she'd looked up to see the Ice Boy witnessing her pathetic attempts to be sexy. What must he think of her? Well – it was obvious what he thought. He'd *left*, hadn't he, rather than have to talk to her. He'd probably felt sorry for her. Gina had moaned and huddled under her duvet, willing herself to fall asleep and forget it all, but the scene had kept replaying itself in her brain.

When at long last the sky grew lighter, Gina had wondered whether to call Uncle Toni and tell him she felt sick. How could she face the bar, with Uncle Toni clucking round asking if she'd had a wonderful time at the club and whether the atmosphere was up to the standard of Antonio's Top Karaoke Bar? And what about the Ice Boy – how could she look at him again? Gina twisted her duvet even tighter round her. She couldn't. It was just too much.

But if she stayed at home, it would be even worse. Her mum would keep asking why she looked so pale and miserable, if anything had happened at the club, and what *was* it that she'd seen Gina wearing as she'd crept up the stairs last night?

At least she might be able to escape Uncle Toni's questions by clearing up in the bar or helping Vince with the karaoke. And perhaps, if she was very cunning, she might avoid meeting the Ice Boy altogether. Suppose she told Uncle Toni she was having problems about the ice supplies, that a top executive decision was necessary? Her mind made up, Gina had tumbled out of bed ready to face the day ahead at Antonio's Bar.

'Yes, Uncle Toni, dancing would be great,' she told him now, but obviously she didn't say it with enough enthusiasm because a cloud passed over his face.

'Tired, *cara*?' he asked tenderly. 'Ah, I know.' His face cleared. 'You have been staying late at your club, enjoying yourself with your friends.' He chuckled. Uncle Toni liked to think of his niece having a good time, and was anxious to hear every detail of her wonderful evening.

'Too much dancing, yes?' he continued. 'What you say: inflicting serious damage on the floor-boards?' He chuckled again. As proprietor of the trendiest bar in Bexington, Uncle Toni prided himself on keeping up with the latest phrases. 'Ah, to be young again . . .' He was only joking, of course: he knew himself to be in the prime of life. 'Everything so exciting . . .'

Gina picked up a plastic tomato filled with ketchup and wiped it with her stripy cloth. Little crusty bits of dried goo fell on to the table. She wanted to sweep them on the floor, but since she'd only have to brush them up later she scrunched them in her cloth instead.

'Yeah,' she said drearily. She looked at the clock. The Ice Boy was due in about twenty minutes. There was no way she could face him today. Uncle Toni would *have* to do it.

'Uncle Toni,' she said hesitantly.

Humming to himself, Uncle Toni had started untwisting the lead to the microphone. He looked up enquiringly as Gina stood in front of him, her eyes beseeching.

'Uncle Toni,' she repeated. 'Could you see the Ice Boy when he comes? I don't know how much ice to order – we had some left over yesterday. I think *you* should decide.' She was proud of herself for having thought up such a convincing excuse.

Uncle Toni's eyebrows shot up. He thought for a moment, then put down the mike and shook his head.

'No, no, Gina,' he said. 'You must make this decision yourself. This is why I give you the responsibility. Always so shy,' he said fondly. 'Uncle Toni will not be cross if you make a mistake. We all have to learn. You and this young man must decide between you.' He snapped his fingers impatiently. 'What he called?' he enquired.

Gina gazed at him dumbstruck.

'His name, *cara*?' Uncle Toni repeated.

'I don't know,' said Gina faintly.

At this, if it had been possible, Uncle Toni looked almost severe. He waggled a finger at Gina. 'You not know his name? You must find out *now* – when he comes. Always know the names of your business associates, *cara*. Ah, Gina, Gina, so much to learn. What a good thing you come to work with your Uncle Toni. Soon you will be top businesswoman of Bexington!'

Gina nodded, keeping her eyes on the floor in case Uncle Toni noticed the tears that had sprung to them. Did he mean it? Would he really make her see the Ice Boy? And worse – ask his name? Uncle Toni's arms were folded across his chest and he was regarding her steadily. It very much looked as if he did. Perhaps I could trip over someone's foot and sprain my ankle, thought Gina wildly.

Uncle Toni glanced through into the kitchen. His face lit up and he waved his hand. He turned back to Gina. 'Come, Gina, come,' he said. 'Decision time, *cara*.' He shooed her into the kitchen and, smiling and shaking his head, closed the door firmly behind her.

The Ice Boy was standing in the middle of the kitchen, waiting. Gina gave one quick look at his face to see if by any chance Lou had been right and he was prepared to laugh last night away. But when she saw his expression her heart dropped like a stone. It was even frostier than usual.

The Ice Boy regarded her in silence. He had obviously no intention of speaking first. Gina dropped her eyes and forced herself to address his trainers.

'Erm,' she said. Her voice was husky and she tried again. This time it had gone squeaky. 'No ice today,' she told him. She'd no idea if the ice supplies would run out or not, and at this moment she didn't care. She had made an executive decision as Uncle Toni had instructed her and she was prepared to take the consequences.

The Ice Boy pondered for a moment. 'I'll come tomorrow, then,' he said as, without a second glance at Gina, he turned and left.

Gina remained staring at the space he'd occupied. She felt unable to move. She was completely gutted. He could obviously hardly bring himself to speak to her after the fool she'd made of herself last night. And, now that it was all totally hopeless, she could admit it to herself. Even though she hadn't got round to discovering his name, she'd still hoped deep in her heart that somehow, some day, she and the Ice Boy would get together. Well, she could forget that now – she'd blown her chances with him for ever.

When Uncle Toni came into the kitchen and looked at her enquiringly, Gina forced herself to move. Before he could ask, she said quickly, 'I've cancelled the ice today, Uncle Toni. And I haven't asked him what his name is.' Her voice was as bleak as the Ice Boy's, and again Uncle Toni looked at her with concern.

'You not well, *cara*?' he enquired gently, and the kindness in his voice made the tears rush to Gina's eyes again.

'I – I'm alright, Uncle Toni,' she said. 'I just don't feel like talking much. I'll get back to the bar.' At least she knew exactly where she stood now. The only time she'd ever see the Ice Boy smile at her again was in her dreams.

*

293

The next day wasn't quite so bad at first. The emotions she'd gone through in the last twenty-four hours had exhausted Gina so much that she'd fallen asleep almost as soon as her head touched the pillow. And, since all hope had gone and nothing mattered any more, it wasn't quite so much effort to get up and go to the bar. The only surprise was that it was such a beautiful, sunny day, when it should have been cold and grey, with rain stinging Gina's face as she walked around the bay.

But in spite of the heat, Gina felt cold. The usual losers kept trying to come on to her, but she ignored them. She'd got no better at handling the lairy lads and their comments, but if they ever showed any real signs of getting out of hand Uncle Toni was there to sort them in a flash.

A group of guys Gina had never seen before were gathered round the karaoke equipment, poking it experimentally. It seemed to have packed up altogether now. Gina glanced around, hoping that Uncle Toni would appear to put them in their place.

'When's the karaoke starting?' one of them asked Gina. He picked up a microphone and started whirling it round his head. Another lad snatched it from him and began crooning into it. When nothing emerged from the speakers, he started tapping, then banging them.

At that moment Uncle Toni poked his head round the door. Unfortunately, the creeps were out of his field of vision. 'Gina,' he called out, 'I leave you in charge – ten minutes only, *cara. Ciao!*' Before Gina could draw his attention to the lads' antics he had disappeared.

'It won't be long,' Gina told them. She hoped that when they learnt this they would stop mucking about and settle down. 'Can I get you anything?' she asked, hoping to divert their attention from the karaoke.

One of them winked at the others. 'Yeah,' he leered. 'You can get me anything anytime, darling.' They moved towards the bar, dragging the mike with them. Gina retreated behind it.

'I'll have – that,' he continued, pointing to a bottle with a green label. Gina reached for it and he shook his head. 'No – that, darling,' he said, pointing to one further along. Gina picked it up and he grinned. 'Changed my mind,' he said, pointing to the first bottle. 'I'll have that one after all. This is a karaoke bar,' he went on. 'We've come here to sing. No – wrong again,' as Gina pushed the bottle towards him.

Gina put her hands down on the bar counter and tried to look cool and unconcerned. She'd no idea what she'd do if they got any more out of hand. She wasn't cold now; she felt hot and flushed and her heart was jumping. She longed for Uncle Toni to return. But suppose he didn't?

The lads had put their arms round each other's shoulders and were swaying from side to side. 'Baby love – ooo, baby love!' they wailed, making eyes at Gina. Their voices got louder and louder and Gina had to fight with herself not to put her hands over her ears.

'Come and join us,' one of them stopped to urge Gina, who pressed herself against the wall, shaking her head and trying to smile.

'Aw, come on, Gina, sing for us!' shouted a guy at the pool table, then the whole bar joined in.

'Yeah, sing for us, Gina. Sing!' they yelled. They started pounding the floor and the tables. The room was full of stamping and singing. Gina had no idea what to do. Come *back*, Uncle Toni, she pleaded silently.

As if in answer to her prayer, the door into the kitchen opened. Gina turned thankfully towards it. There, outlined in the doorway like a character in an old-style Western, stood the Ice Boy. He looked even more wonderful than ever, frowning, his grey eyes chilly, and Gina's stomach did a double somersault. He looked coldly round, taking in the creepy gits and Gina's flushed and anxious face. At the sight of his broad shoulders and frosty look, a silence descended on the bar.

'Having trouble?' he asked her, and Gina gulped and nodded. Except for Uncle Toni, she couldn't think of anybody she'd have been more pleased to see. She knew instinctively that the Ice Boy would sort everything out. At the same time, she thought how pathetic she must seem to him again.

The Ice Boy surveyed the rowdy lads, who shuffled uncomfortably. Under his frosty gaze they started disentangling themselves. He watched as they put back the mike, draping it carefully across a speaker. Gina gazed at him in total admiration. How marvellous he was, how strong and – how sexy! The Ice Boy gave one final look around, nodded sternly and then disappeared back into the kitchen. At the same time, Uncle Toni pushed open the door and beamed at his quiet, orderly bar.

'All well, Gina?' he enquired. 'No trouble? Naturally not,' he reassured himself. 'Soon we fix the karaoke.'

'Excuse me, Uncle Toni,' said Gina, and slipped into the kitchen. The Ice Boy had his back to her. He had opened the lid of the freezer and was staring intently at the contents. Gina coughed and he spun round.

As she gazed at him, Gina felt the old wibbly sensation in her stomach return, and the dryness in her throat. But she was determined to make the effort of her life. She was going to talk to him. And then she realised that something very strange had happened to the Ice Boy. He was blushing. Gina stared at him in amazement. Could Lou by any chance have been right – *was he shy too?*

She looked directly into his dark-grey eyes. It was one of the most difficult things she'd ever done, but she managed it. Then she took a deep breath and spoke. 'Thank you,' she said. 'Thanks for helping me out there. I don't know what I'd have done.'

The Ice Boy seemed to have difficulty in replying.

He had to clear his throat several times. 'It's OK. I didn't know if you'd want me to butt in, but I could see things were getting out of hand,' he said. And then – it almost seemed as if he was having to make as much effort as Gina – he said suddenly, 'Why did you run away when you saw me at the club?'

Gina's face flamed. Didn't he realise why she'd fled?

'I – I thought perhaps you didn't want to talk to me in front of your trendy friends,' he continued. 'I thought you didn't like me.'

Didn't like him – if only he knew! Gina struggled to explain. 'I – I didn't know what you'd think when you saw me in that outfit,' she said. 'I don't usually wear that sort of thing when I go clubbing.' (She wasn't ready yet to tell him that she wasn't really into clubbing at all.) 'I was . . . embarrassed. But when I came out, why had you left?'

'There didn't seem much point in hanging around once you'd gone,' said the Ice Boy simply. When Gina goggled at him, he explained – and he was blushing again, she noticed. 'I'd been wanting to ask you out since the first time I saw you, but you always seemed so cool and aloof, I didn't think you'd be interested. You always seemed so cool,' he repeated.

He wanted to ask her out! Gina was filled with such unbelievable bliss she could have sung the ice-cream song without accompaniment for the whole of Uncle Toni's bar. The squawks emerging from the speakers now the karaoke had been restored were like a heavenly choir. If Uncle Toni hadn't at that very minute called her name, she felt she would have died of happiness.

'I won't be long,' she told the Ice Boy. 'Don't go away,' she said daringly. He grinned and leaned back against the deep freeze as if he was prepared to wait all day.

Halfway through the door, Gina paused and turned to face the Ice Boy again. 'Isn't it stupid,' she added casually, 'I don't even know your name.'

'Gina!' called Uncle Toni again. A note of impatience had entered his voice. His jaw dropped as – smiling radiantly, her face transformed with happiness and her dark eyes filled with stars – his niece came back into the bar.

'He's called Shane, Uncle Toni,' Gina told him.

Full Circle

On Holly's last day at the Chestnuts Garden Centre, there was a new sharpness in the air. Holly, tipping the crisp, fat daffodil bulbs into wicker baskets, felt restless and unsettled. It was almost as if, instead of things coming to an end, they were only just beginning.

And in a way they are, thought Holly philosophically. Term started on Monday, and who knew what untapped talent was at this very moment checking out the bus routes ready to join Holly's school? As soon as she'd left this dump behind, there'd be no holding her. At least she'd finally succeeded in dampening the ardour of the Gnome Boy. She'd hardly seen him around at all during the last few days – it was almost as if he'd been avoiding her. Holly smiled grimly to herself.

Tonight they were sleeping over at Gina's place again. It was funny how things had turned out – who'd have thought that Nik and Gina would have nabbed a spunk by the end of the holidays while she and Lou stayed ladless? When she'd been at her lowest, Holly had even considered descending on the surf school and scooping up the shy New Zealand boy. Then she'd told herself not to panic. She'd just have to concentrate on getting in first with the new school totty. Once she was free of the garden centre, the whole world of gorgeous boys would be wide open to her again.

Lifting her head from the bulbs, Holly sniffed the sharp and woody air. Yup, two days back at school, and she too might well have netted a gorgeous boy for fireside cuddles.

'So this is your last day with us, Holly?'

Holly jumped. Mentally, she'd already left Derek far behind. Like the other inhabitants of the garden centre, he was now well and truly part of the past. She smiled kindly on him, though – poor Derek, doomed almost certainly to spend the rest of his sad life in this dump.

'Yeah, 'tis,' she told him. She looked towards the gates of the Chestnuts Garden Centre and the open road. A few more hours and she'd be pedalling along that road, free at last.

'We shall miss you,' said Derek. 'It's nice to have keen young people about the place.'

Holly struggled between politeness and the truth, but in the end honesty won. She just couldn't bring herself to tell Derek that she'd miss him, too. She mumbled something vaguely.

'It's an ideal job for youngsters,' Derek continued. 'Out in the open air, tending living things. But no need to despair, Holly. Mr Mack wants to see you. I think he may have some good news.'

Holly was surprised: she'd hardly spoken to Mr Mack during her time at the Chestnuts and the most she'd expected was a farewell nod when she waved goodbye through the glass walls of his office. Was he going to thank her for her efforts and tell her that, since it was her last day, she could knock off early? Holly didn't think so. She'd worked long enough at the garden centre to know it would get every last gramme of work out of her. She propped a yellow and orange label on top of the bulbs and followed Derek into Mr Mack's room.

It was a tiny office and there were four of them

inside it, so it seemed very crowded. There was Mr Mack, Derek, Holly and . . . *wow*! Would you look at that lad standing next to Mr Mack and oozing an easy confidence. *Coo*!! He was tall, dark, and had the most amazing sea-blue eyes Holly had ever seen. They were fixed on Holly now and they had a glint in them that said immediately he was just Holly's type. Wow, wow, *wow*! she repeated to herself as she felt that peculiar lurching sensation in the pit of her stomach that she'd never in a million years expected to experience at the Chestnuts Garden Centre.

'Ah, Holly,' said Mr Mack. Holly tore her gaze away from the delicious dish and fixed it on Mr Mack's speckly beard. The last thing she felt like doing, with her mind totally blown and her tummy in such turmoil, was bend an ear to Mr Mack, but she was willing to try.

When Holly was excited her red hair blazed as brightly as a forest fire. Mr Mack blinked and adjusted his glasses before continuing.

'First, let me introduce you,' he said. 'Holly, this is Alex, he's joining us for some work experience. He's hoping to study horticulture at college. Holly has been helping us over the summer, Alex. She's leaving today.'

Yeah, and isn't that just typical, thought Holly bitterly. On the very day of her departure, the botanical boy of the century turned up. It just went to prove what she had long suspected. Life was totally and utterly unfair. She gazed yearningly at Mr Gorgeous and he raised an eyebrow and smiled lazily back. He looked devastating. Was there any chance she could bag him before the day ended? Holly knew herself to be a quick worker, but even so it was a huge challenge . . .

'Derek's given me good reports about you, Holly,' continued Mr Mack. Holly nodded impatiently. It was nice of Derek, but face it, who cared? If he'd really had her interests at heart, he'd have employed this botanical wonderboy several weeks ago, thus giving her a chance to get to grips with him. Holly's attention wandered as she continued to fill her eyes with what was probably her first and last sighting of him.

'. . . so,' Mr Mack continued, 'we decided that, as Sunday morning is our busiest time, we'd ask you to come in and help us then. It was a choice between you and Stewart, but after that business with the ornamental fish-pond it was clear he was completely unsuitable.' He turned to Derek with a puzzled frown. 'How on earth anybody could be so clumsy as to fall in . . .' he mused.

'He claims he was pushed,' said Derek. His gaze flicked towards Holly, then away again. 'But . . .' Holly stared straight ahead, her face expressionless.

'Ridiculous excuse – as if anybody would do that,' said Mr Mack sharply. 'He could have severely traumatised those fish.'

'The fish were all right,' said Holly. 'And it wasn't very deep.'

Alex looked at Holly with even greater interest as she made this statement.

'So, the field's open for you, Holly,' said Mr Mack. 'Can we take it that you're interested?'

In the past ten minutes Holly's feelings about the Chestnuts Garden Centre had totally reversed. Before then, she would have pitied Mr Mack for deluding himself that any human being apart from Derek would want to spend a minute more than necessary in his plant-infested dump. Now, she could have thrown her arms around Derek's chestnut-decorated sweatshirt and hugged him to death.

'Yes,' she said. 'Yes, yes I am. For a few weeks anyway,' she added hastily. With the sudden serious interest in plant life she was about to develop, she reckoned it wouldn't take all that many Sunday mornings to well and truly bag Alex. 'It depends how much studying I have to do,' she told him, and he nodded approvingly.

It was time, Holly felt, to bring the meeting to an end. 'I'd better get back to sorting the bulbs,' she said, and again Mr Mack smiled and nodded. There was no doubt that as far as he was concerned Holly was flavour of the month. It was a new sensation for Holly, and she basked in it for a moment before returning to business. 'Shall I show Alex some of the work we're doing?' she asked. Passion, which had totally paralysed Gina, caused Holly's brain to work at twice its normal speed. Derek hesitated, but Mr Mack agreed instantly.

'Certainly, certainly, Holly,' he said. 'Take him round the centre, will you? I was going to ask Derek, but that will free him for other things. A girl of initiative, Holly,' he told Alex.

'Come on, Alex,' said Holly firmly. She nodded

at Mr Mack. 'See you on Sunday,' she promised. As she conducted Alex through the garden centre, Holly looked around her with new eyes. 'There's a new type of Californian poppy,' she said, waving her hand towards the seed packets. 'Apricot flambeau,' she told him, reading the name on the packet. 'It's an F1 hybrid,' she added knowledgeably. 'Brilliant colour, isn't it? It's apricot.'

'I see,' said Alex seriously. 'You're obviously very interested in plants, Holly.'

'I'm *really* interested,' Holly told him. 'Erm, you *are* coming in on Sunday mornings, aren't you, Alex?'

'I am,' said Alex, crinkling his dark-blue eyes at her.

Holly breathed a sigh of relief. Fate, in this matter, seemed on her side for once. And about time too.

'I'll be able to tell you lots more then,' she said happily. She was almost sure her dad had a gardening encyclopedia at home, though she'd never looked inside. She might even buy herself a gardening magazine, though perhaps that was going a bit far. Who'd have thought she'd need to start swotting up on plants at the end of the summer holidays? Still, some things were worth it . . .

'I'll look forward to it,' said Alex.

'It was a funny summer, wasn't it?' said Nik, as they sat around in Gina's kitchen that evening. Nothing really turned out like we expected.' She thought of Matt, as she did most of the time she wasn't with him, and her eyes grew dreamy. It *was* strange how she'd set out on the love hunt with the others and then come back full circle to the guy she'd told everyone was just a mate. Remembering those wonderful moonlight walks on the beach – Matt's hands in her hair, and his lips, tasting of sea and salt, on hers – Nik shivered. She could hardly wait till tomorrow to see him again.

Holly grinned at her. 'No prizes for guessing who Nik's thinking of,' she said. 'But for a sussed-up girl, it certainly took you a long time to see sense, Nik.'

Nik laughed. 'Yeah, yeah, I admit it,' she said. 'You were right and I was wrong.' She smiled round at them all and took a gulp of hot chocolate.

'What about when school starts?' asked Gina. 'Will you be able to see Matt then?'

'Oh, he doesn't live that far away,' said Nik. 'There's the weekends, and the holidays . . .' She hugged her knees, her eyes shining.

'So Nik's got her man lined up for the autumn,' said Holly briskly. 'Likewise our Gina.' Gina blushed and stared down into her mug. 'Didn't I tell you it would all turn out OK, Gina? And I must say,' she said approvingly, 'you've done very well for yourself. That is one cool guy. I couldn't have picked a more delicious boyfriend for you myself,' she added generously.

'He – Shane's – very sensitive really,' said Gina happily. 'He always works delivering ice during the holidays 'cause he's so big and strong.' She blushed again. 'He's at that boys' school at the other end of town, so it'll be quite easy. It was a *beautiful* summer,' she added. She seemed to have totally forgotten the horrors of Uncle Toni's bar.

'Yeah, it was good,' said Lou unexpectedly. She wasn't as radiant as Nik or as glowing and excited as Gina, but she looked confident and happy.

'Erm, we did set out to get you a new boy, Lou,' said Nik delicately. 'I mean, that was the original idea. But – perhaps you haven't really got over Guy yet?'

'I have,' said Lou. She nodded several times. 'I've definitely got over Guy,' she repeated. 'Isn't it great?'

'Are you sure?' asked Nik. 'You were so down at the beginning of the holidays.'

'I'm sure,' said Lou. For the last few days she'd been thinking she'd probably recovered from Guy. But it wasn't until that morning that she'd known it for sure, when she'd gone to answer the door and found him standing on the doorstep.

The summer sun had bronzed Guy's skin and bleached his hair, and he was looking even more fetching than usual. Lou didn't feel a thing. She looked at him enquiringly.

'Hi – hi, Lou,' he stammered. 'How are you?'

'I'm fine,' she said. They weren't going to go through all that again, were they? 'What do you want, Guy?' she asked, getting straight to the point.

'Can I talk to you Lou?' he said.

Lou opened the door wider. 'I haven't got long,' she said. 'Digger's expecting me to take him for a walk.'

'He can wait,' said Guy impatiently, striding inside and plonking himself on the sofa. Same old Mr Egoist, thought Lou. She perched herself opposite and waited.

Guy leaned forward and stared hypnotically into Lou's eyes. She looked coolly back at him. 'Lou,' he said, 'Lou, I – I made a big mistake at the beginning of the summer. I've missed you and I want you back. You're the only girl for me, I've decided. Can you ever forgive me?'

He folded his arms and leaned back again. From the self-satisfied look on his face it was obvious he had no doubt that she'd fall straight into his arms, overcome with gratitude. Now was the opportunity for her revenge.

Lou had rehearsed this scene loads of times in her mind, imagining how much she'd enjoy telling Guy exactly what she thought of him. But now it had finally arrived, she no longer wanted to make him suffer like she had. She couldn't be bothered. All she wanted was for Guy to leave her alone and let her get on with her life. 'I'm sorry, Guy,' she said firmly. 'I don't want to get back with you. Ever.'

She'd thought that was clear enough, but it seemed Guy just couldn't get his head round the fact that she was turning him down.

In the end, 'You've met someone else,' he accused her.

'No, I haven't,' Lou assured him. 'I just don't want to go out with you again, Guy. I prefer it on my own,' she added, but this only seemed to make things worse.

Only when she stood up and told him she was off to collect Digger did he finally stop arguing and pleading. 'I've blown it, haven't I, Lou?' he said humbly. His voice was choked and he could hardly speak. Lou was pierced by an emotion she'd never imagined feeling for Guy. She was desperately sorry for him.

'Goodbye, Guy,' she said gently, and he shook his head and stumbled out of the house. Watching him walk slowly away, it occurred to Lou that perhaps she should be grateful to Guy. He'd taught her that she didn't have to have a boyfriend to enjoy herself. Until the right boy came along, she knew that with a little help from her mates she could go it alone.

'So thanks, everybody, I'd never have made it without you,' Lou continued. 'I'm sorry it didn't work out for you, though, Holly.'

'Aww, you never had a chance at the garden centre, did you, Hol?' said Nik consolingly. 'But just wait till all that new totty hits school.'

'Hey, hey, not so fast,' protested Holly. 'The idea was to bag a boy by the end of the holidays, wasn't it? Well I've got news for you: term doesn't start till Monday. That leaves most of the weekend. By the way, I'm working at the Chestnuts on Sunday mornings now. For a week or two anyway.'

The others stared at her open-mouthed. Holly was always full of surprises. She pushed herself off her stool, got to her feet and stretched. 'Let's take our drinks up to your room, Gina,' she said. 'Here – put them on this tray.'

Curled up on Gina's bed, they waited for Holly to explain herself. But she seemed in no hurry. She looked round them all and grinned. 'So, we had a few surprises, but basically we all got sorted, didn't we? In our different ways. So everyone's OK?'

'If you are, Holly,' said Gina worriedly.

'Don't worry about me,' said Holly. 'Just wait and see. Like Nik said, summer didn't exactly turn out like we thought it would. But it was fun.'

'Everything's fun with your friends,' said Lou softly. She giggled. 'Remember the Bexington Beach Babes? And we've even had a laugh about the Kiss Club, haven't we, Gina?'

'Right!' said Holly. 'So how do we follow that? Just one term to go, girls. We'll hardly notice it if we shut our eyes and don't let it get to us. And then, *ta-boom* . . . it's Crimbo time!! And have I got some great ideas for Christmas! So listen, everyone . . .'

Love Games

Jacqui Deevoy

Libby In Love

My beautiful Libby,
 How long is it since I last saw you? I'm sure it is only weeks, but it seems as if years have passed since we last touched. Now I can't wait to touch you again . . .

'God – I'm having a hot flush!' Libby giggled, theatrically mopping her brow with the letter.

'Me too,' said Ellie. 'And he's not even my boyfriend.'

'I'm not sure if he's mine either . . . well, not yet anyway,' sighed Libby as she bounced onto her bed.

'Sounds keen though,' said Ellie encouragingly.

'Mmmm.' Libby flopped back on the white lace-edged pillows and let the letter drop to her side. Staring at the bobbly ceiling and absentmindedly stroking the ear of her favourite teddy, she sighed again. 'I kind of reckoned the whole thing was just a holiday fling. I'm really surprised he's written actually . . .'

'Yeah, he didn't really seem the letter-writing type, did he?' agreed Ellie. 'So what else has he got to say?' She grabbed the letter impatiently, almost falling out of Libby's wicker chair in the process. 'Hey, get a load of that curly, girlie handwriting!' she burst out.

Libby sat up, snatched the letter back and glared at Ellie. 'If you knew *anything* about graphology,' Libby began condescendingly, 'you'd know that this particular handwriting is the sign of a great romantic.'

'Oh, is that what you call it!' Ellie retorted, leaning back in the wicker chair, her hands behind her head.

'What do you mean?' said Libby knowing full well just what Ellie meant.

'Oh come off it, Libs,' Ellie argued, wide eyed. She stared at Libby. 'Don't tell me you've forgotten already . . .'

Libby tossed her blonde curls and turned her head away from Ellie. She wasn't going to let her spoil her moment of romantic glory. She was still glowing from the warmth of Lars's prose. 'Forgotten what?' she said, with a knowing grin on her face.

'Forgotten how, when we were in Sweden on the exchange trip, he tried to stick his tongue down your throat within five minutes of meeting you?'

'He was just swept away with the emotion of it all, that's all,' Libby replied, smiling to herself.

'Libby!' Ellie exclaimed. 'I just don't believe you sometimes! Anyone would think it was me talking, not innocent little you!'

'Well he's a boy, Ellie, after all, isn't he?' Libby said defensively.

'Not *all* blokes are like that, Libs.'

'Oh yes they are,' Libby argued.

Ellie shook her head. 'What about Alistair?'

'Oh, for God's sake, El! Ali doesn't count!'

'He *is* a bloke though,' said Ellie.

'Only just,' Libby joked.

'Yeah, well, whatever . . . Ali certainly wouldn't try to get you in a love lock before even saying hello first!'

'Well that's OK then,' said Libby. 'Because I wouldn't want him to!'

'Honestly, Libs, anyone would think you didn't like Ali the way you go on about him. He's supposed to be your friend.'

'He *is* my friend. I just don't want to think about him snogging me, that's all.'

'But you think Lars snogging you is OK, do you?'

'Of course. I fancy Lars and, much as I love Ali, I definitely *don't* fancy him. And anyway, Lars is better looking than Ali,' she added rather lamely. 'Anyway, nothing happened: I fought him off.'

'Well done you! said Ellie sarcastically.

'Just because *you* fancied him,' said Libby accusingly. 'Just because *you* fancied him and *I* got him.'

Ellie felt a strange prickling at the back of her neck, the way she always did when Libby had sussed her. But let's face it, it was hardly her fault if Lars happened to be an out and out love-god and it happened to be in her nature to flirt with anything that moved. But, sussed or not, she wasn't going to rise to the bait. 'I'm just trying to prove a point,' she said emphatically.

Libby looked sideways at Ellie. First she narrowed her eyes, then she smiled. 'Point taken,' she said. 'Now do you want me to read out this letter or not?'

Ellie nodded, eyes sparkling. She smiled. 'Yeah, go on. If the first sentence is this passionate, I can't wait for the rest. It's so hot, you should be wearing oven gloves!'

Libby laughed. She picked up the letter and lay back on her bed, holding it at arm's length, allowing the early summer sunshine to stream through the window and the paper, causing the words on both sides to merge, back to front and the right way round. A wistful, almost glazed look, came into her eyes as she began to read . . .

I can't begin to tell you how much I've missed you, Libby. You are in my thoughts as I go to sleep, I dream about you every night, I wake up thinking about you. I'm counting the days until I see your pretty face, hear your musical voice and breathe in your gorgeous aroma . . .

'Your gorgeous aroma?!' Ellie guffawed. 'What's he like? Doesn't he recognise Mum deodorant when he smells it?'

'Oh, very funny!' Libby retorted. 'Just because nobody's ever commented on *your* gorgeous aroma!'

'He obviously hasn't caught a whiff of you in the changing rooms after a heavy game of doubles,' Ellie laughed.

Libby stuck her tongue out at her friend, folded

the letter in half and stuffed it back into the envelope.

'Oh come on, Libs . . .' Ellie leant forward and tugged at the toe of one of Libby's woolly socks. 'I'm only messing around. Read me more of the letter.'

'Only if you promise to stop taking the piss,' bargained Libby.

'I promise,' said Ellie, po-faced.

I've been crossing off the days on my calendar (Libby read) *and can hardly believe that in just over a week's time, we'll be together again. And this time I'll never let you go.*

'Oo-er,' Ellie intercepted.

Libby glared.

'Sorry,' said Ellie quickly, then pressed a finger to her lips.

Libby continued to read.

I miss you desperately and, even though we've had a few snatched phone conversations, simply talking to you isn't enough. I need to see you; to be with you; to hold your hand; to kiss you. Every song I hear on the radio reminds me of you. Even the dreadful poetry we're forced to read at school makes me think of you. In fact, you make me want to write poetry! And love songs! And romantic epic blockbuster screenplays! I've never felt this way about a girl before. Libby, it must be love. Libby, I know it's love.

I love you. I hope you can find it in your heart to love me too. See you very soon. All my love, Lars. XXXXXXXXXXXXXXXX

'How many kisses?' Ellie asked, as she stroked Libby's best 'Plum' nail polish onto her nails.

'Sixteen,' Libby replied.

'One for each year of your life,' Ellie observed idly, without looking up.

But Libby wasn't listening; she was savouring every word of Lars's wonderful letter. He was so gentle and sweet – just the kind of boy she loved. Not like man-eater Ellie: she was always much more up for fun, a definite love 'em and leave 'em sort of girl. But, somehow, even though they were like chalk and cheese, they had always got on. Libby sighed wistfully.

'God,' said Ellie, 'you've got it bad, girl.' And somewhere inside her head she heard an alarm bell ring . . .

The Meaning Of Cool

Alistair pulled a crumpled denim shirt from his chest of drawers. Most of the buttons were still done up, so he pulled it on over his head and walked over to the wardrobe mirror. Looking at his reflection, he cursed the trendy hairdresser who'd given him his latest cut. He ran his fingers through the spiky bit on top, but it still looked crap. He smoothed it back from his face, but the only way it was going to lie flat, he decided, was if he rubbed half a pound of lard on it. Actually, he thought, stepping closer to the mirror, it looked pretty lardy already. He yanked off his shirt, threw it on the bed and headed for the bathroom. He'd only washed his hair yesterday, but it looked like he was going to have to wash it again. He couldn't go to the 'Welcome To The Swedes' party with a lardy head, could he?

Through the rattle of the shower, Alistair could hear the phone ringing. 'Mum!' he yelled. 'The phone's ringing!' Then he remembered that his mum was at work. It was hard to work out what day it was these days, Ali reckoned as he turned off the shower and grabbed a towel. GCSEs finished, there was now a weird gap of a couple of weeks with nothing to do except practise his tennis. Not that that was a bad thing – Alistair loved tennis . . .

He got to the phone about five seconds after it had stopped ringing. He picked up the receiver and tapped out the numbers 1–4–7–1 to find out who'd been calling. He hoped it had been Libby, so was kind of disappointed when the nice lady from British Telecom recited Nathan's number. He rang him back immediately.

'Nathan?'

'Yeah, Al, man – how's it going?'

'I was in the shower.'

'Getting spruced up for all those lovely, leggy Swedish birds, are you?'

'Yeah, something like that.' A second's silence. 'What did you want, anyway?'

'Nothing really, I just wanted to know what time you're heading down to the school – y'know for the *rave*.' He said the word 'rave' in a way that suggested that the welcome party in the school hall was going to be nothing like one.

'At about seven, I suppose,' Alistair replied, not sounding overly keen.

'Want me to pick you up on the Vespa?' Nathan always managed to get his precious scooter into the conversation somehow.

'Nah, it's all right – I'm going with the girls.'

'Libs and Ellie?' Nathan asked.

'Yeah.'

326

'Bad move, man,' he said. Then he sucked in some air – the sort of noise someone might make if they'd picked up something too hot. 'You're hardly going to impress the lovely Kristina if you turn up with two other birds in tow, are you?'

Alistair edged sideways so he could see his reflection in the hall mirror. A tuft of hair was sticking out horizontally. He tried to smooth it down but it wouldn't go. 'To be honest, Nathe, I'm not that bothered about Kristina,' he sighed despondently (although the despondency was more due to the state of his hair than the state of his love-life).

Nathan snorted. 'Don't tell me you're still trying to get off with Libby?!'

Alistair said nothing. There was no point. He could always tell when Nathan was about to launch into one of his rants.

'You're mad, man!' he said. 'You must know by now that she's not interested. You're her mate and her doubles partner but that's it. You've asked her out twice and she's said "no". I think she's made it pretty clear how she feels. How many times do I have to tell you? Don't push it, Al. You'll end up losing her friendship – not to mention your self-respect. Girls don't like guys who hang round them like bad smells. They like guys who are laid back, a bit mysterious, guys who are – '

'– Like you?' Alistair interrupted.

'I'm not saying that,' Nathan said. 'But, I suppose

327

. . . yeah . . . well . . . now you come to mention it, most chicks are more likely to go for someone like me than someone like you. You need to be calm, cool, in control . . .'

Alistair pressed the sticky-out bit of hair hard against the side of his head.

'I mean, let's face it,' Nathan continued, 'you can't even control your hair, let alone your mind.'

Alistair took the receiver away from his ear and peered into the mouthpiece. What was it with Nathan? Could he see down the phone? Or was he just plain psychic? Whatever, he was a pain in the arse.

'My hair looks great as it happens,' Alistair mumbled. 'I had it cut.'

'Good. Well, that's a start. Now, phone Libby, tell her you're coming with me tonight and we'll make a bit of an entrance, OK? We'll show those Swedes what cool really means.'

'I don't know if Libby – '

'Al – come on. She'll understand.'

Al agreed. Nathan was right. Libby *would* understand. After all, she was his best friend.

Girls Can Be So Cruel

The welcome bash wasn't quite as Ellie and Libby had expected.

'Hardly a rave, is it?' Ellie muttered, her eyes scanning the school hall.

'More like a wake,' Libby whispered back. She stared in disbelief at the long table and the row of blond heads along one side of it.

'A wake? They all look half asleep to me!' Ellie let out a small guffaw and with this caused seven of the eight blond heads to turn in Ellie and Libby's direction.

'Ah! The first of our lot!' Steve Elliott, the team's tennis coach stood up at the head of the table and stepped forward. 'Ellie . . . and Libby . . . you remember everyone, don't you? After all, you've only been apart for a few weeks . . .'

He ushered them further into the room, smiling. But neither Ellie nor Libby were paying much attention to what Steve was saying. Ellie was watching Libby. And Libby's gaze was fixed firmly on the one blond head that hadn't bothered looking up. It was Lars. He seemed to be cleaning his fingernails or something.

Her heart was in her mouth as she willed him to look at her. But her powers of telepathy had never really been that good.

She walked over to where he was sitting. 'Lars,' she said, abandoning the psychic approach.

He turned slowly in his seat and looked up sideways, smiling, at her.

'Libby,' he said. Then he stood up slowly and threw his arms around her. 'It's great to see you.'

Libby grinned into the warmth of his sweet-smelling jumper. 'And you.'

He pulled away, and with his hands on her shoulders stared deep into her eyes. A warm shiver tickled her spine. Libby could have stayed like that forever.

'Come and sit down,' he said. 'Move up, Nina.'

Libby recognised the round-faced, pretty girl. 'Hi, Nina,' she said, easing herself into the chair that Lars had pulled up for her.

'Hello, Libby. How are you? Good?'

'I'm fine,' smiled Libby, glancing from Nina to Lars. 'Just fine.'

The sound of a revving engine caused everyone to look towards the door. Suddenly, a helmeted Nathan burst in, almost knocking Ellie and Steve off their feet. 'Guys!' Nathan shouted, arms outstretched in his leather jacket, thumbs pointing skywards. Behind him, trying to undo the strap of a far less cool-looking 'lid' was Ali. Nathan frowned. 'Hey! Where's the party?'

Steve stepped forward. 'I'm just going to do a bit of an introductory talk – get the boring stuff out of the way – and then we'll party,' he explained.

'Cool!' announced Nathan, unfastening and removing his helmet in one deft move and heading for the table. He peered at the spread of food. 'Oooh, a *smorgasbord*!' he laughed. 'As if you guys don't get enough of that at home!' He gave Nina's shoulders a squeeze. 'Here, Nina, give us a smorg!' he muttered in her ear.

Nina shrugged him off, her cheeks reddening.

'Ooh, don't tell me you've gone off me.' Nathan feigned a sad expression which made him look a bit like the circus clown who'd just been hit with the plank.

Nina, now bright red, sighed. 'You know I've got a boyfriend at home, Nathan.'

'Yeah, but you're not at home now, are you?' he grinned, leaning down towards her and nudging her.

Nina rolled her eyes.

'When you two have quite finished . . .' Steve's voice boomed from the head of the table. 'And, Alistair, I'd like to get started so get that helmet off will you? Ellie, give him a hand with it.'

Ellie undid the strap, while a mortified Ali stood there, arms dangling, like a helpless child. He caught sight of the gorgeous Kristina trying to stifle a giggle and he knew there and then, if there had been any chance at all of him copping off with her, that he'd now completely and utterly blown it. Big time. Not

331

that he fancied her anyway, he told himself by way of consolation. Well, not much anyway.

Ellie handed him the helmet and led him towards the table. Unfortunately, the only spare seats were next to the cooing lovebirds, Lars and Libby, and although Alistair tried to manoeuvre Ellie into the seat *right* next to them, something went wrong and *he* ended up there instead. Not that it mattered. The Pope could have sat next to her and Libby wouldn't have noticed – she was that wrapped up in the lecherous Lars. Alistair shot him his most evil glare. It obviously wasn't evil enough because Lars seemed to interpret it as a friendly greeting and smiled.

'Hi . . . er . . .' Lars said in a voice that seemed far too deep for a guy of his age.

'Ali,' said Ali. No one ever remembered his name and he made a point of never wondering why. To be honest, he didn't want to know.

'That's it . . . Ali,' Lars laughed. 'How are you doing? Looking good. Nice shirt.'

Ali fingered the collar of his denim shirt. It was the only bit showing from under the leather jacket Nathan had lent him. How could Lars have liked it? All he could see was a curly collar, for God's sake! Ali took a deep breath. He was getting hysterical. *Chill out, Al man*, he told himself silently. *Just chill out.*

'By the way,' Lars added in a theatrical, behind-the-hand whisper, 'Kristina's here.'

Ali didn't look up. He'd already seen Kristina: he didn't need an ape like Lars to point her out and embarrass them both. He cursed his red cheeks and fiddled furiously with the clip on his crash helmet.

He was going to have to master undoing it himself, and fast. How did he always manage to make such a complete prat of himself.

Lars nudged him heftily in the ribs. 'I said Kristina's here,' he repeated.

'Yeah, I know. I saw her,' Ali mumbled.

Lars turned back to Libby, who hadn't stopped staring at him adoringly for a second. Ali felt sick. When he did look up at Kristina, she was looking back at him . . . Well, not so much *at* him, but slightly up and to the right of his face. Ali self-consciously raised his hand to his head. Oh God, that's all he needed. That strong-hold gel of his mum's hadn't done the trick at all . . . That bloody annoying bit of hair was still sticking out! He swore he was going to get his head shaved. *Yeah, that's it*, he reckoned. *Next time I go to the barber's, I'm going to ask for a number one.*

'Hi, Ali,' Kristina smiled. 'I like your new haircut. It's very nice.'

Ali glowered: girls could be so cruel sometimes.

God, I'm Fickle!

Steve's talk went on a bit, and by the end of it there were plenty of bored expressions and curly edges to the paper tablecloth. By the time the food had been demolished, it was getting dark outside. And once the table had been pushed aside and Steve had dimmed the lights and put some music on, the school hall could have almost passed for a night-club. Luckily, Nathan's dad – who ran a lighting company – had provided some really cool oil lamps, which turned the plain white walls into psychedelic backdrops. From 7.30, other fifth- and sixth-formers started to filter in, so by 9.00 the hall was pretty packed out.

Ellie was leaning against a multi-coloured wall, chewing absentmindedly on the rim of her plastic cup. If she had another Coke she'd be sick – she was sure of it. Across the room, through the crowds, she could see Lars and Libby, dancing slowly, which was pretty stupid really, considering the track they were smooching to was hardly what you'd call a sloppy number. Close by was an agitated-looking Ali, hovering around Kristina (who seemed too engrossed with her mates to even be aware of Ali's presence), still fiddling with that stupid horn of hair. Ellie reckoned he should've kept that crash helmet on. *Done us all a favour*, she muttered. It wasn't that she didn't like Ali – no, he was really sweet and a brilliant tennis player – but he was such a wimp when it came to girls. He wasn't bad-looking (if you like that sort of thing), but he really needed to get his act together in the pulling department. Honestly, talk about puppy-dog eyes! What girl in her right mind would go for that?

But it wasn't really Ali she was looking at; nor was it Lars and Libby. She wasn't even watching Nina and Nathan, who seemed to have engaged in some kind of private dirty dancing competition. It was the team coach Steve who, standing behind a trestle table and a couple of record decks, was the most gorgeous makeshift DJ she'd ever seen. He was great, Ellie smiled to herself. They were lucky to have him, he'd come back from travelling the world and was taking a break earning money for college by coaching them in tennis. And he was damn good at it too. Ever since they'd got back from Malmo, Ellie had had the hots for him. The trip to Sweden had been stressful and she needed something to take her mind off things. At the time, Steve seemed ideal. Not that he'd shown the slightest bit of interest in her. Why would he? OK, so she was pretty, but she was also a bit young for him – or so he seemed to think; she was fit (she'd been told that often enough), but not in the way she wanted to be; nowhere near as cool and sophisticated as the dark-haired, almond-eyed girl she'd seen him hanging round town with.

Ellie had tried flirting with him – she found it hard not to flirt with most guys, let alone one she really fancied – but he was having none of it. It made her really mad. He was only about four years her senior, but he treated her more like a kid sister than a potential paramour. What could she do?

Libby, the only person she'd confided in, was hardly helpful. She said that the only reason Ellie found him so attractive was because he was so completely unavailable. 'And anyway,' Libby had said last time they'd discussed Steve, 'you know he's just a passing phase. All your crushes have never lasted more than a week.' But this one had. This one had lasted three weeks – at the very least.

'It'll end in tears,' Libby had warned in that annoying mumsy voice she used whenever she tried to unravel Ellie's tangled love-life. 'You know what you're like, El. You'll be on to the next one before you know it.'

Maybe Libby was right. Maybe this one *wasn't* going anywhere. And maybe it *was* time to kill the dream and move on.

She glanced at Steve again, but in a more objective way this time. Maybe he wasn't so good-looking after all. *God, I'm fickle*, Ellie smiled to herself.

'Hi, Ellic.' It was Lars. Or so Ellie thought. But when she looked closer, she realised it wasn't Lars at all. He looked like Lars, but his hair wasn't as blond, his eyes were bigger and his nose was a different shape – less aquiline and more ski-slopey. And anyway, it couldn't have been Lars, because Lars was still dancing with Libby.

'Hi, Patrik.' Ellie tried to smile, but she wasn't really in the mood. 'I see your twin brother's not wasting any time.'

Patrik turned to look at Lars, whose hands were slithering snakily up and down Libby's back. Patrik shrugged. 'You know Lars – that's what he's like.'

Ellie nodded. She knew what Lars was like all right. He was good-looking, muscley, an ace tennis player. And although she hated to admit it, the fact that Libby was getting on so well with him was really starting to bug her.

She watched as Lars whispered into Libby's ear and felt her heart rise up into her throat as he kissed and caressed her neck. She was surprised to feel a surge of jealousy flooding through her. *It could have been me*, she thought suddenly. *It should've been me*. And it was true: because it wasn't just Libby Lars had got off with back in Malmo . . .

Patrik took a sip of his drink and continued to watch them. 'I don't know why Libby likes him,' he continued, without taking his eyes off them. His English really was very good, but he seemed to be struggling to find the right words. 'I mean, she seems

337

like a nice – a *really* nice – girl. And Lars . . . well, he's OK, but . . . I don't know . . . I'm just not sure whether Libby can handle him. He's – how do you say it? – kind of, you know, too much. Dangerous. She could get hurt.'

Ellie nodded. It was true. Lars *was* dangerous and, although Ellie had considered warning Libby off him, she decided that doing so would have been rather hypocritical; that if she encouraged Libby to dump him then ended up going out with him herself, it wouldn't exactly look very good. And no matter how much she fancied her best friend's boyfriend, she wouldn't stoop to such devious and underhand behaviour. First and foremost, Libby was her best mate and she was determined not to let anyone come between them. Really she was . . .

'He's more *your* type really.' Patrik turned to face Ellie.

Ellie blushed. Had Patrik been reading her mind? 'What do you mean by that?'

Patrik rubbed his chin. It was rather a small chin – well, it was when you compared it to his brother's model-like square jawline. 'I mean *you* could handle him. *You* know where a guy like Lars is coming from . . .'

'Yeah, I suppose so.' Ellie was not sure whether to feel flattered or offended. What was Patrik getting at exactly? How much did he know about her night with Lars in Malmo? She wondered whether to ask, but decided to play it cool instead. 'But maybe that's not what Lars wants,' she said.

'I know for *certain* that that's not what Lars wants,' grinned Patrik.

Ellie's heart sank.

'He wants a girl who'll fall for him without asking any questions, without challenging him. He likes a girl he can take for a ride. How do you say it in English – something like a pusharound?'

'A pushover,' Ellie mumbled.

'Yes, that's it – Lars likes girls who are real pushovers.'

Ellie suddenly felt very angry. She wasn't sure whether it was because he was insulting her best mate, or because he was trying to make it clear that Lars would never be interested in a girl like Ellie.

'So is that all you reckon Libby is?' she spat. 'A pushover?'

Patrik raised a hand in his defence. 'No, not me,' he said, shaking his head. 'Lars – that's what Lars reckons. Me, I like Libby – I think she's great.' He let his gaze wander in Libby's direction for a second, then back to Ellie. His eyes were the palest blue – gentle and kind, nothing like Lars's. His were diamond bright, searching, intense. 'To me, Libby is perfect,' he said, his English faltering suddenly. 'But I feel she is wasted on my brother. He doesn't appreciate her. He's just messing around, playing games. He loves to be loved. And he knows that a girl like Libby is the sort of girl who falls in love easily.'

She's not the only one, Patrik, Ellie thought ruefully, her own eyes fixed on Lars, Steve becoming more of a memory by the minute. *She's not the only one.*

Altered Egos

Nathan's head hurt. It was pitch black. Where was he? There was a terrible buzzing noise. What the hell was it? The alarm on his clock radio stopped and Nathan emerged from his duvet like a tortoise from its shell. He peered through bleary eyes, first at the black walls (he'd painted them that menacing shade during his metal phase), then at the clock . . . Eight-thirty. He was going to be late for school! Why hadn't his mum woken him up? He sat bolt upright, and was just about to get out of bed when it dawned on him that it was the summer holidays. He didn't have to go to school. He slumped back down on the pillows. Ouch! His head really *did* hurt. But that's what you got for playing the hard man, he supposed. That's what you got for trying to impress a girl by drinking your dad's whisky and trying to cop off with her, even though you know she has a boyfriend at home. And that's what you got for staying up till four in the morning playing 'Crash Bandicoot' with your Swedish mate Patrik, who may not be as cool as you in a number of ways but who can thrash you any time on a computer console. He snuggled back down under the duvet. He was going to go back to sleep and dream about Nina.

'Nathan! Time to get up!' His mum's voice rang shrilly – worse than any alarm – up the stairs.

Nathan ignored her. She called again. Nathan tried to summon up an image of Nina in some sexy underwear.

'Nathan!'

His bedroom door opened and a dust-filled burst of sunshine filled the room. Silhouetted in the doorway was his mum.

'It's only half-eight,' Nathan mumbled.

'But you told me to wake you at half-eight,' his mum said, bustling into the room and pulling back the heavy black curtains. Puffs of dust came off the curtains with every tug. 'Honestly, Nathan,' his mum sighed. 'This room's like a tomb. Why don't you let me give it a little spring clean for you?'

'Because it's summer,' Nathan mumbled through the duvet.

'A *late* spring clean then,' said his mum patiently. She ran her fingers along the window-sill. 'Look at this dust!'

'I like it dusty,' muttered Nathan.

His mum rolled her eyes, walked over to the bed and yanked his duvet off.

'Get off!' Nathan snapped.

She tickled the soles of his bare feet.

'Stop it!' he yelped. 'You're mad!'

'And *you'll* be pretty mad when you miss the first tennis match of the tournament.' She glanced at the clock radio. 'You've got approximately 15 minutes to get down to the school.'

'What?!' Nathan shrieked. He leapt off the bed and stood by the open doors of his wardrobe, staring into the crumpled mass of clothes. 'Where's my tennis stuff?'

Nathan's mum closed the wardrobe doors and folded her arms.

'Don't panic,' she said calmly. 'As per usual, everything's organised. It's all ready for you downstairs in the kitchen.'

Nathan let out a long sigh. 'Thanks, Mum,' he said and gave her a big (and rather uncool, he thought) kiss on the cheek.

It wasn't until he was downstairs that he wondered where Patrik had gone.

'He left ages ago,' said Alex, Nathan's kid brother. 'When I was watching "Rugrats".'

'"*Rugrats*"? What are you on about?' Nathan leant across the kitchen table and made a grab for Alex's cereal.

'Oi, get off! They're *my* cornflakes!' wailed Alex.

'I just want a couple of mouthfuls,' Nathan said, shoving a heaped spoonful into his mouth.

'For goodness sake, Nathan,' sighed his mum. 'Can't you get your own bowl?'

'Sorry, Mum, I'm in a hurry.' He wiped his mouth

on the sleeve of his leather jacket. 'You haven't seen my scooter keys anywhere, have you?'

Nathan's mum dangled them in front of his eyes.

'Oh, right . . . thanks. Look, I'll see you two later, OK?' As he passed Alex, he playfully flicked his ear.

'Ow!' Alex squealed.

'Baby,' teased Nathan. 'Anyone would think you were seven months old, not seven *years* old.'

'You're horrible!' Alex yelled, rubbing his throbbing ear.

'Yeah, and I love you too!' called back Nathan from the hallway before the front door slammed shut.

Halfway to the school, Nathan saw Ellie, jogging along the road, an Adidas holdall slung over one shoulder, her tennis racquet under her arm, fully kitted out in her short white skirt and Fred Perry. He pulled up next to her and revved his engine in what he thought was a suggestive fashion.

The buttons on her Fred Perry were open and Nathan noticed tiny little beads of sweat, like miniature pearls, glinting on her chest. He shifted on his saddle.

'On your own?' he asked.

Ellie nodded, panting slightly. 'Yes – Nina's not feeling too good. Said she had a headache or something . . .'

'Really?' said Nathan, trying his hardest to look surprised. 'A headache? I wonder why.'

Ellie frowned. 'I think you've got a pretty good idea why, Nathan. After all, wasn't it you who kept her up all night? God knows what time it was when she got a taxi back to mine! I had to do a bit of fast talking to Mum this morning as well!'

'She wouldn't go home!' Nathan lied.

'Oh sure,' Ellie said sarcastically. 'I mean, how could a girl possibly go home when you're there impressing her with your wit and wisdom and immense knowledge of scooters? I bet the reason she stayed so long was because she couldn't move – your pathetic attempts at trying to pull her probably paralysed her with boredom.'

'Now, now,' smiled Nathan, wagging a gloved finger at her. 'Just because you're jealous.'

Ellie yawned a big, fake yawn. 'Been there, done that.' She took her hand away from her mouth and gave Nathan a short, sharp, fake smile.

Nathan winced. It wasn't that he wanted to go out with Ellie again – no, he'd really moved on since they were an item – but he hated it when she was off with him. He decided to change the subject. 'Well, I'm glad I'm not the only one who's late for the first match,' he grinned. 'Come on. Hop on the back.'

'You haven't got a spare helmet,' Ellie pointed out.

'That never used to bother you,' said Nathan. 'Don't you remember the time when we – '

'Look, there's no time for all that now,' interrupted Ellie.

Nathan mentally kicked himself. Why did he have to bring it up again? It was ridiculous – whenever he made up his mind not to mention something, he couldn't *stop* mentioning it.

'We can take a stroll down memory lane another day, OK Nathe?' said Ellie, flinging one long, tanned leg over the back seat of the scooter. 'For now, let's just get to the school and get this tournament started, shall we?'

Nathan revved up his Vespa. The engine felt pretty healthy. Which was more than he could say about his ego at that particular moment . . .

Mad About The Boy

It was only nine-thirty, but Kristina could already feel the heat from the tarmac burning through the soles of her trainers. She'd slept well at Libby's house – despite the rather confusing dreams about Ali – so couldn't work out why she was so tired.

She looked across the tennis court to see Ali drinking something out of a can. It was easy to watch him: he was always so busy scrutinising Libby and Lars, there was no fear of him glancing up and catching your eye.

He's a funny guy, Kristina mused. He was such a brilliant tennis player, yet he was so modest. The previous night, for instance, at the welcome party, when she'd said she liked his hair, he blushed to the roots of it, and started jabbering on about some trendy but useless hairdresser Nathan had recommended. He ran his fingers through it so often, his hands were shiny with gel by the end of the evening!

She'd touched him a couple of times at the party – once to point out his shiny hands and later to smooth down a cute little spike of hair that was sticking out from his head at right angles. It was a shame he didn't seem to realise how she felt about him – she made it obvious enough – but he was just too besotted with Libby. Libby was beautiful though – there was no denying that – with her red curls and cute smattering of freckles (just on the bridge of her nose and nowhere else). She had a lovely figure too – slim but curvy. She wasn't very tall – five foot two or three perhaps, but that just made her all the more cute and cuddly. The best thing about Libby though was the fact that she didn't seem to realise just how stunning she was. She never actually put herself down, but she wasn't boastful or conceited either. Even Kristina, as a girl, could understand why guys fell for her, Ali in particular, who'd known her since she was five and who had watched her grow up. They were really close, the best of friends and that, Libby had told Kristina, was why she could never see Ali in any other way. Ali, on the other hand, hadn't actually said anything to Kristina about Libby, but he didn't have to: it was clear that Libby was everything to him. And because of that, there was no way he'd be interested in another girl. Not now. Maybe never.

Sadly, it was the story of Kristina's life: she always seemed to fancy boys who were mad about other girls. She hoped that one day she'd find a guy who was mad about her, but she was 16 now and had never even been kissed properly (Postman's Knock and Spin The Bottle, two games that Libby had shown them, where Kristina got a kiss from Nathan didn't count). She sighed. No, that didn't *really* count. Nathan may be cool, but he wasn't much of a snog. When he'd kissed her, it was as if he was doing it for an audience, like he was acting in a film. He'd kissed her, all smoochy and passionate, but she didn't kiss him back. He'd said afterwards, 'Thanks for the game of tonsil tennis', but Kristina didn't really know what he was talking about. Sometimes, English guys didn't seem to speak English. Anyway, that wasn't what she wanted at all. What she really wanted was a proper kiss, a kiss with feeling, a kiss with someone she really cared about, someone who really cared about her too. She'd often wondered what it'd be like to kiss Ali. She bent down to unzip her racquet from its case, but didn't take her eyes off Ali for a second. He had a really sweet little face – not typically good-looking perhaps, but gentle and kind and sort of sad. Like a lost puppy. A tufty-haired lost puppy. How could any girl resist him, Kristina, wondered idly to herself.

Steve Elliott's loudhailer-enhanced voice broke Kristina's reverie. 'OK, everyone – time for the first match!' He held a sheet of paper in front of him. The bright morning sunshine beat down on it, making him squint. 'Right,' he announced, 'the first match is Nathan and Claire, versus Lars and Lena.'

Kristina moved sideways to allow her friend Lena to pass. Lena looked nervous. '*Lycka till, Lena,*' Kristina smiled, wishing her friend luck. She wondered who Claire was: she didn't remember her from Malmo. A tall, dark-haired girl with stick-thin legs walked towards Steve . . . Oh yes . . . Claire. Wasn't she the one who Lars . . . ? No, that was just a rumour. It couldn't have been true . . .

Steve was shouting through the loudhailer. 'Has anyone seen Nathan?'

Everyone shook their heads. Then Ali pointed. 'Here he comes!' he said.

Through the criss-cross fencing, they could see a Vespa. It was chugging along at a maximum of 20 miles per hour. Minutes later, a grinning Nathan and a rather embarrassed-looking Ellie arrived on court.

'Thank-you for fitting us into your hectic schedule, you two,' said Steve sarcastically, and Kristina could see Ellie wincing.

'I'm sorry,' said Ellie to Steve, 'but we would have got here quicker if it wasn't for that stupid scooter.'

Nathan frowned.

'My *hairdryer* is more powerful that that thing,' she complained. She tossed back her silky dark hair and flashed her best sultry look at Steve. As usual he didn't notice. She knew she wasn't supposed to fancy him any more, but he didn't make it very easy for her – he always looked so fit!

'So where's Nina?' he asked.

'Ill,' replied Nathan – a bit guiltily, Kristina thought.

Ali walked over. 'What did you do to her, Nathe?' he asked.

Nathan put his hands up defensively. 'Nothing to do with me, man,' he said, shaking his head. 'You know what these chicks are like . . . Can't take the pace.' He sighed melodramatically. 'So, Steve,' he said, 'who's playing the first match?'

'You are,' replied Steve. 'But you won't be unless you get a move on. You and Claire will be playing Lars and Lena.'

'Not Love-all Lars?!' Nathan laughed; the Swedish lad's voracious appetite for girls was common knowledge.

Lars, on hearing his name mentioned, stopped nuzzling Libby's neck and glared at Nathan. 'What was that?' he asked through slightly gritted teeth.

'Love-all Lars! The tennis super-stud!' Nathan smirked. God, Lars was so up himself.

Lars disentangled himself from Libby and stood up. 'You're in big trouble now, Brit-boy,' he declared.

'Oooh, I'm *sooo* scared,' said Nathan in a high-pitched voice. 'Please don't hurt me Lars.' He let out a burst of laughter.

But Lars wasn't laughing. Lars wasn't laughing at all . . .

Game On

As Lars waited for his opponent's first serve, he vowed to make this a winning match. He smiled to himself as he thought how good it would feel to give that idiot, Nathan, the thrashing he deserved. He'd think twice before trying to make a prat of Lars again.

Nathan served. The ball hit the net. Nathan swore at the sun, which was shining right in his eyes.

Lars crouched low, moving slowly from one foot to the other. From this angle, he could almost see up Lena's skirt. If he crouched a bit lower, down to net level, he could probably see up Claire's too. He'd always fancied Claire, but she was already spoken for. Not that that would stop most girls. It hadn't stopped Ellie back in Malmo when she was supposed to be going out with Nathan, had it? He could feel a smirk spreading across his face: he hoped Nathan could read his mind. If anything would put him off his stroke, that would.

Smash! It seemed to work. Nathan hit the net again.

'Love-fifteen,' announced the umpire, a geeky guy

from the English school. Lars gave him a cursory glance. God, he was ugly! *If I had a face like that, I'd never go out*, Lars decided. And look at his clothes! He knew these British guys were into – what was it they called it? – nerd chic, but a beige polo-neck sweater and mustard corduroy trousers were going a bit too far. Especially in this heat – he must stink! And the shoes?! Well, only someone English would wear shoes like that ... He didn't know much about the geek – just that he loved tennis and had some heart condition which stopped him playing. What a life!

'Bastard!' Nathan hissed under his breath, looking at the ball, but Lars knew it wasn't the ball he was talking to.

Claire turned around and glared at him. 'Language, Nathan,' she chided.

'I wasn't talking to you,' Nathan explained.

'I should hope not,' said Claire, elevating her nostrils in a way that only Claire could.

Nathan looked really fed up. 'Swearing's good for you actually,' he said. 'It releases tension.'

Claire, who had stepped towards the net and got herself in position for the next serve, looked back at him over her shoulder. 'I don't know about that, Nathan,' she replied condescendingly. 'I mean, *I* don't swear, do I?'

'No – and that'd probably explain why you're so uptight,' he hissed.

Lars burst out laughing. He felt calm and confident:

if the Brits were battling against each other, there was no *way* they were going to win.

Claire's cheeks went pink. She looked angry . . . and kind of sexy, Lars reckoned. She tossed back her dark curls and turned back to face Lars. Her chest seemed to have grown since she was in Malmo, Lars reckoned, his pulse speeding up. That, or she'd invested in a new sports bra. And let's face it, he'd encountered a few of those in his time. God, what he wouldn't give to get his hands on Claire's sports bra . . .

'Suddenly, he thought of Libby – sweet little Libby, who was so completely stuck on him. He looked over to where she was sitting, her eyes all sparkling, her gaze fixed firmly on him. He noticed how Ali was now sitting next to her – quiet and pensive, pretending to do something with the strings on his racquet. Every so often, Ali would take a deep breath. Most people would see it as a sigh, but Lars knew that he was breathing in Libby's sweet smell. He would have felt jealous if Ali hadn't been such a loser.

'Can we get on with the game please?' called Lena.

'Yeah, what are we waiting for?' asked Lars.

Fifteen minutes later and Lars was feeling pretty pleased with himself. Lena wasn't playing too well, but he was more than making up for it.

'Forty-love,' announced the geek.

Nathan threw his racquet on the ground. 'Oh, come off it, Col!' he shouted at the umpire. 'That wasn't out!'

Colin the umpire nodded complacently. ''Fraid it was, Nathan,' he replied.

Nathan bent down and picked up his racquet. 'Who's bloody side are you on anyway?' Nathan muttered, checking the racquet for damage. 'Bloody Swedophile.'

'Another word and you'll be disqualified,' announced Colin, looking more than pleased with himself. 'Now can we get on with the game, please?'

In just under half an hour it was all over: the first match of the tournament was over. The Swedes were triumphant. Game, set and match to Malmo.

Lars winked at Libby and she gave him a tiny, secret flutter of a wave back. Ali was still sitting next to her. Next to Ali sat Kristina, looking depressed.

Lars walked over to Libby and ruffled her red hair. But his eyes were on Claire, who'd run joyfully (well as joyfully as a snooty tennis team captain could run) into the arms of her cherubic-looking boyfriend – *Jamie, the Brit team's answer to me*, Lars deduced. He watched as Jamie pulled her into his lap and stroked her head in consolation. Her dark curls glinted blue in the early afternoon sunshine and her long legs appeared even longer as she draped them over Jamie's. But all the while he was observing Claire, he was aware of someone else's gaze drilling a hole in the back of his head. He thought at first he'd been caught out by Libby. But when he turned around, it wasn't Libby who was looking at him at all. No,

355

Libby was deep in conversation about tennis racquet strings with Ali and Kristina. Then he thought that perhaps it was Patrik, his jealous twin. But Patrik was nowhere to be seen. As he scanned the assembled company, he realised that the girl who was gazing at him so determinedly and so blatantly was none other than the girl he'd spent a secret evening with back in Malmo; the girl who he thought only had eyes for another guy; the girl who once gone out with his arch-rival Nathan . . . Ellie.

Nothing's Going On

When Nina had answered the door, she didn't look too good but, Patrik decided, she was looking a lot better now.

'Thanks for coming over,' she said in their native Swedish, as they sat in Ellie's kitchen.

'I was concerned about you,' said Patrik. 'When I heard Ellie say you weren't well, I came round right away. I didn't like to think of you all alone here.'

'It's not been too lonely,' she smiled. 'Ellie's mum was here for most of the morning. She was really nice – gave me some Paracetamol and chicken soup.'

'Mmm, nice combination,' Patrik laughed.

Nina smiled again.

'So where is she now?' he asked.

'Oh, she's gone to the hospital.'

'Hospital? Is she OK?'

'Yes, yes, she's fine,' said Nina. 'She works there.'

'Oh, I see . . .' He paused. 'What about Ellie's dad? Is he still – '

'No,' said Nina, shaking her head. 'He's gone now.'

Patrik nodded. 'About time.'

They were quiet for a moment, both thinking about all the stuff Ellie had told them back in Malmo about her dad.

'So what about the tournament?' Nina asked, changing the subject. 'Aren't we supposed to be –'

Patrik patted her pale hand. 'Don't worry about a thing,' he said. 'I got down to the school really early this morning and checked with Steve. We're not playing till tomorrow.'

'That's a relief,' sighed Nina. 'I don't think I could face it today – not with this headache.'

'So what did you and Nathan get up to last night? It must have been a late one – I mean, I didn't go to bed until two.'

'Nothing really.' She got up from her chair. 'Fancy a coffee?'

'Er . . . yes . . . OK.' Patrik was watching Nina closely. She was being cagey. Just what was going on? 'You and Nathan, did you –?' he said to Nina's back as she plugged in the kettle.

'Honestly, Patrik!' she said without turning round, trying her hardest to sound offended. 'I said nothing, and I meant nothing!' But she didn't sound very convincing.

'You can tell me,' Patrik said. 'I'm your friend.'

'Yeah, but Peter's your friend too,' said Nina, referring to her boyfriend back home.

'Well, I'm hardly going to rush back and tell tales to Peter, am I?' said Patrik. *He* was sounding offended now.

Nina shrugged and stared out the kitchen window. She still didn't turn around: Patrik guessed she was blushing. 'I don't know,' she replied.

'So, tell me,' he urged. 'What *is* it with you and Nathan?'

Nina suddenly spun round. 'Nothing!' she almost shouted. 'There's nothing going on with me and Nathan, OK?'

'All right, all right,' Patrik said, leaning back in his chair. 'Calm down. I was only asking.'

'Yes, well don't,' snapped Nina. She stirred the milk into the coffee. It was the loudest cup of coffee Patrik had ever heard. She slammed two cups down on to the table. Coffee sloshed over the edges. She went to the sink and brought back a cloth. As she mopped up the mess, Patrik noticed that there were two circles of red on her white cheeks.

When she'd finished wiping, she threw the cloth back into the sink, wiped her hands on her jeans and stared at him, her eyes glittering blue and diamond bright. Then she sighed and sat down. 'I know you mean well, Patrik,' she said, 'but there are some things I just don't like talking about.'

'Some *people*, you mean,' corrected Patrik. He took a slurp of coffee.

Nina nodded. 'OK,' she began, 'let me tell you something. Me and Peter aren't really getting on that well at the moment.'

Patrik nearly choked on his coffee. 'What do you mean?' he spluttered. 'You and Peter are the perfect couple – love's young dream! You'll be together for ever.'

'Yeah, so everyone keeps telling me,' Nina grimaced into her cup. 'If you want to know the truth, I'm kind of bored of it.'

Patrik's eyebrows almost touched his hairline. 'What about Peter – is he bored too?'

Nina shrugged again. 'I really don't know. I mean, Peter doesn't really think about those sorts of things, does he? He just kind of plods on. He likes things on an even keel. And I thought I did, but now, since I met Nathan in Malmo . . .'

'So you *do* fancy Nathan then?' Patrik said, almost accusingly.

Nina shook her head and stared into the depths of her coffee cup.

'Oh, I don't know,' she sighed. 'It's just that Nathan's so different from Peter.'

'You can say that again,' mumbled Patrik.

'He's so much fun . . . a really good laugh,' Nina continued. 'Peter wouldn't recognise a joke if it hit him in the face.'

'I suppose he *is* a bit lacking in the sense of humour department,' admitted Patrik. 'But, Nina, he's a nice guy. Nathan . . . well, Nathan's a joker. He doesn't take anything or anyone seriously. Especially not girls.'

'I think that's where you're wrong,' said Nina, looking straight into Patrik's eyes. 'I think, underneath that big jokey exterior lies a really nice, caring bloke.'

'You do?' asked Patrik, genuinely surprised.

'Yes, I do,' said Nina. She was deadly serious.

'Oh,' said Patrik. He didn't know what else to say. If he was a girl, he'd never fall for someone like Nathan. He liked genuine people – people who were kind and interesting and beautiful through and through, from the outside right through to their very soul.

'What's up?' asked Nina. 'You've gone all soppy-looking.'

'I was thinking,' Patrik said quietly.

'About who?'

'No one,' he replied.

But Nina knew as well as he did that he was lying. Because he was thinking about someone – someone special and interesting and beautiful through and through. Someone not very far away . . .

Girl Talk

After Patrik had gone, Nina began to wonder – not about Nathan (she'd spent all day thinking about him), but about that faraway look in Patrik's eyes. Who was it he fancied? She thought about the four British girls: there was Libby, pretty and romantic; Ellie, sexy, beautiful and cool; Claire, the team captain, tall and haughty, all legs and nostrils; and Emma pale and quiet, with a high forehead and low self-esteem – not, it seemed, interested in boys at all.

The trouble with Patrik, Nina decided, was that he wasn't really like all the other boys. Whereas most guys would go for someone obvious – like Ellie perhaps – Patrik was just as likely to go for a real individual, a girl who presented more of a challenge – someone like Emma maybe.

Then, of course, it may not be one of the Brits he was after at all. Maybe it was one of the Swedish girls. She immediately discounted herself (for no real reason other than they'd known each other since they were kids). Kristina? No, she knew them both well enough to know that there was nothing going on there. Lena had been with her boyfriend (and tennis team captain)

Anders for years and because Anders was built like Arnie Schwarzenegger, no boy would be crazy enough to make a play for her. That only left man-eater Orsa, who would gobble up Patrik for breakfast if he ever got within a ten-metre radius of her!

Nina's musings were disturbed by Ellie's return.

'Feeling any better?' asked Ellie, letting her holdall fall to the kitchen floor and yanking off her towelling headband.

Nina smiled. 'Much better thanks. Patrik's been here most of the afternoon.'

'Oh really?' said Ellie, looking suddenly interested.

Nina shook her head. 'It's nothing like that,' she said. 'Me and Patrik are just good friends – we go back years.' She pushed back a strand of flaxen hair from her face. 'So how did it go?' she asked, deliberately changing the subject.

'Well, it seems we're pretty evenly matched so far,' replied Ellie. 'Lars and Lena thrashed the living daylights out of Nathan and Claire, but me and Daniel slaughtered Kristina and Jonas.'

'Daniel? The guy with the ginger hair?' Nina frowned.

'Yeah, that's him. Fancies himself as a young Boris Becker,' Ellie laughed.

'He's a pretty good player though, isn't he?' said Nina in his defence.

'Yeah, well I have to admit, he *did* play well this afternoon,' smiled Ellie. She paused. 'Nathan was awful though! I don't know what was wrong with him. I think he's got a real problem with Lars, to be honest.'

'Most guys have,' said Nina. 'I know Peter doesn't like him much.'

'How *is* Peter?' asked Ellie, flopping into a chair. 'I didn't get to chat to you much last night.'

'Oh, he's fine. Same as ever,' said Nina dismissively. Silence for a few seconds. 'Fancy a coffee? I was just about to make myself one.'

'That'd be great. Thanks, Nina.' Then Ellie jumped up. 'Actually, let me do it: I *am* supposed to be the hostess after all.'

'OK.' Nina handed her the kettle. They were quiet as Ellie filled it with water.

Then Ellie said: 'Lars was brilliant today.'

'He's always pretty good,' commented Nina.

'Mmm . . .' Ellie stared dreamily out of the window.

Nina frowned. Surely Ellie didn't have a thing about Lars. Nina really respected Ellie: she'd certainly go down in her estimation if it turned out she was just like all the other girls – that she fancied Lars too.

'I'd never noticed how good-looking he was before,' Ellie said, more to herself than to Nina. 'He really *is* something special.'

So she *did* fancy him! Nina couldn't believe it. 'Him and Libby are well suited then, aren't they?' she said, rather pointedly.

Ellie turned around to face Nina. 'Well, that's just

it,' she said slowly. 'I don't think they are ... I mean, Libby's my best mate, she's fantastic, but ... I don't know ... there's just something not quite right about her being with Lars. He's not her type. He's more ...'

'*Your* type maybe?' Nina said, eyebrows raised.

Ellie placed her hand on her chest. '*My* type?' she laughed (rather falsely, Nina thought). Then she paused and crooked a finger against her chin. 'Well actually, now you come to mention it ...'

Suddenly Nina burst out laughing. 'God, Ellie, you're so transparent! It's really obvious you fancy him.'

'Oh, so what if I do?' said Ellie resignedly. 'What's wrong with that?'

Nina sighed. She was disappointed, but she couldn't hold it against Ellie. After all, every girl had a crush on Lars at some point. Now it just happened to be Ellie's turn. 'Nothing, I suppose,' she replied. 'Apart from the fact that he's going out with your best friend.'

'Oh, I know and I wouldn't do anything to break them up,' said Ellie.

'Really?' said Nina.

'Really,' said Ellie.

Nina looked over at Ellie. There was something about the glint in her eyes that made Nina think that maybe, just maybe, she wasn't *quite* telling the truth ...

The Green-Eyed Monster

Ali had persuaded Libby to stay behind for some practice. The lunky Lars had gone without too much fuss, so Ali finally had Libby all to himself.

For half an hour they volleyed, but having Libby all to himself again, Ali couldn't really keep his mind on the tennis. He didn't want to stop playing though, because that might have meant Libby would go straight home. He needed to keep her for a bit longer. He studied her every move and every minute fell in love with her a little bit more. She really was the loveliest person he'd ever known. He loved her so much, he could even forgive her for going out with Lars.

As the sun went down and the sky turned from pink to purple, Libby suggested calling it a day.

'Shall we go for a coffee in town?' Ali suggested. He didn't want to let her go.

'I'd love to, Al,' Libby replied, looking beneath her towelling wristband at her watch, 'but I need to get home and get showered and changed. I promised Lars I'd meet him round at Ellie's tonight . . . you can come if you like.'

'No, it's OK,' Ali said, sounding more abrupt than he'd meant to. He knew Libby meant well, but the last thing he wanted to do was watch her and Lars slobbering over each other all evening. 'I've got a lot on tonight,' he lied. 'I'll walk you home if you like though.'

Libby nodded and smiled. 'OK, that'd be nice.'

There was a definite nip in the air as they walked down the main road outside the school, so Ali draped his sweatshirt around Libby's shoulders. It was a good 20 minutes back to Libby's house but that wasn't long enough as far as Ali was concerned.

'So where are you lot off to this evening?' he asked, not really wanting to know.

'Not sure,' Libby replied, swinging her racquet as she walked. 'We might just stay in . . . you know, watch a few videos. Nina's going out with Nathan, but Kristina's coming over. It's going to be a bit of a girls' night in.'

'A girls' plus Lars night in, you mean,' corrected Ali.

'That's true . . .' Libby frowned. 'It *is* going to be a bit unbalanced, isn't it? Oh, come on Ali, why don't you come too? It'll be fun.'

'No,' he sighed. 'I told you – I'm busy.'

'I think Kristina might like to see you,' Libby said in a teasing tone.

'Really?' said Ali flatly.

Suddenly, Libby stopped walking and stood facing

him, her tennis racquet over her shoulder, one hand on one hip. 'Honestly, Ali, I don't know what's the matter with you. Kristina's really nice. It's obvious she fancies you: why don't you do something about it?'

'Don't want to,' he replied sulkily.

Libby rolled her eyes and started walking again. They were quiet for a while, then Libby said: 'Lars is bringing a video of him playing a gig with his band in Malmo.'

'Oh, he's a pop star as well as a tennis champ, is he?' said Ali.

Libby seemed oblivious to Ali's sarcasm. 'Seems so,' she said. 'He's the singer I think.'

'How nice.' He paused. 'It's funny,' he said, straining to get a little laugh out (just to prove how funny it was exactly),' but I've hardly seen Lars since he's arrived. He's supposed to be staying at my place, but his bed hasn't actually been slept in yet.' He bit his lip, not wanting to hear what Libby was going to say next.

'No, he's been staying at mine,' she answered gaily, confirming Ali's worst fears. 'On the sofa-bed, downstairs.'

Ali silently cursed Libby's liberal parents. They let her do whatever she liked, including having Swedish Love-gods who were obviously using her to stay. They must be mad to even let him in the house.

Ali felt that his nose was being seriously (and metaphorically) pushed out of joint. Libby's place was more his territory than Lars's: it was part of his childhood. He loved hanging out there in that big, messy house, with all Libby's brothers and sisters. Since they'd started secondary school, they'd all meet up in Libby's attic room on Sunday afternoons. They'd sit around on beanbags, listening to music and chilling out. Sometimes, Nathan would bring his guitar and they'd listen to him strumming. In the summer, with the windows open and the birds singing outside, it was really mellow. Ali had the feeling that this summer – the next couple of weeks in particular – weren't going to be that much fun though. They stopped outside Libby's house.

'Come in while I get ready, if you like,' she offered. 'Then you can walk me over to Ellie's.'

For a moment, Ali felt he was being used, but one look at Libby's sweet, innocent expression confirmed that Libby wouldn't do a thing like that. Not deliberately anyway.

They entered the house through the side door. Libby's mum was sitting with her feet on the table, watching a portable TV. Her long flame-coloured hair was tied back with a paisley-patterned scarf and her jeans were spattered with paint.

'Hi, guys,' she smiled, a rather badly rolled cigarette waving between her lips as she spoke.

'Hello, Mrs Lawrence,' said Ali politely.

Libby's mum took the cigarette out of her mouth and, taking her feet off the table and leaning forward on her elbows, tapped it into an ashtray on the large pine table. 'How many time do I have to tell you, Ali?' she grinned. 'Call me Angie.'

Ali blushed apologetically. 'Sorry . . . yes . . . Angie,' he mumbled.

Libby laid her tennis racquet on the table. 'I'm off for a shower. Mum, you don't mind entertaining Ali for a bit, do you? I won't be long.'

Angie waved a hand dismissively. 'You take your time, darling. Ali will be just fine here with me . . .' She smiled at Ali, 'especially if he gets the kettle on and makes me one of his wonderful cups of tea.'

Ali jumped to attention. 'Oh yes. OK,' he said, grabbing the old-fashioned kettle from the stove and heading for the sink.

'See you in a minute, Al,' smiled Libby, as she skipped out of the kitchen.

By the time Libby came back down, Ali had been treated to a private viewing of her mum's paintings. They were pretty good, Ali reckoned, even if he couldn't tell what half of them were supposed to be. As they'd strolled around the conservatory (which Angie had converted into a studio), he'd heard all about Angie's inspirations – from the brightness of the summer sun to the darkness of her regular bouts of depression, much of which she blamed on the departure of Libby's father, Alan, ten years ago. Painting, she'd explained, was a way of exorcising Alan's ghost. Very therapeutic, she said. She told him that things were much better these days though, especially since she'd met Charles, Libby's stepdad.

Ali felt uncomfortable: he wasn't sure whether he wanted or needed to know all this. But he just smiled and nodded in what he hoped were the right places and willed Libby to hurry up. It wasn't that he didn't like Angie, and it wasn't that he didn't know her; it was just that he couldn't get used to her. She was so unlike a mum – unlike *his* mum anyway, with her sculpted perm, Marks & Spencer dresses and old-fashioned values.

'Ready!' Libby chirruped from the kitchen.

Ali followed Angie from the conservatory. 'Your mum was just showing me her pictures. They're very . . .' he paused, not knowing quite how to describe her work, '. . . arty,' he said finally.

Angie smiled, sat down at the table and started rolling another cigarette.

Libby shook her head. 'Come on, Al,' she grinned. 'Let's get going.' She took him by the hand, sending shivers of excitement up through his arm and down his spine. As they left the house, she said: 'Lars will be really annoyed if I'm late.'

Ali snatched his hand away.

'What's up, Ali?' she asked, as innocent as ever.

'Nothing,' replied Ali grumpily. 'Nothing at all.'

But he knew that even Libby, in all her innocence, knew that that wasn't the case at all.

All's Fair...

Ellie waved goodbye to Nina and watched her walk down the wallflower-edged path. *She's almost skipping*, Ellie smiled. *She's obviously looking forward to seeing Nathan.*

She shut the door and sauntered back down the hallway. Before entering the living-room, she paused to examine her reflection in the hall mirror. Smoothing back her thick dark hair, she studied her face. On the shelf by the mirror was a tiny pot of kiwi-flavoured lip gloss. She opened the lid and smeared some across her slightly chapped lips. *Best to stay kissing sweet at all times*, she smiled to herself. You never know . . . As she put the lid back on the pot, she leaned closer to the mirror. She looked different, she decided – her skin was positively glowing and her eyes were sparkling like pieces of jet. There was no denying she was looking good. And she knew why too . . .

Back in the living-room, Lars was stretched out on the sofa. 'Hi, there,' he purred. He patted the cushions next to him. 'Come and sit with me.'

Ellie looked at the space next to him: there wasn't much room, but that didn't really matter – she was slim. What *did* matter though, she decided, as she tried to get comfortable, was the fact that she was getting rather cosy with her best friend's boyfriend. She remembered an old saying that her mum often used – 'all's fair in love and war' – and then tried not to think about Libby too much.

With her head resting on Lars's broad shoulder, she brushed her fingers across his chest, tracing the outlines of his muscles with her fingertips. She knew it was wrong but she couldn't help herself, she was being drawn towards him by same strange irresistible force. She snuggled into his armpit. He smelt musky and warm . . . A shudder of excitement ran through her body. God, he was sexy! God, what was she doing!

'Cold?' asked Lars, pulling her closer.

'No,' Ellie whispered. Then she smiled what she liked to think was her most alluring smile. 'I'm feeling pretty hot actually.' On cue, Lars turned and leant his head towards her. She looked up towards him and he planted a kiss, as light as a butterfly, on her tanned cheek.

When she made no effort to resist he wasted no time in taking hold of her chin and tilting her face up towards his. Then he clamped his mouth, warm and wet, on hers. As they kissed, he manoeuvred her until she was trapped securely in the corner of the couch. His kiss was firm and professional and Ellie melted into it, trying to ignore the pictures of Libby that kept flashing through her mind.

Lars's weight pressed down on her and his legs

pushed more closely against hers. There was part of Ellie – the best friend, loyal and sensible part – that wanted him to stop. But other parts of her that desperately wanted him to go on . . . and on . . .

'Ellie,' he murmured, pulling his lips away from hers. He looked down at her, his eyes glinting with desire. 'You're so beautiful.' Ellie smiled. She didn't like to admit it, but she was a sucker for compliments. Especially from a guy as gorgeous as Lars.

'You're different from the other girls,' he continued and although Ellie wondered what he meant, she didn't ask; she didn't want to interrupt him. 'More mature,' he went on. 'Like you know what you want.'

Ellie narrowed her eyes. God, he was a smooth-talker.

'*Do* you know what you want, Ellie?' he asked.

At that moment, the doorbell rang, making them both jump. *Saved by the bell*, Ellie thought, as she wriggled out from beside Lars and straightened her skirt and T-shirt. Her face felt hot and her knees felt decidedly weak – this was getting dangerous.

'Who the hell's that?' Lars said, moving into an upright position and pulling a face that made him *almost* unattractive.

'Libby, most probably,' Ellie replied as lightly as she could, making her way to the hall and trying to sound as cool as possible.

As she passed the mirror, she noticed her cheeks were slightly flushed. Too late to do anything about that though.

She opened the front door. 'Hi, Libs,' she smiled, a rush of guilt consuming her. She felt a complete fake. 'Hi, Ali,' she added. 'Come in.'

They followed her inside.

'Lars is already here,' she said, trying to control the wobble that was threatening to rise in her voice, as they entered the living-room.

Libby rushed towards him and kissed him on the mouth. Ellie's heart flipped in her chest as she wondered whether Libby could taste the kiwi-flavoured lip gloss. This was awful; she was such an awful person. The trouble was, she just couldn't seem to stop herself.

Ali stood at the door. He was looking kind of pale. 'You OK, Al?' Ellie asked. 'You don't look very well.'

Ali nodded. 'I'm all right,' he replied.

'You can leave your tennis stuff in the hall if you like,' she offered, taking his bag and racquet from him. She realised she was acting jumpy and talking far too quickly, but Ali didn't seem to notice. He smiled at Ellie, but his smile was as false as hers had been moments earlier.

'So what can I get everyone to drink?' Ellie called from the hallway.

But only Ali answered. Lars and Libby were too busy . . .

In the kitchen, Ellie poured Ali a large Coke. He hadn't looked at her once since he'd arrived. If he had, he might have noticed that she was feeling pretty much the same as him. Sick.

'How was practice?' she asked, trying to help them both take their minds off what was going on in the next room.

'OK,' mumbled Ali. Suddenly, he stood up. He hadn't touched his drink. 'Actually, Ellie, I think I'd better go home. You were right – I'm not feeling too good.'

The doorbell rang.

'That'll be Kristina,' Ellie said. 'Sit down, Ali. Stay a bit longer. And drink that Coke: it might make you feel a bit better.'

She went to answer the door. She could hear soft murmurs coming from the direction of the sofa. She suddenly felt as sick as Ali looked. As quietly as possible, she clicked the living-room door shut.

It wasn't Kristina at the door at all. It was a vaguely familiar-looking girl – sort of Oriental, with long, straight, black hair, an olive complexion and almond-shaped eyes.

'Are you Ellie?' the girl asked.

Ellie nodded in reply.

The girl reached into her bag and pulled out a sheet of paper. 'I want to have a word with you,' she said firmly. 'About this.' She waved the paper in front of Ellie's face.

'What is it?' Ellie asked, genuinely puzzled.

'Don't come the innocent with me,' hissed the

girl accusingly. 'Steve's told me all about you. But this . . .' She waved the paper again. 'This is going too far,' she said.

'I think you'd better come in,' said Ellie nervously.

But the girl – or Steve Elliott's girlfriend, as Ellie had finally recognised her to be – was already inside.

First Date Nerves

Nathan was peering out of his bedroom window. He was sure he'd just spotted Steve Elliott's girlfriend – the sexy, Japanese-looking one – walk down his street. He'd only ever seen her in the town centre before, and wondered what she was doing over this way.

It was almost eight o'clock, yet it was still swelteringly hot. As hot as it had been on the tennis court this morning. Nathan wiped his brow with the back of his hand: it made him come out in a sweat just thinking about how badly he'd played earlier. The humiliation of losing to Love-all Lars – it was more than a guy could stand! He was pleased Nina hadn't been there to witness his downfall.

After the game, he'd hung around to see Ellie and Daniel play Kristina and Jonas: that had been a pretty tense match. Daniel was on top form, but Ellie was even better. She was a great tennis player. Come to think of it, she was great at everything. He often wished – as he was wishing now – that they'd never split up . . .

But they *had* split up and Nathan knew he had better come to terms with that. *Better to have loved and lost and all that*, he told himself. He yanked back the black curtains as far as they would go, sending clouds of dust in all directions, and pushed open the window. It seemed to be getting hotter by the minute. He stuck his head out of the window, but there was less fresh air outside than there was inside. At that moment, he saw Nina at the top end of his road, and all thoughts of Ellie were forgotten as he rushed downstairs.

'Whatya doing?' a small voice piped up behind Nathan, as he stood at the foot of the stairs, smoothing back his perfectly gelled hair.

'Get lost, face-ache!' Nathan snapped at his little brother.

'Got a girlfriend coming?' Alex asked, swinging on the banister. He looked disgusting, Nathan thought. He'd just had his tea and his face was all covered in orange cack.

'Well?' persisted Alex. 'Have you?

'Have I what?' Nathan wasn't really paying too much attention to Alex. He was too busy trying to fluff up the front of his hair into a presentable quiff.

'Have you got a girlfriend coming?' Alex said again, rolling his eyes.

Nathan tapped the side of his nose. 'Might have,' he said.

'What does she look like?' Alex asked.

'She's very pretty,' Nathan said.

'Like a princess?' asked Alex.

Nathan sighed: he didn't want to tell Alex, the baby, *anything*, but there was something about Nina – when he thought about her – that made him feel all kind of romantic and poetic. He couldn't resist describing her. 'Well . . .' he began, his eyes misting over. 'She's all blonde and pink and kind of sugary-looking. Like a marzipan pig.'

Alex frowned. 'I don't like marzipan,' he said sulkily.

There was a rap on the door. 'Is that her?' Alex asked.

'Yes,' said Nathan. 'Now clear off, will you?'

'No – I want to see your girlfriend,' Alex said.

'She's *not* my girlfriend,' Nathan sighed. 'And probably never will be with you hanging around,' he muttered. He opened the door and Nina stood there beaming. She looked really sweet. All blonde and pink and smiley. *Just* like a marzipan pig.

'Come in,' he said politely, feeling suddenly nervous. 'Don't mind him,' he added, nodding in Alex's direction. 'He came with the house. We're hoping to get rid of him soon.'

Alex scowled. 'He says you're not his girlfriend,' he sang, a sneaky smile spreading across his face.

Nina gave an embarrassed little laugh and her cheeks went even more pink. 'Oh,' she said.

'He says you never will be,' continued Alex.

Nina's expression changed. 'Oh,' she said again, glancing from Nathan to Alex.

'Just ignore him,' Nathan insisted, taking Nina by the arm and steering her upstairs.

'You can be *my* girlfriend if you like,' Alex offered.

'Thanks,' Nina replied. 'I'll think about it.'

Just as Nathan and Nina reached his bedroom door, Alex called: 'Nathan!'

'What now?' sighed Nathan, leaning over the banisters, feeling more than exasperated.

'*I* don't think she looks like a pig . . .' he smirked.

'Alex?' said Nathan, not daring to look back at Nina.

'Yes?'

'Just shut it, will you?'

'What's he saying about a pig?' asked Nina, as Nathan closed the bedroom door behind them.

'Oh, nothing. He's mad,' said Nathan.

Nathan rubbed his hands because he couldn't think of anything else to do with them. Nina looked around the room awkwardly, as if she couldn't decide whether – or where – to sit down.

Nathan pushed his computer magazines off the bed. Nina watched them slither on to the floor. She looked at the dusty, black duvet cover, but didn't sit down. 'So what are we going to do?' she asked – slightly nervously, Nathan thought.

'Do?' What on earth did she mean? What did she *want* to do? Did she want to start snogging straight away? Nathan knew Swedish girls had a reputation for being up for it, but this was ridiculous! He took a deep breath: he was having an anxiety attack – he was sure of it – but tried his hardest to appear cool.

'Yes . . . do,' she repeated. 'Tonight,' she added.

'Oh . . . well . . .' To be honest, Nathan hadn't really worked out much of a plan. 'I thought perhaps we could listen to a few CDs . . .'

'Mm-hm,' said Nina, still scanning the bedroom.

'Then . . . we could . . . erm . . .' Nathan was at a bit of a loss. 'Well . . . I dunno . . . what would *you* like to do?'

Nina shrugged. 'We could go out somewhere, I suppose,' she suggested.

Oh my God – she hates my room, Nathan panicked. *I knew I should have tidied up.* He spied a pair of grubby socks poking out from under the bed. He could have at least picked those up.

'How about a cheese pizza?' he asked. He cringed: he hadn't needed to say 'cheese'. It was just that he was still thinking about the socks.

Luckily, Nina didn't seem to make the connection. She nodded and smiled. 'OK,' she said.

'Right,' said Nathan, grabbing his leather jacket off the mounted goat's skull he always used as a coat-hook and kicking the cheesy socks under his bed at the same time. 'A pizza it is! Shall we go on the Vespa?' he asked.

Nina shook her head. 'No, let's walk,' she said, making Nathan wonder exactly what Ellie had told her about his precious scooter.

*

Nathan hadn't realised how crowded The Pizza Palace was going to be. And he hadn't really expected to see anyone there that he knew either. So he was surprised when Nina nudged him as they entered and said: 'Isn't that Claire over there?'

'Where?' Nathan asked. He peered around the restaurant.

'Over there.' Nina tried to point discreetly with her elbow. 'In that alcove.'

'Oh yeah,' said Nathan. 'But who's she with?'

Nina stood on tiptoe and squinted. 'I'm not sure, but he's got dark hair, so it's definitely not Jamie.'

Nathan tried to see who the bloke was, but he was half-hidden behind a big rubber plant. He could see Claire though and she looked really different – kind of twinkly and glamorous. He'd never seen her wear big earrings like that before. Or lipstick. She looked quite pretty. And her nostrils didn't look quite so obvious. He wondered if she'd spent the afternoon with a cosmetic surgeon. Maybe that was him now – the bloke in the alcove. Maybe they were discussing a leg-shortening operation for her . . .

The waitress came over and indicated for them to follow her. She sat them at the table in the alcove next to Claire. Now they couldn't see Claire and the mystery man at all. But Nathan could just about hear them.

'They're talking about tennis,' he said.

'That's all Claire ever talks about though, isn't it?' commented Nina.

Nathan nodded. 'Yeah, I suppose it is.' He paused and pressed his ear to the wooden panel behind him. 'Hold on a minute,' Nathan whispered. 'They've gone all quiet.'

Nina looked suddenly mischievous. Then she knocked her knife to the floor.

Nathan chuckled: he knew exactly what she was up to.

As Nina bent to retrieve the knife, she craned her neck to get a better look. She was back sitting up in a flash, her eyes wide and her mouth open in mock horror. 'They're kissing!' she breathed.

'Jamie will kill her!' Nathan breathed back. 'Mind you, I always thought that those two were never really suited.'

'Me too,' agreed Nina.

'Did you see the guy?' asked Nathan.

'Just the back of his head,' Nina replied.

'He won't have a head at all if Jamie catches them,' Nathan said, eyebrows raised, not envying the mystery bloke at all.

Nina giggled. Nathan smiled. He was feeling pretty relaxed, especially as he'd discovered that he and Nina had so much in common.

'I like a bit of a scandal, don't you?' Nina smiled over the top of her menu.

Nathan nodded slowly – he hadn't really considered it before. 'Yes, I suppose I do,' he said.

'We should go out more often,' she grinned.

Nathan grinned back. 'I think we might just do

that,' he said. And he was suddenly aware that it wasn't hunger that was making his stomach feel so funny. No, it was something much more than that . . .

What An Awful Night!

'What was all *that* about?' asked Libby. She and Lars hadn't emerged from the living-room, but when Libby had heard voices from the hallway and got up and opened the door slightly, she'd seen Steve Elliott's girlfriend standing on the doorstep. Minutes later, they'd heard raised voices in the kitchen.

'She accused me of writing a love letter to Steve,' Ellie said, shaking her head.

Libby gasped, so shocked that she momentarily removed her hand from Lars's knee. 'You didn't, did you, El?' she asked.

Ellie screwed up her face. 'What do you take me for, Libs?' she said. 'You *know* that's not my style.'

Libby raised her eyebrows in apology. 'S'pose not,' she said. 'Sorry.' But she wasn't sure she believed her. Ellie was her best friend but she was more famous for romantic adventures than her capacity for truth telling.

'So what did the letter say?' Kristina asked from her prone position on the rug, her pale eyes gleaming with curiosity. Ellie sat down in the armchair opposite the sofa. 'It was *well* passionate,' she revealed, exaggerating slightly.

Ali glanced up from where he was squatting on the floor behind the sofa. He was going through Ellie's CD collection – looking for something morose to put on no doubt, Ellie reckoned. Nevertheless, she was pleased that she'd managed to engage everyone's attention.

'Go on,' Libby urged.

Ellie leant forward and said in a low and suggestive whisper: 'It kind of implied that Steve and whoever had written the letter had . . . you know . . .'

'No!' shrieked Libby.

Lars sighed loudly and started picking at his finger-nails. 'I don't know what all the fuss is about,' he said flatly.

'You wouldn't – you're Swedish,' said Ali grumpily, studying the front of a CD.

Lars ignored him. Thanks to Nathan, he seemed to be getting used to these anti-Swede insults.

'Oh, come *on*,' said Libby. 'It's pretty scandalous. I mean, it's *got* to be someone we know . . .'

'Yeah, but who?' asked Ellie. 'Who could it be?' But, even as she spoke, she had a pretty good idea . . .

In the end, they decided that the writer of the letter could well be Emma.

'The quiet ones are often the worst,' said Libby in her mumsy voice.

Ellie nodded pensively. 'It's just hard to imagine her

387

coming up with all that stuff though, isn't it? Who'd have thought she had it in her? She must be the least experienced of the lot of us.'

'You don't have to be experienced to be able to write like that,' said Libby knowledgeably. 'Look at the Brontë sisters. Not one boyfriend between them and their novels were *really* passionate.'

'My favourite's *Wuthering Heights*,' said a voice from behind the sofa.

'Mine too,' sighed Libby wistfully.

'It's *so* sad,' said Kristina. 'Especially the bit where it's clear that Isabella really adores Heathcliff, but he's so in love with Kathy that he barely notices her. And poor Isabella – well, she just kind of wilts away . . .'

Ellie stared at Kristina. How could she come out with all that stuff? It was obvious she saw herself as a modern-day Isabella. She *was* Isabella. Libby was Kathy. And Ali was her very own real-life Heathcliff. Ali was probably cringing behind the sofa.

'I like the bit at the end best,' sighed Libby, 'when Kathy's on her death-bed and Heathcliff turns up and starts ranting on about how he's always loved her. Then he carries her to the window to look at the heather for one last time, and she dies in his arms.'

Oh my God, thought Ellie, *I think I'm going to be sick*!

She obviously wasn't the only one. A spluttering noise from behind the sofa caused them all to look round. Ali's red face popped up. He held up his glass of Coke. 'Sorry, guys,' he apologised. 'Coke went down the wrong hole.' And everyone laughed.

Soon, everyone had forgotten about Heathcliff and Kathy. Everyone apart from Ellie – who was watching Kristina and slowly realising why she always looked so sad.

'So what do you all reckon?' Libby was shouting above the sound of some very loud thrash metal – a CD that Ellie was convinced Ali must have brought with him. It was nothing she would admit to owning. 'Party at my place next Thursday night – the night before you Swedes all go home?'

'Don't you think you should ask your parents first?' Kristina asked.

'Oh, Angie and Charles won't mind,' laughed Libby. 'They love a good party.'

'You mean they'll be *there*?' asked Lars, unable to hide the horror on his face. The sort of party he had in mind, parents – even pretty cool ones like Libby's – would be the last thing he'd want around.

Libby nodded. 'Yeah,' she replied. She put her arm around Lars's broad shoulders reassuringly. 'Look, don't worry about it – they'll be fine.'

Lars nodded but didn't look too convinced.

'Sounds good to me,' Ellie said. She was always up for a party. 'Who shall we invite?' she asked, immediately assuming the role of co-hostess.

'Everyone,' said Libby grandly.

'Even Emma?' asked Ellie, wrinkling her nose.

'*Definitely* Emma,' said Libby. 'We'll be able to corner her and ask her all about this letter.'

'What about Steve?' asked Ellie tentatively. She was actually overdoing the tentative bit, because she wanted Libby to believe that she still had the hots for him and in some strange way it made her feel less guilty . . . like she could almost believe it herself if she tried hard enough. Unfortunately, Lars chose that moment to flash one of his drop-dead gorgeous smiles and all Ellie's rather weak resolutions once again melted into nothing.

'Don't push it, El,' smiled Libby interrupting her reverie. 'I don't think that'd be a good idea considering the current circumstances, do you?'

'S'pose not,' Ellie sighed theatrically.

'I suppose we should invite Colin,' Libby said – rather generously, Ellie thought.

'Colin?' barked Lars. 'That nerdy umpire guy. You *are* joking, aren't you?'

Libby took her arm away from Lars's shoulders and turned to face him. 'Colin's all right,' she said in his defence. 'OK, so he's not that good-looking and he can't play tennis, but . . .'

'The guy's a jerk,' Lars interrupted aggressively. 'If *I* had a face like that, I'd *never* go out,' he added, delighted to be able to voice the thoughts he'd had earlier that day. He burst out laughing. The laugh was harsh. No one else joined in. He looked surprised. Then he coughed. 'So who wants to see my video?' he said.

The CD had stopped playing and the room was quiet.

Lars jumped up and disappeared from the room.

Libby made an apologetic face.

Ali emerged from behind the sofa, leapt over the back and nabbed Lars's place on it.

Kristina smiled up at Ali.

Lars reappeared clutching a video cassette. 'Here it is!' he announced. 'Wait till you see this, guys! We really rock!'

'Don't be too modest, will you?' mumbled Ali into his glass.

Ellie could see Libby cringe. But Libby was a loyal person, so she made an effort to be interested. 'So what are your band called?' she asked.

'Lars,' said Lars in all seriousness, bending down to study the workings of the video recorder.

'Lars?' repeated Ellie incredulously.

'Yes,' he replied. 'It's named after me.'

'Yeah, I think we managed to work that much out,' muttered Ali.

Lars stood up. 'Do you want to see Lars in action or not?' he said huffily.

Kristina stifled a giggle. Ali rolled his eyes.

'Of *course* we do,' Libby insisted, smiling sweetly. 'Go on, Lars, put it on.'

'Give us all a laugh,' said Ali. But Lars didn't seem to hear him.

The video machine made a whirring sound and an image flashed onto the screen. But it wasn't a

391

band that came into view. It was an image of a half-dressed girl in a room that was quite obviously Lars's bedroom back in Malmo.

The girl on the video giggled and folded her arms across her bra. Lars's voice could be heard saying something in Swedish. In a state of panic, Lars attempted to cover the TV screen with one hand. With the other, he fumbled for the stop button.

Ellie looked around the room. Everyone – even Ali who'd been totally unimpressed with the proceedings so far – was open mouthed.

Kristina was the first to speak. 'Wasn't that Ulrika?' she asked.

Lars pulled the cassette out of the machine, but said nothing.

'Ulrika?!' said Libby quietly, her cheeks almost purple with anger. 'Who the *hell* is Ulrika?'

'Ulrika?' Kristina repeated. 'Ulrika? Oh, just a girl from school. No one special.'

Ellie wasn't surprised. It was exactly what you'd expect from a guy like Lars. After all, she knew he was a two-timer so a three-timer – or a four-timer even wouldn't be that much of a shock. But what an idiot getting caught out like that! Still, maybe it was for the best. At least Libby might now realise that he *really* wasn't her type.

Lars opened his mouth to speak, but it was obvious that he couldn't think of anything to say. It was obvious too that, although his expression was more than jaded, he couldn't quite bring himself to apologise.

Ellie could see that. And the tears welling up in Libby's eyes were proof that she could see it too.

Lars put his head in his hands. It seemed Mr Cool had for once suffered a serious loss of composure. Ellie was itching to tell him to pull himself together. Surely, as far as he was concerned, it wasn't that big a deal. Still, all things considered maybe now wasn't quite the right time.

Ali put his arm comfortingly around Libby. Kristina's naturally sad expression became even sadder.

What a night! thought Ellie. *What an awful night!* She'd have gone home if she wasn't already at home.

The ring of the doorbell disturbed the silence. Ellie rushed to answer it.

'You'll never guess what!' gushed Nathan, charging into the hall, Nina following close behind.

'You won't believe it!' breathed Nina.

I don't know if I can take any more, Ellie thought, shaking her head, feeling on the brink of hysteria. *I really don't know if I can take it . . .* Then she let out a giggle. What did one more scandal matter? 'Come on through,' she said, linking her arm through Nina's, 'and tell me all about it.'

And, bypassing the living-room, all three of them headed for the kitchen.

Keep Smiling Through

It was gone midnight when Libby and Kristina got back to Libby's house. They'd walked home in silence – Libby in a state of shock and Kristina feeling guilty, simply because she was the one who'd revealed the identity of the girl on Lars's home movie.

In Libby's room, the girls undressed and got into bed. Kristina didn't usually mind sharing a bed with Libby, but tonight it felt different: there was a kind of cold aura around Libby and Kristina felt totally shut out. Still, she supposed it was understandable, Libby had been pretty badly shaken by the evening's events.

'I'm sorry about what happened,' Kristina said. She was lying on her back staring up into the black space.

Libby had curled up, embryo-like, her back to her friend. 'It's OK,' she said in a muffled voice. 'It wasn't your fault.'

Kristina was silent for a moment. 'I don't know,' she said. 'I feel sort of responsible.'

'Don't be silly,' said Libby quietly into the duvet.

Silence again. Kristina didn't know what to do.

Should she have warned Libby about Lars? Maybe. Perhaps she shouldn't have said anything while they were watching the video. Perhaps she should have pretended that she didn't know who the girl was. God, she had a big mouth sometimes! 'Libby?' she whispered into the darkness.

But the only reply was the sound of Libby's steady, rhythmic breathing. Kristina sighed. It was obvious Libby didn't want to talk about it. The whole thing was so awful: she really did feel bad. But at least it had helped her take her mind off Ali for a while.

The tear that rolled down her face at that point took her quite by surprise. Before she knew it she was sobbing quietly. But she quickly realised that the tears weren't being shed for Libby alone. She was crying for herself too – for herself and Ali and the love that looked as if it would never be . . .

During the night, Kristina dreamt of a tennis match, between herself and Libby. Ali, in Colin-style polo-neck and cords, was the umpire. Lars was the ball-boy. Libby kept hitting the net and smashing the ball way out of the court, Lars would run and fetch and Ali would award her points. Kristina was constantly trying to get Ali's attention – shouting that Libby was losing not winning, that hitting the net didn't deserve points but that her own shots did – but Ali refused to look at her . . . Even if he had, he wouldn't have been able to hear her complaints over the roar of the crowd.

It was the sound of her heart, beating in frustration, that woke her. She looked at Libby, now facing her, in the blue moonlight. Her brow was smooth, white and unfurrowed; her curls spread out on the pillow like a red, rippled halo. Her nostrils flared slightly with every out-breath, and a small smile danced on her lips. Her sleep, unlike Kristina's, was clearly untroubled. Untroubled, because she had nothing to fear. Untroubled, because she knew she was going to win. Untroubled, because she knew, just as everyone else knew, that a girl like Libby just couldn't lose. And what was more, she was so lovely, no one even *wanted* her to lose. That was the problem.

Kristina sighed and pulled the duvet up around her ears, blocking out the sound of Libby's gentle purring. Then she closed her eyes tightly and drifted back to her dreams, hoping against hope that this time they'd be sweeter than last.

June sunshine and the sound of a spoon clanking in a cup woke Kristina. Standing next to the bed, fully dressed, her smile brighter than the sun itself, was a grinning Libby. She was holding a tray.

'What's this?' asked Kristina, her hand shielding her eyes.

'Thought I'd bring you breakfast,' announced Libby. 'I *am* your lovely hostess after all.' She proudly placed the tray on the bed beside Kristina. 'Did you sleep OK?' she asked politely, stirring the spoon around the cup again. Then, without waiting for an answer, she added: 'I thought I heard you crying in your sleep.'

Kristina pulled herself up to sitting position. 'Really?' she said. She reached over to the tray and pulled it up onto her lap. Cornflakes, coffee and half a grapefruit, complete with a glacé cherry in the middle . . . What a feast!

'What were you dreaming about?' Libby asked.

Kristina shrugged and sprinkled some sugar on her grapefruit.

'Can't remember,' she lied. A second of noticeable silence. 'Aren't you having breakfast?' she asked, changing the subject.

'Already had it,' said Libby. 'I've been up for ages.'

'Oh.' Kristina dug a spoon into the grapefruit. Libby was obviously determined to be steadfastly cheerful despite what had happened, so Kristina assumed she still didn't feel like discussing it. 'What time is it anyway?' she asked.

'Nine,' Libby said, still with a fixed smile on her face.

Nine on a Sunday morning. Kristina thought Libby was definitely behaving strangely – still she supposed it was only to be expected. As she slurped grapefruit juice from the spoon, she continued to think about the previous evening. She glanced up at Libby and wondered whether she was thinking about the same thing. It looked as if she might be, as her 'good morning' smile had crumpled into rather a sad and pensive expression. As Kristina watched and Libby realised Kristina was watching, the smile snapped back into place.

'So ...' said Libby perkily, 'what shall we do today?'

'How about some sightseeing?' Kristina suggested. 'I was reading about Hampton Court recently. I'd love to visit the tennis courts there – they sound fantastic.'

Libby nodded thoughtfully. 'Yeah – that's not a bad idea,' she said.

'Would it take us long to get there?' asked Kristina.

'I don't think it'd take too long,' Libby replied. 'Maybe I could persuade Charles to take us in the van.'

That wouldn't be a problem, Kristina reckoned: Charles was a total pushover when it came to doing favours for his step-daughter. 'So who shall we bring with us?' Kristina asked, shovelling cornflakes into her mouth and edging dangerously close to the subject of Lars.

'Well,' began Libby, 'Ellie and Nina might want to come.'

Kristina nodded and took a slurp of coffee. 'And Nathan and Patrik,' she suggested.

'And what about Ali?' said Libby. 'We mustn't forget dear old Ali ...'

Kristina looked up immediately. Did Libby suspect something, she wondered? Judging by the expression on her face, Libby didn't have a suspicious thought in her head.

'I'm sure he'd enjoy it,' Kristina said cautiously, not wanting to sound too desperate. But she couldn't help it – she *was* desperate – and that's what made her add: 'I'll phone him if you like.'

'OK,' Libby smiled, but Kristina was smiling more. Because, although she felt a bit pathetic even admitting it to herself, she was already missing him . . .

She sipped her coffee and wondered how Ali and Lars were getting on. It couldn't be easy, especially after last night. Then, before she had time to check herself, she said: 'What about Lars?'

The smile fell from Libby's lips. 'Lars can take a hike!' she snapped.

'Right,' said Kristina. 'Good for you!' and Libby smiled gratefully back at her friend. Kristina finished the last of the cornflakes in silence, then pushed the tray aside and jumped out of bed. 'Hampton Court, here we come!' she declared, trying to lighten the atmosphere.

'Yeah, right,' said Libby. But Kristina noticed that, all of a sudden, Libby didn't seem quite so keen.

Pride Comes Before A Fall

Lars hadn't heard the phone actually ringing, but as he poked his head out from beneath the sheets and blankets, he could now hear Ali chatting to someone.

'That'd be great,' Ali was saying. 'It'd make a change to do something a bit cultural . . . Yeah, OK . . . Do you want me to call Nathan and Patrik? Yeah, sure . . . I'll do that . . . OK, Kristina . . . I'll meet you round at Libby's at eleven . . . OK . . . See you then. Bye!'

Lars kicked back the covers and jumped out of bed. The first thing he did – as he did every morning, whether he was at home or away – was check out his physique in front of the mirror. He ran his hands through his hair and flexed his muscles. His arms were looking particularly good today – tanned and shapely. Just get a load of those biceps! His shoulders and chest were broad and his pectorals were so well-defined, they looked almost rectangular. He didn't know exactly what a washboard was but, according to the many English girls who'd seen him shirtless, apparently his stomach resembled one.

He thought it looked more like one of those slabs of toffee – brown and divided into neat squares. Mmm, delicious! He turned sideways slightly and edged his black Calvins down a fraction. There was a triangular-shaped tendon just to the front side of each hip that ran downwards towards the groin: that was his favourite muscle. Even though he said so himself, it was incredibly sexy. There was a movement just to the right of his shoulder and beyond his own reflection he could see Ali standing in the doorway of the bedroom. Ali wore an amused and bemused expression – one Lars couldn't quite fathom. Lars frowned, relaxed his pose and turned to face him.

Ali shook his head.

Lars wondered what his problem was. Did Ali expect him to be embarrassed or ashamed? *There's nothing wrong with admiring your own body*, he thought indignantly, *especially one as perfect as this*. 'Heard you talking to Kristina,' Lars said. 'Going out for the day?'

Ali entered the room and walked over to the sink and shelf unit in the corner. 'Yeah,' he said. 'Something like that.' He was being deliberately vague – Lars could tell.

Ali picked up a bottle of cologne. It was labelled 'Stallion' and he smirked.

'Hey, don't touch that,' Lars objected. 'It's expensive.'

'Stallion, eh?' said Ali teasingly.

Lars scowled. He felt he had to defend himself

somehow even though he didn't really know why. Ali was laughing at him and he had no right.

Ali suddenly looked directly at Lars, a rather strange glint in his eye. He gave him the once-over, up and down, from the tips of Lars's neatly trimmed toenails to the top of his coiffed yellow hair.

He wants a physique like mine, Lars reckoned smugly. *That way he could impress Libby too.*

Ali must have been reading his mind, because the next time he spoke he said: 'I don't think Libby was too impressed with you last night.'

Lars shrugged. 'That's her problem,' he said.

'I don't think it is,' said Ali, stepping closer.

Lars took a step backwards: it wasn't that he was afraid of Ali – it was just that Ali looked like the type of guy who might have bad breath. Lars sniggered to himself.

'You see,' Ali continued. 'Libby's a really nice girl and you've well and truly blown it. So really it's *your* problem, don't you think?'

'There are plenty more girls like her,' Lars said defensively.

'But that's where you're wrong, Lars,' he hissed. Ali was so close now that Lars could feel his breath on his face. It wasn't bad at all: in fact, it smelt kind of fresh, like fruit – peaches or something. Weird for a guy, Lars decided.

'Libby's special,' Ali continued. 'She doesn't deserve to be treated this way by a git like you.'

Lars shrugged again. Just what was Ali's problem?

He grabbed his white shirt from the back of a chair and, his eyes still on Ali – who knows what a guy in this kind of mood could do next; he might make a lunge for him . . . anything – he pulled it on.

'Girls are girls,' sighed Lars nonchalantly, fastening the buttons on the shirt with one hand. It felt tight, good, his body building was really paying off. 'There's plenty more where she came from.'

Ali's face was getting red: it was clear he was becoming angry. Lars really wasn't in the mood for a fight – not over a girl anyway – so he made an effort to change the subject. 'So where are we all off to today then?' he asked casually.

'Hampton Court Palace,' Ali replied.

'Great!' grinned Lars.

'Thing is,' said Ali, through clenched teeth (and looking – quite surprisingly, Lars thought – like Clint Eastwood in one of those old cowboy films), 'you're not invited.'

Lars felt all the muscles in his body deflate, but he did his best to pump himself up again. 'Fine,' he said. 'I've never been interested in your sad English history anyway.' For some reason – and even *he* didn't know what it was – Lars started tucking the white shirt into his boxer shorts.

Ali smirked lopsidedly and went to leave the room.

'So you're going without me, are you?' Lars asked the back of Ali's head, knowing he sounded a bit panicky.

'Looks like it,' replied Ali without looking back.

'Well give my love to Libby,' Lars said mockingly.

'To be honest, mate,' Ali said, turning towards Lars, 'I don't think she needs it.'

'Yeah, like I don't need a day out at Hampton Palace or whatever you call that crap pile of medieval bricks,' Lars blurted out. He took a deep breath – he'd nearly lost control for a moment there and that was something he didn't *ever* like to do. 'I've got a pretty busy day ahead of me anyway,' he said, as coolly as he could. He waited for Ali to enquire about his agenda, but Ali was silent. He just stood there with his arms folded across his sparrow-like chest, staring unswervingly with those big watery blue eyes. 'Yeah, I've got a *really* hectic schedule,' Lars continued. 'First, I'm going down to the courts to get some practice in for the semi-final of the tournament,' he said, picking up the tennis racquet he always kept beside his bed. He swiped it deftly from side to side. 'Not that I *need* to practise of course,' he boasted. 'I'm going to thrash the lot of you.'

Ali shook his head and went to leave the room again. He said nothing until he reached the door. Then he turned round. 'Oh and by the way, Lars,' he said calmly.

'Mm-hm?' said Lars, pretending to concentrate on his backhand technique.

'You're wearing my shirt . . .' And, with that, he left the room, leaving Lars wondering how a guy as uncool as Ali could make him – Lars, tennis ace, pop star, every girl's dream and all-round hero – feel such a jerk . . .

What's With Ellie?

Nina woke up feeling terribly guilty. At first she couldn't work out why, but then she remembered Peter back home in Malmo and realised ... She thought of his cute, smiling face and that little bit of blond chin-fluff that he liked to call a beard. She remembered the last day at the airport, when Peter had kissed her goodbye and had told her to be good. Back then – a whole three days ago – Nina had no intention of being anything else. Back then, the only thing on her mind was the tennis tournament. Back then, Nathan wasn't on her mind at all. It was only when she set eyes on him again that she forgot about Peter, forgot about being good, forgot about tennis – well, almost. Her heart missed a beat at the mere thought of Nathan, with his dark, tousled hair and tanned skin. It made her smile just to think of him. And when she thought of some of the stupid things he got up to she nearly laughed out loud. They'd had a fantastic night at the Pizza Palace the previous night. Even seeing Claire with that mystery man, and Ellie's scandalous story of Lars and the scantily clad Swedish girl couldn't overshadow the fun she'd had with Nathan.

She glanced across to the other side of the room, where Ellie was still sleeping. She was frowning in her sleep and Nina wondered what – or who – she might be dreaming about. Downstairs, the phone rang and Nina could hear Ellie's mum answering it. Minutes later, there was a light rap on the bedroom door.

'Ellie . . . Nina . . .'

Nina climbed out of bed and went to the door. 'Good morning, Mrs Lester,' Nina smiled.

'Hello, Nina,' Ellie's mum smiled back. 'Your friend Kristina just called. Could you call her back?'

'Sure,' replied Nina. She grabbed her navy silk dressing-gown from the back of the door, slipped it on and made her way downstairs.

Within minutes, she was back upstairs, trying to wake Ellie. 'Ellie . . . Ellie, get up,' she urged, sitting on the bed and gently shaking her friend's shoulder. 'We're going to Hampton Court Palace.'

Ellie opened one eye. '*Where?*' she croaked.

'Hampton Court,' Nina repeated enthusiastically.

'Great,' said Ellie, shutting her eye again.

Nina sighed. 'Oh, come on, Ellie, it'll be a laugh.'

Ellie opened both eyes this time. 'I suppose so,' she agreed.

'Well get up then,' Nina insisted.

'I can't,' replied Ellie.

Nina frowned. 'Why not?' she asked.

'Because you're sitting on my hand,' she smiled.

Downstairs, the phone was ringing again. 'Ellie, it's for you!' Mrs Lester called up the stairs. 'And can you hurry up please – I'm not your secretary, you know!'

Ellie sighed, heaved herself out of bed and plodded down the stairs.

Nina wondered what to wear. Peter always liked her to look really pretty, in flowery dresses and the like. But Peter wasn't around. She delved into her suitcase, pulled out Peter's favourite dress and flung it to one side. She got the feeling that Nathan wasn't that bothered about clothes – he seemed to like her whatever she was wearing. Ellie had told her in the past though that he was keen on the biker-chick look – that he thought it looked good, a girl in leathers on the back of his scooter.

Nina looked at herself in the full-length mirror on the front of Ellie's wardrobe and tried to envisage herself in a black leather catsuit. *Yeah*, she reckoned, *I'd look pretty cool in one of those.* Sadly, though, she thought sarcastically, her mum hadn't packed her leather catsuit, so she'd have to make do with her Levis and a T-shirt instead. She pulled both on and looked in the mirror again. She sighed – she didn't feel right. Not special enough. Ellie came back into the room.

'Ellie,' said Nina in her best 'I'm-about-to-ask-you-a-favour' voice.

'Yes?' replied Ellie, sitting herself down on the edge of her bed and looking rather distracted.

'Could I borrow something from your wardrobe?'

Ellie was biting her fingernails. 'Yeah, sure, what-ever . . .' she said between nibbles.

Nina opened the wardrobe and pulled out a short denim dress.

'Can I wear this?'

Ellie had got back into bed. 'If you like,' she replied without looking at the dress.

Nina held it up to herself and studied her reflection. 'I suppose it looks better with something underneath it,' she mused. 'What do you usually wear with it?'

Ellie was silent.

'Ellie?'

'What?'

Nina turned around. 'I said what do you usually wear under this?'

Ellie looked at the dress. 'Oh, I don't know,' she sighed. 'Maybe that red and white stripy T-shirt. That one, up there, on the shelf.'

Nina stood on tiptoe and reached up to the top shelf in the wardrobe. 'This one?' she asked, pulling out the T-shirt.

'Yeah, that one,' said Ellie, closing her eyes.

Nina got dressed and put on her make-up before realising that Ellie was about to go back to sleep. 'What are you doing, Ellie?' she asked. 'Aren't you coming to Hampton Court?'

Ellie, eyes still firmly shut, shook her head. 'Don't really feel up to it,' she mumbled. 'Got a head-ache.'

Nina wondered if her headache was anything to do

with the last phone call. 'Who was it on the phone?' she asked.

'Libby,' Ellie replied.

'What did she want?' asked Nina.

'Nothing much,' answered Ellie.

'Well, she must have wanted something,' said Nina.

'She just wanted to make sure I was coming,' said Ellie, opening her eyes.

'And what did you tell her?' persisted Nina.

Ellie sighed. 'God – what is this – the Spanish Inquisition?' she snapped. 'I told her that yes, I was coming.'

'But you're not,' said Nina.

'No, I'm not,' said Ellie. 'And you can pass on the message for me . . .'

Nina frowned at Ellie and wondered what was going on. Then baffled, but always good at taking a hint, she left without her.

Mix 'n' Match

'What's up, mate? Don't you like Weetabix?' Nathan's voice interrupted Patrik's daydream.

'Sorry?' said Patrik, stirring his spoon around in his cereal bowl.

'Weetabix . . .' Nathan repeated. 'Don't you like it?' He peered into the bowl. 'To be honest, I wouldn't want to eat that. What have you done with it?'

Patrik looked down: he'd stirred his breakfast into an unsavoury looking mush.

Nathan poured himself a glass of milk and pulled out a chair. Patrik looked up and made an effort to appear with-it. 'Nice shirt,' he commented.

Nathan, a sucker for flattery and always ready for a bit of a boast, said: 'Oh, what . . . this? It's just some old thing. Bought it ages ago.'

Patrik nodded. 'It's nice,' he repeated.

Nathan sat down. 'So you don't fancy Hampton Court then?'

'Who?' frowned Patrik.

Nathan rolled his eyes. 'God, you're slow today, Pat,' he laughed. 'Hampton Court . . . Don't you remember? Libby phoned and invited us on a day out . . . to Hampton Court . . . you know, where Henry the Eighth used to live.'

Patrik forced a smile. 'Oh yes,' he said. 'That'll be fun. When are we going there then?'

Nathan shook his head despairingly. 'Today,' he said. 'This morning . . . Now. Are you ready or what?'

Patrik pushed his bowl of mush across the table. 'Yes,' he said. 'I'm ready.'

'Then grab this!' ordered Nathan, glugging down his milk and tossing Patrik the less-than-cool-looking helmet, 'and let's scoot!'

'Where are you going?' Alex appeared, sleepy-eyed and pyjama-clad on the stairs.

'To see the king!' shouted Nathan.

'*I* wanna see the king,' Alex whinged, his face scrunched up, his finger firmly embedded up his nose.

'Well, the king doesn't want to see you!' laughed Nathan. 'Come on, Pat,' he said, yanking Patrik by the arm. And before their ears were assaulted by the sound of Alex bursting into tears, both Patrik and Nathan were on the Vespa, on their way to Libby's.

Ali and Nina had already arrived. They were sitting around the big pine table with Libby, Kristina and Libby's step-dad Charles. Libby's mum, Angie, was sitting on top of the washing machine, legs crossed, rolling a cigarette. Patrik hadn't been to Libby's house before, but it was pretty much as he'd imagined it.

412

Libby stood up and introduced him to her parents. Then she grinned and said, 'Charles has kindly offered to give us a lift to Hampton Court.'

'I don't think "offered" is quite the right word,' said Charles, rubbing his beard pensively.

'Well, whatever,' shrugged Libby. 'We're going in the van,' she added.

'I hope you're all going to fit in,' said Charles, standing up, his chair making a scraping noise on the stone floor.

'We'll manage,' said Libby. 'If it's too squashy, the girls can always sit on the boys' laps.' She winked at Patrik and his heart nearly leapt out of his chest. He could feel someone's eyes on him and he scanned the room until he met Ali's glare. He felt uncomfortable, even though he wasn't sure what he'd done. He turned away from Ali and fixed his gaze on Nina.

'I can always take the Vespa if there's not enough room,' suggested Nathan.

'I think we'll be OK, Nathan,' said Libby.

Nina stood up. 'I can't believe it's getting so hot already.' It's going to be a real – what do you call it? – a real scorcher today.' She smiled at Nathan and unbuttoned her denim jacket.

Nathan baulked as she slipped the jacket from her shoulders.

'Are you OK, Nathan?' she asked.

But Nathan was too busy staring at her chest to reply.

Patrik noticed Nathan's expression and was puzzled: what was up with him? It wasn't as if he hadn't seen Nina in tight clothes before. She'd never left much to the imagination on the tennis courts, in her tight white T-shirt and tiny white skirt, so why was Nathan reacting like this now?

'Come on then,' said Charles. 'Let's get you all in the van.'

'Have a good time!' called out Libby's mum as they left.

'We will, Mrs Lawrence,' said Patrik.

'Call me Angie,' she smiled.

Ali climbed into the back seat of the van and Kristina quickly followed, wedging herself in next to him, as close as possible. In the seat in front sat Nina and Nathan.

'Do you want to sit in the front?' Libby asked Patrik.

'I don't mind,' he replied politely. 'Where would *you* rather sit?'

Libby tilted her head – the way she always did when she was required to make a decision. 'Um . . . I'll go in the front,' she said. 'You sit there, next to Nina. Is there enough room?'

'Yes,' Patrik replied. 'Yes, there's plenty of room.'

'Lucky me,' giggled Nina, moving her jacket from the seat beside her to the floor. 'A Nina sandwich!' She wriggled as Patrik sat down next to her.

Nathan stared out of the window.

'Are you *sure* you're OK, Nathan?' asked Patrik.

Nathan nodded. 'I just feel a bit sick, that's all,' he said quietly.

'Car-sick already?' said Ali from the back seat. 'What are you like?! The engine's not even on yet!'

Everyone laughed. Everyone apart from Nathan, Patrik observed as they pulled away.

'So where's Ellie?' Patrik asked Libby, after they'd said goodbye to Charles and tramped their way to the Palace across the car-park.

'At home,' she replied. 'Nina says she's got a head-ache . . . But I'm not so sure.' She paused. 'I reckon she's not coming because she's upset over that Steve thing . . . Did you hear what happened, by the way?'

'Last night? With the letter?' said Patrik. 'Yes, I did. Nathan told me all about it.'

'Where were you anyway?' asked Libby suddenly. 'I thought you were coming over to Ellie's place.'

'Oh, I didn't fancy it,' said Patrik. 'It's just my brother . . .' Patrik said tentatively, 'well, I know you like him, but . . .'

'Hmmphh!' interrupted Libby suddenly looking like she was going to cry.

'Oh right, of course,' said Patrik. 'I'm sorry, I heard about the video thing too. What an idiot!' He sighed loudly and shook his head, as if he genuinely despaired of his twin. Then he glanced at Libby. She'd folded her arms tightly across her chest as if in an effort to contain her rising emotions.

'I suppose you're pretty mad with him,' said Patrik.

415

'It's finished,' said Libby in a choked voice. 'In fact, I don't know how or why I ever got involved with him. I suppose it was his looks and his letters that did it . . . He seemed so . . . different in them . . . So, oh, I don't know . . .'

Patrik coughed awkwardly. It was difficult for him talking about his brother like this, especially to Libby. 'So what about this letter to Steve then?' he said, deliberately changing the subject. 'You don't think it was Ellie who wrote it, do you?'

Libby sighed and allowed her arms to fall to her sides. 'Well, Ellie says it wasn't her and because she's my best friend, I really want to believe her, but . . .'

'But she's the most likely person to have done it,' said Patrik, reading her thoughts.

'I suppose so,' said Libby, nodding slowly. Patrik was so easy to talk to, she thought, she wondered why she'd never noticed it before. 'She's mad about Steve you see – she told me so herself.'

'What happened when Steve's girlfriend accused her of writing the letter then?' Patrik was enthralled and Libby noticed a bright sparkle in his eyes.

'Ellie just denied it,' said Libby. 'Said it must have been someone else.'

'Like who?'

'Who are you talking about?' Kristina drew level with Patrik and Libby.

'Ellie . . . and that letter to Steve,' Libby replied.

'Old news,' said Kristina matter-of-factly. 'I'm more

interested in your team captain Claire and the mystery man in The Pizza Palace!'

'Oh yeah – I forgot about that,' said Libby, wide-eyed. 'Jamie will kill her!'

'Kill who?' asked Ali, catching up with them, eager to join in the gossip.

'Claire,' said Libby. 'Well, he'll kill her if he finds out that she's been seeing someone else.'

'Not if he doesn't get to find out about it,' Kristina said.

They all glanced back at Nina and Nathan, who were lagging behind. They were the ones who'd seen Claire canoodling: if anyone was going to say anything to Jamie, it'd be one of them. Libby shook her head. 'I doubt that,' she said. She stopped walking and looked back at Nathan and Nina again. Patrik stopped and followed her gaze. They seemed to be arguing. 'What's up with them, I wonder?' said Libby.

'I don't know,' Patrik replied, 'but they don't look too happy.'

Suddenly Kristina, slightly ahead of them now, shouted out: 'Look, there's a sign to the Hampton Court tennis courts! Shall we go and have a look, Ali?'

Ali smiled. 'Don't see why not,' he said. He gave Libby a kind of apologetic smile as he allowed Kristina to take his hand and drag him away.

'Looks like those two are finally going to get it together,' Patrik commented, looking longingly at Libby.

'And it looks like those two are going to split up before they even get started,' said Libby, indicating the arguing couple behind them and smiling at Patrik.

'Love, eh?' sighed Patrik, blushing as he awkwardly placed his arm around Libby's shoulders. 'It's weird how things turn out, isn't it?'

Libby felt herself blushing too, though she wasn't quite sure why. She fliched a sky glance at Patrik and noticed how the sun had really brought out the gorgeous little freckles across the bridge of his nose and as his warm strong arm guided her forward, she felt herself gently pressing against his firm torso, and thoughts of Lars faded further and further from her mind . . .

Ali Wakes Up

By the time Ali and Kristina had entered the big barn-type building which housed the Hampton Court Palace tennis courts, something strange had happened . . . Whereas Ali hadn't given Kristina the time of day before, he had now begun to look at her . . . *really* look at her. And, to his surprise, he truly liked what he saw.

In the past, he'd always thought of her as having a rather sad face; but now, suddenly, all that seemed to have changed. *She* was shining out and everyone else around her seemed to be fading into oblivion.

Ali wondered why: perhaps it was because he'd finally started to notice her in the way she wanted to be noticed. The radiance that she was now exuding was because of him and that made him feel really good. Or perhaps it was nothing to do with him at all.

He watched her as she wandered around the courts. No one was playing but, even so, Kristina was completely fascinated.

'I've never seen a tennis court like this,' she enthused, her azure eyes sparkling. 'It's so weird and old-fashioned looking.'

Ali smiled: he wasn't really listening to what she was saying or taking in the old-fashioned tennis courts – he was too busy thinking about how pretty she was and how he wanted to take her in his arms and kiss her on those full pink lips. His heart was pounding in his chest, the way it did whenever Libby stood too close to him . . .

Libby . . . Ali realised that for the first time in ages, he hadn't thought about Libby for a good ten minutes. Up until this afternoon, she was *always* on his mind. During the day, she filled his every thought; at night she starred in his dreams. But now . . . it was different. He could see her in a new light. Libby was great – a really lovely person – but something had gone. It was if at long last, he was free of her spell. And it felt fantastic.

Kristina turned to look at him, her blonde hair falling around her face, 'It's fantastic, isn't it, Ali?' she breathed. 'To think, the king played tennis here all those years ago . . .'

Ali stepped towards her and took her by both hands. 'Fantastic,' he echoed quietly.

Kristina blew a stray strand of hair from her eyes and smiled. Her cheeks were as pink as her lips and her skin was as smooth and unblemished as an egg . . .

Ali let out a small laugh. *An egg*! he thought. Why couldn't he have more poetic thoughts?

'What's so funny?' Kristina asked.

Ali shook his head. 'Nothing,' he said. 'I just feel happy today.'

'Me too,' said Kristina.

Ali was still gazing at her: he couldn't stop. She was so beautiful. 'I'm really sorry, Kristina,' he said suddenly.

Kristina frowned. 'Sorry?' She paused. 'About what?'

Ali hung his head. 'I'm sorry I've treated you so badly,' he apologised. 'It's just that Libby – '

Kristina pressed one of her long, elegant fingers to his lips. 'Ssh,' she said. 'It's OK . . . I know.'

Ali nodded. 'Well, it's been a long time, you know. For the last few years the only girl in my life has been Libby. I've never even *looked* at anyone else. But now you've come along and changed all that. You've made me realise that, although Libby is special, she might not be the girl for me after all.'

Kristina pulled Ali towards her and they wrapped their arms round each other's waists in a long, silent and affectionate hug. Ali rested his chin on the top of Kristina's head and breathed in the scent of her hair. It smelt gorgeous, like a pine-forest in the spring – warm, spicy and fresh.

'Libby's a fool,' murmured Kristina softly into Ali's shoulder. 'She doesn't know what she's missing.'

A pleasant shudder ran down Ali's spine. No one had ever said anything that nice to him before. Kristina's breath on his neck made him feel weak with longing. He pulled away from her and looked deep into her eyes. For the first time, he could see beyond the blue sparkle. 'You make me feel so good, Kristina,' he sighed. 'About myself, about everything.'

421

'I can make you feel even better,' she whispered provocatively.

'You can?' Ali wondered what was going to happen next, but he didn't have to wonder for long. Catching hold of his chin and standing on tiptoe, Kristina pressed her soft lips against Ali's slightly quivering mouth and kissed him, gently at first, then harder, more urgently. Her mouth on his felt wonderful, unlike anything Ali had ever experienced. Ali had never been kissed like that before. But he wasn't complaining. This was great. The best. He wanted it to go on for ever. And when they finally broke apart, it was as if someone had turned off the sun.

'I think perhaps we should go and see the Palace now?' Kristina suggested, her cheeks flushed with passion.

'OK,' he grinned, his heart, which had been frozen for so long, finally melting. He held out his hand to her. 'I'll be the king and you can be my lovely queen.'

'How would you like me – with or without a head?' Kristina giggled.

'Oh, *with* a head – most definitely,' Ali replied, laughing.

'Then with a head it is!' announced Kristina.

And with their fingers entwined they made their way of the tennis courts and towards the Palace.

The Plot Thickens

'I'm really not sure about this, Lars.' Ellie sat up, fiddling with the buttons on her blue chambray shirt.

From his prone position on the bed, Lars reached up and placed a patient hand on Ellie's shoulder. 'You don't *have* to be sure,' he smiled – rather snakily, Ellie thought. 'It's just a bit of fun.'

'We should be at Hampton Court with the others,' she said.

'But you wanted to be here with me,' he drawled. 'Well, I *thought* you did anyway.'

Ellie sighed. 'I *did* . . . I *do* . . . But, well . . .'

'What?' snapped Lars, suddenly not so patient.

'It's just that, well, it doesn't feel right.' Ellie felt a bit pathetic. Lars was right. She *had* wanted to spend the day with him – 'have a bit of fun' as he'd put it – but it wasn't working out. It felt all wrong and there was no way she was going to stay here with him if her heart wasn't in it. Absentmindedly, she picked some fluff off her leggings. 'I've got a lot of things on my mind at the moment,' she said weakly. 'I'm not sure I need this.'

Lars propped himself up on one elbow and looked

ceilingwards. 'Girls,' he muttered to the light fitting. 'They're all the same.'

Ellie glared at him. 'I thought you said I was different.'

'Yeah, well I thought you *were*,' he said gruffly. 'But I've obviously made a mistake.'

Ellie could feel anger welling up inside her. She got to her feet. 'No, Lars, it's me that's made a mistake,' she said aggressively. 'I thought maybe we could have some fun together, but I should have realised your ego would get in the way. I'm sorry Lars, but I'm worth a lot more than someone like you's got to give.'

Lars sighed in half-hearted self-defence, lying back with his hands behind his head. He was silent for a while. Then he said: 'The trouble with you, Ellie, is you don't know what you want.'

'I know what I *don't* want though,' she countered quickly.

Lars ignored her. 'One minute you want me,' he said, 'the next you want Steve Elliott. You really should make up your mind.'

Ellie glowered at him.

'All that stuff about the letter to Steve,' he said. 'Why don't you just admit that you wrote it? It was hilarious watching you trying to blame someone else last night. Who was it you reckoned was the authoress? Poor little Emma, wasn't it? As if she'd do such a thing! Why can't you take responsibility for your own actions?'

'Shut up, will you?' she said.

'Touching on a sore point, are we?' teased Lars.

'No, we're not,' she replied. 'Now, if you don't mind, I've got things to do.'

'Are you sure you wouldn't like to do a few more "things" with me first?'

Ellie was amazed at how full of himself Lars could be. What on earth had she ever seen in him in the first place? 'Get out, Lars,' she said, pointing to the door. 'Just get out, will you?'

Lars lazily slid off the bed. 'You'll be sorry,' he smiled. 'You'll never know what you missed.'

'I'm sure I'll survive,' replied Ellie sarcastically. And she would – she knew she would – because she suddenly realised that losing Lars would actually be no loss at all.

After Lars had gone, Ellie sat in the kitchen, her head in her hands, going over the previous hour in her mind. It had seemed like a good idea inviting Lars round and getting him all on his own, all to herself. But once she had him there, in her room, his appeal kind of disappeared. It wasn't just that she felt bad because of all that had happened with Libby – no, there was more to it than that.

The thing about Lars, she reckoned, *is that he's a sort of trophy lad. He's good-looking, sexy, brilliant at everything and all the girls fancy him.* But that's what it was all about – all the girls fancying him. To go out with a guy like that and be the envy of all your friends is great, she realised, but it doesn't mean things are necessarily going to be that great once you've got him behind closed doors.

And that's exactly how it was with Lars. Once on his own, away from an audience, Lars let the act drop and, because it was the act that was the most attractive thing about him, he'd turn out to be not so great at all – in fact, he was distinctly *un*-great. And even more worryingly, despite all her promises to herself *and* last night's fiasco, she still found her thoughts returning more and more to Steve. Why was life always so complicated?

She thought again about Lars and his relationship with Libby and wondered what *she*'d seen in him. Libby was a pure romantic – nothing like Lars at all. Ellie reckoned it was the distance between them and the fact that Lars wrote such passionate love letters that made him so alluring.

But Ellie had seen another side to Lars – the lustful, grabbing, won't-take-no-for-an-answer side – and coming face-to-face with that had been a deeply unpleasant experience. Ever since Malmo, she'd been aware that he'd rated himself as a bit of a stud (to say the least). She'd even known about poor Ulrika, his long-suffering on-and-off Swedish girlfriend. Actually, to tell the truth, she'd only found out about Ulrika when she'd walked in on her and Lars at that party in Malmo and caught them mid snog. Then, a few days later, when he'd shown an interest in Libby, Ellie approached him and asked him what the hell he was playing at. Libby was very sensitive and sweet, she'd told him, and although he seemed to think it was OK to mess girls around, Ellie was determined that Libby wasn't going to be one of them. She told him to back off, to leave her friend alone, but Lars had just laughed, accused her of being jealous, and proceeded to woo Libby anyway.

He'd sent Libby flowers, wrote her poetry and told her he was writing a song for her. Libby had fallen for it completely and look where that had got her.

Ellie paced between the hall and kitchen. She was itching to do something, see someone, but she didn't know what or who. Then, after a bit more pacing, she decided she *did* know. She sat on the stairs, picked up the phone and dialled Steve's number . . .

Somewhat to her surprise, an hour and a quarter later, Ellie and Steve were sipping cappuccinos at the café in the market square. It was the first opportunity Ellie had had to talk to him about the letter. Amazingly, Steve didn't seem to know anything about it.

'What letter?' he asked, clearly puzzled.

Ellie started to tell the story. 'Your girlfriend – what's her name again?'

'Yuki,' said Steve.

'Yes, that's it – Yuki.' Ellie repeated the name as if she was tasting it. She wrinkled her nose; it didn't have a good flavour. 'Well, she came round to my place last night, waving this letter and accusing me of all sorts of things.'

Steve appeared to be totally baffled now. He shook

his head as if it really didn't make any sense at all. 'So what did this letter say?' he asked.

Ellie blushed slightly. 'Oh, all sorts of stuff,' she mumbled. 'It was a love letter really.'

'Oh, I see,' said Steve, looking a bit taken aback. 'A love letter, eh?'

Ellie took a deep breath and continued the story. 'Well, I had a look at it, but I didn't recognise the writing . . . But then anyone sending a letter like that would probably disguise their handwriting, wouldn't they?'

Steve shrugged. 'I don't know,' he said. 'I'm not much of an expert in this particular area.' He paused, took another sip of coffee, and added: 'I can't say I'm not flattered though.'

Ellie frowned. She wasn't really listening to Steve: she was trying to work out why the letter hadn't actually got to him. She voiced her dilemma.

Steve shrugged again. 'Well, I suppose Yuki *is* very protective of me,' he said. 'She's quite a jealous person and is always asking me about you girls. She doesn't seem to realise that I'm just doing my job . . .'

Ellie's heart sank. She couldn't understand why she felt so disappointed – she'd always known that he thought she was too young to be a serious contender for his affections. She knew that it was silly to expect Steve to fancy her (he'd always made it clear that schoolgirls weren't of any interest to him), but still, she thought, there was no harm in fantasising . . . She hadn't needed Steve to spell it out and blow away all her hopes and dreams in one sentence . . .

Ellie nodded, in a way she hoped made her look wise and mature.

'She's always telling me how she wished I did a different job, one where I wasn't surrounded by females in short skirts all day,' he laughed.

'She *does* sound possessive,' said Ellie. 'But, possessive or not, she shouldn't be riffling through your mail, should she?'

'To be honest, she *has* done this kind of thing before,' sighed Steve. He ran one hand through his dark curls. 'She can be a real nightmare to live with sometimes. Sorry Ellie, I really shouldn't be burdening you with all this.' He paused, his eyes narrowed, deep in thought. 'The letter may have been sent to *her* of course,' he said suddenly.

'Mmmm . . .' Ellie was quiet for a moment as she thought. 'That's a possibility, I suppose. But why would anyone want to do that?'

'To stir up trouble?' Steve suggested.

'Yeah, maybe,' said Ellie. 'But who on earth would want to break up you and Yuki?'

'I wonder . . .' said Steve, staring directly into Ellie's eyes and sending a shiver of unease down her back. 'I wonder . . .'

Better Off Without Them

'You should have come to Hampton Court with us yesterday!' Libby said to Ellie. They were in the locker rooms at school. Libby was getting ready for Game 3 of the tournament and Ellie was there to give her some moral support. 'We had a great laugh,' she added, pulling off her T-shirt and replacing it with a whiter-than-white Fred Perry. 'And you'll never guess what . . .' Libby could easily make her eyes gleam, but she couldn't stop her mouth from twitching.

'What?' said Ellie in anticipation.

Libby forced a grin. 'Ali got off with Kristina,' she whispered, glancing from side to side to make sure no one was eavesdropping.

Ellie looked unimpressed. 'Pretty inevitable really,' she said pragmatically.

Libby frowned. 'I don't know,' she argued. 'It kind of took *me* by surprise.'

'Anyway, never mind about them,' said Ellie. 'What about you?'

'What *about* me?' asked Libby, deliberately naive.

'Got over Lars yet?'

Libby nodded. 'I'll be all right,' she said. And she

really meant it. She was beginning to realise that what she had with Lars amounted to nothing: friendship with a guy who was genuine and sincere (someone like her old mate Ali, for example) was far more important than a few lusty snogs with an egotistical love-god.

'I saw him yesterday actually,' said Ellie.

'Who – Ali?' asked Libby, still miles away mentally.

'No – Lars,' said Ellie, frowning.

'Really?' said Libby. 'I thought you had a bad headache.'

'I *did* have a headache,' she said.

'Oh. So where did you see him?' asked Libby, still slightly distracted.

'He came round . . . to mine,' replied Ellie.

'Did he? That must have been nice for you.' Libby hadn't meant it to come out sounding so 'off', but it seemed odd that Lars should just casually pop round to Ellie's like that. 'What did he want?'

Ellie looked her friend straight in the eye. 'Me,' she said simply.

'Oh.' Libby was lost for words.

Ellie turned to the mirror on the locker and proceeded to get an eyelash out of her eye. 'I told him where to get off,' she said coolly.

'Good for you,' said Libby. But still she felt confused. Just *what* was going on between those two? She thought there'd be no harm in asking . . . 'So what's going on with you two exactly?' she said, trying to stop her voice from shaking.

'Nothing,' said Ellie flatly, examining the extracted eyelash on her fingertip. 'Absolutely nothing.' And for once, she was telling the complete truth.

Game 3 was Ali and Libby versus Orsa and Anders. Orsa looked terrible, like she'd had a bit of a rough night. *There's no way she's going to play too well today*, reckoned Libby, feeling quietly confident.

She glanced back at Ali, behind her on the court, but Ali was waving at Kristina at that particular moment so missed Libby's confident smile. Libby felt weird – no, *more* than weird: if she was honest with herself, she'd admit that she felt really put out. Ali was always watching her; he'd watched her more or less constantly for years . . . What was the matter with him? She hoped he wasn't going to become a pain just because he had a girlfriend.

She crouched down in preparation to receive the first serve from Orsa, as Colin, the umpire, announced the start of the game . . .

'What a doddle!' Libby exclaimed, rubbing her damp face with a white, fluffy towel. 'Two sets to one! And all thanks to you, Ali . . .' She peeped out over the top of the towel, but Ali had already disappeared into the distance with Kristina. 'Bloody lovebirds!' Libby muttered.

The sun beat down. It was hotter than ever.

'Has anyone seen Jamie?' Steve called out across the court. 'He's supposed to be playing in the next game!'

'I don't think he's turned up,' called back Emma, Jamie's doubles partner.

'Yes, I have,' said a voice.

Everyone gasped. Because there was Jamie, grinning from ear to ear and looking very different, due to the fact that his cherubic blond curls were blond no more.

'Your hair!' squealed Emma. 'What have you done?'

Jamie smiled. 'Claire dyed it for me,' he said. 'On Friday.'

Claire appeared behind him. 'Looks good black, don't you think?'

'So *you're* the mystery man!' laughed Libby. *How brilliant!* she thought. *Claire wasn't with a mystery guy at all. She was with Jamie all along.*

'Who? What mystery man?' frowned Jamie.

'Nothing,' giggled Libby. She couldn't wait to tell Ellie and Nina the news.

'At least you won't be mistaken for a Swede now,' laughed Sarah.

'No bad thing, I can assure you,' said Jamie in hushed tones.

Steve clapped his hands to get their attention. 'Right,' he said, 'We've got Jamie and Emma. Has anyone seen Patrik?'

'He was in the locker room. I think he was writing his diary or something,' said Jamie. 'Do you want me to go and hurry him up?'

'Yeah – that'd be great,' said Steve gratefully. 'Thanks, Jamie . . . Now what about Nina? Libby, have you seen Nina anywhere?'

Libby shook her head. 'She's probably off snogging an English boy somewhere,' she mumbled to herself dejectedly. 'That's all these Swedish girls seem interested in doing. They've certainly not been practising their tennis, that's for sure.' She looked across at Orsa, who had a pained expression on her face as she pushed a couple of Paracetamol out of their silver wrappers.

Ellie arrived on court. 'Nina's just coming, Steve,' she smiled. Libby frowned. Ellie just didn't know when to give up.

Nina emerged from the school into the bright sunshine. Her eyes were red-rimmed, like she'd been crying.

'Is Nina all right?' Ellie asked Libby.

Libby nodded. 'I think she's OK now. She had a bit of a row with Nathan yesterday, that's all,' she explained. 'When we were at Hampton Court.'

Ellie seemed to forget about trying to attract Steve's attention for a moment and turned to Libby. 'Really? What about?'

Libby smiled wryly. 'As if you didn't know ...' she said.

'What?' said Ellie, innocence personified.

'You mean you didn't dress Nina up like that on purpose?' said Libby.

'What are you talking about?' Ellie squeaked.

'The denim dress, the red-and-white stripy T-shirt. Don't tell me you didn't do it deliberately ...' Libby tilted her head back and looked suspiciously down her nose at Ellie. 'Surely you can't have forgotten . . .' she said.

'Forgotten what?'

'What you were wearing when you dumped Nathan in Malmo,' Libby said finally.

Ellie clamped her hand over her mouth. 'Oh my God!' she whispered. 'I *had* forgotten.'

'Shame Nathan hadn't,' sighed Libby. 'He accused Nina of doing it to wind him up. He said that she was there when you finished with him and deliberately wore the same outfit yesterday to upset him.'

'But why would she do that? It's a ridiculous accusation to make!' said Ellie.

'God knows!' replied Libby. 'If I knew what went on in a boy's mind, I'd probably have a boyfriend right now.'

Ellie laughed a sardonic little laugh. 'Yeah, right,' she said. 'They're a mystery to me too.'

They both looked at Nina's miserable face. 'I think we're better off without them really, don't you?' Ellie said, slipping her arm round her friend's waist and giving her a little squeeze.

'Definitely,' smiled Libby.

And although they found some comfort in telling each other such things, Libby knew they both had their fingers crossed behind their backs.

If It's Not One Thing...

'You *must* sort it out,' advised Patrik. 'I mean, you're staying at Ellie's house. You can't not talk to her.'

Nina sighed and took a long sip of her milkshake. She looked across the burger bar, to where Libby and Ellie were engrossed in conversation. 'But it's because of her that Nathan won't see me,' she whined.

'It was a misunderstanding,' said Patrik. 'If you can just make out that it doesn't really matter – and it doesn't really, does it, not in the scheme of things? – Soon everyone else will see it the same way.'

Nina nodded. Patrik – her dear, sweet, kind friend – was always right.

'Nathan's just being stupid,' he smiled reassuringly. 'He'll soon see the error of his ways.'

'I suppose so,' Nina agreed.

'So let's go over and talk to them, shall we?' suggested Patrik.

Nina nearly choked on her hamburger. 'What? Now?' she said.

'Now's as good a time as any,' grinned Patrik. He pulled her out of her seat. 'Come on.'

*

A few minutes later, Nina and Ellie were friends again. 'I'm really sorry about what happened with my clothes,' said Ellie. 'To be honest, I wasn't really paying attention when you were borrowing my stuff.'

'I know,' smiled Nina, taking a bite of apple pie. 'And *I*'m sorry too. I don't know why I thought you did it on purpose.' She stopped mid chew. 'It's just Nathan . . . will you talk to him for me?'

'It'd probably be best if Libby does it,' suggested Patrik. 'To be honest, I don't think he's quite got over Ellie yet.'

Nina flinched.

'Don't worry, Nina,' said Patrik. 'Libby's a good person to talk to – I'm sure she'll be able to sort things out between you.'

Libby smiled. 'I don't mind having a word with him if you think it'll help.'

Patrik reached across the table and placed his hand on top of Libby's. 'You're great,' he whispered. 'You really are.'

And, if Nina wasn't mistaken, she was sure she could see something more than just gratitude in Patrik's blue eyes.

Later that evening, the phone rang at Ellie's house.

'Nina – can you get that?' called Ellie from the shower.

'OK – I've got it!' Nina yelled back from the hallway. She picked up the receiver. 'Hi,' she said.

'Is Ellie there?' It was a female voice – high-pitched and abrupt.

'Ellie? Well, she is, but she's in the shower. Can I give her a message?'

'Yes, tell her Yuki called and I want a word with her. She's got my number – it's the same as Steve's.'

'Yeah, OK. I'll tell her. No problem,' said Nina. It didn't register until she had put down the receiver who Yuki was . . .

'Oh God, what does she want *now*?' Ellie wailed, rubbing her hair vigorously with a small, pale-pink towel.

'She just said she wanted a word with you,' replied Nina. 'She didn't sound too happy though.'

'I suppose I'd better phone her back,' Ellie sighed resignedly. She tightened a larger pink towel around her chest and made her way downstairs.

Nina put some music on: she didn't know what it was, but it was kind of soothing. She thought about Nathan and wondered if Libby really *could* help patch things up for them. She hoped so, because she was beginning to realise just how much Nathan meant to her. She was terrified of losing him. Peter just didn't come into it any more. As far as she was concerned, he was part of the past. Nathan was her present and, she hoped, her future too.

Ellie appeared in the doorway. 'I can't believe what that woman is doing!' she exclaimed.

'Why – what did she say?' asked Nina, turning down the volume on the stereo.

'She said that a friend of hers had seen me and Steve in the café in town, and that that was proof enough that I was the one who wrote the letter!'

Nina was quiet for a moment. Then she said: 'But you *didn't* write it, did you, Ellie?' She looked closely at her friend. 'If you did, you know you can tell me.' She was treading carefully, but not carefully enough.

'No, I didn't write it!' Ellie snapped. 'How many times do I have to tell everyone?!'

'OK, OK,' said Nina. 'I was just checking.'

Ellie regained her composure. 'Anyway,' she said, 'that's not the worst of it. Yuki told me that another letter had been sent, and this one says they're going to reveal all to Mr Madres, the head.'

'No!' gasped Nina.

'Yes,' said Ellie. 'And, according to Yuki, this letter is even *more* explicit. It goes into really gory detail about what Steve and this girl have been up to. And it says there have been other girls too – other students . . .'

Nina put her hand to her mouth.

Ellie continued: 'Yuki reckons if it goes any further it could get Steve the sack. She's furious.'

Nina shook her head in disbelief. 'But whoever would want him to lose his job?'

Ellie paused for a moment, then frowned. Then a look of enlightenment washed over her face. She smiled knowingly. 'Actually,' she began, 'there's someone I can think of who would *love* him to lose his job. And, before I say another word to anyone else, I'm going to do everything I can to make sure Steve knows all about it . . .'

'But you can't phone him at home: Yuki will be there,' Nina said, making a huge effort not to be more nosey. She desperately wanted to know who the culprit was.

'I'll speak to him tomorrow,' said Ellie, 'before the semi-final of the tournament. I just hope he believes me . . .'

Who'd Have Thought It?

For the first time in weeks, Nathan had dreamt about someone other than Ellie. In his dream, Nina had been sitting at a window, crying. And, although he'd wanted to comfort her, he couldn't get off his Vespa. It was like he was glued to it or something. He woke up feeling agitated. He tossed and turned and tried to get back to sleep, but he couldn't, so he threw back the duvet and got up. It was only seven o'clock.

Downstairs, the TV was blaring.

'Nathan!' cheered Alex, jumping to his feet, his pyjama bottoms sliding down his skinny-whippet bottom. He hoisted them back into place. 'You're up!' he shrilled. 'Brilliant! Come and watch 'Rugrats' with me!'

Nathan grunted. He wasn't sure if his vocal chords worked this early in the morning and he wasn't going to risk trying. He staggered into the kitchen and poured himself a big glass of milk.

He pulled up the roller-blind and recoiled in horror: the sun was blazing, so Nathan grunted at that too.

He'd forgotten it was daylight at seven in the morning: he'd half-expected it to still be dark.

After he'd eaten a huge pile of toast and Marmite and watched 'Real Monsters' with Alex, he considered going up to the spare room and waking Patrik. Then he remembered that Patrik was playing in the semi-finals of the tournament today (unlike Nathan who'd been knocked out in the first match, thanks to Love-all Lars) and decided that maybe it was best to let him get some rest.

Just as he'd reached that decision, however, Patrik appeared in the doorway, fully dressed in his tennis gear, as spritely as most Swedes seem to be first thing in the morning. Nathan, still in his dressing-gown, a neat crust of dried Marmite around his mouth, felt a right slob.

'Morning!' beamed Patrik.

'Morning,' croaked Nathan. It was the first word he'd spoken that day and he was mildly impressed that his voice functioned at all. He hauled himself to his feet and followed Patrik into the kitchen.

'Are you coming to watch the semi-finals today?' asked Patrik, pouring some orange juice into a glass.

'Why, who's playing?' Nathan really had lost track. He supposed he should have gone to watch yesterday's games, but he couldn't face it – not after his row with Nina.

Patrik sighed. 'Well, the first game is Lars and Lena versus Ellie and Daniel.'

'Oh yeah?' said Nathan, only half interested.

'And the second game is Ali and Libby against me and Nina.' Patrik gulped down the juice and rinsed the glass out under the tap.

At the mention of Nina's name, Nathan's heart had suddenly leapt into action. 'How *is* Nina?' he asked cautiously.

'A bit upset,' said Patrik. It was obvious that, as Nina's mate, Patrik didn't want to give too much away.

Nathan sighed. 'I think I've been a bit of a jerk, don't you, Pat?' he said.

Patrik grinned. 'Yes, I think you have.'

Nathan smiled and Patrik picked up his holdall and racquet, which he'd packed the previous night. 'Now, I'm going down to the courts to get some practise in. Will I be seeing you later?'

Nathan nodded. 'Yeah, you'll be seeing me all right,' he replied.

'Good,' nodded Patrik. He walked towards the door, then stopped. 'Oh and by the way,' he said, 'Libby might be coming round to see you this morning. She wants to talk to you about Nina.'

Nathan wasn't surprised. 'I'll look forward to that then,' he joked, because being told off by Libby at this time of day – or, in fact, at *any* time of day – wasn't his idea of fun.

'See you later then,' said Patrik.

'Yeah – see you.'

*

Nathan had just about pulled on his jeans, T-shirt and trainers when the doorbell rang. Libby ... He leapt down the stairs three at a time (that way it only took four steps, he'd deduced a long time ago), opened the door and reeled backwards in shock. Because it wasn't Libby standing there at all ...

'Nina!' he said. 'I was expecting – '

'Yes, I know,' she interrupted. 'But I thought I might as well come myself. I want to talk to you.'

'Good,' said Nathan, 'because I want to talk to you too ...'

It wasn't long before Nina was sitting on Nathan's lap, her arms wrapped tightly around him. They'd talked all about the misunderstanding with Ellie's clothes, and then Nina went on to tell him about the previous night's drama with Yuki. She explained how Ellie was planning to turn up at the tennis courts extra-early this morning to have a chat to Steve.

Nathan wasn't really paying too much attention to what Nina was saying – he was just happy to have her in his arms again. 'I'm glad you came round,' he grinned, feeling a bit uncool for saying such a thing, but not really caring *too* much.

'I'm glad too,' Nina whispered, leaning down to kiss him on the lips.

As they kissed, Nathan spied Alex's cheeky face peering around the kitchen door. 'Bleeurgh!' he said, then disappeared. Nina and Nathan looked at each other and then burst out laughing.

Nina leant back. 'Libby's been great, don't you think?' she said.

Nathan nodded. 'Patrik's been great too,' he commented. 'Really loyal . . .'

They were silent for a moment. Then Nina said: 'Don't you reckon those two would be really well suited?'

Nathan hadn't really considered it before, but now Nina came to mention it . . . 'Yes,' he replied, nodding slowly and pensively. 'Yes, I reckon they'd get on pretty well together . . .'

'Maybe we should do something about it?' suggested Nina, a twinkle in her pale eyes.

'Like what?' asked Nathan.

'Well, I've got an idea,' smiled Nina. 'Tell me what you think . . .'

By ten o'clock, everyone had assembled at the school tennis courts. The atmosphere was tense and the air was humid and stifling.

'I can't believe that guy,' laughed Lars, pointing at Colin the umpire. 'Does he wear that high-necked jumper *all* the time?'

Colin didn't hear what Lars said, but realised that he was talking about him. He grinned and gave him the thumbs-up sign.

'What a prat!' sighed Lars. 'The guy thinks I *like* him.'

Nathan glared at Lars. OK, so Colin might not be the sort of bloke you'd want to hang round with, but that was no reason to constantly take the piss.

Nina headed for the locker rooms – she wanted to talk to Ellie, she said – and left Nathan out on the court. Lena was standing on the sidelines, limbering up, seemingly confident. Libby had brought a tiny battery-operated television with her and was sitting on the ground watching it. Nathan wandered over to her.

'Cool TV,' he commented.

'Thanks,' said Libby, glancing up over her shoulder. She quickly turned back to the television. 'I got it for my birthday.'

Nathan sighed: he wished *he* had rich parents. 'What's on anyway?' he asked, unable to see the picture due to the glare of the sun.

'Wimbledon, of course,' sighed Libby, not looking up this time. 'It's the men's singles today.'

'Oh right,' Nathan sighed. Last summer, he would have known that. This year, somehow he'd lost interest.

He felt warm breath on his neck and an even warmer body pressed up behind him. It was Nina.

'Have you told Libby about our little get-together tonight?' she asked.

Nathan frowned. 'Get-together?' he said.

'Yes . . . *get-together*.' Nina nudged him hard.

'Oh, right – *that* get-together.' Luckily, Libby wasn't paying any attention to them. On the small TV, the Australian player was about to serve.

'Libs . . .' he said, squatting down beside her. 'Fancy coming over to mine for a little party tonight?'

The TV tennis game finished and Libby turned around. 'Brilliant!' she sighed. 'I knew he'd win . . . Sorry, what were you saying? A party? Yeah, that'd be fab! What time?'

Nathan shrugged and looked up at Nina.

'About seven,' said Nina.

'Yeah, great,' said Libby, grabbing her racquet and jumping to her feet. 'Let's hope we have something to celebrate, eh?'

'I'm sure we will,' said Nathan. 'In fact,' he continued, grinning at Nina, 'I'm almost certain of it.'

Everyone watched in silence, while Lars and Lena played Ellie and Daniel. It was a very tense game – and there seemed to be some particular tension between Lars and Ellie. A couple of times, Lars quietly spat the word 'bitch!', but Nathan wasn't sure whether he was talking to the ball, his racquet or to someone else . . .

Ellie looked distracted and wasn't playing as well as usual. She kept glancing over at Steve for moral support. That reminded Nathan . . . He turned to Nina and whispered: 'So did you find out what happened between Ellie and Steve?'

Nina nodded. 'Yes,' she said. 'Ellie worked out that it was Yuki writing the letters and told Steve as much.'

'No!' said Nathan, a bit too loud.

'Ssshhh!' scolded Colin, purple-faced, beads of sweat trickling from his forehead, down his cheeks and into the polo-neck of his jumper.

Once everyone's eyes were off Nathan, he turned back to Nina and said: 'So what did Steve reckon?'

Nina replied in a whisper: 'Well, apparently, Steve had pretty much worked out the same thing. He'd found the original letter and recognised Yuki's handwriting ... He told Ellie that they're splitting up. Yuki's moving out of Steve's flat today. She's obviously a complete head case. Apparently they'd been on the rocks for ages, he'd tried to break it off with her before and she'd gone nuts and accused him of all kinds of stuff, but this time she's gone too far. That's it as far as he's concerned.'

Nathan shook his head. 'Wow!' he said. 'What a scandal!'

'More scandalous than that though,' continued Nina, 'is that Steve has asked Ellie out.'

Nathan digested this new morsel of information and waited for a surge of jealousy – the surge he usually felt when he heard about Ellie being involved with anyone else. But nothing happened. There was no surge, no jealousy ... nothing. 'Oh,' he found himself saying. 'That's good.'

He looked across at Ellie as she smashed the ball

into the net once more. *Steve and Ellie, eh?* He pondered the new partnership. *And me and Nina. Who'd have thought it?*

Truth Will Out

Libby was surprised at how quiet Nathan's house was when she arrived that evening. She stood at the front gate and checked her watch: eight-thirty. She was hardly early. She'd spoken to Ellie, Ali and Kristina earlier and they all said they were coming, so what was going on?

She pushed open the gate, walked up the front path and pressed the doorbell.

Nathan answered. 'Well, hello, Miss Libby,' he said, bowing theatrically in greeting. '*Do* come in.'

Libby stepped inside, not knowing quite what to expect. If it had been her birthday, she would have suspected some kind of surprise: there was that kind of air about the place. But it wasn't her birthday.

'Let me take your overgarment,' offered Nathan.

Libby wriggled out of her cropped linen jacket and let Nathan catch it. There was music coming from the living-room, but it was soft and gentle – more suitable for the winding-down, smoochy end of a party than the start of one.

'Go on in,' said Nathan, ushering Libby into the room.

Sitting on the sofa was a rather nervous-looking Patrik in a very smart checked shirt. She hadn't seen him since she and Ali had thrashed him and Nina in the semi-final earlier that afternoon. It had been a good game – very friendly – all things considered. Unlike the Lars and Lena/Ellie and Daniel match in the morning, which the Swedes had won hands down.

In the armchair beside the sofa sat a grinning Nina.

Libby turned back to Nathan. 'So where *is* everybody?' she asked.

Nathan shrugged. 'Dunno,' he said. 'Quite a few people said they couldn't make it at such short notice . . .'

'Maybe no one's going to turn up,' Patrik said.

'Maybe,' said Nina.

Nathan rubbed his hands together. 'Oh well,' he said, 'It doesn't really matter does it, we can still have a good time on our own.'

Libby was quiet: she was thinking, a half-smile hovering on her lips, and beginning to put two and two together. Oh well, what the hell, she *did* like Patrik after all and it was obvious from the way he was constantly gazing at her – much like Ali used to – that he was pretty keen on her too.

'The less, the merrier, I say,' said Nathan.

'Yeah,' grinned Libby. 'I'll second that.'

And it had been fine. Nathan's mum and dad had been banished to the kitchen, his little brother was asleep upstairs, and the four of them had ended up having quite a laugh. And Libby and Patrik seemed to get on like a house on fire, as predicted. As it neared eleven o'clock, Libby decided it was time to leave.

She saw Nina nudge Patrik.

'I'll walk you home if you like, Libby,' he said.

Libby grinned. 'OK,' she said. 'That'd be nice.'

The night sky was purple and the clouds were bobbly. Patrik put his arm protectively around Libby's shoulders. It felt warm and comfortable and natural, Libby thought, as they fell into step together.

'So it's all over with my brother then, is it?' asked Patrik.

Libby nodded. 'To be honest, I don't think there was really anything there to start with,' she sighed.

Silence, apart from the sound of their footsteps on the pavement.

'It's weird though,' continued Libby, 'because when I first met him, he seemed so lovely. Do you remember – he sent me flowers and everything?'

'Yeah – I remember,' said Patrik. 'How could I forget?' he added quietly.

'Then there were all those romantic love letters . . .' She sighed. 'It's hard to believe a guy as cold-hearted as Lars could write so passionately.'

Suddenly Patrik stopped walking and, turning to face Libby, he said: 'Actually, Libby, I've got a confession to make.'

'What's that?' She was sure he was going to tell her that he was in love with Ellie or something. That was just the sort of thing guys did to her. First she'd lost Lars, then Ali, and now this . . . But her thoughts were racing way ahead.

'It was me,' said Patrik shyly.

'What was?' said Libby, baffled.

They started walking again.

'It was me who – who wrote all those letters,' he confessed.

'*You*?!'

Patrik nodded. 'Yes, it wasn't Lars at all. He asked me to do it.'

Oh no. This was worse than Libby had expected. She'd been made a complete fool of and she'd fallen for it all hook, line and sinker! 'I can't *believe* this!' she said. 'I really can't.' She suddenly felt very bitter – towards Lars, towards Patrik, towards everyone.

'So how did he persuade you to do it?' she asked, venom in her voice. 'Did he pay you or something?'

Patrik shook his head. 'No, I did it for nothing. I didn't mind. In fact, I *wanted* to do it.' He put his arm around her shoulders again.

'Oh, leave me alone!' she gasped, shrugging off his arm and storming off up the road towards the bus stop.

'Libby – wait, you don't understand!' he called after her.

'Oh, I understand all right!' she yelled back. 'I understand completely. You must have been having

a really good laugh about me behind my back . . .
God, I'm stupid!'

Patrik ran after her and caught up with her by the
bus shelter. He placed his hands on her shoulders
and turned her towards him. 'Wait, Libby,' he said,
panting slightly. 'Please let me explain.'

'There's nothing to explain as far as I can see,'
Libby said huffily, her arms folded, her face turned
away from him.

'But there *is*,' he said, leading her into the bus
shelter and sitting her down on the moulded plastic
bench inside. 'There's a lot to explain.'

So Patrik explained. He told her about how he'd
been in love with her since the first time he'd seen
her in Malmo: about how Lars, of course, had seen
it, and how, as he always did with his twin brother,
had taken it as some sort of challenge.

'Lars has always been better at attracting girls than
me,' Patrik said, 'so I knew that when he started
flirting with you, I didn't stand a chance. So I backed
right down.'

Libby nodded slowly. She was trying to take all
this in but it wasn't easy.

'When you returned to England, Lars said he
wanted to write to you, but as letter writing isn't
really one of his strengths, he asked me to do it. At
first, I didn't want to,' admitted Patrik, 'but then I
realised at least it would be a good way of conveying
my feelings to you – even if you *did* think they were
the feelings of someone else. It sounds a bit stupid

now, but at the time it seemed to make sense. I was crazy for you, Libby, and it seemed the only way to let you know.'

'Why didn't you just tell me?' she asked.

Patrik shook his head. 'It's not that easy for someone like me,' he said. 'Lars can do that sort of thing. I can't. I'm just not made that way. I couldn't tell you I loved you, especially as you seemed to be so smitten with Lars. But I *did* love you. I still do.'

Libby was flattered – *hugely* flattered – but still wasn't sure she could trust Patrik. What if he turned out to be like all the other boys? What if all this was just another lie? 'How do I know you're telling the truth now?' she asked.

'Well,' smiled Patrik. 'I always knew there'd be a moment like this – a time when I could tell you the truth. And I knew that I'd need proof.' He paused. 'If you look closely at the letters, you'll see that the kisses at the bottom always add up to 16. That's because there are 16 letters in the sentence *Patrik loves Libby*.'

Even in the purple darkness, Libby could see he was blushing.

'That's really sweet,' she said, finally believing him. 'In fact, *you*'re really sweet.'

'Not as sweet as you,' said Patrik.

'Come here,' said Libby, catching his arm and pulling him towards her so he slid along the bench. She snuggled up to him, resting her head on his shoulder.

Patrik kissed the top of her head.

They said nothing, not because there wasn't anything to say, but because, at that particular moment in time – a moment that would be freeze-framed in both their memories for ever – there was no need to speak.

Winners And... Losers!

Wednesday: the day of the final. Lars was feeling as confident as ever. He'd never lost a game and certainly had no intention of losing today either. His opponents – Libby and Ali – were pushovers and, although he liked that in a girlfriend, he liked it even more in tennis rivals. His doubles partner Lena had been on top form throughout the tournament and, even though she was a bit on the plain side looks-wise, he had to admit she was a good tennis player – for a girl anyway. Lena was OK: unlike all the English females, *she* wouldn't let him down.

But that's where he was wrong. When Lars turned up for their morning practice session, Lena was nowhere to be seen. There was no sign of Orsa or Anders or that ginger-haired Brit-boy either.

Steve appeared, clipboard in hand.

'Hey Steve – where *is* everyone today?' called Lars.

Steve looked up. 'Oh, Lars, glad you're here. Lena can't make it, I'm afraid. She's sprained her ankle. Daniel phoned me first thing this morning, but I knew all about it anyway.'

'How come?' Lars frowned.

'Oh, I found out when I picked Ellie up this morning,' said Steve casually, flicking through the sheets of paper attached to his clipboard. 'Her mum works shifts as a receptionist at the hospital. She told us about it when she got in from work.'

'You picked Ellie up this morning?' Lars tried not to sound jealous (or too interested), but he was. How could Ellie turn down Love-god Lars (isn't that what they called him?), then start dating an old guy like Steve – who, let's face it wasn't even blond *or* muscular.

Lars was seriously miffed – was he losing his touch or what? This had certainly never happened to him before – these English girls were obviously all crazy.

'Yes . . . anyway,' Steve continued, going back to the Lena story, which Lars really couldn't care less about at that moment, 'apparently, four of them went out last night and Lena ended up in a dustbin or something.'

Lars presumed he was supposed to be surprised and exclaim 'a dustbin?' at this point, but he couldn't be bothered.

Steve carried on as if he *had* said that anyway. 'Just don't ask,' he said. 'I didn't know what Daniel was going on about either. He sounded a bit worse for wear himself . . .'

'You wouldn't get me staying out late like that,' said Lars, all proud of himself.

'No,' grinned Steve, 'you probably need more beauty sleep than most.'

Then he walked away, leaving Lars to wonder whether that last comment was a compliment or an insult.

'So who's playing in Lena's place?' Lars asked Steve half an hour later.

'I think Kristina should,' he said. 'I've just called her and she's coming down with Libby right away.'

'But Kristina got knocked out in the first round,' complained Lars. 'She's really not up to scratch for the final.'

'I think she'll be just fine,' argued Steve. 'Anyway Lars, it's not up to you – it's my decision, OK?'

Lars was doubly miffed now and all the more determined to win the whole tournament. *I'll show them who's the tennis king*, he said to himself. *Then they'll be sorry.*

Lars felt like he'd been ready for hours and was pacing up and down the edge of the court impatiently when Libby and Kristina finally arrived. Ali had been hanging about for ten minutes or so, but he never seemed to say too much, even when Lars made a serious attempt to engage him in conversation.

Colin was settling himself into the umpire's chair. Lars watched him as he unwrapped some curly-edged sandwiches. As he chewed, melted butter oozed out of the corners of his mouth. Every so often, he'd stop – either to pick his nose or scratch around down his trousers.

Colin became slowly aware of Lars watching him. 'Hi, Lars!' he called out, crumbs spraying in all directions.

Lars cringed. He really didn't want to be friendly with this disgusting guy, but he was the umpire and being matey with the umpire was no bad thing . . . Lars took a deep breath and gave Colin one of his biggest, broadest, chummiest smiles. 'Enjoying your lunch?' he asked.

'It's more elevenses really,' grinned Colin, big chunks of cheese between his teeth. 'Nice,' said Lars, even though he hadn't the faintest idea what 'elevenses' were.

'Do you want one?' Colin waved a soggy sandwich at Lars.

'No thanks, Colin,' Lars replied. 'Not before a game . . . Thanks though – it looks delicious.'

Lars could feel Ali glaring at him and, although he wasn't particularly telepathic, he somehow knew what Ali was thinking.

Lars and Kristina positioned themselves on the opposite side of the net to Ali and Libby. Ali seemed different today, Lars reckoned. Bigger, a bit more aggressive. Libby didn't seem to be her usual timid self either. The way she was trying to stare out Kristina was distinctly un-timid, in fact. Lars had heard the gossip about Ali and Kristina – that they were now an item – and that made him wonder about Libby's feelings for Ali. Maybe they'd been more than just good friends, Lars thought. Maybe

Libby was the two-timer. He quickly dismissed the idea. The thought of her fancying Ali bordered on the ridiculous. He – Lars – was her type, and if that was the case, there was no way she'd have the hots for a loser like Ali.

'Yes!' Nathan, who'd been watching Libby's tiny telly, leapt up. 'It's a win for us,' he announced.

'It's going to be a different story here though,' called out Lars. 'I'm not letting any Brit beat *me* at tennis.'

Steve appeared next to Colin. 'Right! When you've finished your breakfast, Colin . . .' he said.

'It's elevenses actually,' said Colin.

'Yeah, whatever,' said Steve, patting Colin's corduroy knee. Colin finished his sandwiches, pulled off his pullover (revealing a nasty grey T-shirt), and got comfortable in the umpire's chair once more.

And then the game began.

The final was pretty fraught, but Lars wasn't going to lose. If there was one thing he was certain of, it was that. It was getting tense now though; the whole tournament hung on this one last game.

The 'crowd' were on tenterhooks.

Libby to serve. Smash! Into the net.

'Get it together, Libby!' teased Lars.

'Shut it, Lars,' snapped Ali.

Colin waved a lanky arm, displaying an unsavoury-looking damp patch in the armpit area. 'Alistair, watch your language please,' he ordered officiously.

'He started it,' complained Ali, pointing at Lars.

'I think not,' said Colin smugly.

Lars winked at Colin.

Colin smiled back.

Libby's second service. Smash again. Into the net.

'Love – fifteen,' announced Colin smugly.

'Bastard,' Libby muttered.

Lars heard. Libby served again and Kristina returned it. A volley commenced between the pair of them. Kristina whacked the ball in Ali's direction but Ali failed to whack it back.

'Love – thirty,' said Colin.

'That was nice of you,' smiled Lars. 'Letting your girlfriend win that point.'

Libby and Ali ignored him and the game started up again. Mid volley, Lars laughed out loud. 'Maybe *my* girlfriend will give me the next point,' he joked, taking a well-aimed swipe at the ball.

'You haven't got a girlfriend,' said Libby, puffing slightly as she hit the ball back. 'Not here any-way.'

Lars wasn't expecting such a quick comeback and missed the ball.

'Fifteen – thirty,' said Colin, not hiding his disappointment.

Lars flexed his biceps and pretended not to be embarrassed. 'I'd prefer it if my opponent didn't harass me verbally,' he said to Colin.

'Too right,' agreed Colin. 'Libby, could you stop harassing Lars please?'

'Ha!' said Libby, serving once more. 'That's a turn-up, isn't it? A girl harassing Lars: it's usually the other way round.'

'Thirty – all.'

'You'd be lucky to be harassed by any guy,' hissed Lars, as he smashed the ball over the net.

Libby, furious now, tripped over her own feet and missed the return shot.

'Thirty – forty.'

Libby served, a spectacular, point-winning serve.

'Deuce.'

She served again. 'Do you know something?' she said as the ball sped back and forth between herself and Lars. 'You're not as special as you think.'

'I'm special all right,' Lars replied.

'You're not,' said Libby, hitting the ball.

'I suppose you think my inferior brother is special, do you?' he countered.

Libby cringed, praying that Patrik hadn't heard his twin's nasty comment. She glanced sideways to locate Patrik and the ball whizzed straight past her.

'Advantage to Lars – I mean Malmo,' said Colin.

Lars grinned as play began. This was getting easier by the second. One more insult like that and the game would be his. He looked at the back of Kristina's head: she might as well not have been there, the amount of help she'd been. He was going to win this tournament and, what was more, he was going

463

to win it alone. He didn't need anyone else. It was just him, Super-Lars, against the world.

Suddenly it was all over.

'Game, set and match,' said Colin, clambering down from his high-chair.

'Yes!' yelped Lars, jumping up and punching the air with both fists.

Ali and Libby stepped towards the net and shook hands with Kristina, but Lars was too wrapped up in his own personal glory to do any such thing – tradition or not.

Colin patted Lars on the back and congratulated him. 'You were great, mate,' Colin said.

But, Lars couldn't fail to notice, Colin seemed to be the only person who thought so.

Love All

'I thought we should have this in here.' Ellie entered the kitchen and plonked a ghetto-blaster down on the big pine table. 'Parties are better if there's music in *all* the rooms.'

'Yeah, right,' said Libby. She wasn't really listening properly: she was wondering how the party was going to go. She smiled to herself: she had a good feeling about it.

'So how's the carrot chopping?' asked Ellie.

'Fine,' sighed Libby.

'Isn't Kristina supposed to be helping?'

'She's making some tapes of dance music upstairs with Ali.' Libby stopped chopping for a moment: she was cutting the pieces far too thin.

'Making tapes my foot!' laughed Ellie. 'I'll be surprised if they even get *one* done.'

Libby smiled dreamily. 'Oh, it doesn't really matter. I've got some good CDs . . .'

Ellie walked a semi-circle around her friend. 'Look at you!' she teased. 'You're in a little world of your own!'

Libby put down her knife and stared out of the

window. The sun was shimmering in the evening sky and everything outside had been given a kind of hazy quality. 'Oh, I'm not on my own in my little world,' she grinned.

Ellie smiled. 'Yeah, and I bet I can guess who's in there with you,' she laughed.

'Maybe you can . . . maybe you can't,' said Libby, teasingly tight-lipped.

'It's OK,' Ellie said. 'I know exactly how you feel. Being with Steve these last few days has made *me* feel much the same way.'

Libby turned round, her thoughts not on herself any more. 'Oh my God!' she exclaimed, 'I just can't believe you two – it's amazing!'

'Yeah I know.' Ellie nodded. 'I can't quite get over it myself.' She was quiet for a moment. Then she grinned. 'He's not bad for an old bloke is he?!'

Libby laughed out loud. 'Yeah, right!' she said. She picked up the knife and started to chop again. 'So what was all that stuff about him not fancying schoolgirls then?'

'Oh, it's true – he *doesn't* like schoolgirls,' said Ellie, all serious. 'But *I'm* not a schoolgirl any more, am I? The exams are over, I'm not going back. In fact, Steve's been giving me some advice on how to become a tennis coach . . .'

'I bet that's not all he's been giving you either . . .' Libby giggled.

'Libby!' screeched Ellie. 'What's got into you?'

'I don't know,' she beamed. But she *did* know . . . well, she had an idea anyway. Since Patrik had told her he loved her, she'd felt different, liberated, like she could stop being 'sweet Libby' all the time and now be just Libby. 'I really don't know . . .' she said again. 'But whatever it is, it feels great!'

Patrik was in a dilemma. In the past, he'd never really bothered much about clothes, but tonight he just couldn't work out what to wear. While he was trying to decide between the two clean T-shirts he had left, there was a knock on the door and Nathan's head poked round.

'Fashion crisis?' he asked.

Patrik smiled: it seemed Nathan could read his mind sometimes.

'Here . . .' Nathan flung a navy shirt at him. 'Thought you might like to borrow this.'

Patrik picked it up off the floor. It was the cool number he'd admired on Saturday morning. 'Don't *you* want to wear it?' he asked, stunned.

Nathan shook his head. 'Nah,' he said.

'It's great,' grinned Patrik, pulling it on. 'Thanks a lot.'

Nathan sat on the bed. 'So what's happening with you and Libby?'

'It's been great,' Patrik sighed. 'We went out last night – just to that pizza place, nowhere fancy, but we had a nice time anyway,' he said. 'Then we spent most of the day today together, just messing around at Libby's house, getting stuff ready for the party tonight.' He paused, looking embarrassed 'Thanks, by the way,' he said. 'For getting me and Libby together. I don't think it would have happened without you . . .'

'Don't be stupid,' Nathan shrugged, blushing. 'It was mostly Nina's idea. Anyway, it would have happened sooner or later: it was obvious Libby fancied you.'

'I'm not so sure about that,' said Patrik. And it was true: he wasn't.

As far as he was concerned, Libby only had eyes for his brother up until the other night. But that wasn't her fault. He sighed as an image of her came into his head. Libby was gorgeous. Sexy, sweet and pretty. He could hardly wait to see her again. He fastened the bottom two buttons of his – or rather Nathan's – shirt, then ran his finger around the collar. He was getting a bit hot under it.

'You can keep it if you like,' said Nathan, getting to his feet.

'What?' asked Patrik, his reverie over.

'The shirt,' said Nathan. He left the room. 'It looks better on you anyway,' he called from the landing.

Patrik smiled and did up the rest of the buttons.

Ali pressed the stop button on Libby's cassette deck. 'There!' he said. 'One first-class party tape!'

'Just one?' gasped Kristina. 'Is that all we've done?'

'Well, it *is* a highly complex procedure,' grinned

468

Ali, sliding the cassette into its box and tossing it onto the bed.

'Oh, is it now?' smiled Kristina, holding out her slender white hands to him.

Ali looked at her: she looked so beautiful, sitting there in Libby's wicker chair, her pale eyes gleaming with mischief, her freshly washed hair glittering as the last rays of the evening sun streamed into the room.

They'd had a great day – perfect in fact . . . Larking around in town, a sandwich and milkshake at his favourite café, then back to his place. They *had* intended to watch videos but . . . well, that didn't quite happen . . .

'What are you looking at?' Kristina asked, still smiling.

'You,' replied Ali, pulling her out of the chair and into his arms. And, although he knew she had to leave the following day, at that moment he believed that he wouldn't be able to let her go . . .

Lars placed his silver cup on Ali's chest of drawers. Although it wasn't as ornate as some of his previous trophies, he reckoned it'd still look pretty cool on his mum's mantlepiece back home. He stroked it (for what he thought must have been the hundredth time) and stood back in admiration. He was pleased he'd got it – typically stingy of the Brits to supply just one cup for a doubles win. Kristina had had to go without. Mind you, he thought, she *had* got herself a trophy of sorts – that pallid-faced Brit-boy with the terrible haircut. (Lars couldn't remember his name.) He shook his head. Some girls had no idea . . .

He caressed the contours of his cup once more. (*One hundred and one*, he thought, amusing himself immensely.) So he was a winner . . . again. He sighed a big, satisfied sigh and, turning sideways, studied a perfectly developed bicep in Ali's full-length mirror

He was a winner, he told himself again, so why was he feeling so – he struggled to find the right word – so . . . empty? Maybe he hadn't managed to ignore what Libby had whispered in his ear as he'd walked off court yesterday. Maybe when she'd said 'winning a game of tennis is one thing, Lars, but winning the game of life is quite another', it'd hit a nerve. And maybe, when everyone paired off and went their separate ways and only that ugly umpire guy Colin was there last night to offer to go for a celebratory drink with him but Lars hadn't quite sunk *that* low . . . yet), maybe he'd realised that perhaps Libby was right . . . But no – that was silly. Because she wasn't right.

'I'm a winner through and through,' said Lars out loud to his reflection. But, for the first time ever, the reflection didn't look so convinced.

Nina was rushing to get ready. Although she'd only left Nathan's two hours ago, she couldn't wait to see him again. She thought back over the last 24 hours . . . Yesterday evening they'd gone on Nathan's Vespa to a little village nearby and she'd treated him to a delicious candle lit dinner. It was a really pretty little place and, as the evening was warm, they'd sat outside over looking the village green – very romantic.

This morning, they'd had a had a real laugh when they'd gone to collect Lena from the hospital. Emma and Jonas had turned up too. Everyone reckoned they'd make a great couple but because they were both so shy, they seemed to be at a bit of a standstill. Daniel and Orsa were there too, but they were so wrapped up in each other that they really weren't much help.

Anders helped Lena along on her crutches, while they – Nina and Nathan – had called a taxi. Considering Lena had quite a bad sprain, she was in pretty good spirits. She wasn't even that worried about having missed playing in the final, claiming that Lars was an awful doubles partner anyway.

Nina thought back to the final match. Lars had played brilliantly, but his head had seemed to grow with every serve. *Thank goodness Libby finally saw sense*, she thought. Patrik would make a much better boyfriend. Like Nathan . . . Now he really *was* something else. OK, so the Swedish team were all going home to Malmo tomorrow, but they'd be back soon. Nina was certain of that . . .

Tournament Results

Nathan and Nina – knocked out.
Ali and Kristina – a real smash.
Libby and Patrik – won in straight sets.
Ellie and Steve – simply ace!
Claire and Jamie – a match made in heaven.
Lena and Anders – game, set and match.
Daniel and Orsa – a crazy mixed double if ever there was one!
Emma and Jonas – deuce.
Lars – played some games, loved all. Score? Double fault, regular winner but all-round loser.
Colin – the umpire strikes back!
Yuki – Distinct *dis* – advantage!